GIVEN

ALSO BY ELAYNA R. GALLEA

The Binding Chronicles

Tethered

Tormented

Treasured

Troubled

The Ithenmyr Chronicles

Of Earth and Flame

Of Wings and Briars

Of Ash and Ivy

Of Thistles and Talons

Of Shale and Smoke

The Choosing Chronicles

A Game of Love and Betrayal

A Heart of Desire and Deceit

A Curse of Stars and Storms

A Tempest of Wind and Fate

Romancing Aranthium

A Court of Fire and Frost

A Court of Seas and Storms

A Court of Wind and Wings

GIVEN

ELAYNA R. GALLEA

Podium

Cover design by Artscandare Book Cover Design
Map by Eternal Geekery

ISBN: 979-8-3470-2173-4

Published in 2025 by Podium Publishing
www.podiumentertainment.com

To those who hate running
but always thought being chased would be hot . . .
This one's for you.

CONTENT NOTES

Welcome to Myreth!

I am so glad you decided to join Wren and Gabriel for the beginning of their journey.

Please note: The following content warning may contain slight spoilers.

Given takes place in an epic high fantasy setting that contains violence in several different forms, including but not limited to: death, blood, human sacrifices, whippings (off-page mentions), sexual assault (threat of), being hunted, and physical and emotional child abuse.

Please take care of yourself as you're reading; your mental health is important to me.

—Elayna

N
W
E
S
GHOST LAKE
Van
Woodmarket
THE DARK FOREST
Tretfall
MYRETH

PROVINCIAL CAPITAL
COUNTRY CAPITAL
HOME VILLAGE
CITY
Rosebridge
SAPPHIRE COAST
SALT RIVER
Moorn
Saltwater
Mivat
Mora
THE CELESTIAL MOUNTAINS
THE BLACK MOUNTAINS
RIVERBEND FOREST
Grenbloom

PRONUNCIATION GUIDE

Hello dear readers,

Myreth is part of a fantasy world. I have included this pronunciation guide in case you find it useful. (But as always, please feel free to ignore me and pronounce the words as you see fit.) After all, the beauty of reading is that we all create worlds in our minds.

Adros: *Ah-dros*
Alara: *Ah-lar-ah*
Dehena: *Day-heh-nah*
Etelle: *Eh-tell*
Eses: *Eee-sees*
Eskana: *Es-kah-nah*
Esyn: *Eee-sin*
Fyona: *Fee-oh-nah*
Kadyn: *Kay-den*
Maia: *My-yah*
Mareeth: *Mah-reeth*
Mivat: *Mih-vah-t*
Myreth: *Meer-eth*
Nakisha: *Nah-key-sha*
Nilam: *Nigh-lam*
Nyna: *Nee-nah*
Rya: *Righ-yah*
Tarna: *Tar-nah*

GIVEN

1

NOTHING BUT A FUCKING LIE

Wren

I despise heights.

Unfortunately, I only reached this realization moments ago. Perhaps even more unfortunately, I'm trapped in a small alcove three stories above the temple's shining white marble floor with a plan I'll probably regret later.

I'm on my stomach, and my feet are stretched behind me as I peek over the thin ledge. The delicate slab of wood is the only thing keeping me from plummeting to what I'm certain would be a very painful death. My slippery palms struggle to find a firm grasp, and the floor seems so far away.

Suns, why did I think sneaking into a Giving was a good idea? There's probably a reason these ceremonies take place behind closed temple doors.

Even though the glowing blue Mark on my forehead signifies that I'm gods-blessed, I'm not supposed to be here today. I just wanted a glimpse of my long-awaited future, not to tumble to my death and crack open my skull the day before my own ceremony is scheduled to take place.

Mistress Fyona, one of the three teachers at Grenbloom's village school, always encouraged us to breathe through our fears. I haven't attended school since my eighteenth birthday two years ago, but I'll never forget her advice. She used to say that breathing through fear builds character.

I try to follow her counsel, but it's practically impossible. Every time I peer over the ledge, a fist squeezes my lungs. Perhaps my character is strong enough.

Doubtful, though.

If anything, trying to breathe steadily is making things worse. My head is light, and my heart is a stampeding horse in my chest. No matter what I do, I cannot force the fear away.

It's probably the darkness. Esyn's temple is typically packed wall to wall with parishioners. The windows are usually open, allowing the twin suns to shine upon the villagers as they worship the gods and thank them for their benevolence. Statues usually line the walls, standing against the columns supporting the roof, and stone pews typically take up most of the floor space.

The statues and the pews are gone, having been removed for this sacred ceremony. Save for a few candles, the temple is cast in shadows. The holy space is utterly silent except for the sounds of my unsteady breaths.

Maybe I'm just imagining how bad the distance is. I squeeze my eyes shut, count to three, then open them and peer over the ledge again.

A moan crawls up my throat, and I barely contain the sound. My stomach twists into painful knots, and I can't pull my eyes away from the ground. Has it gotten further away? It shouldn't be possible, but it feels like it has.

Bad idea.

My head spins as I stare at the white marble, frozen in place. Sweat slides down the back of my homespun dress. The soft, pale green skirts stick to my legs as if today were the middle of the hot, humid summer and not partway through the Giving Season.

The massive stone altar at the other end of the temple catches my attention, and I lock my gaze on it. Hopefully, the stationary object will help ground me and stave off my panic. Unfortunately, as I sweep my eyes over the intricate leaves, vines, and flowers carved into the side, my heart starts beating *faster*.

Gods above. There's just something about the vacant temple that feels off.

Or maybe I'm overreacting. Honestly, no one would be surprised to hear that *I* was being overly dramatic about something. If anything, they'd nod in sympathy because of course Wren Nightingale is being a lot.

Honestly, they're right. I'm not, nor will I ever be, the perfect Given. I ask too many questions, and I'm too curious. My presence here is proof of that, but it's only cementing what I already learned a decade ago.

My tenth birthday had just passed, and I'd accidentally broken one kitchen table leg and cracked another right before dinner. I hadn't been misbehaving on purpose, but I'd been chasing my latest stray cat, Brownie, and not paying attention to my surroundings.

That was typical for me. Unfortunately, my behavior didn't go unnoticed that day. Mother sat me down in front of the hearth to discuss my lack of awareness.

"It's a miracle you're Marked, Wren Lilith Nightingale, because out of my five children, you've caused most of these." Mother points to the streaks of grey in the indigo braid trailing over her shoulder. "What will the gods do with you, child?"

I've been asking myself the same question from the moment I understood what the Mark on my forehead meant.

"I don't know, Mother." I blink up at her, tucking an unruly indigo curl behind my ear in a futile effort to tame it. It springs back almost immediately, and my bottom lip wobbles. "Will they like me?"

It's one of the many questions I wrestle with on a daily basis. What if the temple where I'm assigned has taken a vow of silence? What if they keep their Given locked up and I never see the suns again? What if I have to travel to another province, one where it snows nearly every month of the year? I like the snow, but I don't know if I could handle that.

I have so many questions and no answers. All I know is that taking a vow of silence would likely be the death of me.

The gods wouldn't make me remain silent for the rest of my days, would they? Mistress Fyona says they care about us. Well, if that's the case, they know how much I love to talk. Hopefully, that means they'd never take that away from me.

Mother's smile softens, and she sighs, gathering me in for a hug. Her embrace is warm, and I melt into it. After all, these hugs will stop soon. I should enjoy them while I still can.

"Of course they will, Birdie." My family's nickname for me makes me smile, and I burrow my face against her chest. "Everyone likes you, even when you're a lot."

Mother is right: I am a lot. Over the years, I've tried to tone myself down, but it hasn't really worked. This is just who I am, and I hope I'll be enough for the gods, even if I ask a lot of questions.

Yanking my gaze from the altar, I take in the long white candles lining the temple perimeter. They cast ominous flickering shadows on the walls, reminding me far too much of the monsters I used to think lived beneath my bed.

The presence of shadows far outweighs the light, and the temple lacks the comforting air I typically associate with being in the gods' house. Where is the safety, calm, and joy that usually resides within these four walls?

My heartbeat is growing louder by the second, and I want to bang my head against the floor. How did I ever think this was a good idea?

I look over my shoulder, where my feet are brushing up against the top of the thin white ladder I climbed earlier. Going down will be a feat in my heavy floor-length skirts. The green garments are constrictive on the best of days, but they're mandatory for the gods-blessed to wear.

Constrictive dress or not, I shouldn't be here, and I need to leave. I'll just have to be patient and wait for my ceremony tomorrow. Bracing myself for the long climb down, I shimmy back. I've barely made it an inch before the clock above the temple starts tolling, marking the noon hour. The sound is obnoxiously loud, and I wince as the entire ledge vibrates with each ring.

Blessed suns, this was a terrible idea. If Mistress Fyona saw me now, she'd tan my hide.

The doors beneath me open, and it seems I'll get my wish, after all. I'm going to witness a Giving Ceremony. Drawing as deep a breath as I can manage, I make myself as small as possible. I pull my hair over my Mark, willing the swirl on my forehead not to glow for the next few minutes.

The candles flicker as a cool breeze enters the temple. Footsteps ring through the space, and the doors shut with a resounding *bang* that seems to echo in my soul.

I peer over the decorative ledge, barely breathing as four priestesses come into view. They stride forward as though in a dance, their hooded crimson robes trailing behind them like rivers of blood. Today's guest of honor is walking in the middle, with two robed women on either side of her.

A resplendent vision bedecked in a green so pale it's almost white, Amelia Lockheart's Giving gown flows around her as she strides forward with her head held high. The traditional garment boasts floor-length bell sleeves, pristine lacework, and a four-foot train. I should know. I have one hanging in my own closet for tomorrow.

My best friend's silken golden hair has been braided into a crown, highlighting her soft features. Her pale skin, several shades lighter than my tan, reflects the flickering candlelight. A brilliant pink glow comes from her neck, where her Giving Mark resides.

Amelia approaches the altar confidently, which doesn't surprise me in the least. She's even more eager for her Giving than I am for mine, which is saying something. It feels like I've been living my entire life in anticipation of tomorrow. I can't wait to find out where I'll be Given so I can get started on living the rest of my life.

Most Marked Ones born in Myreth's villages don't have the luxury of growing up alongside another gods-blessed child. Twenty years ago, it was considered highly unusual when two Marked girls were born in neighboring villages. Everyone, from our mothers to the priests and priestesses, was apparently shocked.

Amelia and I learned to walk together, went to school together, and even courted villagers at the same time.

Casually, of course.

Everyone knows not to get attached to the Given. We're here temporarily, lent to our families by the gods until we are returned to them in our twentieth year.

When I turned twelve, my siblings and parents stopped hugging me. It was easier that way, Mother said, since it would prepare me for my future of serving the gods. I would find a new family in the temples; the one I was born into would be a marker of my past.

That was eight years ago. Now, Amelia and I will spend the rest of our lives serving the deities and thanking them for keeping the Kingdom of Myreth safe and prosperous. It's my fervent hope that we will be stationed at the same temple after our Givings. I can't imagine spending the rest of my life without my friend's cheerful laugh, knowing smiles, or witty comments.

Amelia reaches the altar and clasps her hands in front of her. Pride swells in my chest, and I smile at my best friend. Unlike me, she's the picture of a perfect, dutiful Given. Quiet, composed, and prepared to serve the gods no matter what they ask of her. She will excel at this, just like she has with every other task in life thus far.

The four priestesses line up in front of the altar, their backs to me, and then . . .

My brows scrunch together, and I frown. None of the women move or even speak as long seconds pass. A thick silence falls upon the temple. Amelia glances curiously at the women, and I know my friend well enough to recognize the look of confusion flitting across her face.

I don't know these priestesses, since they aren't the typical ones who serve in our village. These ones are blessed by the gods, and they travel across the land each Giving Season, performing the gods' will. I don't see their Marks, but that doesn't mean they don't have them. Perhaps they're on their arms or beneath their robes.

A drawn-out, awkward moment passes, and I fidget in my perch. Is this normal?

Not for the first time, I wish someone had properly prepared us for our ceremonies. No matter how often Amelia and I asked, no one would tell us what they would entail. Not the priestesses, not our teachers, not even our parents. They all said the same thing: *Giving Ceremonies are secrets, and Marked Ones learn about their destinies on their Giving Days.*

Well, secrets are awful, and I want to know now. I've lived with this Mark on my forehead my entire life, and I deserve to know what it means.

A bang comes from the back of the temple as a door slams shut, and the air thickens. Breathing, which was already a chore, becomes more difficult. The hairs on my arms bristle, and I tighten my grip on the ledge.

Two figures emerge from the shadows. Something about them makes me want to fling myself back and run. Their presence is a reminder that I shouldn't be here.

But it's too late to flee. All I can do is watch as, on the right, a woman glides forward. The silver threads lining her scarlet robe mark her as a head priestess.

Inadvertently, I shudder. Something about her sets my entire body on edge.

A taller figure dressed entirely in black stands to the head priestess's left. A hood obscures their face, and even though I narrow my eyes, I can't make out their features beyond the shadows shrouding them.

Shivers crawl down my spine. This is odd, right? It feels that way. My stomach twists into knots as my lookout's height is no longer my primary concern.

The head priestess reaches Amelia and takes her arm. The godly woman's sleeve slides up, revealing a red swirl on the back of her hand. A Mark.

She leads my friend to the other side of the altar but doesn't let go. The shadowed figure stands to the right, a silent observer.

Those knots grow barbs and tighten to the point of pain.

"Welcome, children." The head priestess speaks in a honeyed voice, her words echoing through the mostly vacant temple. "Thousands of years ago, when the skies were dark, and the twin suns were nothing more than glimmers in the distance, the gods came together. They decided to bless Myreth twice over. First, with life. Then, with magic. With a wave of their hands and a river of power, they created the land . . ."

On and on, she recounts the entire creation tale. I've heard it all before, and her words wash over me. Everyone knows how the story goes.

The gods created the land, and seeing that it was good, they blessed it. They drew light forth from the darkness and then created magic. They dragged water out of the depths of the earth, and life took root.

Plants formed, trees grew, and mountains rose.

Once nature presided over the land, the gods created animals. Big and small, each one was blessed as it was formed by hand. Only then, when everything else was complete, did they create people.

In the beginning, everyone was Marked. During those times, magic ran freely through the land, unlike now. Everyone lived in peace and harmony, worshipping the gods and the suns. Some, like me, bore the Mark of the Given on their foreheads. Others, on their necks. Some on their arms. A few were Marked on their legs, hands, or feet.

"As time went on, the Mark became rare," continues the head priestess, removing her hand from Amelia as she gesticulates dramatically.

"Fewer gods-blessed are born each year. No one knows why the number of Marked Ones has dwindled, only that it has. Magic, too, is no longer common in Myreth. Now, only the royals have access to it. It's a gift from the gods, a reminder of what we once had."

The royals are lucky to have magic. How nice must it be to have immeasurable power at your fingertips? No one else in Myreth has magic—just them. This is part of why the royal family has ruled over our kingdom for centuries.

"That's why we are gathered here today," she concludes. "Eight hundred and twenty-seven years ago, in her infinite wisdom, the Mother Goddess Esyn decreed that those bearing the gods' Mark shall be Given in their twentieth year. Each Giving Season, we honor the Mother for her thoughtfulness, and we thank the gods-blessed for their willingness to serve her."

Each of the priestesses turns to Amelia. One by one, they dip their heads and murmur, "Thank you, young one."

The hooded figure remains a statue in the corner, hidden in the shadows. My stomach tightens, and I grip the ledge, forcing myself to breathe. I can't help but feel that I've made a grave mistake in coming here today.

The head priestess places her hand on Amelia's shoulder. "In the name of the gods and His Majesty, King Andreas, we thank you, Marked One."

My chest warms, and I exhale. Okay. The ceremony must be drawing to a close. This is when they'll tell Amelia where she's going, right?

A nervous smile spreads across my friend's face, and she shifts her weight from one foot to the other. Clasping her hands in front of her, she rubs her thumb across her pale flesh and bites the inside of her lip.

Maybe Amelia isn't as confident as she appears. If she's nervous, there's no telling how I'll feel tomorrow. Calm, cool, and collected, I am *not*.

Amelia's eyes shimmer, and she dips her head. "You're welcome, Head Priestess," she murmurs.

This is it. Now, they'll announce where she's going. Then they'll pray, and Amelia will be on her way to her future home. A little anticlimactic if you ask me, but that's fine.

My mind starts whirling as I plan my escape from the temple. As soon as they leave, I'll have to slip out of here and hurry back home to prepare for my ceremony tomorrow.

It will be—

A glint of metal catches my eye as the head priestess reaches into her scarlet robe and withdraws a long, thin silver dagger. The blade glimmers ominously in the candlelight, and my stomach churns.

What? My mouth drops open, and a strangled cry rises in my throat. The sound escapes me before I can stop it, but it's drowned out by sudden chanting. The other four priestesses move, circling Amelia as they pray in a language I don't recognize.

Goosebumps erupt on every inch of my skin. The women's voices crescendo, echoing through the vacant temple.

Wrong, wrong, wrong.

What is going on? Everything seems to happen in the blink of an eye, yet I can make out every detail in agonizing clarity.

Horror and confusion pin me in place, pressing down on me. My breath comes in strangled gasps. I can't move. I can barely think.

All I can do is watch, a thundering drum taking the place of my heart, as the black-robed figure steps forward. They grab Amelia's arms and viciously wrench them back, shoving her upper body over the altar.

My best friend screams. The blood-curdling sound is the worst thing I've ever heard, and the hairs on the back of my neck rise. I cry out, slapping a hand over my mouth to contain the sound.

The hooded person whispers something in my best friend's ear too quiet for me to hear. A glint of something gold catches my eye, and I notice the obscene ring on the cloaked person's finger. It rests on the ring finger of their left hand, and rubies are encased within the heavy piece of jewelry. Amelia sobs, struggling against the mysterious person's hold.

Why are they doing this? This is wrong. Acidic bile rises in my throat, and my vision swims.

Being Given is a blessing.

Being Given is a good thing.

Being Given is a sign of the gods' favor.

Being Given is . . .

No . . .

No . . .

No!

My best friend screams again, but the sound is cut off as the head priestess slashes her blade across Amelia's throat. The godly woman moves with such force that her hood falls back, revealing a shock of straight lavender hair.

A flash of pink light explodes, and then, there's blood.

Rising suns, there's so. Much. Blood.

Crimson rivers pour from Amelia's neck, coating her once-beautiful robe. Staining it forever. The rivers seem endless as they spill from her neck.

Seconds pass. Horrible, awful, never-ending seconds where I can't breathe. I can't think. I can't move.

All I can do is watch as the head priestess calmly wipes her dagger on my friend's dress. The hands holding Amelia release her, and she falls. Her head smacks into the side of the altar, and then she tumbles to the ground, landing in a growing scarlet pool.

The priestesses step back, and the hooded figure follows suit. I'm still frozen. Why isn't anyone yelling? Why aren't they screaming? Shouldn't someone get the Watchers and report this murder?

Then, one of the priestesses *laughs*. The sound is so out of place that it hits the center of my chest like a lightning bolt on an otherwise clear day.

Another woman chuckles, and they move together, bowing their heads like gossips gathering around the village well.

"Did you hear her final scream?" A chittering laugh that has me tasting bile rises from the group.

"Suns save me; I hate it when the Blessed fuss." The head priestess sighs, pulling her hood back up.

"They're just making it harder on themselves," adds a priestess who had yet to speak.

"This is their fate," Amelia's murderer agrees. "Remember the redhead from the north last year?"

The shortest priestess nods enthusiastically, rubbing her neck. "Orcus Midwater."

"It took me days to wash his blood out of my robe," the head priestess says conversationally. "If only he hadn't fought back . . ."

A ringing fills my ears, drowning out their continued chatter. It doesn't matter, though. I will never forget the way they laughed as they gossiped about murders. Gods above, who does that? Who commits cold-blooded murder, then stops to chat about it like it's an everyday occurrence?

Eventually, the priestesses and their shadowed companion filter out through the back of the temple. There's mention of a cleaning crew who will come and deal with the body later as the door slams shut behind them.

The resounding bang is as loud as an axe falling on an executioner's block, and I tremble in my perch. I stare at Amelia's discarded, lifeless corpse for so long, my eyes cross.

A lie. My entire life, everything I've ever been taught, everything I believe in . . .

It's nothing but a fucking *lie*.

2

NUMB

Wren

Being Given is a death sentence.

The phrase runs through my mind for hours. It's all I hear as I slip out the temple, run through the fields, and pass the gallows on my way home. Mother says something as I barge through the front door, probably scolding me for being out for so long on the day before my Giving Ceremony, but her words don't register. I somehow end up with the broom in my hands, and I sweep the main floor of the house as the words cycle through my mind on a continuous loop.

Being Given is a death sentence.

It still doesn't feel real. None of this does. The lies, the unanswered questions, the things I've always wanted to know but no one has ever given me a straight answer for . . .

It all feels like the worst kind of dream.

I should be screaming and crying, curled up in a ball, and unable to move after what I just witnessed. I should be weeping and mourning the loss of my oldest friend, tearing my hair out from its roots as I grieve her untimely death.

I should be a gods-damned mess, but I'm not. I'm just cold.

Numb.

Maybe that's for the better, because by the time the phrase stops repeating through my mind, my entire family is arriving for my farewell dinner.

There's my oldest brother, Markus, with his cropped dark brown hair streaked with violet. He strides into the house, holding his wife Yvette's hand. Her ebony skin is smooth, and her black hair hangs in a single braid down her back. Their four-year-old daughter, Lydia, runs around the house as soon as she steps inside, shrieking in delight.

James and his boyfriend, Philip, follow close behind. James's curls are wild, like mine, although his hair is short and a few shades darker than my own. His partner's blond hair is knotted at the back of his neck. James has his arm around Philip, holding him close. They walk through the door, their heads bent together as they share a quiet moment.

"Hi, everyone," Violet says as she comes out of the kitchen, followed by Marie.

The twins are fifteen, and everyone has doted on them since the day they were born. They're identical, from their hair that was Violet's namesake, to the gentle slope of their noses. The only thing setting them apart is the crown braided around Violet's head, as opposed to the single plait Marie prefers.

The rest of my family laughs and hugs as if nothing's wrong. Not me, though. I just stand in the corner. The numbness prevents me from screaming at them that I witnessed a murder.

It prevents me from doing anything at all.

No one hugs me, which is fine. I haven't been hugged by any of them in a long time. After all, it's not safe to get attached to a Given.

Amelia and I were always told that families are to keep Marked Ones at arm's length during their teenage years to make the Giving Ceremonies easier. We aren't permanent members of our families but simply loaned to them by Esyn.

Once, I asked why our families couldn't know where we were going after our Giving Ceremonies. Why keep it a secret?

I was told, in no uncertain terms, that the gods had made the decree and no one should question them. Not even the gods-blessed who were too curious for their own good. After all, it's easier for Marked Ones to serve Esyn if they don't have any attachments to the outside world.

It turns out that was also a lie. If no one gets attached to the gods-blessed, they won't find it odd when they never hear from them after their Giving Ceremonies.

Because we're all fated to die.

The rest of my family can hug and laugh and kiss all they want because none of them are Marked. None of them are doomed. My fingers find the fabric of my dress, this gods-damned gown that labels me as much as the swirl on my forehead, and I fiddle with it.

My suns-forsaken Mark burns, reminding me of its existence.

Like I could ever forget. My fingers rise, tracing the swirl that's been there since my birth. It's etched onto my forehead, just as Amelia's was so perfectly placed on the side of her neck.

But now my best friend is dead, and I'm going to die tomorrow.

I arrived at that bone-chilling conclusion earlier, right before I lost the meager contents of my stomach in the bushes outside.

I'm going to die tomorrow.

There's a chance I'm wrong. I know that. Maybe not all gods-blessed are murdered during their ceremonies. Maybe Amelia's death was a horrific anomaly.

I don't think so, though. There's something about the way the priestesses spoke so casually after her death that tells me things went exactly as planned.

This is their fate.

The head priestess's words echo in my mind, confirming my thoughts.

No. This wasn't an anomaly.

The gods-blessed are killed during their ceremonies. All of us? Some? The head priestess was Marked, but I've been racking my brain, and I can't remember seeing a Mark on any other temple worker. I've always thought they were just hidden beneath their clothes, but now I'm doubting everything I've ever been told.

I don't understand how the head priestess wasn't Given, nor do I understand how this has been so masterfully covered up for centuries, but I don't have time to figure it out.

In less than a day, I'm supposed to die. Why? Why are they doing this? Why kill us? Why kill Amelia?

If I weren't completely numb, I'd wince at the thought. As it is, my heart twists.

I don't want to die. I have hopes and dreams, and none of them include having my blood spilled over an altar as a human sacrifice. We aren't supposed to question where the gods send us, but I've always hoped I would be Given to a role where I could interact with people and animals. Sometimes, when I was very daring, I used to dream of a future where I'd be trained in the healing arts.

But I'm Marked to be Given, and my fate has been determined since the moment of my birth. I don't think my wants and needs matter anymore.

Maybe they never have.

My parents arrive, and Father calls everyone to the table. My feet somehow remember to function, and I walk to my seat as though in a trance. James is on my right, and Violet is on my left. The food is passed in a blur, and I serve myself without noticing what I'm putting on my plate.

After dinner is served, we all join hands. Mine are clammy. Do my siblings notice?

"Esyn, Mother of all that is good and pure, we thank you for this food." Father's voice rings out over the dinner table as he prays the nightly blessing. He continues speaking, but I don't notice his words.

What good is a prayer when everything I know is false?

Father finishes speaking, and I pull my hands back, picking up my fork. It's the heaviest weight as I dig into a pile of potatoes. I lift the fork to my mouth, swallowing the whipped potatoes without thought.

Dinner passes me in a rush. Everyone else laughs, telling stories about my childhood as they enjoy the roast beef, candied carrots, and potatoes that Mother and the twins prepared. Their words barely register. It's like I'm underwater, a ghost of myself.

Every bite is ash in my mouth, but still, I force myself to finish my plate.

I'm just . . . pretending.

Pretending that I'm tasting the food, pretending that my best friend is still alive, and pretending that my entire life hasn't been built on a foundation of falsehoods.

I don't know if it's working. James keeps glancing at me, his brown eyes unblinking, but he doesn't say anything. Of all my siblings, he and I have always been the closest. He's twenty-one, a year older than me, and he only moved out last year to live with his partner.

Does he know what happens to the Given? Does he know Amelia's dead?

Part of me wants to ask. The questions bubble up inside me, and they almost slip off my tongue. If I weren't empty inside, I'd be screaming at my family.

But I am void of every emotion, and because of that, I can barely move.

Tonight, I'm not a lot. I'm quiet and demure. I'm just . . . existing.

At some point, I look down at my left hand. My brows furrow, and if I weren't in a state of shock, I'd shriek in horror. The bracelet that I've worn for a decade is still on my wrist, but where two wooden suns usually hang, now there's only one.

Deep inside me, where the numbness can't reach, I scream and scream and scream.

"Wren!" Amelia calls my name, and I turn to see her racing towards me, two blond pigtails flying behind her. "Wait for me!"

It's the first day of winter—my birthday. I'm still headed to school because even the gods-blessed can't miss school on their birthdays. I slow down at the sound of my friend's voice, my lunch pail hanging from my right hand as I clutch a library book with my left. Mother gave me a piece of apple cake in my lunch today, her birthday specialty.

"Morning, Amelia." I smile as she runs with a skip in her step, a small package in her hand. "What's that?"

She grins, handing it over. "It's for you."

"A present?" My eyes widen, and I beam. Suns, my best friend is so kind. "Really?"

"Really." She chuckles impatiently, pulling on the twine wrapped in a bow. "Go on, open it."

I rip open the packaging, a gasp falling from my lips. "Oh, goodness. They're beautiful."

Two woven bracelets sit in the box, each bearing wooden carvings of the two suns. I reach inside and run my fingers over them.

"One for you." She bounces on the balls of her feet, and her smile reaches from ear to ear. "And one for me. I found them in a box in the attic, and they felt special. The moment I picked them up, I just knew *they were meant for us. I asked, and Mama said we can have them!"*

Tears rush to my eyes, and I choke them back as I look up at her. "Because the Given stick together."

She helps me slide my bracelet onto my wrist before I do the same for her.

"Always." She throws her arms around me. "Promise to keep it on forever, even after we're Given?"

"I promise," I tell her, squeezing her tightly.

I stare at my wrist, where only one sun hangs from my bracelet. When did I lose the other? It was there this morning, I'm sure of it.

It's gone . . . like Amelia is gone.

Dinner ends, and James and Philip help the twins clear the plates. No one asks me to help because being fated to die means I'm the guest of honor.

I don't speak as Violet passes around a plate of freshly baked chocolate scones, and my lips barely twitch into a smile as she puts one in front of me.

Usually, these are my favorites. What good are favorites now, though?

Marie follows with a special bottle of sparkling wine, pouring it into flutes already at the table. The wine is the color of blood, and my stomach churns as I remember the scarlet pool Amelia landed in.

When the twins are done serving, they reclaim their seats. Mother taps her knife on the edge of her glass, the sound echoing through the dining room. Are the walls closing in on anyone else?

"Father and I purchased this bottle of wine the day Wren was born," Mother announces from the head of the table, smiling kindly at me. "As soon as we realized you were gods-blessed, we knew we would need something to celebrate the momentous occasion when you were returned to them."

Because tomorrow, I'm going to die.

"You've always been a good girl, Birdie," Father says from his seat at the other end of the table. I swing my gaze over to him. His eyes, violet like mine, crinkle. White hair hangs around his shoulders, and there's warmth in his gaze as he lifts his cup in my direction. "Raising you and preparing you for the gods has been the greatest honor of our lives."

An honor? Really?

A crack runs through my numb shell, and then it shatters into a million pieces. I draw in my first deep breath of the night as I stare at the man who raised me. Does he know? Is this a charade for him, like it is for the priestesses?

I grab my fingers and squeeze so tightly I can feel each bone.

How is this my life? How come we're all sitting here like nothing is wrong? If they don't know, if they're in the dark as much as I was yesterday, then I suppose I understand where they're coming from. But if they know and we're still acting like everything is normal, then this dinner is the cruelest thing that's ever happened to me.

I don't think my father is a cruel man. One of my earliest memories is of him sitting on the edge of my bed, reading me bedtime stories. He held my hand and walked me to the village school on my first day. Not only that, but he returns home from the butcher shop every night with a new story to tell.

Father loves me. I know that just like I know the sky is blue and the twin suns rise in the west and set in the east. He loves me, and yet, I'm going to die tomorrow.

My heart races in my chest as my gaze swings from one family member to the next. No one looks upset. No one looks perturbed. They're all just sitting here as if this were any other day.

Gods above. There's no way my parents know that the gods-blessed are murdered, right?

Right?

I stare at Father, trying to determine if he's aware it's all a lie. I can't ask him and reveal I snuck into a Giving Ceremony. It's a crime punishable by death. Which, now that I've seen what happened to Amelia, is fucking laughable.

I don't think my family would turn me into the king's guards . . . but I don't know that for certain.

I don't know anything anymore.

"To Wren!" Father declares in a booming voice that pulls me out of my thoughts. "May her Giving Ceremony be blessed by Esyn herself!"

My family echoes his toast, clinking their glasses together. Even the twins join in. It's a special occasion—I'm going to die tomorrow—so they're allowed to drink.

Red wine swirls. My stomach is a whirlpool.

A long, awkward silence fills the air, and it takes me far too long to realize they're waiting for me. For what? For me to freak out?

I want to. My fingers twitch with the urge to grab the table and flip it over. For a moment, I let myself imagine what would happen if I did. I'd shove myself to my feet and scream.

I know what's going to happen! I know that the Giving is a lie. I know Amelia is dead. I know it all. My cheeks would heat, my fists would clench, angry tears would stream down my face, and my nostrils would flare as I waited for their response.

I don't even know how my family would react. Would they laugh because it's a joke they're all in on? Would they cry? Or would they tell me I'm crazy?

Those are all possible options.

But then I look at my glass of wine and realize why they're really waiting. Forcing my numb fingers to curl around the stem, I shove down the urge to scream. Instead, I lift the cup.

As I do so, a plan starts to form in my mind. Whether my family knows the truth or not, I can't stay here. I can't just wait around to die. I need to leave before my Giving. I may be fated to die, but I won't accept my fate without fighting to live.

First, I need to get through this dinner. That thought has me taking a deep breath as, somehow, I force my lips to curve into a semblance of a smile.

"To being Given." The words taste like chalk as I toast to my death, grin, and clink my glass against theirs.

I toss the contents back in one go. My head spins as I put the glass down. The twenty-year-old wine was meant to be savored and not downed like the ale Father and my brothers sometimes enjoy after a long day at the butcher shop.

There's no time for savoring wine, though. There's no time for anything at all.

I have a fated death to run from.

3

CRYING IS A LUXURY

Wren

Three crescent moons shine their brilliant light through my bedroom window as I hurriedly move through the space that I've always called my own.

My dresser drawers are open, and clothes hang haphazardly out of them. I'm pointedly ignoring the lace ceremonial gown I'm supposed to wear tomorrow, furiously grabbing everything I can think of and shoving it into the satchel I pulled from the hall closet before the twins went to bed.

The house is silent. My brothers left an hour ago, and the rest of the family promptly went to sleep. Not me.

Now that my numb shell has been shattered, anger is burning in my veins. Not only because of all the lies but because I'm leaving my dreams behind. I will never get to learn the healing arts now. Never get to live the life I've dreamed of. Never see Amelia or my family again.

Tears born of rage and grief gather in my eyes, but I don't let them fall. Crying is a luxury people are afforded when there isn't a ticking clock on their lives.

My Mark is hot, and I groan as its blue glow rivals that of the moons. Both the burning and the glowing are new developments. I was born with the swirl on my forehead, but it only started shining last winter, on my twentieth birthday.

A sign from the gods that it would soon be time for my Giving.

At the reminder of the fucking farce that has been my entire life, I shake my head and continue stuffing everything I care about into my bag. I don't have a lot since Marked Ones aren't allowed much in the way of worldly possessions. We were always told that the gods would take care of our needs after our ceremonies.

Like fools, we believed that meant we'd get to live good lives serving the gods. Healing. Working in temples. Being scribes, teachers, or even temple workers. Obviously, that isn't the case, but since dead people don't need anything, it's a very dark, twisted truth.

I'm bringing my notebook, the feather quill James gifted me when I turned fifteen, and the necklace of two golden suns my parents gave me tonight before they went to bed. On a whim, I throw in the romance novel I found at the back of the school library a few years ago. The pages are yellowed and falling out, and the cover is so worn that the title is barely legible. Still, I don't want to part with it.

One of the few blessings I had as a Marked child was that I was taught to read and write. Not many girls in villages like mine are afforded the chance, but Amelia and I learned alongside the boys since there was the possibility we'd have to work as scribes once we were Given.

Another fucking lie.

There are no jobs, no positions for the Given, no blessings at all. I don't understand why they'd put so much work into us just to kill us on the day of our Givings. Why let us live at all? Why nurture us and give us even the semblance of a life before sacrificing us? Wouldn't it be easier, in some twisted way, to kill us before we drew our first breaths?

All questions that don't seem to have any answers.

Furiously blinking away frustrated tears, I turn and glance at the door. My heart aches at the thought of leaving without saying goodbye, but I can't risk drawing targets on my family's backs.

I'm keeping them in the dark for a good reason.

The twins, especially, are young and innocent. They're adored by my entire family, and I want them to get the chance to live normal lives. If they don't know why I'm leaving, hopefully, they'll avoid the gods' wrath.

The gods do not tolerate criminals.

It's one of the first things children in Myreth learn. Everyone knows that the gods detest those who work outside the law, which is why the king employs Watchers and Enforcers to keep the kingdom safe.

I'm not sure if my family would be killed for helping me escape my Giving, but I'm not willing to risk their lives. Bile rises in my throat at the very thought of seeing my parents or siblings hanging from the gallows in the village square. It doesn't require much imagination to picture their bodies swinging from nooses, because I'm no stranger to death.

No one in Myreth is.

Thirteen years ago, the harvest had been particularly bad. To make matters worse, a bitter winter had followed. At seven, I was too young to fully understand what was happening, but an empty belly spoke volumes.

The Giving Allowance my family received did little to alleviate the hunger pangs that winter. All we ate for months was watery broth with potatoes and gristly bits of meat.

What I didn't understand at the time was that we were better off than most of the other families in Grenbloom. Most people didn't have a father who hunted and worked as a butcher, nor did they receive anything extra from the temple.

That winter, there had been a lot of hunger, and there had been many deaths. Four branded bodies had hanged from the gallows in the frigid months following the Giving Season, all convicted of theft.

Leniency doesn't exist in Myreth, especially for criminals. Everyone knows that theft is bad, but missing a Giving? That's much worse. It's the law, codified in the Giving Agreement. I was forced to memorize the legislation as soon as I learned to read.

Being Given is a blessing. Every gods-blessed person is required by law to attend their Giving Ceremony during their twentieth year.

Failure to attend will incur the immediate wrath of the king and the gods.

I swallow, my throat suddenly dry. What kind of punishment is worse than death? I never really paid much attention to the laws because I never thought I'd have to worry about them. After all, my entire life has been building up to this.

My fingers tighten around the satchel, and my knuckles turn white as Amelia's screams reverberate in my ears. The pool of crimson blood flashes through my mind, and my knees knock together.

Oh, gods.

My best friend is dead.

I frantically search within myself for the numbness from before, but it's vanished.

No, no, no. I can't give in to the panic. Not now.

I shake my head, gritting my teeth. The tears have to stay put. I can't cry now, no matter how much I want to. I'll mourn Amelia when I'm safe.

If I can get to safety.

I need to hurry because when the suns crest the horizon, Mother will come to prepare me for the temple. I'm due to be Given at noon, and we'd set aside the entire morning to get ready.

After all, it takes a lot of work to prepare a lamb for the slaughter.

That thought rekindles my anger, and my tears dry up. I'm not the only one who has been lied to. Every gods-blessed who has ever entered the temple expecting their life to continue, only to be murdered, deserves to have someone know what happened to them.

I'm leaving for me, for Amelia, and for all the others like us. I'm not sure where I'm going, but I'll figure it out on the way. At least this way, I'll have a chance at escaping my fate.

Tying the top of my satchel, I place the bag on the bed. My fingers find the laces of my dress, and a few tugs later, the garment is a green puddle on the ground. I reach for the dress I smuggled from Mother's things earlier, knowing she'll realize her second-best dress is missing soon enough.

I'll be long gone before that happens.

I trail my hand over the blue fabric, my heart catching in my throat. Wearing this color wouldn't be an issue for most people, but Marked Ones only wear green. It's our color, designated by the gods.

It is blessed, as we are blessed . . .

And now, I'll never wear it again. It's a dead giveaway that I'm a Given, and it'll draw too many eyes. Just like the suns-damned glowing Mark on my forehead. I can't do much about that, but there's no way I can ignore it. The shining blue swirl is a great way to attract questions I have no intention of answering. It's a problem that I'm not entirely sure how to solve, but I'll have to think of something.

Thank the suns, Mother and I are nearly the same size. The dress is a little tight around the bust and arms, since I'm curvier than she is, but it's not nearly bad enough for people to notice. At least, that's what I tell myself as I lace up the top of the dress. It falls an inch above my ankles, but there's nothing I can do about that right now.

I sling my satchel over my shoulder, adjusting it so it rests on my opposite hip. Grabbing my dark brown cloak from where it's hanging on the back of the door, I pull it on. Next, I grab my walking boots and slide my feet into them, doing up the laces.

I don't look around my room one last time, nor do I slow down to think about what I'm doing. The moment I step outside, I'll be an outlaw. Able to be hunted for bounty; anyone who feels so inclined will be allowed to turn me into the king's soldiers for a reward.

Gods, that's going to make my life so damned difficult. I'll have to come up with a real plan that's more than just "not dying," but for now, my primary objective is surviving the next twenty-four hours. Once I make it past my Giving Day, I can think about what comes next.

I nudge open the door, thanking all the gods that Father always insisted we keep the hinges well-oiled. It opens without a sound, and I tiptoe down the hall, careful to avoid creaky floorboards.

My bedroom is at the back of the house, and I need to pass the twins' room and then the one belonging to my parents on my way out. All of them are fast asleep, their snores rising in a symphony, reminding me that everyone who isn't Marked gets to live a quiet, peaceful life. Jealousy burns in my belly at the thought.

The sound of their slumber accompanies me down the stairs and into the living room. A *meow* pulls me from my thoughts as I creep along the main floor.

Truffle is sitting on the kitchen table, her long tail hanging off the edge and swinging back and forth. She stares at me with her left eye, the other one white and glassy from an injury she sustained in a fight before I saved her from a life on the streets.

"Oh, Truffle." My lip quivers as she rises and arches her back, begging for pets. The tears I've been suppressing threaten to spill, and keeping them back is harder than ever.

I should get going. That knowledge is sharp at the back of my mind, urging me towards the door. Time waits for no one, and the suns will rise no matter what.

But before I can stop myself, I move towards Truffle, picking her up and snuggling my nose into her coarse brown fur. She purrs, licking the back of my hand with her rough pink tongue.

"I have to go," I whisper, blinking furiously to keep the tears at bay. "I'm so sorry, Truff."

She looks up at me and meows.

"The twins will feed you," I say, answering her question. "They promised they'd look after you after I was Given. I'm sure they'll still take care of you even though I'm running away."

I whisper the last words, the hushed confession our secret even though she can't understand what I'm saying.

Truffle meows again, nipping the pad of my finger.

"Ow." Putting my finger in my mouth, I suck on the bead of crimson before bopping her on the nose. "Bad kitty. You know the girls will be nice to you, even if they aren't me."

Another meow, this one louder than the last. Her displeasure is clear, and it's making my heart ache.

"We've talked about this," I remind her, snuggling her closer. "We always knew I'd be leaving."

My voice cracks on the last word, and remaining calm is a struggle. Even when I thought being Given was a good thing, I'd mentally prepared to leave Truffle. She's the latest in a long line of injured strays I've taken in over the years, but our bond is one of the strongest I've ever had.

I love her, and pain fills me at the thought of leaving her. I give myself one more minute to hold her. "I wish I didn't have to go," I confess into her fur, my voice barely audible. "I wish I wasn't Marked. I wish I could stay here and live a boring, happy life."

This time, Truffle doesn't meow. She lifts her head from my chest and stares up at me, her left eye unblinking, before rubbing her head under my chin.

"I'll miss you, too," I whisper, a tear slipping past my defenses. "So, so much."

When my minute is up, I kiss Truffle's fluffy head and place her back on the table. Her tail curls as she prowls to the end of the table and hops to the top of the cabinet. Her favorite spot in the house, she sleeps there more often than not. She turns three times and settles into her perch, her gaze locked on me.

I can't linger here, and there's still one more thing I need to do. Drawing my hood over my head so the material rests above my eyebrows and covers my Mark, I hurry to the cabinet above the sink.

Running water is a luxury not many in Grenbloom have, but a few years ago, Father installed a tap that brings fresh water in from a small cistern on the roof.

The cabinet door swings open, and I scan the contents. On the top shelf, high enough so that tiny prying fingers can't get into them, are several bottles of salves and ointments. I sift through them until I find the two ceramic jars I'm looking for. The lids are sealed, which will hopefully keep them from spilling. Knowing my luck, they'll make a huge mess of my things, but I don't want to leave without them.

The salve they contain is enchanted, created to help the healing process. Something tells me I might need them in the future. After all, Myreth's forests are notoriously dangerous. Three years ago, Father encountered a feral wolf while hunting. He barely got away with his life, and the six-inch scar on his chest is a reminder that if Mother hadn't had any blessed salve on hand, he would've died.

Placing the jars in my bag, I grab a roll of bandages and a canteen. Filling the canteen, I clip it onto my belt. I'm about to shut the cupboard when one of Father's sheathed hunting knives sitting on the middle shelf catches my eye.

Before I can reconsider—or remind myself that I don't have any weapons training—I grab the sheathed blade, sliding it into my satchel. Then I take a small bag of dried meat that Father brings hunting.

That's it. I don't have room for anything else.

Truffle's judgmental eyes drill into my back as I slide the cupboard door shut, but I don't look over at her. She doesn't understand. I need to do this so I can live.

One more door stands between me and freedom.

Dancing my way out of the kitchen and avoiding creaky floorboards, I creep towards the back door. I can't risk using the front entrance. If someone sees me wearing this dress, it'll attract too many questions. Grenbloom isn't a large village, and everyone knows who I am. What I am.

Gods-blessed.

I scoff. Gods-cursed is more like it.

This is their fate.

A shiver runs down my spine, and my fingers shake as I grasp the metal lock on the back door. It's cold, and the sudden change in temperature sends a jolt of awareness through me. I'm really doing this. I'm running away.

There's no time to second-guess myself. I turn the lock slowly, wincing at the loud tumbling sound that comes as I flip it upwards. Did anyone hear that?

My heart is a booming drum as I pause, waiting for the telltale sounds of people waking up. I hold my breath, seconds passing in agonizing slowness, but the house remains silent.

I release the lock and turn the knob.

This door isn't as well oiled as the others, and part of me wonders if Father did that on purpose to make it harder to sneak out. Easing it open far enough so that I can slip through the gap takes precious seconds, and I release a low breath as I step outside.

The night air is cold as it slams into me. It's a reminder that the Giving Season will end in a few weeks, and winter will take its place. That's usually my favorite season. Not only is my birthday on the first day of winter, but I've always loved the first snow. There's little that brings me more joy than taking long walks the day after a blizzard, when the untouched snow glistens beneath the light of the suns.

None of that matters now. I don't even know if I'll survive the Giving Season, let alone celebrate my twenty-first birthday.

With one final glance at my childhood home, I slide the door shut and draw my cloak tighter around myself. The moons are high, and the stars twinkle as I draw in a deep breath, pray for strength, and bolt towards the trees.

4

I NEVER ASKED FOR THIS

Wren

Running is worse than heights. It's worse than pretty much anything else I can think of, too. Especially running at night when every single sound makes me think a predator is about to jump out of the trees and eat me.

Why in gods' names would anyone ever do this for fun?

James and Philip run every day, and they claim it's enjoyable.

Good exercise, James said the last time I asked why they willingly do this to themselves. *It's fun,* Philip added.

Well, I don't know how this wasn't abundantly clear to me before, but my brother is obviously insane. He used to be my favorite sibling, but I'm rescinding that title. No one who enjoys this devilish, suns-damned activity can be my favorite anything. The twins will be my new favorites.

There is *nothing* enjoyable about running.

I've been racing through the woods for hours, trying to put as much distance between myself and my home as possible. I've come up with a plan, and even though it isn't great, it'll have to do for now.

Staying in Myreth with a glowing Mark is basically a death sentence, so I won't do that. I can't go south—the damned Relentless Mountains are there. I don't know much about this land, but I know they're impossible to cross.

I'm heading north to the Sapphire Coast, where I'll find a boat to take me across the sea. I'm not entirely sure how far the coast is, but it's a better plan than waiting around to be killed.

It feels like the forest goes on forever, even though I know that isn't the case. I've overheard my brothers talking about an enormous city to the north, but I've never been there.

I've never been anywhere.

The trees have lost the emerald leaves they bear during the summer, and I'm surrounded by long brown trunks with spindly branches sticking out on all sides. Green moss covers most of the forest floor, including the fallen logs that seem to be placed in ideal tripping locations. The remaining leaves are shades of yellow and orange.

Thank the gods, the moons provide decent lighting and I don't impale myself, which, honestly, seems like something I'd do. However, they don't stop branches from attacking me. I have more cuts on my hands, cheeks, and calves than the wooden carving of a bear that Truffle claimed as her own and scratched until it was unrecognizable.

My heart is slamming against my ribs, and it's been making a concentrated effort to escape the confines of my chest for hours. My lungs feel like they're on fire. Every breath is like inhaling flames.

I've thrown up three times since I left the house, and my muscles are burning and shaking. As if that isn't bad enough, my hip feels like it's permanently bruised from my satchel smacking against it.

Running is fucking awful. I'd curse, except I don't have the energy to speak.

I duck beneath a branch, my head swiveling from side to side as I use the moons to guide me north. I'm mostly guessing, if I'm being honest, since I've never tried navigating by the suns and the moons before.

I'm so unprepared for this journey, it's actually laughable. Not only am I out of shape, but no one has ever taught me about the land where I live. I was never allowed to go hunting with Father, even when I begged. Before, that just annoyed me, but now I realize that's going to be problematic.

If someone had asked me yesterday morning if I knew all there was for me to know about my kingdom, I would've said yes. I've spent my entire life preparing to be Given, and part of that included learning about Myreth. Unfortunately, the past twenty-four hours have made it clear there were enormous gaps in my education.

While I know that Myreth is a vast kingdom consisting of five provinces ruled by lords who answer to His Illustrious Majesty, King Andreas Bloodthorn, I'm unable to name the strange plants I keep passing. Some have small speckled green leaves, while others boast brilliant orange ones the size of my hand. Even with the late hour, they stand out among the rest of the forest.

I know that Lord Malachi Darkwater rules the province of Eskana, where I live, and he's been married to his wife, Lady Isobel, for twenty-four years. They have four children, ages twenty-three, eighteen, seventeen, and eleven, and they spend a month every summer in the capital with the royal family.

What good is that information now? Lord Malachi isn't here to tell me where I'm going, nor does that knowledge help me identify edible plants. My lack of education in this department will soon be a big problem. It's not like the dried meat I took from the house will last long.

As if imminent starvation isn't bad enough, I have a bigger issue on my hands. There are other towns and cities in Eskana, of course, but other than the one located north of the forest, I have no idea where they are. I don't know how to find them, nor do I know where the nearest body of drinkable water is located.

Burning suns. I'm torn between the urge to scream and cry, but I don't have time for either one. All I can do is keep putting as much distance between myself and my village as possible.

So that's what I do. My feet pound the forest floor as I run and run and, you guessed it, fucking run.

The longer I run, the more everything hurts.

You're going to die on this trek, you foolish girl, a small voice at the back of my mind whispers. *You should give up now and turn around.*

I don't know whether this voice is the product of my own negative thoughts or something else entirely, but I try to ignore it. It's wrong. Turning back isn't an option. I have to stay alive.

At first, the voice is merely annoying, but as exhaustion creeps over me, it gets louder and louder. Eventually, it's roaring in my head. The effort to keep it quiet is nearly as draining as running, and I'm not sure how much longer I can keep going.

Nothing about this is easy.

By the time the suns crest the horizon, painting the sky above the trees in pastels, my throat is dry and scratchy. Every single part of me hurts. I scowl at the sky peeking through the trees, never ceasing my movements. It's bright and cheerful, and the day will be beautiful.

That sucks. I was supposed to die today. It should be raining. The sky should be dark and cloudy, and a thick fog should be sweeping through the forest. A thunderstorm would've been appreciated.

At least then, the sky would've mourned the end of my life with me.

As it is, I glare at the rising suns as a branch whips me in the face. Fucking perfect. Even though every part of me wants to stop moving and lie down on the forest floor, giving in to my exhaustion, I don't. I force my legs to keep moving because my parents will be waking soon. I wish I didn't know what would happen, but I do.

I leap over a fallen log, picturing Mother's face as she opens my bedroom door to find me gone. She'll gasp, and the door will slip shut as she hurries to get Father. He'll confirm that my room is empty, and they will exchange a worried look.

Father will see if I'm getting in one last goodbye with my brothers before my ceremony, while Mother will walk past the gallows to the village square. She'll keep her head down and try not to attract attention as she searches Grenbloom, looking for me.

It won't take them long to realize I'm not there.

Mother might cry because I've run from my fate. Father will hold her. But then they'll go to the temple and report me missing. That's what any good citizen would do. Then it will be official: I'll be an outlaw. A gods-blessed who has missed her calling, guilty of one of the greatest crimes in the land.

Will my parents understand why I left? Will the twins? I wish I knew the answer, but I don't. I have no idea what they'll think of me, and I'm not sure I want to. I'd like to believe that none of them know that the Given are being ritualistically slaughtered, but I just . . . don't.

It feels like I don't fucking know *anything* anymore, and I'm not entirely sure what to do with that information. I still don't know why the Given are murdered or why the priestesses killed Amelia and then talked about it so casually. I don't even know how such an elaborate ruse was created.

Giving Ceremonies have been conducted for centuries—have the gods-blessed been murdered this entire time? What was that pink flash that filled the temple when Amelia died? Who was the cloaked figure?

My chest aches with the pain of all my unanswered questions. All I know is that my life has been irrevocably changed.

My eyes burn, and a single frustrated tear slides down my cheek. This was supposed to be *my* day. For so long, I looked forward to my Giving. It should've been the beginning of the rest of my life.

Instead, what do I have?

A murdered best friend, an aching body, and no real plan for how to survive now that I've run away. As if it's mocking me for my current predicament, my Mark starts to itch. It thrums beneath my skin, and if I were a betting woman, I'd put several gold coins on the fact that it's glowing brighter than normal right now.

Of course. Why is it doing this *now*, of all times? I'm on the run, and a glowing Mark is the last thing I need. Why won't it dim?

Wishing that for once in my life something would come easily to me, I adjust my hair over my forehead as best I can before drawing my hood further down. I can't tell if the Mark is completely covered, but it's better than nothing.

What did I do to deserve this?

I never asked to be gods-blessed. I would've been content with a normal life instead of this. Maybe the gods hate me. As another branch slaps me in the face and I feel the sting of drawn blood, I scowl.

That's probably the case.

Mareeth and Nilam, the two suns, are high when I finally allow myself to take a break.

Sitting on a moss-covered rock that comes up to my hip, I chug water from my canteen. The cool liquid runs refreshingly down my throat, and I drink too fast. Coughing, I slap my hand over my mouth, forcing myself to keep the water down.

As soon as I'm finished drinking, I nibble on a few pieces of jerky. They're somehow both over-spiced and bland, which seems impossible but tracks with the direction my life has taken. Keeping the food down is difficult, and I take another drink of water to try to rid myself of the taste before shoving away from the rock and standing.

"Fuck!" I shout as searing pain runs through my entire body.

The break was a bad idea. I never should have given my body the illusion of stillness. I thought I was in pain before, but that has nothing on how I'm feeling now.

My feet feel like I'm walking on coals, even though I'm just standing. My muscles are shaking, and my stomach is churning. Stopping would be the wise thing to do, but I can't risk it. I need to keep going.

This time, running is pure, unmitigated torture. The only good thing about the constant pain is that it keeps my mind off the time, for the most part. In the back of my mind, I note that the suns are sitting in the middle of the sky.

It's noon. My Giving Ceremony should be happening right now. As of this moment, I'm living on borrowed time.

I keep going. Lifting my feet and placing them one in front of the other consumes every ounce of concentration I possess. My run has slowed to a stumbling jog. My feet are two burning flames attached to my legs, and the bottom of my dress is covered in mud.

Hours pass. By the time the suns are setting in the east, I no longer feel like a person. I'm a jumbled mess of pain, nothing more.

At some point, tears start flowing down my cheeks. I can't stop them. I should probably be concerned about the large cats, bears, and man-eating snakes that are rumored to reside in Eskana's woods, but honestly, if they eat me, I won't have to run anymore.

Maybe that would be better than this.

5

A TRUE SENSE OF PEACE

Gabriel

Earlier that day

Nothing in Myreth is as calming as a forest midway through the Giving Season. Especially not when there's no one else around.

Some people thrive in cities, but not me. I was always meant to be here, surrounded by nature in the middle of the woods with only the animals for company. They understand me far better than anyone back home ever did. Besides, here, I'm choosing to be on my own. There's no forced isolation, no snide comments made behind my back, and no one sneering at me as they realize who I am.

Here, I can be myself.

Gabriel Moreau, Hunter.

The title brings a smile to my face, as it has every day since I was first appointed as a Hunter nine years ago. The smile grows even wider as I imagine what my new title will soon be—Gabriel Moreau, the youngest Master Hunter the Kingdom of Myreth has ever seen.

I'm so close to achieving my promotion that I can practically taste it at the back of my mouth. Becoming the youngest Master Hunter in the history of the kingdom will be nice, but what I'm really looking forward to is the look on the king's face when he's forced to honor me in front of the entire court.

For once, he will have to show me respect. For once, he won't be able to ignore me.

As soon as I complete my fiftieth hunt.

Raking a hand through my hair, the blue so dark it's almost black, I stride forward. My sword hangs at my side, and my bone dagger is in its sheath as my gaze swivels through the forest. A few days ago, I completed my seventh successful hunt of the year, bringing my total up to forty-nine.

Instead of returning to the capital after catching the runaway prisoner and returning him to Whitewater Prison, I decided to spend a few days out in the wild with Mist.

I can't see my familiar, but our bond thrums with delight as she undoubtedly chases whatever poor animal has caught her attention. I know from experience that she'll return in a few hours, pleased with herself and licking her paws triumphantly as her latest meal settles in her belly. She tolerates the city for me, but the woods are where she comes alive.

The midafternoon suns are retreating behind stormy clouds, taking the warmth of the day with them as I draw my cloak tighter around myself. I enjoy the woods, but I won't be able to stay here forever. Unless I get another hunt, I'll be expected to report back to Rosebridge within the week. I shudder, knowing that means I won't be able to avoid my family.

Shoving those thoughts aside, because I refuse to give them any time when I don't have to, I focus on my surroundings.

Myreth is beautiful this time of year. Most of the trees have lost their leaves, and the forest's animal inhabitants are running to and fro, storing food for the impending winter. Some people don't like it when the trees have lost their leaves, but I do. There's a peace in the woods during the Giving Season that I can't find anywhere else.

My bond vibrates, and in the distance, a roar fills the air. Moments later, an animal cries out, and I know Mist has caught her prey. Sitting on a fallen log, I send a message down our bond letting her know to come find me when she's done. Once she's back, I'll find us a shelter for the night.

Tomorrow—

A shrill bird's cry shatters the silence of the forest, and my head jerks up. I scan the horizon, my gaze sweeping through the trees until I spot the black speck on the horizon. It's careening towards me, leaving a crimson trail of sparks in its wake. A signature of the king's magic, it's a sure sign that this bird is one of his enchanted messengers.

"Well, there goes my peace and quiet." I chuckle to myself as I glimpse the parchment clasped in the bird's talons.

I'm not upset. Not really. Tugging on my bond with Mist, I tell her to return to me quickly. I know what that piece of paper means.

We have another hunt.

As the falcon lands on my outstretched arm, delivering the paper to me, a burst of excitement comes to life in my stomach. Not only will this be my fiftieth hunt, but something about this one feels different.

Life-changing.

I unfold the paper as soon as the falcon flies away, my eyes widening as I read the contents. A gods-blessed has fled from their Giving Ceremony, and their actions have called down the wrath of the gods upon them.

My lips tug into a smile as I pull on the bond again, energy rushing through my veins. This is my chance. I can feel it.

I'm going to catch this Given, and when I do, the title of Master Hunter will be mine.

Nothing will stand in my way.

6

I'M GOING TO LIVE

Wren

The night passes in a painful blur, and before I know it, the suns are washing away the darkness. I'm still running—stumbling—and tears have been streaming down my face. Who knew a body could produce so many tears or hurt so much? As dawn arrives, I know two things for certain.

One: I never want to run again in my entire life.

Two: I might be a mess of pain, but I'm *alive*.

I am alive, and it feels like a gods-damned miracle. I was never meant to see dawn, but I'm here and I'm not going anywhere. My bracelet is still on my arm, and the solitary sun dangling from my wrist reminds me of everything I'm fighting for.

The Given stick together.

Amelia would be proud of me. *I'm* proud.

That's the thought that has me slowing to a staggering walk. I grip my sides as shooting pain runs up them, and I wheeze. Miraculously, my feet keep moving.

This time, I don't focus on the way everything hurts. Pain is temporary, but my lungs are still drawing breath, and my heart is still beating. I've defied the odds, broken though I may be, and I'm still here. My plan shifts, becoming less of a hope and more of a rough semblance of something I can actually accomplish.

I will find the Sapphire Coast, leave this gods-damned kingdom, and live a full life. Not just for me but for my best friend and all the other Given whose lives have been cut short.

My lips twitch upwards. It's not much, but it's the first approximation of a smile I've had since Amelia's untimely death.

"I'm going to live," I declare, needing to hear it out loud.

The forest is unsettlingly quiet around me, and shivers crawl down my spine. I repeat the sentence again, and again, and again. I keep going until it's ingrained in the marrow of my bones.

I, Wren Lilith Nightingale, middle child of Charles and Rya Nightingale, am going to *live*.

There are a plethora of barriers in my way. Money, for one. I have none, nor can I think of a way to acquire it without drawing attention to myself. Food, for another. My stomach chooses that moment to grumble, reminding me that a few pieces of jerky stretched over a day doesn't make a sustainable meal. Not to mention my lack of geographical awareness. I need a map, but like money, I have no idea where to find one. And then there's the issue of keeping the glowing spiral on my head hidden.

Even though my problems feel insurmountable, I refuse to let them bring me down. I will not let death claim me like it has the other gods-blessed.

My most pressing issue is shelter. I need to sleep. I've put it off for far too long, and I'm more exhausted than I've ever been. On top of that, clouds are systematically rolling in, bringing in a storm. Judging by the brisk air, coupled with the wind blowing the colorful autumn leaves in every direction, it will be a bad one.

The last thing I need after the past two hellish days is to get stuck in a rainstorm. Being wet would make this already awful situation ten times worse.

I stumble forward, my gaze sweeping through the forest, searching for a spot to call home for the next few hours. I'm not picky—at this point, I'll take anything that somewhat resembles a shelter.

It's amazing how quickly one's standards fall when one's life is on the line. Two days ago, I would've told anyone who asked that I didn't enjoy the outdoors. Now, I don't even have the mental fortitude to care about dirt or bugs.

I duck under a massive branch with long, thin green needles that brush against my skin and gasp. Hanging off a nearby bush are red berries each the size of my thumbnail. My stomach growls, and I hurry over as quickly as my aching feet allow.

Finally, something in these woods that I recognize. We have a moonberry bush outside our home. Amelia and I used to pick them every year. Moonberries are delicious, a little sweet and tart at the same time. They get their name because, at night, they shimmer in the moonlight.

I drop to my knees in front of the bush and grab a handful. The berries are squishy, and their juices paint my hand red, but I don't care. It's been nearly two days since I've eaten anything fresh.

Tossing them into my mouth, I rock back and forth on my heels as the familiar flavor coats my tongue. I groan, the sound echoing through the forest. Esyn help me, but food has never tasted so good.

I feast on three more handfuls of berries before a rumble of thunder reminds me of the impending storm. I rise to my feet, and with one parting glance at the moonberry bush, I continue searching for a place to sleep. Now that I've taken care of one need, my others are more insistent than ever.

Judging by the movement of the suns, it takes another half hour before I find something that will work. It isn't exactly a cave, more like a rough overhang cut out of the side of a mountain, but it's close enough to a shelter that I exhale a sigh of relief.

Maybe the gods don't hate me, after all. If I'm lucky, I might even be able to get a few hours of sleep. My body sags at the thought. I've never wanted to fall asleep more than I do at this very moment. Even though I know this isn't a bad dream, the thought of escaping the horrible reality that is my life, even for a few hours, makes me smile.

The shelter is less than ten feet away when I hear it.

A groan. It's so different from the sounds of the forest that I freeze. Was that real, or am I losing my mind?

I haven't slept since before Amelia's Giving Ceremony. Maybe this is my brain's way of saying that enough is enough. Or maybe my sanity is slipping away. That seems equally plausible, considering the events of the past two days.

"Get a grip, Wren," I whisper, shaking my head and taking a step towards the shelter. Chances are, it was just in my head.

But then, I hear it again, and this time, I know it's real. Something, or someone, is out here.

My breath catches in my throat, and my heart thunders. Oh, gods.

Ignoring the sound would be the smart thing to do. I'm exhausted, and every part of my body is urging me to sleep. Even if I wasn't ready to fall over, I'm an outlaw, for gods' sakes. I need to start looking out for myself if I want to survive.

Yet when an agonized moan rises through the air, it tugs on my heartstrings. Someone nearby is in serious pain. How can I ignore them?

The same part of me that encouraged me to save countless strays and injured animals has me taking a step away from the shelter. Then another. And another. With one last longing look at the spot poised to give me refuge, I sigh and turn towards the sound.

"Seriously, Wren?" I mutter, pushing branches aside. "Why can't you leave well enough alone?"

It would be so much easier than this.

The problem is that I *can't.* Something deep within me is encouraging me to help this injured being. I can't ignore the call to assist them any more than I can wish away the glowing Mark on my forehead.

Now that I've made up my mind, I move swiftly. The sky is darkening, and thunder rumbles in the distance. I keep my eyes trained on the forest floor, searching for the source of the sound. They must be around here somewhere. I just—

There.

Two boots, so dirty the brown is nearly black, are sticking out from under a thorny bush. Honestly, I'm surprised it's a person and not an injured animal since I haven't encountered anyone else during my run. Another agonized, pained sound rises, and I lift my skirts and hurry over.

Dropping to my knees in the fallen leaves, I ignore the sharp twig that prods my leg as I reach for the feet and pull. The body doesn't move at all. I grunt, tightening my grip on their ankles.

Suns, this person is heavy. Or maybe I'm just weak. Honestly, it's probably the latter. Either way, my already aching arms burn as I yank the person out inch by inch, releasing them from the bush's thorny grasp.

It's more of a struggle than I'd like to admit, and the thorns put up a big fight, but eventually, I'm victorious. The person is a man, a rather attractive one if I'm being honest, and his muddy tunic is ripped beneath his cloak.

Purple and black bruises bloom on his chest, and blood is oozing out of a laceration on his forehead. An empty sheath is on his hip, where a sword presumably once hung.

Who, or what, would do something like this? I'm not entirely sure, but it looks like he's been here for hours. Hopefully, whoever did this is long gone.

A frown tugs at my lips as I reach up, brushing a lock of blue hair so dark it's nearly black away from the man's stubble-covered cheek. He looks like he's a few years older than me, and the hard edge of his features is equally rough and attractive.

I'm not a healer, as much as I used to wish I could be one, but I know the laceration on his forehead needs to be looked after.

My heart twists, and I already know what I'm going to do. Wishing I'd been born with a heart of stone, I hook my hands under the man's armpits and begin the laborious process of dragging him back to my shelter.

By the gods and everything I've ever held holy, I hope I don't regret this.

7

THIS DAY KEEPS GETTING WORSE

Wren

I haven't even made it ten feet before the clouds open up and water pours from the sky. Because, of course, *now* it starts raining.

Grumbling a slew of curses under my breath that would have Mother fainting, I heave the man back to my shelter. It feels like he's getting heavier with every step, and when the stone overhang finally comes into view, I can barely breathe.

My cloak and dress are plastered to my body, my feet slosh through mud, and wet strands of hair are sticking to my face. Drowned rats probably look better than me.

I blink rapidly, trying to clear my vision enough to see.

It seems inconceivable, but things keep getting worse. Someone must have it out for me. That's the only explanation I can think of.

By the time I reach the shelter, being dry is a distant memory. I drag the unconscious man beneath the overhang, and a groan slips from his mouth.

"I'm sorry," I tell him, reaching down and wiping a wet lock of hair away from his skin. "I'm being as gentle as I can, but you weigh so damn much."

He doesn't answer, which is just as well. My muscles are screaming from the burden of having to bring him across the forest, and I'm not sure I could hold a conversation at the moment.

It's not like I haven't carried injured beings before, but a mewling cat doesn't compare to a heavy, impaired man. Thank the gods, I get him situated without too much trouble.

The ground is elevated, so the rain can't get to us, although it's a close call for him. He's so tall that even with the top of his head grazing the stones, his toes barely miss the rain. Other than the occasional moan, the rise and fall of his battered, muscular chest are the only signs that he's alive.

Now that we're beneath the shelter, I take a moment to breathe and study the man I rescued. His skin is pale beneath the blue-black scruff decorating the bottom half of his face, his jaw is sharp, and from what I can see, which is a lot, thanks to the torrential downpour, he's covered in muscles.

He probably wouldn't have any trouble running for days on end. If I had to guess, he might even choose to exercise for fun.

I frown. No, thank you. I'll take my curves and disdain for exercise any day.

Still, there's an undeniable pull about the man that makes me want to get closer to him. It's not all that surprising, since even unconscious, he's undeniably handsome, in a rugged *I can survive in the woods for a month by myself* sort of way.

Is it wrong to think of someone I just dragged through the woods as good-looking? Probably. Do I have it in me to care? Not really.

I do, however, force my thoughts away from his attractive face to focus on his injuries. He needs help, and I'm the only one around to give it. At least this, I can do.

Dropping down beside him, I undo my cloak and pull my satchel over my head before drawing my hood back on. Miraculously, even though the exterior of my bag is wet, the inside has remained fairly dry.

I sift through it until I find one of the jars of blessed salve. Drying my hands on my dress, I untwist the lid. A floral aroma floods the air, mingling with the scent of fresh rain from all around us. The creamy ointment is a stark white tinged with flecks of green. I reach in with one finger, careful not to take too much. After all, the ointment is worth its weight in gold. Enchanted medicine is both rare and expensive.

The royals are the only ones with magic. Queen Lucille, the suns protect her, only blesses a specific number of salves each year. Mother has used a portion of my Giving Allowance to purchase a jar of blessed salve once a year for as long as I can remember, accumulating a tiny stock of it at home. That's why she was able to save Father after the wolf attack.

It doesn't escape me how odd it is that the prized healing salve comes from the same court that is rumored to be soaked in blood. Even in Grenbloom, isolated though the village is, we often heard tales of the king's cruelty.

Some say King Andreas bathes in the blood of his enemies. Others say that he took his first life when he was merely ten years old, and he hasn't stopped killing since. There are arguments about how bloodthirsty the king truly is and disagreements about how many lives he's actually taken, but the one thing people can agree on is that King Andreas is not a man to anger.

And yet, his wife makes this salve that is sold all across the kingdom.

Musing about what I'm sure must be a complicated relationship between a dangerous man and his wife, I lean over my unconscious patient. My heart beats harder in my chest from my proximity to him—it's not like I've been around that many men in my life, other than my father and brothers—but I ignore it as I carefully apply the cool salve to the laceration on his forehead. His skin thirstily drinks in the cream, and I dip my finger back into the jar twice more before the cut is fully covered.

Now that the worst of his injuries is looked after, I stare at the man. Even unconscious, there's no hiding the fact that he's so much bigger than me. I pat him down, careful to avoid any major injuries and check for weapons. When I'm satisfied that he's unarmed, I shuffle away and rest against the stone wall.

My feet are killing me. They've been hurting for what feels like an eternity, but I've been ignoring the pain. Unfortunately, the time has come to see what exactly I'm dealing with.

Leaning down, I undo the laces and ease my boots off. They're surprisingly resistant to my efforts, and a low moan rises in my throat as I lift my right foot in the air.

My once-white stocking is red with blood. Wincing, I peel it off my foot before moving to the other one. I try to keep the fabric away from my skin as much as possible, but they're both so wet with blood that it's a losing battle.

"Oh, suns," I moan.

My feet are red and angry. Popped blisters line my soles. No wonder it felt like I was walking on embers.

Tears prick my eyes again, and I don't have the energy to stave them off. I'm too tired, too wet, and in too much pain.

I don't even care that there's a witness to my weakness—although he's unconscious, so thank the gods for that small mercy, I suppose. Wet, salty tears pour down my cheeks as I lift my feet and apply the cream to my raw skin.

At the first touch of the salve, the fire that had been burning beneath my skin dulls from a roaring blaze to a slow burn. Thank the gods I had the foresight to bring this with me. When I'm done, I replace the lid on the jar and stare at it. Guilt is creeping up inside me for taking this from my family, but I shove that emotion down, down, down.

I can't acknowledge it right now because if I do, it will devour me from the inside out. This isn't the time for things like grief or homesickness; I need to focus on my goal of staying alive.

To that end, I shove a piece of jerky into my mouth. The meat is stringy and tastes like a mélange of dried spices, but I can't afford to be picky and go hungry. Luckily, I'm past the point of caring what I eat, so it's not difficult to pretend the jerky is a rare delicacy and force it down. I continue until the piece is all gone, and by the time I'm done, my tears have dried up.

That's good. Tears have no place in the wilderness.

Needing to occupy myself with something in order to forget that a single strip of meat doesn't make a filling meal, I turn to the man I saved.

My breath hisses through my clenched teeth. Rugged handsomeness aside, he's in bad shape. Now that I'm paying attention and we're out of the rain, I count more bruises than before. His shirt is ripped, and I can make out the edge of a nasty bruise that is as dark as a night sky on his pale chest.

This isn't the work of an animal. One of the bruises on his chest looks an awful lot like a boot print, and a few others echo the shape of a very large fist. Whoever attacked this man must've wanted him dead because it looks like they kicked and punched every part of his body.

Even though I've already patted him down and felt for weapons, I don't pull his cloak and tunic away to look more closely at his chest. That seems like an invasion of privacy.

I lay my hand across the uncut part of his head to check for a fever and exhale. His skin is cool. Hopefully, I got the cream on in time.

When I was eleven, I rescued a limping kitten in the woods behind our house. She'd been so tiny, barely the size of my hand, and she'd cut her paw before I found her.

I brought her home and cleaned her wound as best I could, but it was so dirty. Even though I begged, Mother refused to let me use the enchanted cream on her. She said we couldn't waste such a valuable resource on a stray.

The cat died a week later, and I cried for a month.

I don't want the same thing to happen to this man. Not only because he looks like he has a lot of life left to live, but because witnessing Amelia's death was enough for me. Even though it's a natural part of life, I've had my fill of death.

Grabbing my canteen, I untwist the lid and carefully bring the vessel to the man's lips. I ignore the way his mouth seems so perfectly formed and lift his head with one hand, slowly pouring the liquid into his mouth. Water sloshes, and half of it dribbles down his scruff-covered chin, but the rest seems to go in.

That's better than nothing, and honestly, it's all I can manage right now.

Once my attractive patient has had water, I apply more salve to his forehead. The laceration seems to be the worst one he has, although there's another on his chest that must've hurt. I also coat that one in medicine, trying not to think about the firm muscles beneath my fingers. There's no doubt in my mind: This handsome man must love exercise because it feels like he's made of iron beneath his skin.

I move to replace the lid on the jar once again when my lips tug down. Bloody hell. I've already used a third of the salve.

This does not bode well for my survival. If I want to make it to the Sapphire Coast, I'll have to be more careful in the future. My resources are extremely limited, and I need to remember that.

I repack my satchel and grab my stockings. Holding them in one hand, I crawl to the entrance of the shelter. My knees ache from kneeling on the hard stone, but it's nothing compared to the way my feet felt earlier. I hold the stockings under the rain, letting them get soaked before I wring them out. Red rivulets run down the stones as the material fades to a light pink. I repeat the process several times until my hands are shaking and my eyes are drooping.

Crawling back, I lay the stockings out beside me to dry before placing my satchel on the rocky ground. Stretching out a few feet from the stranger, I draw my cloak tighter around myself. The material is wetter than I'd like, but I can't afford to take it off and let it dry.

I think it's early evening, although the sheets of rain make it hard to tell, and I'm done with this day. I take out Father's knife and hook the sheath onto my belt, thankful I have something to protect myself with.

Resting my head on my bag, I shimmy around until I find a semi-comfortable position. By *comfortable*, I mean that the rocks are only digging into part of my back and not all of it. This is nothing like a real bed, but with the direction my life has taken, even a wisp of comfort is better than nothing.

I stare into the trees, listening to the sounds of the forest. It's hard to hear over all the rain, but that doesn't stop my mind from remembering that dangerous predators call Myreth's woods their home.

Are they coming for me?

My heart races in my chest, and I jump at every cracking branch, every skitter of paws on the forest floor, and every whistle of wind.

I'm not sure how long passes as I stare into the rain, but eventually, the heaviness of my eyes is impossible to ignore. Sleep drags me into its embrace, momentarily freeing me from the hell that has become my life.

I don't dream at all, and the next time I open my eyes, the suns are shining brightly in the west. Well. They're shining as brightly as they can, since rain is still pouring from the heavens.

I didn't get eaten.

One would think I'd be delighted by that, but I barely manage a smile. Not getting eaten is great, but it doesn't help me with the mess that is my life. As if reminding me of that fact, my Mark is burning again. Can't I catch a single break?

My clothes are damp, which is an improvement from earlier, but it's still not great.

Rather than wallowing in pity for the terrible circumstances of my life, I turn my attention to the man beside me. He's just as handsome as I remember him being last night, but he seems bigger now that I've rested. More imposing and more good-looking, which shouldn't be possible.

I frown, gnawing on my bottom lip as I stare at him. I'm not entirely sure that bringing him back here was the best idea I've ever had. What will I do if he wakes up and sees my Mark?

The thought has me grabbing my hood in a rush, yanking it over my head, and covering the blue swirl. The movement sends fire running through me, and I swallow a strangled cry as tears prick my eyes.

The past two days were bad, but today? Today is going to be worse. I can feel it in my bones . . . and in my feet. They're going to be a problem. The open wounds have healed, thanks to the salve, but the skin is red.

When I gingerly touch my right foot, my finger might as well be the fire poker we used at home to stir the flames in the hearth.

"Fucking gods-damned suns," I hiss, drawing my finger back.

Stupidly, I poke the left one next. Unsurprisingly, it's fucking worse.

One touch, and it feels like flames are licking at my feet. A scream crawls up my throat, but I slap a hand over my mouth. I can't afford to attract attention, especially when I'm injured. The threat of predators seems even worse now. I'm stuck here for the day.

When the fire has abated to a more manageable burn, I apply more salve to my feet. I wish I didn't have to, but right now, I can't imagine walking to the edge of the forest, let alone the length of a kingdom.

Once that's done, I dig through my bag and pull out the white roll of bandages. Thank the gods I brought them with me. I wrap them around my feet, careful not to touch the inflamed flesh.

One time, I rescued a dog whose leg had been bitten by a wolf. When I brought him home, Mother showed me how to wrap his leg tightly—after she yelled at me about how foolishly sentimental I was, and couldn't I let someone else take care of animals, for once? Well, the dog's leg healed, and with any luck—not that I think there's much of that on my side—my feet will, too.

After they're wrapped, I ease my feet back into my boots. It's a much tighter fit than before, but I make it work. Just in time, too. I've been ignoring the call of nature, but I can't any longer. Using the rocks to help steady myself, I stand on wobbly legs.

A mangled scream rises in my throat, but I manage to shove it down. Hobbling away from my patient, I slip into a nearby grove of trees to relieve myself. I manage to stay mostly dry as I take care of my needs and find some leaves to wipe my hands before stumbling back to the shelter.

Every step feels like I'm walking on burning coals in bare feet, and I know deep in my soul that I won't be going anywhere today. I wish I could, because I need to put as much space between myself and the king's soldiers as possible, but that won't happen.

As soon as I can get off my feet, I do. Resting my back against the shale, I slip off my boots once more. Stretching my legs in front of me, I adjust my hood before letting my head fall back. There's nothing to do now but wait for the rain to stop and my feet to heal.

I hate waiting almost as much as I hate secrets. The suns seem to creep along the sky, and the day crawls by. Every hour feels longer than the last.

Waiting is *exhausting*. Or maybe it's all the running I did. Either way, sleep is pulling at me, trying to drag me back into its embrace.

I don't want to sleep, though. I'm not sure if it's the size of the unconscious man beside me, the realization that I can't go anywhere today even if I needed to, or the series of howls that I heard in the forest a short while ago, but I'm fighting sleep as best I can.

I'm using so much mental energy to stay awake that I can no longer fight against the thoughts that have been vying for my attention since my escape.

I left my family.

I'm an outlaw.

This isn't fair.

Everything is a lie.

What is the point of my Mark, anyway?

And on top of all that, there's one that's louder and more persistent than the others.

Amelia is dead.

She'll never smile, never laugh, never do anything again.

My chest aches, and I shove those thoughts away. I don't want to think about the Giving or my family or Amelia. If it won't help me survive, it's not worth worrying about right now. Making it past today, then tomorrow, and the next day. That's all I can handle right now.

Maybe in the future, I'll consider what more I want. The people I'd like to meet, the life I want to lead. Whether I still want to be a healer or if there is something else I want to do. I don't know. For so long, my identity has been wrapped up in my fate—I'm a Given, nothing more.

Now, I have no idea who I am. Not really.

"Gods above, Wren, get a grip." Thoughts like these aren't helpful in the slightest. I don't need to think more about how dire my situation is. All that will do is pull me into a pit of despair that I'm not certain I'll be able to get out of.

In an effort to distract myself, I check on my patient. His bruises are growing lighter, tinged in green and yellow, and his skin is a bit warmer than yesterday. His cuts are healing, and his breaths are more even.

He's going to make it.

Profound relief fills me, and a knot I hadn't realized existed loosens in my stomach. I may not know the man or anything about him, other than the fact that he was traveling in the woods all by himself, and he's extremely good-looking, but I don't want him to die.

Now that my patient is firmly on the path to health, I start thinking about what's to come. I can't leave yet—my feet are still far too sore—but once I can walk, I will go. I shouldn't wait around for this man to wake up. What do I know about him, really? He could be dangerous or ask too many questions. No, leaving before then would be best.

Going over my plan for the next few days, I gnaw on another piece of jerky and drink water. At least the rain is drinkable—I learned that from Markus—so I fill my canteen and drink as much as I want.

Eventually, despite my best efforts to remain awake and watch for predators, the drumming rain lulls me back to sleep.

The brush of a wet nose against my cheek pulls me out of my dreams. I wake slowly, my eyelashes fluttering against my cheek as I swat the animal away.

"Go away, Truffle," I mutter, my voice rough. "I thought I told you to stay home."

She presses her nose more firmly into my cheek, and my brows furrow. Truffle's nose isn't this big. It's cute and tiny, like the cat she is.

Frowning, I pry open my eyes.

A half gasp, half scream crawls up my throat, and I barely swallow it. My heart races in my chest, and any vestiges of sleep vanish.

The suns are rising, casting the forest in dim light. Somehow, I slept the entire night away. That isn't what has my heart hammering in my chest, though.

No.

That's all thanks to the massive feline standing in front of me. The animal's silky midnight fur shimmers in the morning light. It tilts its head, looking at me curiously. It's easily ten times Truffle's size, and at the end of its paws are claws that look like they could tear through my skin in a heartbeat.

"G-g-good kitty," I whisper, trying to keep the fear out of my voice.

Animals know what you're feeling, and the worst thing I can do is show the enormous cat that I'm terrified of it. I've been scratched by a regular house cat before, and it hurt. I cannot imagine how much it would hurt to be scratched by one of those claws.

It takes a moment, but the creature's name eventually crawls out of the recesses of my mind.

Panther.

Silver eyes that are pools of shimmering moonlight stare at me for so long that my mouth dries. I like cats, I do. But this panther isn't just a cat, it's a predator.

Well, it's official: My day has somehow gotten even worse.

My hand creeps towards the knife sheathed on my hip. I don't want to hurt the panther, but if it comes at me, I'll have no choice. I didn't run from my awful fate, only to die at the paws of an oversized cat.

"Please leave," I beg the panther, pulling out my knife and twisting the hilt in my hand. It's a foreign weight, and I hate the way it feels in my palm. "I really don't want to hurt you."

That would be a new low, even for me.

The longest moment passes before the feline cants its head and slowly backs away. Did it understand me? I don't dare look away as its paws move soundlessly over the shale. The panther pauses at the injured man, bending its head and licking the dried blood off his forehead.

Disgusting. I shudder as the cat continues its ministrations, only stopping when the man's skin is clean. Then, with a final glance of those silver eyes in my direction, the panther bounds off into the forest.

I shiver, staring into the trees long after the panther's disappearance. The entire encounter has left me feeling strange, and I won't be able to fall back asleep. Not that I particularly want to. Nightmares of being caught had filled my slumber, and it had been less than peaceful.

The rain has slowed to a gentle pitter-patter, and the forest is calm in the wake of the storm. The trees glisten, their leaves an array of brilliant yellows and oranges. Tiny brown and grey squirrels hop from one branch to another. Gentle birdsong lilts through the air, insects chirp, and a rabbit darts by. The forest is coming to life before my eyes.

There's a beauty in it that I cannot stand. How can beauty exist in a world built on a foundation of lies?

It hurts to watch the trees swaying in the wind, to hear the beautiful symphonies the birds sing, and to see the lush plants growing all around me.

I'm mourning the life I thought I'd have as a gods-blessed, and the world doesn't seem to understand. Everyone else is going on with their lives as if my world isn't crumbling around me.

It isn't fucking fair.

None of this is.

I tug my hood further over my head and gather my cloak around myself, wishing I could burrow into the fabric. If I possessed magic and was capable of disappearing into thin air, I would. Vanishing and never dealing with the absolute hell that has become my life sounds perfect right now.

I've never wished to be royal more than I do at this very moment. Why did Esyn decide that they would be the only ones blessed with magic?

Rude, honestly.

What makes the royals so special, anyway? Besides the obvious facts, of course. They have magic; I don't. They rule over the kingdom; I'm on my own. Perhaps most notably, considering my current situation, they aren't on the run for their lives; I very much am.

What a mess. If I had even a drop of power, I'd use it to save myself.

I scoff, shaking my head to clear it of these ridiculous thoughts. I'm not royal, and I never will be. My veins are devoid of power, just like the majority of the population in Myreth. To top it all off, I'm in a far worse situation than most.

I'm a Given on the run, and chances are, I'm going to die before I ever find freedom. I decided to live, and to be honest, yesterday, that sounded great. But now that I've slept and survived an encounter with a panther, I'm realizing how difficult and lonely it will be. Not to mention the soreness that will inevitably plague me if I have to keep running.

Living seems like so much more work today than it did yesterday.

I stare into the woods, wondering if I should try to call the panther back. Maybe I should let it rip out my throat. At least then I'd be dead, and I'd no longer have to deal with this.

Maybe—

A groan comes from my patient, breaking through my spiral of despair. That's good.

Feeling sorry for myself and my circumstances is another luxury I don't have time for. Wishing to be royal won't help me survive, and hoping for magic won't miraculously infuse my veins with power. If wishes worked, my Giving Mark would be gone, and I'd be free.

But they don't, so I'm stuck with my shitty circumstances. I can't do anything about them, but I can help my patient.

I crawl across the shale, careful to keep my weight on my knees. My feet feel . . . better.

Well.

Better is probably an overstatement. A rather large one, if I'm being honest. But at least, instead of burning, they're throbbing incessantly. It's progress, though, and I'll take it.

I reach the man as he groans again.

Frowning, I quickly sheathe my knife and brush back a lock of his hair. From afar, it appears black, but up close, there's a blue tint to it like a raven's cloak caught in sunlight. His laceration has healed, and his skin isn't nearly as pale as it was when I first found him.

That magnetic pull seems stronger than it was before, and I couldn't pull my gaze away from my patient, even if I tried.

His face is chiseled and well-defined, his cheekbones are strong, and his eyes . . .

They blink open, and suddenly, two shimmering emeralds are staring right at me.

8

A GLOWING BEACON

Wren

My brain stalls, and it's like I forget how to speak, let alone move. Taking this man in and helping him seemed like a good idea at the time, but he'd been unconscious then, and I'd been exhausted.

I'm afraid that the tiredness may have slightly clouded my judgment because now that he's awake and looking right at me, I'm realizing just how bad an idea this was.

On the outside, my face is blank, but inside, I'm panicking. I knew this was risky. Why didn't I leave with the panther? What in gods' names possessed me to stay?

I reach up and tug my hood, making sure my Mark is covered as I hold the handsome stranger's gaze. I probably should've planned for this, but I didn't. Not really.

What do I say? What should I do? I should probably be calm, right?

That seems like a good idea. I should pretend that everything is normal. Like *I'm* normal. The problem is that I'm so acutely aware of how not normal I am that I'm not sure I could ever pretend to be otherwise.

My palms grow slick as anxiety twists around my heart, squeezing tightly. Not for the first time since I snuck into Esyn's temple and witnessed my best friend's gruesome murder, I realize how completely unprepared for life I am.

It's probably too late to just back away, right? This man, whoever he is, would probably find that suspicious, and raising suspicion is the last thing I want to do.

Since running is out of the question, I breathe deeply and try to remain calm.

You can do this, I tell myself. *Just remember, you're relaxed, normal, and not on the run for your life.*

The thoughts don't do much to calm me.

"Hi." The monosyllabic word is the first that comes to mind, and wow. That's delightfully inarticulate.

Rocking back on my heels, I force myself to keep my face calm, even though internally, I'm slapping myself for being such an awkward mess. I pulled this man out of a bush and healed him, and the first thing I can think to say is *Hi*?

Suns save me from myself.

Those emerald eyes stare at me for another long moment before the corners of his lips quirk up into a smile. If he was ruggedly handsome before, now he's downright captivating. My stomach flutters at the sight, which is a wholly inappropriate reaction since the man was on the brink of death a short while ago.

Add that to my list of problems, I suppose. Not only am I awkward, but I keep having inappropriate thoughts about the man I saved in the woods, of all people.

"Hi," he rasps in a baritone voice.

Something deep within me twists at the sound, and if I weren't in a dire situation, I'd probably take the time to appreciate the way it makes me feel. Like warmth and sunshine and something . . . more. Like I'm drawn to him in a way that I haven't been drawn to anyone before.

But how in gods' names could one word make me feel like that? I don't understand. We just met.

My patient tries to sit up, hissing and grabbing at his stomach.

"Careful." I reach out on instinct, gently pushing his shoulder back to the shale.

I definitely don't pay attention to how well-built he is, nor do I notice that even though I've always been on the curvier side of things, he's so tall that he makes me feel small. Noticing these types of things would be inappropriate, considering our circumstances.

Reminding myself that I'm supposed to be acting normal, I add, "You were badly hurt, and you shouldn't be moving right now."

"What?" His eyes widen, and his chest heaves as he tries to sit up again. Gods, does this man not know how to listen? He was a much better patient when he was asleep. "What happened?"

His panic is palpable; and I can't help but feel bad for him.

"I'm not sure," I admit. "I found you beneath a bush, and it looks like you were beaten up."

"I . . . I don't remember." His brows come together, and anxiety leaks into his voice. "What woods are we in?"

Well, that's a very good question, isn't it? I'm not entirely sure of the answer, but I'm guessing that I unfortunately haven't gone too far from home yet, so I take a guess and say, "River Bend Forest."

Named for the enormous river that runs through the province, the forest spans most of Eskana. Since I haven't made it that far, it would make sense that this is where we are.

My patient exhales. The name must bring him some comfort because some of his panic subsides. "Okay. Thank you. That makes sense, even though I still don't remember."

My heart twists at the pain in his words. Even with the horrible turn my life has taken, I've never lost my memories. I can't imagine how frightening it would be to wake up and not know that something has happened to you.

There's a strange need within me that I don't fully understand. It wants me to comfort him, help him feel better, and assure him that he'll be okay. His pain feels like my pain in a way that I'm not entirely clear on. I've never felt like this for any of my patients before. To be fair, they were animals and not humans, but still.

This is different.

"No, I figured you might not. You had a bad laceration on your forehead." I indicate the spot on my own head—above my hood, of course—but drop my hand as he tries to speak but breaks out into a cough instead. "Suns, I'm sorry. You must be parched."

He nods, and I reach behind me, grab the canteen, and offer him a drink. After he dips his head, I unscrew the lid and bring the vessel to his lips. He opens his mouth, and I pour the liquid in as slowly as I can. This time, every drop makes it in.

My patient swallows, and I definitely don't notice the way his throat bobs, nor do I pay attention to the way his emerald eyes track my movements. That would be ridiculous.

"Thank you," he says when I pull the water away. His voice sounds better, and there's a sincerity about him that makes me feel comfortable. Or maybe that's the loneliness talking.

Is it possible to go insane from being alone for a few days? I'm not entirely sure, but based on the way I've been dealing with my newfound status as an outlaw, it seems plausible.

"You're welcome." I bite my lip and shuffle backwards.

I should leave; I know that. Carrying on a conversation with this man is stupid for a plethora of reasons. For one, I don't know him. For another, as previously mentioned, I'm an outlaw.

These are all great points, but I can't make myself move. The same part of me that ached at the thought of his pain doesn't want to leave. It's urging me to stay, to talk with him, and form a connection. It wants me to do something that I don't quite understand.

Besides, getting up and leaving mid-conversation would raise alarm bells, which is the last thing I want to do.

"You saved my life," he says before I can figure out how to get away without being suspicious.

"I couldn't leave you to die." No one with a heart could do that. "I brought you back and used some blessed salve on you. It seems to have worked."

Obviously. I barely contain my groan, and my cheeks heat. Gods above. Maybe my normal is just being awkward as hell. It certainly feels that way as I stumble through this conversation.

He either doesn't notice my awkwardness, or he's too polite to point it out. Either way, he tilts his head, his hair falling over his eyes in an attractive way that makes it difficult to concentrate on his words. "Queen Lucille's salve?"

I nod, unwilling to speak again in case my tongue continues to betray me. I can't risk saying something even more awkward and embarrassing.

Intrigue sparks in the man's gaze, and I try not to shiver as he studies me. My Mark is hidden. I can feel the brim of my hood above my eyes, assuring me it hasn't shifted. Even so, my fingers itch to make sure the swirl is covered. I don't move, though, because I don't want to draw attention to it.

"Then I suppose I'm in your debt . . ." His voice trails off, clearly waiting for my name.

Seeing that I still possess a modicum of sense, even though I'm still sitting here, I don't give him my name. I drop my eyes to my lap and twist my fingers together. "I just did what anyone would do."

Who could leave someone in pain? Even in my current predicament, I can't imagine being so cold and unfeeling. For the same reason that I've never been able to leave a wounded animal behind, I had to help him.

"Still, you have my thanks." He pushes himself up into a sitting position, even though he winces, resting his back against the shale.

I want to tell him that moving so much is probably a bad idea since he's been recently healed, but I keep the words inside. The sooner this conversation is over, the better. I really need to get going. Every second I'm here is another where my secret can be revealed.

I'm sweeping my eyes over the forest, trying to think of a way out of this, when he holds his hand out between us. "My name's Gabriel."

Gods, that's a nice name. It fits him—he's big and strong and sturdy, just like the moniker suggests.

He wiggles his fingers in my direction, clearly waiting for me to put my hand in his and shake it. Damn it. Refusing to do this will arouse suspicion, but something within me is warning me that shaking his hand is a bad idea.

I don't know why, exactly, only that everything within me is urging me to run in the opposite direction. I can't pinpoint the reason, since Gabriel doesn't seem all that threatening.

Sure, he's bigger than me and clearly has an exercise regime that would probably have me crying on the floor within five minutes, but his scabbard is empty, and he doesn't have a bow.

He certainly looks less dangerous than the Watchers that patrol Grenbloom on a regular basis. Not to mention the way I'm drawn to him. Why would I be drawn to someone who could hurt me?

Gabriel clears his throat. Oh, gods, he's still waiting for me. So much for not being awkward. Before I can continue overthinking things and potentially make them worse, I slip my hand into his, bad ideas be damned.

Except . . . oh, suns. The moment his warm hand envelops mine, my stomach flutters. Sparks seem to jump between us, and every part of me wants this moment to continue forever. My breath catches in my throat, and my eyes fly up to his.

It's like the lightning from yesterday's storm has been bottled up and infused into this brief contact. Every part of me yearns to get closer to him, the feeling much stronger than before.

I don't understand how all of this is coming from a simple touch. Every rough callous on his hands feels amazing against my smooth skin.

Does he notice the sparks, too? I'm afraid to ask because it's probably just in my head. A side effect of everyone keeping their distance from me for years. That's it. I'm starved for touch, unused to getting attention. There's absolutely nothing else happening here.

Gabriel shakes my hand, and I exhale. Okay. That wasn't so bad. Now, I can go.

When the appropriate time for a handshake comes and goes, I try to pull my hand from his. "It's a pleasure to make your acquaintance, Gabriel."

Instead of letting me go, those calloused fingers tighten around mine. My treacherous heart jumps as I glance down to where he's touching me.

"Wait," Gabriel says, the word echoing around the clearing as his thumb rubs the back of my hand. He's still touching me, and this is . . . unexpected.

I'm not sure whether it's good or bad, but I can't deny that holding his hand is nice. That's a strange thought to have about a man I barely know, but it is what it is.

I lift my gaze back to his. "Yes?"

"I gave you my name, but I still don't know yours." Gabriel raises a brow and smirks, his thumb continuing its trail down the back of my hand.

For a moment, I'm taken aback by the way the expression transforms his face. Before, he was handsome, but now, it's like he's a statue that's been chiseled by the gods. I could stare at him for hours and not get bored.

He continues, "How can I owe you a debt if I don't know what to call you?"

My stomach drops, and if I'd eaten anything more than jerky recently, it would've risen in my throat. My tongue grows heavy, and the fingers of my free hand twitch at my sides.

This.

This is exactly why I should've left the moment he opened his eyes and stared at me. Awkwardness be damned, it would've been better than this current situation.

Panic twists my heart, and I barely avoid gasping for breath. Burning suns, I've been so stupid. Who cares if his stupid hand feels nice holding mine? I can't give him my name. I might not know much about being an outlaw, but I do know that my name is unique.

Why couldn't my parents have picked a simpler name for me, one that wouldn't stand out? It's not like the swirl on my forehead makes blending in easy, but by naming me Wren, they made it practically impossible.

Even if this man has no idea who I am—and suns, I'm praying that's the case—I don't want him to know my real name. There are too many ways that that could go wrong.

Instead, I tell him the first thing that comes to mind. "Most people call me Birdie."

According to Mother, James was the one who came up with the nickname when I was a baby. It caught on quickly, and my entire family called me that before I could walk. It was even Violet's first word.

A pang of sadness lances through me at the thought of the family I've left behind, and I send a quick prayer to Esyn for their safety.

I ran away all on my own, I remind the gods, in case they're listening. It's doubtful, but I need to try. *They didn't have anything to do with it.*

Unaware of my inner turmoil, Gabriel smiles. "Pleasure to make your acquaintance, Birdie."

He doesn't seem to question the unusual name, and I exhale. Okay. This is going . . . not terribly. My Mark is hidden, and I'm carrying on a normal conversation with this handsome, kind man. My shoulders relax an increment, and I settle more deeply into a sitting position.

I can do this.

"How are you feeling?" I ask in an effort to maintain the normalcy of our conversation even though he's still holding my hand. I should be yanking my fingers back, but I don't.

I could say it's because I want a moment where things are normal, but I'm not sure that's true. His fingers are much longer than mine, and there's something comforting about his touch and the way he's looking at me. I don't hate being the object of his attention at all.

Besides, it's just hand-holding. How bad could it be?

"I've been better," he replies, arching a brow. "But I have a feeling that I would be in much worse shape without you. You're a good caretaker."

Heat rushes to my cheeks, and I chew on the inside of my lip as I drop my gaze to my lap. "It's easy to take care of someone when they're such a good patient."

"Oh?"

I look back up and nod. "You didn't try to bite me once, which I'm eternally grateful for."

Gabriel's lips twitch, and gods, it's a handsome sight. Part of me wants to reach up and trace the smile, but I don't because I haven't lost all my senses.

He asks, "Have you been bitten by your patients often?"

I *laugh*. The sound takes me by surprise, and for a moment, I can't even believe it. How can I be laughing when my best friend was just murdered? My smile slips as I recall the way her head slammed against the altar.

Keep it together.

"It's only happened once," I tell him. "But it was enough."

Last year, I was walking down the path behind my home when I heard a low moan from beneath a pile of fallen leaves. The sound had tugged on my heart, and when I moved the brush aside, I discovered a small raccoon with a bleeding paw. I promptly named him Sir Hardwell and brought him home to help him heal.

The problem was that unlike most of my other patients, Sir Hardwell hated being cared for. He let me hold him, but every time I tried to look at his paw, he attempted to remove a chunk of my hand with his teeth. When Mother found out about Sir Hardwell's carnivorous tendencies, she banished him to the small shed out back, where he resided until he healed.

"Well, rest assured, I don't bite." Gabriel's eyes twinkle, and he leans in conspiratorially. He releases my hand and inches closer, waggling his brows. "Unless you want me to."

My eyes widen at his suggestive tone, and my mind is more than happy to supply me with plenty of mental images of what he means. The two of us with far fewer clothes, tangled together, close in the most timeless of ways.

My core heats at the thought, and a wave of warmth passes through me, taking me by surprise. I've never experienced this kind of reaction before. It's not that I haven't been around men, but the boys from my village were just that—boys.

All my romantic and sexual experiences, including losing my virginity, were brief. They didn't inspire much emotion in me beyond feeling normal for a few minutes. Certainly, none of them ever brought me close to feeling like this. Who is this man that he inspires such a strong reaction in me?

"I . . . uh . . . maybe later." My cheeks heat, and I fight the urge to hide my face in my hands.

Oh my gods. Did I just tell him he could *bite* me? What in Esyn's name is wrong with me?

It's Gabriel's turn to chuckle, and the deep sound has my core tightening once more. Gods, this is good. *Easy*.

Maybe I was worried for nothing. Maybe I might be able to survive as an outlaw, after all. It doesn't seem *that* difficult. All I need to do is keep my hood on for the foreseeable future, use a new name, get new clothes, and leave the country.

I can do this.

In fact, not only can I do this, but I must do this. If I'm going to live, I need to get used to talking to people without each interaction being a lesson in awkwardness.

With that thought in mind, I reach into my satchel and pull out the pack of dried jerky. Just over half the rations remain. I take a piece for myself, handing another to Gabriel.

Gratitude shines in his green eyes as he takes it, his fingers sweeping over mine again. Am I imagining things, or did his fingers rest over mine for a moment too long? I can't help but wonder if he feels the same urge to close the distance between us.

"Thank you, Birdie."

The sound of my nickname coming from this stranger's mouth is a jolt to my system, a reminder that even though this man is ridiculously rugged and handsome, I'm still an outlaw. I need to be careful.

I dip my head, trying to get a grip on my emotions. "You're welcome."

I take a bite of jerky, trying not to frown at the taste. The flavor hasn't improved, but food is food, and I'm grateful for anything right now.

Relaxing further against the stone, I nibble on my meal. "So, Gabriel." He glances at me. "Where did you come from? I assume you don't spend all your time in the middle of the forest getting attacked."

That would make for a rather awful existence.

A guffaw bursts out of him. "No, you're right. I come from Rosebridge."

I lower my jerky and stare at him, wide-eyed. "The kingdom's capital city?" Even Father, well-traveled though he is, has never been to Rosebridge. "That's so far."

Gabriel smiles, and a hint of emotion flashes through his eyes. "It is, but distance isn't always a bad thing."

It sounds like there's a story there.

"What's it like?" I ask, taking another nibble.

"Have you never been?"

I shake my head, my cheeks flushing. "Never."

He makes a sound in the back of his throat and shifts, seeming to get more comfortable.

"Rosebridge is enormous," he says after a moment. "There are people everywhere. The royal family lives there, of course, and most noble families have a residence in the city." He gestures to our surroundings. "Imagine the forest, but instead of trees, there are hundreds of buildings."

My eyes move from Gabriel to the trees, then back.

"There must be hundreds of thousands of people there," I breathe. I can't even picture that many people in my mind.

He agrees. "It can be a lot, if you don't like people."

"And do you?"

"Hmm?"

"Like people."

His brows bend, and he takes another bite, seeming to ponder the question. "Not usually," he admits after a moment. "My family life is . . . difficult."

His words echo with a deep pain that has an insane part of me wanting to hug him, ignoring the fact that we've basically just met.

That doesn't seem like something a normal person would do, though, so instead, I say, "I'm sorry."

He dips his chin. "Me, too."

Silence stretches between us, but it isn't uncomfortable. There's a familiarity between us that feels like we've known each other for years, not less than a day. Several minutes pass, and I finish my jerky.

"So, what brings you to the area, Gabriel? You're a long way from the capital."

He smiles, and whatever pain had been on his face before is gone. "I'm working."

Well, I suppose that makes sense. Marked Ones don't have jobs, for obvious reasons, but it stands to reason that Gabriel is gainfully employed.

I eye him. He definitely works with his body—maybe he's a blacksmith or a farmer? Part of me wants to pry and find out more, but it feels like it would open up a topic of conversation I'm not sure I'm ready to deal with. If I ask him too many questions, he might do the same. What if he wants to know something I'm not comfortable sharing? I have a world of secrets to protect.

"Do you enjoy your work?" I ask instead, taking a sip of my water.

Not everyone likes what they do, but there's a sparkle in Gabriel's eye that intrigues me and makes it feel like a safe topic of conversation.

"Yes." He smiles, leaning in closer to me. "There are certain aspects that aren't pleasant, but for the most part, I enjoy it immensely. Being out in the woods, traveling throughout Myreth, meeting people." He gestures to me when he says the last part. "It's all enjoyable."

The relaxed look on his face reminds me of Father when he talks about the butcher shop. The corners of my lips tilt up, and I imagine that one day, I'm going to find something that gives me as much joy when I talk about it.

"That must be nice."

"It is." Gabriel finishes his jerky, and I pass him the canteen of water without thinking. Our fingers brush once again, and another spark of awareness runs through me.

A niggling voice inside my mind tells me I should probably question *why* I feel so comfortable with Gabriel, but I shove it aside. These are the first true moments of peace I've experienced since Amelia's murder, and I don't want to lose them.

There will be time for questions later.

He brings the water to his lips, and I unashamedly watch as he swallows. For someone so big, he moves with so much ease. Like the panther from earlier, there's a grace to his movements.

When he's done drinking, he hands the canteen back to me with a thanks. His stomach grumbles loudly, and my cheeks burn. Gods, he must be starving. Whatever he does for work must be physical, and I'm sure he has to eat a lot to maintain a physique like his.

I hold out the bag of dried meat. "Want another? I don't particularly enjoy these."

He grins as though I've offered him a feast. "I'd love that."

He eats the next piece in record time, as if it's the last meal he'll ever enjoy. It's not like I've never witnessed a man eat at incredible speeds—I do have two older brothers, after all—but there's something different about Gabriel that I can't quite put my finger on.

I . . . smile. Not a twitch of my lips, but a full smile. Like the laugh from earlier, it feels so strange that I can barely believe it.

Earlier, I was feeling so depleted, but now, things are looking up.

I hand Gabriel another piece of jerky, and while he munches on it, I wiggle my toes experimentally. My smile widens when I discover that instead of throbbing pain, there's a mere hum in my feet. The pain is still there, but it's manageable. I slip my dried stockings over the bandages, studying the forest while I do so.

The rain has turned into a drizzle, and shards of sunlight are breaking through the clouds. One such sliver of light falls on the forest, illuminating a small cluster of white mushrooms growing at the base of a tree not far into the woods.

The mushrooms are small, about two inches tall, and their stems look to be the size of my pinky finger. I think I recognize them, but I'm not certain.

But Gabriel . . .

"You've spent a lot of time in these woods, right?" I ask, turning to the rugged man.

He nods, and my smile widens. It's practically a grin at this point, which feels . . . odd.

I point to the fungi. "Do you see those?"

"The mushrooms?"

"Mm-hmm." I glance back at him. "Do you recognize them?"

His eyes narrow for a moment before he dips his chin. "They look like blossom mushrooms. Why do you ask?"

My stomach growls in response before I can tell him, and he chuckles. "Ah. You're hungry." He leans forward, resting his arms on his knees as he studies the cluster from here. "I think they're safe to eat. You should make sure there isn't a red mark on them, though. Blossom mushrooms can sometimes be mistaken for their cousin, butterfly mushrooms. Those aren't for eating unless you plan on dying a painful death."

"Dying is the last thing I want to do." My words ring with truth as I wiggle my feet back into my boots. They're tighter than before, between the bandages and the stockings, but I get them on.

Gabriel goes back to chewing on his jerky as I gingerly stand. My feet are still sore, but the pain isn't awful, and I take a few trial steps. Since I don't feel like screaming or crying, I will count this as a victory.

My smile remains as I pick my way across the forest floor, careful not to trip on the plethora of roots sticking up out of the ground. The last thing I need right now is a twisted ankle. It would make an already bad situation even worse.

The ground squelches as I move, the spongy earth shifting as I put my weight on it. I avoid puddles, and soon, I reach the cluster of fungi.

Blossom mushrooms. Up close, I can see where they get their names from. They look like upside-down flowers in bloom. Each has a round bulb and white petals that fan out underneath.

I crouch, picking one and turning it over carefully as I study it. I don't see any discoloration, and it looks safe enough.

"Well, here goes nothing," I mutter before tossing the entire mushroom into my mouth.

It's chewy and has a definitive earthy flavor, but it tastes significantly better than the jerky. I swallow and wait, several moments passing in silence. Since I don't drop dead, have a splitting headache, or feel a sudden onset of sharp pain, I decide the blossom mushrooms are safe to eat.

Gathering as many as I can carry, I cradle them against my chest and stand. Keeping my head down, I navigate my way across the forest floor, cautious of the roots. The last thing I want to do is scatter my food all over the ground and let it go to waste.

"Do you like mushrooms?" I ask, carefully maneuvering over the stones. "These are a little earthy, but they're tasty. At least, I think so . . ."

My voice trails off as I lift my head and meet Gabriel's gaze. An angry growl rumbles through his chest, and he's shifted into a crouch. His hands are balled at his sides, his eyes are wide, and he's staring at me as though he's seen a ghost.

I freeze, one foot on the shale and the other midair. Is there an animal behind me? Oh, gods. Did the panther come back? Or is it a bear? Or maybe a pack of wolves?

"Um, what . . ." I ask.

At the same time, he angrily rasps, "You're Marked to be Given."

Fuck.

My smile plummets, and my arms fall open. The mushrooms tumble to the ground, plunking as they hit the shale, and I stare at Gabriel.

Sweat gathers at the back of my neck, and I can't breathe.

Suns save me. I reach for my hood with trembling fingers, only to realize that it's slipped back. It must have moved when I climbed the rock.

Oh gods, oh gods, oh gods.

My mouth dries, and my stomach churns. The mushroom I just ate threatens to come up as Amelia's lifeless body flashes before my eyes. My throat is closing in on itself, and a fist is compressing my lungs. They burn as I try and fail to draw breath.

The air thickens as those damned green eyes drill into mine. I wish I could move, but I'm frozen in place.

He's seen my Mark. It's a fucking glowing beacon, telling the world *This gods-blessed is twenty and ready to be Given.*

I'm not sure what I hate more right now—the blue Mark on my forehead or my fucking compassionate heart. If I had left well enough alone, I wouldn't be standing in front of an angry man who knows I'm gods-blessed.

Gabriel rises to his feet, his movements shockingly steady for a man who was on the brink of death not long ago. His gaze is unwavering as he steps towards me, and my stomach swoops.

"You're Marked to be Given," he repeats.

A dark gleam enters his eyes, and a hardness takes over his face. My stomach twists into a tight knot, and every part of me is crying out for me to get out of here.

But it's too late to flee. It's too late to do anything.

Before I can think of a single thing to say, he growls, "It's you."

There's a knowing in his words that has me screaming inside. I take a trembling step back, squishing a mushroom beneath my foot.

It doesn't matter. None of it matters anymore. Maybe it never did.

"What?" I whisper hoarsely, my lungs still struggling to work. Why didn't I run when I had the chance? "No."

I don't even know what exactly I'm refuting, only that it's imperative that I deny whatever he's claiming. I stumble back, trying to create space between us, but Gabriel doesn't let me.

For every step I take, he moves as well.

His green eyes sharpen, studying me with an assessing gaze that seems far too perceptive. "What did you say your name was again?"

A whooshing fills my ears, and my lungs tighten, tighten, tighten. Black spots appear in my vision. In my mind, I can hear Mistress Fyona reminding me to breathe, but I can't.

What fucking good will breathing do now?

Gabriel has seen my Mark, and he *knows*. I don't know how he does, but it's reflected in his eyes.

"Tell me your name," he barks.

His voice is so loud, and his command is so powerful that my mouth automatically opens. "Birdie."

He snarls, the predatory sound causing my flesh to prickle, as he stands to his full height. Suns, have mercy on my soul. How could I have ever thought that he didn't look threatening? Clearly, I've been a gods-damned fool.

Gabriel stands over half a foot taller than my nearly six feet, and an aura of violence radiates off him. A lethal sense of power flows around him as if it cannot be contained in his body. I've been in the presence of dangerous men before, but Gabriel . . .

Something about him makes my soul quake in terror. I've never felt fear like what is currently coursing through my veins.

I take another trembling step back.

He advances with deadly grace.

I move to the left.

He mirrors my actions.

Gabriel is a predator, and somehow, I know I'm his prey. Esyn save me. I'd been so worried about the creatures that call the forest their home, yet I unknowingly saved the most dangerous one of them all.

"No," he growls, the deep tenor of his voice sending tremors running through me. "Your *real* name."

My heart is racing so fast, I'm afraid it's going to erupt out of my chest.

"My name is Birdie," I insist, even as the lie tastes bitter on my tongue. I don't like lying. I never have. But it's better to lie and live than tell the truth and die. At least, that's what I tell myself.

He shakes his head and laughs. The cruel sound fills the air, and shivers cascade down my spine.

"It's Wren, isn't it?" He reaches inside his cloak, pulling out a crumpled piece of parchment. A red emblem is stamped on the back, and blood drains from my face.

An eagle and two suns. The king's sigil. It's different from the other times I've seen it, though. A sword is in front of the eagle, the tip pointing down. I should probably know what that means, but I can't remember. My stomach still churns at the sight, though, and it can't be good.

"'Wren Nightingale,'" he reads, his voice devoid of the warmth and charm that had been present earlier.

I hate the way he says my name in that deep voice of his. I hate the way his lips form the words. I even hate the way his stupid, unmarked hands clutch the parchment.

I hate it all.

He continues. "'Twenty years old. Marked to be Given on the fifteenth day of the eleventh month.'"

"It's not—"

He flashes me a withering glare and continues, speaking the words that make me wish I was anywhere else.

"'Fled the morning of her Giving Ceremony.'"

My fingers inch towards the knife sheathed at my hip. What are the chances I can stab him and get away? I don't know, but right now, I'm willing to try anything.

"Don't," he snarls, looking up from the note.

As if I'm going to listen to him. Self-preservation is the only thing on my mind as I ignore his warning and grab the blade. I pull it out of the sheath, keeping the knife between us.

"Who are you?" I demand.

Father's blade looks laughably small compared to Gabriel's size, but I can't help but feel a bit better having *something* between me and him.

A stupidly handsome brow lifts. "You know who I am."

I stare at him, my mind putting together the pieces that I suspected but haven't been ready to acknowledge. The sealed note. The knowing look in his eyes. The fucking fact that he was in the woods in the first place.

I should've realized who he was from the moment I first laid eyes on him.

My mouth dries, and I stumble back. The black spots in my vision worsen. The knife trembles in my grip. My head is light, and it takes everything I have not to be sick.

I know who he is. What he is. But to say it out loud . . . to admit it . . .

I'm not sure I can.

"You're a . . . a . . ."

"Say it," Gabriel growls, stepping towards me.

My heartbeats are like butterfly wings, flapping wildly in my chest.

He's right. I know exactly who he is, which is how I can now say with certainty that the gods have never favored me. They've never cared for me. I'm the only one looking out for me, and clearly, I haven't done a great job.

I'm unable to keep fear from leaking into my voice as I whisper, "You're a Hunter."

The king employs four types of soldiers: Watchers, Enforcers, Protectors, and . . . Hunters.

Whenever Mistress Fyona spoke about the Hunters, her voice would be tinged with a sense of awe. They're revered, she always said.

Special soldiers whose only task is to track down outlaws and ensure they meet justice.

And I'm standing in front of one.

He jerks his chin. "I am."

My fingers spasm around my knife, and I rasp, "Fuck."

What else can I say?

"Yeah." His nostrils flare, and his hands flex at his sides. "Fuck."

9

A SUNS-DAMNED MORAL QUANDARY

Gabriel

Rising suns, this is fucking bad.

Any lingering soreness that had been plaguing me is long gone, having evaporated the moment I saw that incriminating blue swirl on her forehead. It's been replaced by a raging headache that's getting worse by the fucking second.

I can't pull my gaze away from the Marked One in front of me.

How is this possible? The Kingdom of Myreth is home to millions of people. How in gods' names did the girl who saved me end up being the one I'm hunting?

No.

Not a girl. A woman, and a beautiful one, at that. Her face has a sharpness that I noticed as soon as I woke up. She's curvy, which is how I've always enjoyed my women. Indigo curls match the fire in her violet eyes.

I enjoyed talking to and getting to know her, and I even let down my guard and told her a bit about myself. She's clearly kind because she saved me. For a few minutes, I relaxed in her presence, and I rarely do that around other people.

But none of that matters because she's gods-blessed. Her Mark is glowing, a dead giveaway that she's ready to be Given this year.

Burning suns, how did this happen? First, the fucking attack. I've been putting bits and pieces together of what happened to me ever since I woke up. I'm not entirely sure how it happened, but a mere hour after the enchanted falcon delivered the message about my newest hunt, Mist and I were attacked.

Robbers and other criminals aren't exactly scarce in Myreth's forests. After all, life in the kingdom is hard at the best of times, and people have been known to grow desperate. I fought back, but they must've overpowered me somehow.

My memory is still foggy, but I remember telling Mist to get help before I lost consciousness. The last thing I remember before falling into darkness was watching her run into the forest. I'm not sure how much time passed before I woke up to a pair of stunning violet eyes inches from mine.

At first, I thought the suns had blessed me. Birdie was an angel in disguise who saved me from death and healed my wounds. Her scent had faint traces of jasmine and vanilla, and from the moment I woke, there was a connection between us that I'd never felt before.

Now, though?

I'm doubting whether the infernal suns have ever cared about me at all. In my twenty-seven years of life, I've never encountered such a gods-damned awful situation. She saved me, but she's the one I'm hunting.

The Given—Wren—moves to step away from me, and I snarl, "Don't."

The sharp word echoes through the forest, a command that demands attention. She freezes, her damned violet eyes unblinking as she studies me.

A growl rumbles through me. "Don't fucking move."

I need to figure out what to do, and I can't do that if she's running away. Suns, have mercy on my soul. How is this happening? If I didn't know any better, I'd say that one of the gods was having fun fucking up my life. The hunt was supposed to be easy. Catch her, bring her back to Grenbloom, and finally achieve my new status as Master Hunter.

Her mouth pinches in a line, and her gaze is unwavering. Even though she's obeying my order—something that makes me far too happy for such a fucked-up situation—her chest is heaving, and the air is heavy between us.

Esyn's tits, everything I've come up against in my life pales in comparison to this.

My other hunts were relatively simple, all things considered. Escaped prisoners rarely get far before they're caught, thanks to the generally malnourished state they're kept in. The king's prisons aren't known for providing three square meals a day, after all.

And then there's the gods-blessed. There are far fewer Marked Ones who run compared to fleeing criminals, and they're usually caught within a day before being returned to their respective temples.

I know what I'm supposed to do.

I *should* lunge forward, grab her, and tie her up with whatever vines I can find. Throwing her over my shoulder, I should carry her back to her village. No one would fault me for gagging her or even roughing her up along the way if she decided to fight back.

After all, she's an escaped gods-blessed. A felon, in the eyes of the Ruby Crown.

She's broken the law, run from her fate, and disobeyed the will of the gods. For that, she's forsaken any rights she might once have had. The glowing Mark on her forehead gives me permission to do whatever needs to be done.

Even though returning her to her village is the right thing to do, I fucking can't. She saved my life, and for that, I owe her a debt.

I've spent the past decade working towards becoming a Master Hunter, and now this happens? Gods, bad luck doesn't even begin to describe how awful this situation is.

This is a suns-damned moral quandary the likes of which I never could've anticipated, which brings me back to my original statement.

Fuck.

Long moments pass as Wren and I stand there, staring at each other. The wind blows past, howling in my ears. Branches crack, each brittle snap a reminder that the Giving Season will soon give way to winter, and leaves rustle. Deep in the woods, far from us, a wolf howls. A moment later, another one joins in. Birds tweet, and squirrels hop across branches, but I barely pay them any attention.

I may be the youngest Hunter in our kingdom's history, but my training never covered this. Now, I'm at a complete fucking loss. Gods above.

The problem is that even though I'm a Hunter, I also have morals. If I lacked them, this entire situation would be a moot point because I'd already have grabbed her and we'd have been on our way.

"What are you going to do to me?" My prey breaks her silence, her voice frustratingly soft and sweet.

Why does *she* have to be the one I'm hunting? Heat runs through me at the sound of her voice. My muscles tighten, but I pointedly ignore the way she makes me feel.

Moving my eyes from hers, I glance at the knife she's holding with white-knuckled fingers. Even with the weapon, she's no match for me, and we both know it.

"I don't know," I say honestly, returning my gaze to hers.

She draws her bottom lip through her teeth and chews on it. That action has no right to be so attractive or distracting. "You could let me go."

I choke on a laugh, thinking she's joking, but she doesn't crack a smile or even look away from me. Suns, have mercy on me, she's serious. "Impossible."

Her eyes widen. "It isn't. All you need to do is close your eyes, and I'll leave. I promise you'll never have to see me again."

"No," I growl, balling my fists.

She's wrong. I cannot let her go. I am a Hunter, and she is an escaped Given. The very nature of our positions in life sets us at odds with each other. There is no room for bargaining here, nothing she could offer me. Even if my promotion wasn't on the line, I've never negotiated with those I've hunted.

She doesn't seem to realize that, though, as she shakes her head. Are those tears lining the bottoms of her eyes? Gods above.

"Please," she whispers, holding my gaze. "I'll do anything. Just let me go. Do you need money? I don't have any, but I can get some and—"

"I said no," I repeat. "There's nothing you can say that will change my mind."

It's not like I have a choice here. The gods-blessed *must* be Given. It's the law, the very foundation upon which our country is built. The temples need the Given, and Myreth needs the temples. The gods-blessed and their contributions to society are vital to our kingdom. Everyone knows this.

The Giving is the way of our land. The gods, in their infinite wisdom, declared it to be true. It's why we have a Giving Season, why the gods-blessed are venerated, and why I cannot release Wren.

Doing so would paint a target on my back as much as there is one on hers, and I can't let that happen. I didn't work hard for years to reach this position, only to throw it all away because a Given with violet eyes asked me to.

She must decide she's done standing still because she steps to the right. I follow suit. Her left hand creeps down to her side, and my hackles rise.

Clenching my fists, I snarl, "What are you doing?"

I'm so far from relaxed that I can't remember what it's like to not be tense. Each inhale is sharp, like I'm inhaling shards of glass, and I'm far too aware of my movements. It's like I'm dancing on the edge of a sword, and one wrong move will result in a painful death.

"I'm thirsty," she murmurs. "Can I get a drink?"

I'm not sure whether it's the plea in her voice or the way her violet eyes seem to look directly into my soul, but I jerk my chin.

Exhaling, she steps backwards, picking up her canteen off the shale. Unscrewing the top, she lifts it to her lips and drinks. Her throat bobs and swallows, but her gaze is locked on to mine.

Her stare is unnerving, but I can't look away. She tilts back her head, and her hood slips again, revealing her Mark. Every gods-blessed has one, but they're not usually on their foreheads. I can't remember the last time I saw a Mark on someone's face.

The brilliant swirl mocks me, a reminder of what I'm meant to do, and tension radiates through my entire body.

Every minute we spend in this strange standoff is one where I'm decidedly not doing my job. I need to come to a decision quickly. After all, I'm not the only Hunter the king employs. Others undoubtedly received the same message I did. They're probably converging on Grenbloom now, searching for the woman standing in front of me.

When she puts the cap on her water, I've reached a decision.

It's stupid, and I honestly can't believe this is what it has come to, but I don't see any other way forward. At least, not one that will simultaneously allow me to do my job while fulfilling my life debt.

"One day." My words seem to boom through the forest, echoing the thundering of my heart.

A crease forms between her brows, and her nose scrunches as she blinks. "What?"

I step away from my prey, my chest heaving as my fists clench at my sides. It feels unnatural to put space between us, but it must happen.

"In payment for my life debt . . ." The words are acidic at the back of my mouth, but I force them out. "I will grant you one day."

I shouldn't be doing this. Gods, if King Andreas ever learns that I've done such a thing, I'll undoubtedly suffer his wrath. But it's the only way I can repay her for what she did while still fulfilling my obligations.

I'm not sure why she's running from being Given—maybe she doesn't believe in the gods?—but in the end, it doesn't matter. She's fated to work with them, and it's my job to bring her back.

It feels like an eternity passes as her eyes sweep over mine, finally filling with understanding. She swallows. "You mean—"

"One day, little bird." My nails cut into my palms as I force myself to keep the distance between us. "I'll give you one day's head start before I come find you."

And when the day is up, I will hunt her like I've never hunted anyone before. I will catch her before any of the other Hunters and bring her back to the temple. I'm going to become a Master Hunter. Then I'm going to find the people who attacked me and make them pay for putting me in this gods-damned position in the first place.

Her breath catches, and her eyes widen as fear settles into them. Blood leaches from her face. Her fingers tremble as she stares at me.

Good.

She should be afraid. Once I set my sights on something, I never let it go. It's part of what makes me so good at my job.

"But—"

"No buts. You saved my life, and for that, I owe you a boon." There's a roaring in my ears, but I keep going. "This is it. My gift to you."

It's far more than what I should be giving her, but now that I've laid out my terms, I can't take them back.

She still hasn't moved. Why hasn't she moved? I point to the sky, where the canopy of trees breaks enough to give a glimpse of the suns sitting directly above us.

"When the twin suns reach this point tomorrow, I'll be coming for you, Wren Nightingale." I arch a brow and snarl, "Now, *run*."

10

ONE DAY'S HEAD START

Wren

One day's head start.

Gabriel's words echo all around us, louder than any sounds of the forest. For the longest moment, all I can do is stare at him. The *Hunter.*

Is he serious?

As soon as the thought appears in my head, I know the answer. Of course he is. Why wouldn't he be? He's a gods-damned Hunter, for suns' sakes. This is his *job.* The same one I was asking him about. The same one he was smiling about.

It's fucking laughable that a few minutes ago, I was enjoying this man's company. Those feelings of comfort and ease have vanished because he's not a random person I saved. He wasn't just out in the forest for a stroll. He's *hunting* me.

Oh, gods.

A quiver of fear shoots through my belly, and my legs wobble. Suns save me. Could I be any more unprepared for this? I'm a healer at heart, not a warrior. Gods, I don't even know how to use this knife I'm still holding between us.

I'm just a woman in way over her head.

And this . . .

And he . . .

Pressure builds behind my eyes as I remain frozen in place. I blink the tears away furiously, refusing to let this man see me cry. Not now. Not after what he just said.

He rakes his hand through his hair, the light making it seem more blue than black, his eyes flashing with something akin to fury.

"Run, damn you!" he yells, his nostrils flaring. As if he's angry. As if *he's* the one being hunted. "Go!"

Oh, gods help me. He isn't joking, and this isn't some awful nightmare that I can wake up from. This is real, Amelia is dead, Gabriel has seen my Mark, and he's going to *hunt* me.

I don't have time to inhale, let alone pray to the gods—although, to be fair, I don't think they'd hear a word I said. Something deep within me reacts to his command and stirs me to action.

My Mark starts burning, which is bloody inconvenient but tracks with the way my life has gone. I shove my knife back into its sheath, grab my satchel off the shale, and spin on my heels. I nearly trip on the mushrooms scattered on the ground, but I don't dare stop or even slow down.

Run.

Gabriel's command is still woven through the air, and the fury in his voice hits me deep in my soul. And so, I don't beg him to reconsider. I don't ask him to let me go. I don't bargain or plead or scream for him to reconsider.

I just run.

Again.

My feet pound the shale, then the squishy forest floor. I can feel the weight of his gaze as his eyes drill into the back of my skull.

"Run quickly, little bird." The wind carries Gabriel's voice to my ears as I disappear through the trees. "I'll be coming for you."

An ominous promise. A vow. A reminder of who he is.

Fear scrapes its nails down my spine, and bile coats the back of my throat. I skid to a stop beside a bush and empty the contents of my stomach. I wash my mouth out with water before running again.

I force my feet to move.

Left. Right. Left. Right.

The repetitive movement is the only thing I can focus on because if I think too hard about what just happened to me, I'm going to lose whatever semblance of sanity I have left. I'll scream and cry and curl up into a ball, never moving again.

A bird chirps above me, and it feels like the gods are laughing at me. If running on my already aching feet didn't require every ounce of energy I possess, I would curse the gods for this awful fate.

One day, little bird.

Gabriel's words echo in my mind, and his mockery of my family's nickname burns me up inside.

At some point, the tears I'd tried to suppress start streaming down my face, but I don't stop to wipe them away. I just run and run and fucking run.

Hours have passed since I left the Hunter, and I've been racing blindly through the woods. My lungs feel like they're home to burning embers, my heart is hammering against my ribs, and I stopped feeling my legs a long time ago. My canteen is empty, my throat is scratchy, and everything that isn't numb hurts. Mother's dress is splattered with mud, and my petticoat is torn in several places.

To say that this is a day from hell would be a fucking understatement.

Every so often, I swear I can feel the weight of someone's gaze on my back. A few times, I've stopped and looked behind me, but I don't see anything amiss.

Great. On top of everything else that's gone wrong, my mind is betraying me. Of course. I would laugh, but doing so would take too much energy.

I just. Keep. Running. Thoughts of getting away from the Hunter preoccupy my thoughts so thoroughly that I don't hear it at first. A trickle, breaking through the forest's endless symphony of life. A call to all who hear it that nourishment is nearby.

Water.

My breath catches, and I'm suddenly aware of just how long it's been since I've had a drink. My throat is no longer just scratchy. It feels like I swallowed handfuls of dust. I try to breathe past the dryness, but now that I've noticed it, it's all I can think about. I used to think I knew what it meant to be hungry and thirsty, but the past few days have taught me that I was wrong.

A raspy chuckle escapes me as I stumble forward towards the water. Gods, I was a bloody fool. I didn't know anything. Not really.

The weight of all the things I don't know, combined with everything I've been forced to learn far too quickly, presses me down. It threatens to shove me to the forest floor, rendering me incapable of moving.

As appealing as it sounds, I can't give up. Not just for me, but for Amelia.

I need to live for us both.

Even though the Hunter's so-called gift is laughable, I will use it to my advantage. He won't win—not if I can help it.

Digging deep within myself for strength, I quicken my pace. I shove branches aside, ignoring the way they slap me in the face as I stumble towards the rushing water. It's growing louder by the second, encouraging me forward.

Come, come, come, the water seems to say.

I heed its call, my thirst becoming more prominent with every passing step. I'm not sure how much time passes before a blue glimmer appears through the trees.

Releasing my breath in a ragged exhale, I shove the last branch aside to reveal a rushing, gurgling river. The fast-moving water is clear. Smooth, rounded rocks line the bottom of the riverbed.

I drop to my knees, a cry of relief pouring from my lips. Cupping my hands, I dip them into the water. It's cool, and most of it slips from my fingers as I lift my hands to my mouth, but the small amount I'm able to get slides refreshingly down my throat.

The water tastes clean, free of sand and grit. It's so cold, it's almost sweet. Part of me had worried that it wouldn't be drinkable, but I've never been happier to be proven wrong.

I need more. Grabbing my canteen, I unscrew the top. My movements are unstable, and the lid almost falls in the water. I curse and grab it, dunking the vessel into the water instead.

In my haste, I don't wait for the canteen to fill. I yank it from the river after a few seconds, gulping down the meager contents as quickly as possible.

The water is delicious, like a decadent wine. It runs smoothly down my throat, filling my belly. I repeat the process, drinking until I can't imagine consuming even one more drop. Then I hold the canteen underwater. Bubbles rise as water replaces air until my container is full again.

I reseal the lid and dry the canteen on my cloak before sliding it back into my bag. I need to get going, but I'm not sure when I will get a chance to wash up again. I splash water on my face and arms, and then I unlace my boots. Placing them on the riverbank beside me, I'm about to slip off my stockings to wash them when the hairs on the back of my neck prickle.

I'm not alone. Awareness slithers down my spine like a snake, and I rise to my feet.

Grabbing my knife, I look around. Did the Hunter change his mind? Has he decided to come after me now? My blood chills at the thought, and my hands grow clammy. I've been monumentally stupid.

I don't know anything about Gabriel other than his name and his job. Why did I think I could trust a *Hunter*, of all people? I'm his prey.

Everyone knows that Hunters are the most dangerous of the king's soldiers. The things they'll do to me if they catch me will make me wish I'd never run away in the first place.

A branch snaps across the river, the sound pulling me out of my thoughts.

Oh, gods.

Gabriel is here. He's found me, and I'm going to die before I even have the chance to live. Frigid fear courses through my veins as I adjust my grip on my knife and ready myself to do everything I can to remain free. I won't go willingly. He has to know that.

Even though I'm an untrained gods-blessed, I'm still capable of putting up a fight. I was too scared to fight back earlier, but that's no longer the case.

"You suns-damned bastard. You said you'd give me a day . . ." My voice quiets as a pair of silver eyes meet mine from across the river, and I whisper, "You."

The panther is a statue, its eyes locked on mine. The creature is sleek, and its shimmering coat reflects the setting suns. It's the same one I encountered before, I'm sure of it. I'm filled with so many questions I hardly know where to start. Why is it here? Did it follow me? Why won't it stop staring at me?

The feline's moonlit gaze drops to my knife and stays there for a long time before slowly rising back to mine. There's a spark of intelligence in the animal's eyes that has my chest tightening. It's a cat, but . . . more. If I didn't know any better, I'd say there was an air of magic around the animal, but that doesn't make sense.

Only the royals have magic.

The panther looks at me as if it knows I have no idea how to use Father's knife, but how is that possible?

Then those silver eyes widen. A heartbeat later, a snarl rises—not from the panther, whose mouth remains shut—but from behind me. The deep, inhuman sound is far lower than anything I've ever heard, and it rattles me to my core. The water churns uncomfortably in my stomach as something rustles behind me.

At the same time, the panther slowly shakes its head back and forth as if confirming that it didn't make that sound.

Unease sweeps over me, and I swallow past the growing lump in my throat as I adjust my grip on my weapon. I force myself to turn around and see what's behind me.

A whimper slips from my throat before I can stop it, and I suck in a shaky breath. My Mark is burning again, embers embedded beneath my temple. Gods help me.

Why does this keep happening at the most inopportune of moments? A question for a later time. All I can do is focus on the massive beast looming in front of me.

"I . . . Oh, suns." The words escape me on a broken whisper as my neck cranes up, up, up to take in the creature before me.

It's a bear . . . or at least, I think it is. It's a little hard to tell because it's so damn huge.

Once, Father and Markus took down a bear while hunting. That animal had been malnourished, and the two of them had still struggled to bring it home. It had fed us for a month.

The beast standing in front of me clearly has no problem feeding itself. It's far larger than any bear I've ever seen, towering several feet above my head.

This is the kind of creature that nightmares are made of. Its thick brown fur is matted and lumpy. The bear's fur isn't as worrisome as the white, bubbling foam gathering at its mouth. I might not know much about this land, but I know enough about animals to realize that white foam is never good.

A feline snarl comes from behind me, and I glance at the panther. It's pacing across the opposite riverbed, eying the black stones spread along the river. Is it thinking of crossing?

The bear rumbles, and I yank my gaze back to it. Looking away from a predator is stupid. I can't make the same mistake again. Especially now that I've noticed the madness in the creature's black eyes. Death is peering back at me, and my muscles tremble in the face of a true predator.

The bear roars, and the sound echoes through the forest. A scream rips from my lips as the predator lifts a paw. Sharp black talons glisten in the light of the setting suns. I move back quickly, needing to put space between me and the bear.

Except, nothing is behind me.

My foot lands in water, the cold a shock through my thin stockings, and my eyes widen as my arms flail. A moment of sanity has me shoving Father's knife into the sheath so I don't cut myself, and another scream slips from my throat as I fall into the water fully clothed.

The bear lets out a mountain-shaking bellow.

A black streak seems to fly above the river, but then my back smacks something hard. Water fills my vision and my lungs.

The river swallows me whole, dragging me into its cold embrace.

11

TIME IS RUNNING OUT

Wren

"Hewwo? Are you awive?"

The muffled words sound strange, as though I'm deep underwater. They take too long to reach my ears.

I'm alive, I want to shout. *I'm here. Help me.*

The words get stuck on the tip of my tongue, and I can't seem to make my mouth work. My entire body aches, and there's a heaviness in my limbs that I can't quite place. My eyes are squeezed shut, and something squishy is beneath me. That's odd. Squishy is better than the hard rock I slept on last, but it's not right.

Scorching suns. Where am I?

Something prods my shoulder, and I groan. Fuck, that hurts. In fact, everything hurts. Did I fall out of a tree? The moment the thought appears, I dismiss it. I've fallen out of a tree before, and this hurts far more than that.

"She made a sound!" a childish, high-pitched shriek explodes in my ear. "Mama! I heawd it, I sweaw!"

Wincing, I will my body to listen to my commands and *move*.

It takes far too much effort and mental fortitude, both of which are in extremely short supply, but eventually, I'm able to lift my head. I force my eyelids to move, and I blink, trying to clear my vision. My hair is covering my face and my Mark. It feels like rocks are in my mouth, and I lick my lips as I instinctively pull on my hood.

A small shape is crouched in front of me, seeming to vibrate with excitement. They're definitely a person, but I can't see more than that. A massive grin is spread across their face, and their eyes are wide.

I blink again, and the shape comes into focus.

A little girl, no older than five or six, is clutching a woven basket in front of her chest. Dark pink hair hangs in two braids that reach her waist, freckles dust her olive skin, and she's wearing a white apron over a brown cotton dress. She's barefoot and standing in mud.

The same mud I'm lying on right now. Well, that explains the squishiness.

Water laps at my feet, making me groan. I remember taking off my boots on the riverbank and then . . .

My heart races as my close encounter with the bear flashes before my eyes. Gods above. I must've fallen into the river.

Wait. What time is it? My eyes fly upwards, and I gasp. The blue sky is gone, replaced by a dusky grey, and the moons are rising. Already, a few glistening, overeager stars peek out from behind the clouds. Their brightness mocks me, and my stomach twists. Hours lost. Just like that.

The Hunter's warning echoes in my mind, and my throat dries. I'm running out of time. Soon, he'll be coming for me. Soon, it'll be too late.

I need to go. Placing my palms on the mud, I try to push myself up. My drenched clothes are weights, dragging me down. Every movement hurts, but eventually, I pull myself into a seated position. My head is heavy, and I clench my fists, attempting to breathe deeply and gather myself.

Why do these things keep happening to me?

The only positive here is that even though I've lost my boots on the riverbank, a quick inspection tells me I've kept the rest of my belongings. My soaked cloak hangs on my shoulders, and I still have my knife and bag. That's a small silver lining, but considering that I'm drenched, I'll take it.

"Mamaaaaaaa!" the child in front of me screams, the sound inconceivably loud coming from such a small person. "She's awake! I towd you, someone's hewe!"

"Nakisha, what are you shouting about? There isn't anyone out—Oh, blessed, burning suns." A woman in her mid-twenties appears in my peripheral vision, her pink hair and freckles marking her as the child's mother. Unlike her daughter, the woman's forehead is wrinkled beyond her years, and there's a deep sorrow in her eyes.

She crouches in front of me, reaching out to touch my face. Instinctively, I duck my head and tug my hood on further, making sure the brim is resting on my eyebrows. Even now, I have to worry about that gods-damned swirl.

Seeming to understand I don't want to be touched, the woman places her hands in front of her, palms up.

"You poor thing, you must be freezing." Her gaze sweeps over me, but there's no judgment in the way she looks at me. "I can't believe you survived going over the waterfall."

Well, damn. At least that explains the aches and pains. Honestly, I can't believe I survived, either. I learned to swim as a child, but it's been years since I stepped foot into a body of water with the intention of doing anything but bathing. Swimming isn't an appropriate activity for a gods-blessed child. Why should we have fun before they kill us?

I open my mouth to reply, although I'm unsure what to say, when my teeth start chattering. I shut my mouth, drawing my arms around myself.

"Eses have mercy on you," the woman murmurs, calling on the god of strength and healing as compassion fills her brown eyes. "Our cottage isn't far from here. We don't have much, but you can dry off and join us for dinner if you'd like. It's already on, and we have a fire going."

"I was cowwecting gweens!" Nakisha proudly proclaims, holding up a woven basket with a few leaves poking out over the top.

Her enthusiasm is contagious, and even though I just survived an encounter with a bear and fell over a waterfall, my lips slant up.

"Good job," I tell her.

She grins at the praise, hopping from one foot to the other. I chew on my lip, mulling over this woman's offer. I shouldn't take her up on it. Joining them would be dangerous for all three of us. But walking around in drenched clothing isn't conducive to health, and the call of a warm fire is too strong to resist. I nod, agreeing before I can talk myself out of it.

"Wonderful." The woman's smile is kind, and it warms something deep in my soul. She gestures to her daughter, then herself. "You've already met Nakisha, and I'm Alba."

More introductions. Hopefully, this interaction will go better than my last—not that it will be difficult, considering how my time with Gabriel ended. In an effort to be normal, I force myself to smile and cast all thoughts of the Hunter aside. "It's a pleasure to meet you both."

If Alba notices that I refrain from giving her my name, she doesn't remark on it. Instead, she offers me a hand and helps me to my feet. I feel like a newborn colt, especially when she releases me. A smaller hand quickly takes its place, steadying me.

"Come, come, come!" Nakisha proclaims enthusiastically, grinning and tugging me towards a grove of trees. I glimpse a small barn tucked in the trees, where a few sheep and chickens are milling about in a pen.

Not far from the animals sits a log cabin. Even though it's unwise, I curl my fingers around Nakisha's and follow her lead.

The log cabin is small and quaint. Built for two, there's a cozy homeyness about it that warms my heart. A bed rests against the wall in the corner, and there's another in the loft upstairs, accessible by a small ladder. Bundles of wool are scattered around the space, and a spinning wheel rests near the bed.

A bowl of eggs sits on a wooden counter near an empty clay pitcher. Red curtains are pulled back, allowing the remaining sunlight to filter inside. A roaring fire fills the large, redbrick hearth, and the small table has two wooden chairs.

Nakisha quickly drags another over from the corner for me, patting the seat. "Sit!"

Her bossiness makes me smile. She reminds me so much of my sisters Violet and Marie when they were younger. The twins look identical, but their personalities are about as different from each other as they can get. Violet is loud, like Nakisha, and Marie is much quieter. Calmer.

Mother always said the twins balanced each other out in uncanny ways.

A pang runs through my heart at the thought of home. Gods, I pray they're all right. Knowing no good will come from thinking of the home I left behind, I banish those thoughts, dropping into the offered chair. Alba throws two logs onto the fire, the crackling heat caressing my skin and chasing away the cold from my unexpected dip in the river.

I've never truly appreciated the warmth that comes from being indoors and out of the wind, but being on the run for my life has taught me how much I used to take for granted.

Food, shelter, heat, clean clothes, and even seemingly simple things like pillows.

Never again. If I ever find myself in the unlikely position where I have these things in my possession, I'll never forget how it felt to go without them. Comfort, it seems, is something that cannot truly be appreciated until it has been taken away.

The fire crackles in the background as I take in the room. Dried bundles of herbs hang from strings stretched across the wooden walls. I recognize a few of them, but most are foreign to me, which is unsurprising. Glass bottles and jars are scattered through the space, taking up room on every available surface. Some are filled with colorful liquids, while others hold various herbs and spices for cooking.

Warmth seeps into my bones with a speed I hadn't expected. Feeling significantly better after a few minutes of sitting by the fire, I dig through my satchel. Surprisingly, apart from my now-waterlogged and ruined romance book—poor Valissa and Roark, their love story is one I'll never read again—everything has survived my fall.

Pulling out the half-empty jar of ointment, I twist the lid.

A chair scratches the wooden floor, and when I look up, Nakisha is sitting less than a foot away from me. Her feet dangle above the floor, and she's leaning so far over, it's a miracle she hasn't fallen off her seat.

"What's that?" she asks. Her brown eyes are wide as she stares at the jar.

Her curiosity draws another smile to my face.

"It's medicine." I remove my stockings and bandages before applying more salve to my feet. The burning ceases immediately, and I exhale in relief. Nakisha is still staring at the jar in awe.

Leaning forward, I crook my finger in her direction. "Want to know what makes it special?"

She nods so vigorously that she nearly topples out of the chair.

Biting back a laugh, I hold up the jar. "This is blessed by the queen herself."

Nakisha's eyes widen impossibly further. "Weally? The queen?"

She reaches out a hand to touch it, but before she can, her mother calls her name in a scolding manner. "It's not yours," Alba adds. "Don't touch it."

Replacing the lid, I hand the jar to Nakisha with a smile.

"It's okay," I murmur. "Take a look. Just be gentle."

Technically, it's not mine, either.

Nakisha beams as if I handed her one of the suns, and she turns the jar around in her small hands. Her pink brows furrow as if I just gave her a complex puzzle, and she studies the container intently. After several moments, she removes the lid, swiping a finger through the cream.

"Look with your eyes, not your fingers, Nakisha," her mother admonishes from across the room.

I chuckle, the words almost identical to something Mother used to say. "It's okay, just be careful. The cream is enchanted."

The child's head jerks up, and she gasps, revealing an adorable gap in her teeth. "It is?"

I nod. "Yes. That's what makes it blessed."

Nakisha stares at the white cream on her finger for several minutes, turning it one way, then the other, before she looks at my feet. The skin is red, and even though there are no new blisters, my soles aren't pretty to look at. "That looks like it huwts."

"It does, but I'm getting used to it." It's really all I can do at this point. Who knows how much farther I'll have to run?

She extends her finger towards my right foot, where the skin is reddest. "Can I put this on?"

Once I agree, she swipes the cream on the base of my foot. It tickles, and I smile as she hands back the jar. Less than a minute later, Nakisha jumps from the chair, proclaiming in a loud voice that there's a carving she left outside and I simply must see it. She races out, the door slamming behind her as she says she'll be right back.

Slipping the ointment back into my bag, I turn to Alba. "Do you need any help with dinner?"

I should've asked the moment we stepped inside, but I got distracted.

My hostess looks up from where she's stirring a pot that had already been simmering when we entered. "Of course not, dear. You're our guest. Just warm up."

The fire is keeping the chill away, but her kindness is what truly touches my soul. I thank her, but before I turn back to the crackling flames, a thought pops into my mind.

"Alba, if you don't mind me asking, how far is the nearest town?" I try to keep my voice casual, as if this information won't be the first real geographical clue I've gotten. I'm not sure what I'll do with it, but it seems like it would be good to know.

"Grantville is half a day's hike through the forest," she says, not looking up. "Sometimes more, if the weather is bad. It's not a town, though. Just a small hamlet. We get provisions there from time to time."

"Thank you." I tuck the information into my mind. The name isn't familiar, but that isn't a surprise. Still, it's good to know.

My new life motto is "The more information, the better."

Even so, I don't ask Alba any more questions about our location or whether she has a map. I don't want to risk endangering her further by asking the wrong questions. She's already done so much for me.

Rubbing my hands together, I focus on getting warm. Thanks to the blazing fire, it isn't long before my cloak dries. My stockings and dress soon follow. Thank the gods, most of the mud landed on my cloak, and the dark fabric hides the worst of it. One benefit of the water is that some of the mud seems to have washed out of my dress. Once my stockings are dry, I pull them back over my feet.

"Dinner's ready!" Alba declares as Nakisha comes barreling back inside, cradling a small carved bear in her palm.

Now, this bear is cute. A far cry from the one I encountered earlier today.

I fawn over the carving appropriately, making sure Nakisha knows how beautiful it is, before she grabs my hand and leads me to the table. She drags my chair behind her, even though my legs are much steadier now. I take my seat as Alba hands out three steaming bowls of stew.

"This smells heavenly," I tell them honestly, folding my hands in my lap. "Thank you so much."

When I left my parents' house in the middle of the night, I never thought I would eat homemade food again. And this isn't just any meal. Sweet potatoes and carrots float alongside parsnips and leeks in a creamy sauce. It smells like it's been bubbling over the fire for hours, and my stomach grumbles in anticipation.

"Of course." Alba waves her spoon in the air, the skin around her eyes crinkling as she smiles. "Dig in."

I do as she asks; it tastes even better than it smells. Despite my best efforts to savor this unexpected, delicious meal, it disappears quickly. I can't help it. Compared to the jerky and blossom mushrooms from earlier, this is a feast, and I am ravenous.

Nakisha talks nonstop over dinner, carrying the conversation single-handedly. She and her mother live here alone, she tells me moments before launching into a story about a fish she caught in the river yesterday. Her energy seems to have no bounds, and several times, I find myself smiling at her stories.

I don't say much, but the child doesn't seem to mind. She chatters until our bowls are empty, and even then, it seems she could talk all night. When Nakisha pauses to take a breath, I exhale, placing a hand on my full stomach.

"Thank you so much for dinner, Alba." Who knows when I'll get another chance to eat like this? "I appreciate it more than you'll ever know."

Sitting there with my full belly and the warm fire at my back, I renew my vow never to forget again how valuable the small things in life are.

Alba smiles softly, and her eyes gleam. There's a knowing look in them that has me raising my hand surreptitiously, adjusting the brim of my hood. It's still in place, but I can't shake the thought that, somehow, she knows something about me.

"You're very welcome," she says. "I'm glad we found you."

"I found her, Mama!" Nakisha interrupts, pointing at her chest.

"That you did, child." She pats her daughter's hand, smiling fondly. "You did very well."

It's clear that Alba loves her daughter, and even being in their presence for a short period of time has lifted my spirits. Gods above. Things could have turned out so differently if I'd washed up on another shore. Someone else might've seen an unconscious woman and done unspeakable things to me. Or they could've uncovered my Mark and brought me to the nearest temple.

A frisson runs through me as more scenarios cross my mind, each worse than the last. I could've woken up and been halfway to Grenbloom. Or worse—someone could've turned me over to a Hunter.

Suns, are the walls closing in on me? The fire doesn't seem as warm; the cabin feels less cozy and more confining.

Dinner was nice, but I need to leave. My very presence here is a danger. Harboring a fugitive is a serious crime that could result in punishments ranging from a severe fine to death.

I can't let that happen to Alba and Nakisha.

"I appreciate everything you've done for me." I stand, drawing my cloak tighter around myself and stepping towards the door. "But it's time for me to go. I won't put you out any longer."

My feet ache at the thought of running through the woods in just my stockings, but I have no other options. My head start is slipping through my fingers like sand, and I'm running out of time. I'll have to make do with what I have—but at least I'm alive.

There's a scraping of wood on the floor as Alba pushes back her chair and gets to her feet.

"Wait." She turns to Nakisha and places her hand on her shoulder. "It's bedtime, little one."

"What?" The little girl's bottom lip wobbles, and her eyes widen, pulling at my heartstrings. The twins used to do the same thing, and Mother always gave in. "Mama, no."

"Yes." Alba gently pushes her daughter towards the ladder. "Climb up, and I'll come tuck you in soon."

Nakisha sniffles and complains, as all children seem to do when they've stayed up too late, but she does as her mother asks, taking the tiniest, most reluctant steps. Pausing on the top rung, she waves at me. "Night!"

Knowing this will likely be the last time I see her, I wave back. "Night." It's hard to ignore the burning in my eyes as I turn back to my hostess. "She's a good girl."

Just like the twins.

Alba smiles fondly at the loft, and the love she holds for her daughter is evident. She gestures to the door. "Why don't we talk outside?"

That's fine with me, since I'm leaving anyway. I nod and grab my things, slipping out of the cabin. Alba follows, pausing to pick up something near the entrance before she shuts the door behind her.

The cold air carries traces of the impending winter, and it's a shock to my system after the cozy heat of the crackling fire. I shiver, twisting my hands together. I should've grabbed some mittens before I left home. Yet another item I won't take for granted, should I ever be lucky enough to have it again.

At least once I start running, I should warm up. But I'll be running, so . . . that's unfortunate.

With that depressing thought in mind, I turn to my hostess. "Thank you so much for your hospitality, Alba. It's far more than I could've ever asked for."

It's far more than I deserve, when my presence endangers her.

Alba's eyes sweep over me, and once again, I'm struck by the thought that she knows something about me. A long moment passes before she steps forward. Her dark pink hair rests over one shoulder, and she places a hand on my arm, guiding me further away from the house.

Out of earshot.

"Here." She holds out a pair of worn, brown leather boots with her other hand. "Take these."

I stare at them. They look a little big, but they would be infinitely better than the stockings I'm currently wearing.

Still . . .

"I can't take these." I shake my head, frowning. Alba has already fed and warmed me when she could've left me on the riverbank. Taking anything else from her would be wrong. "This is too much."

"I want you to take them." She pushes the boots at my chest, and I have no choice but to grab them.

My frown deepens, and I try to return the boots. "Alba, I—"

"Did you know that I've been raising Nakisha on my own for the majority of her life?" she asks, interrupting me.

I freeze, my hands on the boots as I stare at her. "No . . ."

I don't quite understand the rapid change in conversation. My brows come together as I try to follow her train of thought.

"Six years, almost to this day," she tells me.

I'm not sure if it's her tone or the look of sadness that's been in her eyes since I arrived, but a pit forms in my stomach. I'm not sure what she's about to say, but I have a feeling it won't be good.

Cautiously, I ask, "What happened to her father?"

My education may be lacking in several vital areas, but I'm well aware that two people are required to make children.

"Gone." Her soft tone is one I haven't heard from her before, and the forlorn look in her eyes has the stew churning in my stomach. "I lost him in the Giving Season six years ago."

The air thickens, and my fingers grow slick around the boots. I slowly raise my eyes to hers, searching her gaze. Lost?

"I—"

A wistful smile graces Alba's face, and for a moment, she appears much younger than she did before. Her wrinkles vanish, her eyes shimmer, and her cheeks turn rosy.

"We knew better," she whispers, her gaze seeming to peer into my soul before it drops to the ground. "It was a bad idea from the start, but even though we tried, we couldn't stop seeking each other out."

That pit in my stomach becomes a gaping hole, and I suck in a breath.

"The gods-blessed are here temporarily before they're returned to the temples. Draven and I were aware of that. We always knew that our time was limited. It was always there in the back of my mind. A reminder that we would never get forever." Alba sighs, the sound filled with years of pain and heartache. She drags her gaze upwards, meeting mine. "We knew we wouldn't get to stay together, but love . . . love doesn't understand."

Oh, gods. I already know where this story is going. My heart aches, and part of me wishes I could ask her to stop, but I don't. She's chosen to tell me her story, and I won't do her the disservice of refusing to hear it. Not after everything she's done for me.

"I'm so sorry," I murmur.

"Me, too." Her eyes water, and she draws in a shuddering breath. "We should've been more careful. When his Mark started glowing and his Giving drew closer, we should've stopped and thought about what might happen." A rueful laugh fills the air, and knots take up residency in my stomach. "We couldn't help ourselves."

It's not safe to get attached to the Given.

Mistress Fyona's warning echoes through my mind, and my heart clenches.

"How old was Nakisha when he was Given?" I ask, already dreading the answer.

A long pause. Just when I think Alba isn't going to answer—which is her right—she murmurs, "Four weeks had passed since her birth."

My eyes widen. A month? Oh, gods. I draw in a breath, feeling like I've been punched in the heart. I remember the twins at that age. They were so small, having been born a bit earlier than they should've been, and they resembled the dolls Amelia and I used to play with.

"I'm sorry." The words aren't enough, but they're all I have.

"Me, too." Alba wipes a finger beneath her eyes and squares her shoulders. In a heartbeat, she seems to draw strength from deep within. Her voice is firmer as she says, "These boots were his."

My breath catches in my throat, and I shake my head, trying to give them back. "I can't take these."

They're more than just boots. They're memories. Reminders of a man long gone—one who will never return.

"Yes, you can." Alba's tone is forceful, and I hitch a breath, freezing. "I won't ask for your name, where you came from, or where you're going, but I want you to take these."

She knows. I don't know when she figured out what I am, but she knows. I had an inkling before, but now I'm certain.

My chest tightens, and every breath hurts as fear of what will happen if she turns me in washes through me. A dark temple. Being shoved over an altar. Chanting coming from above me. A silver blade. Pain. Blood.

"Alba, I can explain. But please—"

"If someone comes asking after you, we never saw you." Her smile is watery as she looks at me with sympathy in her eyes.

"Why?" I breathe, my heart racing in my chest as I try to banish the thought of being Given.

The monosyllabic word is all I can manage right now.

Why not turn me in? Why not collect a reward for capturing me? Why help me, feed me, give me boots? Why do any of this?

Alba moves towards me, clasping her hands around mine. Her warm touch is grounding, pulling me out of my fear.

"The day before Draven's Giving Ceremony, I asked him not to go. I begged him to run away with us, to make a new life away from the temples. We argued for hours, but in the end, he chose the gods." Her voice wavers on the last words, an echo of the deep pain in her eyes. "Now, I'm raising our daughter on my own while he serves the gods somewhere in this vast country."

He isn't serving them anywhere, but I don't say that. Why add to Alba's pain?

I squeeze her fingers. "I'm so incredibly sorry."

Sorry for the Giving. For her heartache. For these Marks that ruin lives and rip apart families. For everything.

"I couldn't stay in our village on the Black Mountain after that. Draven was everywhere I looked. After that Giving Season, Nakisha and I left. We moved here, and I vowed to myself that if I ever came across a Marked One who needed my help, I would do whatever I could."

For him.

The unspoken words echo through the night, and my heart squeezes.

"Thank you," I whisper brokenly. This is the closest I'll come to admitting that she's right about everything.

"Go ahead." Alba releases my hand and gestures to the boots. "Put them on."

How can I keep arguing with her? Even if I had any fight left in me, I can't disrespect Draven's memory. Not after everything else Alba has done for me. I slide the boots on, and even though they're a little loose, they fit well enough by the time I tie up the laces.

I straighten, adjusting my cloak and dress. "I cannot thank you enough."

Alba takes my hands in hers and squeezes, slipping something into my palm. "You don't have to, dear. Just take these and find what you're looking for, whatever it is."

Before I can reply, she steps away. Taking a deep, composing breath, she wipes her fingers beneath her eyes again. She holds her head up high and draws in a deep breath.

Her face shifts, hardening before my eyes as she rebuilds walls around her heart, gathering the strength it takes to raise her daughter on her own. Only then does she walk back into the cabin, leaving me beneath the moons on my own.

My heart is still pounding as I slowly pry my fingers open and look at what she gave me. Three gold coins rest in my palm, glimmering in the moonlight. This kind of money can't be easy to come by, especially out here in the woods. How much yarn did Alba have to spin to earn this?

A lump grows in my throat, and the coins grow blurry as I stare at them.

The Given stick together.

Amelia's mantra echoes through my mind, but this time, I add something to it.

The Given and their families stick together.

A tear runs down my cheek, and I make no effort to stop it. How many people have been hurt by the Giving? How many people dread the Giving Season and feel nothing but pain? It seems that everywhere I turn, there are more people affected by it than I ever could've imagined.

Eventually, I move. Opening my satchel, I slip the coins inside and pull out the full jar of enchanted ointment. I place it on Alba's stoop, hoping that she understands this for what it is—a gift. Blessed salves are expensive, and I pray this will help them in the future.

Keeping the half-empty jar for myself, I turn around and walk into the night. I'm tired, and I should sleep, but I can't lose any more time. I need to start running again.

The Sapphire Coast is far away, and the Hunter is coming.

12

MORE MONSTER THAN MAN

Gabriel

Time has never moved more slowly than it has in the hours that have crawled by since I commanded the Given to run. Every minute feels like an eternity, giving me ample time to think over and regret my actions. I still can't believe I let Wren go. What in Esyn's holy name was I thinking?

One day's head start.

Groaning, I run my hands through my hair for the hundredth time since she left. The deal was made by a foolish, desperate man, and it might very well have been my final act as a Hunter.

A lesser man would've broken his word and gone after his prey early. It would've been the easier and smarter thing to do. But gods help me, I can't get my grandmother Marilla's voice out of my head.

Of all my relatives, she and I were always the closest. Not that she had much competition—the fact that she looked at me with kindness in her eyes automatically put her at the top of the list. Sometimes, hers was the only smile I received in a day. When I was a young boy, she'd invite me to sit with her in the afternoons. She'd embroider while I studied, and then she would share whatever sweet treat came on her tea cart that day.

A man without morals is more monster than man, Gabe.

Grandmother would often say that to me, especially on days when my father was crueler than usual. She's since passed across the Veil and joined the god of death, Adros, in the Underworld. Her death doesn't stop her advice from acting as my leash, though. The problem is, she's right. I might be a Hunter, but I'm a man of my word, first and foremost.

So, as much as it pains me, I don't follow Wren.

Rather than pursuing my prey, I spend most of the day searching for my missing weapons. My sword never turns up, and I'm assuming the assholes who accosted me took it. After several hours of combing through the forest, I locate my small bone dagger beneath some fallen leaves. Thankful to be armed again, I forage a handful of berries and some edible greens before returning to the shale where it all went to shit.

"You're a suns-damned idiot, Gabe," I chide myself, staring at the scattered mushrooms on the rocks. A few grey squirrels are picking at the easy meal, but they scurry off at the sound of my voice, leaving their snack behind.

Dropping down and resting my back against the rock beneath the overhang, I groan. My head falls into my hands, and I resist the urge to scream. This is an unmitigated disaster, and with every passing minute, it feels like my promotion is slipping further away.

I'm not sure how long I stay like that, but the air has cooled by the time I lift my head. The suns are setting, and no matter how hard I try, I can't pull my mind away from the little bird.

Wren.

I hate that I know her name for the same reason that I hate that, for a few minutes, I saw her as something other than a gods-blessed. It felt like a connection was growing between us before I saw her Mark. I would've liked to get to know her more; interacting with her had been easy in a way I never experienced before.

Knowing her as anything other than a Given will make doing my job so much harder. I can't think of her having a name, nor can I think about our blossoming connection, because I need to bring her back. I can't think about why she seemed desperate to get away, can't wonder whether she hates the gods or simply doesn't want to serve them for the rest of her life. Those thoughts aren't going to help me at all.

Instead, I wonder where Wren is right now. Is she racing through the woods, or has she decided to try and hide? Will she find people and try to blend in, or will she take her chances in the wild? Will she sleep or run through the night?

There are so many paths she can take, so many choices she can make, and I'm just sitting here while she gets further away.

"Fuck!" I bellow, slamming my fist into the rocks beneath me. My hand stings from the impact, and I curse again.

No one is around to hear my outburst. Even Mist hasn't returned from wherever she ran off to after the attack. My bond with her thrums in my chest, and I rub my fist over it. She's far enough away that the thrum is quiet, but I can still feel her.

Mist and I bonded nine years ago when I turned eighteen and joined the Hunters. Each Hunter has a bonded animal, a gift from the gods to help us connect with the land. The king's magic forms the bond, and both the animal and the Hunter must approve of and desire the connection. It's old magic, the kind whispered about in the corners of taverns late at night.

I knew Mist was destined to be my familiar the moment we first locked eyes. We've been together ever since our fateful meeting, and she's joined me on every hunt. Even though she sometimes disappears for a few days to feed, she always returns.

She seems on edge, though. There's a franticness to our bond that wasn't there earlier, and my brows crease as I prod at our connection.

"What are you up to?" I murmur.

I can't hear my familiar's thoughts, but I send some inquisitive feelings down the rope that ties us together. A few moments later, heat suffuses my chest.

I'm fine, she seems to say.

Is she? I'm not sure.

Come back to me, I reply after a moment.

The bond hums, and I choose to assume that means she's going to do as I asked. Instead of worrying over my familiar, I stretch out on the ground and cross my arms behind my head. I have nothing better to do—the Given's day is still underway.

Stars shimmer in the night sky, twinkling as if they know something I don't. And they probably do. Somewhere in this kingdom, Wren is looking at the same stars. Does she know their names?

That thought makes me growl in frustration, and I slam my eyes shut. Gods. Why can't I get her out of my head? No one has ever gotten under my skin so quickly or so thoroughly before.

When I was younger, I used to love looking at the constellations. Studying their names and the stories behind them was nearly as fun as tracking their patterns across the sky.

Now, those stars just remind me that I've been a fucking fool.

I close my eyes and try to fall asleep, but rest is just out of my reach. My mind won't stop whirling, wondering where the Given has gone. Eventually, minutes drag into hours.

My thoughts shift from the present to my past. Memories I'd long since buried force themselves to the forefront of my mind.

The first execution I remember witnessing. I was five when a courtier spoke out of turn in King Andreas's court. The king used his magic to behead the man that very hour.

My first kill—a wild stag.

And the first time I saw a Hunter face repercussions for failing their task. I will never forget his name: Yves Thornhill.

He had failed to retrieve a criminal who'd escaped from the Ice Prison, and the king had convened the court, along with the entire company of Hunters, to witness his trial. I'd been ten at the time, altogether too young to be a part of something so dark, but darkness is a part of life in King Andreas's court.

Even though I was young when the trial took place, I'll never forget it. Fear had wafted off the Hunter as he'd walked down the aisle towards the angry king. I sensed it from my position at the back of the throne room. I will never forget Yves's cry of shock when the king played judge and jury, sentencing the Hunter to a year without his familiar. That was the first time I'd seen a grown man cry.

That memory, more than any of the others, haunts me as I toss and turn, trying to fall asleep. Tonight, I will remember why I cannot fail, because tomorrow, my hunt begins in earnest.

"Gabriel Moreau." King Andreas's booming voice echoes through the throne room as he calls me. "Step forward."

What? My head and limbs feel heavy as if they don't truly belong to me.

I blink, trying to figure out how I got here, but I'm not entirely sure. Looking down, my torn clothes are gone, replaced by traditional black Hunter's garb. The forest has vanished, and I'm standing in Rose Palace.

I have no idea how this is happening, but there's no time to question it because the king's command is ringing through the throne room. Just like when I was ten, the space is filled with hundreds of courtiers and the entire company of Hunters.

But this time, I'm not a small child watching Yves's trial. This time, *I'm* the one who failed. I know that, just like I know that making King Andreas wait is a bad idea. Dream or not, I can't risk evoking his ire.

I do as the king commands, striding past hundreds of courtiers. All dressed in the latest fashion, they're silent, faceless blobs as I pass them by. My boots click on the stone floor, and I keep my eyes trained on the gold stone that sits directly in front of the stairs leading up to the Ruby Thrones.

Even though I don't look at the crowd, the gathered Hunters, or the guards, I'm aware of their presence. Their gazes follow me as I stride through the expansive throne room, just like they followed the other Hunter all those years ago.

Then, like now, the court was completely silent. A pin dropping would be as loud as a boom of thunder, and my footsteps echo off the white walls. My failure is an anvil hanging around my neck, and each step is more difficult than the last. Being in the king's presence has never been so intimidating.

When I reach the golden stone at the front, I drop to my knees. I don't have to look up to know that the king is perched above me, scowling. He's always doing that.

What is a surprise, and what sends my stomach twisting into a tight knot, is the queen's unusual silence. She usually has a lot of say about me, but little of it is good. I can feel her eyes drilling into the top of my head.

The silence stretches as the monarchs choose not to speak. This didn't happen the last time. Yves's trial was fast. He came in, the king declared him guilty of failing, and his sentence was read.

Today, it seems the king wants to play . . . and I'm his favorite toy.

I kneel for so long that my knees ache, but I still don't move. Doing so without permission would only incur the king's displeasure, which I am intimately familiar with. My back tenses, reminding me that angering the royal is a bad idea.

King Andreas, the ninth of his name, delights in bloodshed, pain, and death. I know this more than most, not that anyone in Myreth is unfamiliar with the king's unusual aptitude for death and darkness.

How could they be when public executions take place weekly for the smallest of offenses? Some days, there is so much death that Rosebridge's cobblestone streets run red with blood. On those days, King Andreas seems the happiest.

It feels like an eternity passes before the king clears his throat. The sound echoes through the throne room and reverberates in the depths of my soul.

"Look at me, Hunter Moreau," the royal orders.

The air thickens, and the collective intake of breath at my back sounds like a clap of thunder. My heart pounds, and I draw deep breaths as I force myself to follow the king's command and meet his dark gaze.

His eyes bore into mine, lacking any hint of kindness. His face is hard and merciless, a reflection of his black soul. Skin as pale as snow clings to his frame. His black hair makes the stark whiteness of his flesh stand out even more. The ruby crown on his brow seems to absorb the light, becoming darker with every passing moment. His royal robes are as dark as his soulless eyes.

Is this a dream? I can't tell. Real or not, looking at the king for more than a few seconds hurts. I pull my gaze over to Queen Lucille. Pale blond, almost white hair falls in an intricate, gem-studded braid over her right shoulder. Her velvet gown is made of a blue so dark it's almost black, and her russet skin seems to glow in the light of the flickering candles.

A third, currently vacant throne sits on the king's right. The crown prince must've decided there was a better use for his time than this. He was there for Yves's trial, but apparently, I'm not to be afforded the same courtesy.

On either side of the thrones, flanking them like celestial soldiers, are a head priest and priestess. The hems of their crimson robes are lined with silver, and their expressions are hard as they stare into the crowd. The priest on the left bears a green Mark on his collarbone, and the head priestess's red Mark is on the back of her hand.

Is this a dream?

I can't tell.

"Gabriel Moreau, you have been accused of failing your gods-given duty." The king's deep tenor fills the throne room, pulling my attention back to him as he utters the same words he did the day of Yves's trial. "How do you plead?"

"Your Majesties, I found the runaway Given," I say, arguing my case.

Even now, she flashes through my mind's eye. I'll never forget her for as long as I live.

"And yet, records show that she was not returned to her village temple." The king's cold voice causes goosebumps to erupt on my flesh, and I bite back a shiver. "Do you dispute these facts?"

This is all my fault. I never should've given Wren the head start. Morals be damned, I should've just grabbed her and taken her in. I knew letting her go was a bad idea the moment I opened my mouth, and now . . .

Now, I'll be the one to suffer King Andreas's wrath. My position as Master Hunter was right there, but it slipped away . . . just like the Given.

The silence in the throne room presses down on my shoulders. My ears echo with the pulsing of my heart, and streaks of phantom pains run down my back. I hate being this close to the king. There's a reason the woods bring me peace—I'm far from him.

My voice is hoarse as I force myself to rasp, "No, my king. Your records are infallible, and I do not dispute them."

The king slams his fist down on the armrest of his throne. The sound is a booming crash. Crimson sparks dance around his hand. For a split second, it seems like the throne room wavers around him before solidifying.

Dream or not? I don't know.

"You failed me," he snarls. "You failed the Hunters." His voice deepens, and ghosts of past hurts dart down my back. My scars are coming alive beneath the king's furious gaze. "You failed *the gods*."

That knot in my stomach twists tighter and tighter as the king's words find their mark, sharper than any sword. I don't need him to remind me that my mission was a failure. I've been telling myself the same thing every suns-damned day since the gods-blessed ran into the woods.

The king doesn't want an apology. I know that. The soldiers know that. The court does, too. It's too late for things like apologies now.

Wren is gone. I have failed. Everything is about to come crashing down.

More time passes. I'm not sure whether minutes or hours crawl by. The air is heavier, and each breath is harder to take than the last. I pinch my leg, trying to wake up, but it isn't working.

Maybe this is real?

When the king breaks his silence again, his voice is deeper. Colder. In my heart of hearts, I know I made a grave mistake in letting Wren Nightingale go.

"Gabriel Charles Aiden Moreau, by the power of my crown and the Ruby Thrones, so bestowed upon me by the gods, I hereby strip you of your titles and your position as a Hunter."

Ice cascades down my spine, and my stomach lurches. I thought I was prepared for this, but I was wrong. Gods above, I was so wrong.

And then, as if that isn't punishment enough, the king continues, "Additionally, your bond with your familiar will immediately be severed."

What? My head jerks up, and a collective gasp of horror comes from behind me. My fists clench, and my nails slice half-moons into my palms, but I barely register the pain.

I must have misheard him. There's no way the king would've commanded such an awful thing. Yves's punishment hadn't been nearly this severe.

My heart races in my chest. Mist isn't just some animal. We've been bonded for nine fucking years. Stripping us of our connection would be devastating for both of us since bonds grow stronger the longer they exist. Forcing us apart now would be akin to ripping our souls in two and leaving us to die.

The queen sucks in a sharp breath, placing her hand on the king's. Her manicured nails are black, a stark contrast to her husband's pale flesh. I'm not accustomed to hearing her speak up for me, so it's a shock when she says, "Andreas, perhaps this is—"

"Silence!" the king roars. He shoves himself to his feet, shaking off his wife's touch. "I did not ask for your opinion."

The queen wilts in on herself, her face paling as her lips slam into a thin line. My jaw clenches, and I wish for both our sakes that she hadn't spoken up. No one, not even the queen, deserves to have the king's wrath pointed at them.

"I have made my ruling." The king's voice booms, and he flicks his hand towards four guards at a side entrance. "Bring in the creature."

The soldiers, all dressed in matching black uniforms, step through a door cut into the wall.

No. This cannot be happening. This has to be a dream. Please.

I squeeze my fists and try desperately to wake up. My surroundings don't shift, though. The throne room is still here, the cruel king is still in front of me, and my failure is still weighing me down.

This can't be real. But if it is . . . I return my gaze to the king. "Your Majesty, I know I failed you, but—"

"Unless you wish for your head to be removed from your shoulders, soon-to-be-former Hunter Moreau, you will cease speaking *immediately.*"

The king prowls down the steps and leans over me, his frigid breath brushing against the shell of my ear. He lowers his voice, his next words meant for me and me alone.

"You will take this punishment as a man, Gabriel, or Esyn help me, I will toss you into the dungeons myself and throw away the key. Forget about ever seeing the suns and moons again. You will be lucky to be fed and clothed."

I hate him.

I hate him so fucking much that I can barely breathe.

Red tinges my vision as I force myself to dip my chin. This is my fault for letting her go. Burning suns, I fucked up so badly.

The sound of a struggle comes from my right as the king straightens and steps back. The four guards from before reappear, holding silver chains. Their faces strain as they pull Mist towards the Ruby Thrones.

She's digging her claws into the stone, gouging long marks, and she snarls at her captors. The predatory, feline sound echoes through the throne room, and behind me, a woman shouts in alarm. Someone else screams.

I barely hear them over the roaring in my ears. Mist's black coat is usually shiny, but today, it is matted with blood. She's limping, and anger is reflected in her silver gaze. Fury fills our bond, a tempest of pure rage.

The guards drag my struggling panther across the floor, and my chest warms with pride at her fight. She's growling and biting at their legs. One of the guards slams the blunt side of his sword against Mist's flank, and I mark his face. I will kill him for this.

The vow echoes in my soul as my familiar lets out a pained howl. My heart aches as though it's been stabbed with a hundred daggers.

I'd take any punishment over this. A thousand lashings. Continuous beatings. But this? Why did King Andreas have to pick *this*?

I glare at him, hoping he can feel the contempt rolling off me in waves.

One day, I will drive a knife through your heart and kill you, I silently promise. I will hold him close and twist the knife, letting his blood coat my hands so he knows *I* am the one who finally bested him, finally killed him.

But that day isn't today.

The guards stop a few feet away from me, keeping Mist just out of my reach. King Andreas stands in front of the dais, making some bullshit speech about how all crimes within Myreth must be punished, but I don't listen to him.

Instead, I turn my attention to Mist and look into her silver eyes.

I'm sorry, I tell her through our bond. *I'm so fucking sorry.*

She shouldn't have to pay the price of my failure.

The king's eyes glimmer with malice as he finishes speaking and turns to me. The bond in my chest tightens, and agony is a tsunami flooding through me. Mist knows what's happening, I'm sure of it.

My heart is breaking into a million pieces. This was never supposed to happen. Becoming a Hunter was supposed to give me a purpose and a way out of the life I was born into. It was never meant to end like this.

I'm so sorry.

I repeat the words over and over again, sending them down our bond. It's pointless. No apology will save us now, but I can't seem to stop.

King Andreas spreads his hands, his palms outstretched at his sides and facing the ceiling. Crimson sparks rise, and a muted red glow surrounds him as if he's painted in the blood of the countless souls he's taken.

Silence blankets the throne room, save for a single inhale of breath at the back that sounds like a stampede of elephants.

The king's mouth moves as he murmurs words too low for me to hear. Sparks continue rising from his hands, hovering in the air. More of them gather until hundreds of them float around him.

His mouth stops moving, and time seems to slow for one long, never-ending moment. It's a heartbeat and a lifetime. A second and an eternity. I gather all my love, care, and hope, shoving it down the bond. I give it to Mist, hoping she understands what I'm trying to do.

If this is real, I need her to know she's the best thing to ever happen to me. The *only* good thing to ever happen to me.

The king's lips curl upwards, a cruel smile. It's the same one that has haunted my nightmares for as long as I can remember. He turns his palms until they're facing me.

"*Break*," he commands.

Crimson magic flings itself at me and Mist. The red sparks are tiny daggers of death as they embed themselves into my flesh and burrow beneath my skin, burning a path to my soul. I'm being flayed apart from the inside out as pieces of my very being are ripped from me.

I *roar*, the sound utterly animalistic as it echoes through the throne room.

The king's magic weaves through my body, leaving a crimson trail of destruction in its wake. Each moment is worse than the last as he digs his claws into the essence of my soul.

My chest heaves, and I fall forward, slamming my hands against the tile. There isn't a single part of me that is left untouched by the king's powerful magic.

I am pain, and pain is me. My chest burns, burns, burns as the embers weave themselves into the tapestry of my soul.

Mist howls, the sound worse than anything else I've ever heard. Something deep within me frays, and it's like I'm being torn in two.

The king says something, but I can't hear him over the cacophonous roar in my ears. At first, I think the sound is in my head, but then I realize it's coming from my mouth.

My panther wails, the never-ending sound one of pure agony as it stretches on and on.

And then, it all stops. The roaring. The burning. The pain. It vanishes, and I'm left with . . .

Nothing.

The king lowers his hands and steps back as Mist collapses, unmoving. I take deep, shuddering breaths, staring at my hands in despair.

The bond is gone, and now, I have nothing.

I wake with a roar, jolting into a sitting position. My chest heaves, and my fingers grapple at the cold shale beneath me.

"Mist," I groan, her name sounding shattered as it slips from my lips.

I search within myself for our bond, and it's . . .

There. The rope is still present within me, and our connection hums as I poke and prod it disbelievingly. It feels the same as it has every day since we bonded.

Fucking hell.

Pressing a hand against my racing heart, I force myself to breathe. It was just a nightmare, but by the gods, it felt so bloody real.

I can still feel the king's magic crawling against my skin like bees, still feel the agony of having my bond ripped from my chest. My ears still echo with the remnants of Mist's pain.

It doesn't matter whether the nightmare was a warning, a premonition, a message that I'm not ready to think about, or simply a bad dream conjured by my stupidity.

I will never forget the feeling of emptiness in my chest or the horror of having everything I care about stripped from me. Finishing this task is the only thing I can do, because I refuse to allow that future to come to pass, no matter the cost.

When my heart has calmed, I look up. I've slept longer than I thought I would, and the suns are approaching the midway point in the blue sky. I gather my things, staring out into the forest as if the act will conjure the Marked One.

"I hope you ran quickly, Wren, because I'm coming for you."

I won't stop hunting until I've caught her. This isn't just about my promotion anymore—I can't risk losing Mist.

The king has left me no other choice.

13

TRYING TO FUCKING SURVIVE

Wren

Three days have passed since I left Alba's cottage, and I'm still in River Bend Forest. Gabriel never confirmed it, but it's the only thing that makes sense.

If I didn't know there were other towns and cities in Myreth, I'd be convinced this forest is endless.

The trees all look the same, with long trunks and bare branches. Very few leaves remain, a sure sign that winter is drawing near. The gurgling river to my left assures me I'm not going in circles. It's been my guide for days, and I'm trusting that it will lead to a larger body of water. Maybe even the Sapphire Coast?

It's unlikely, but I'm hoping that might be the case. To be honest, I have to cling to what little hope I have left with all my might because, with each passing day, survival seems more and more unlikely.

Ducking beneath yet another branch, I huff as I continue forward. Always forward. I've hardly slept. Yesterday I ate my last piece of jerky. Even the blossom mushrooms I've foraged along the way haven't been enough to sate my hunger.

My body feels like one massive bruise, and I've stopped using the blessed salve on my feet. They still hurt, but I don't want to risk running out.

A few times, I heard voices carrying through the forest. Each time, I tugged up my hood and hid, praying to the gods that they wouldn't find me. They haven't yet, but that doesn't mean they won't. I'm acutely aware that I might be discovered at any moment.

Not only that, but over the past few days, I've uncovered several pieces of evidence speaking to the presence of predators in Eskana's forests. Claw marks on trees, fresh dung, and low, deep howls at night. Now more than ever, I'm acutely aware that I'm not the only one in the forest.

And then there are the nightmares. The meager hours of sleep that I've been able to manage have been filled with awful dreams. Each time I fall asleep, I wake with a scream on my lips.

The Hunter is coming for me.

His warning is loud in my mind, and it's the only thing I can think about. When my body is exhausted and all I want to do is collapse and cry, I hear his voice in my head.

Run.

His command pushes me, urging me forward when everything else feels dire. And to be fair, there isn't a single part of my life that *doesn't* feel dire right now.

With every passing minute, the chances of the Hunter catching me and dragging me back to Grenbloom become more likely than the last. I'm sure there are other Hunters after me, too, but it feels like I *know* Gabriel. That short time we spent together was nice . . . and now he's chasing me.

Knowing his name makes this even worse.

Fear has me startling at every cracking branch, every whisper of wind, every fish jumping in the river, and every animal running through the forest. I've looked over my shoulder so often that my head might become permanently stuck in that position the next time.

The past few days have been a lot, but I woke up an hour ago, and something felt different. I wasn't sure why when I started walking because I'm always walking these days, but now the trees ahead of me are thinning.

Is this . . .

Have I reached the end of the forest? I hurry forward until I can see beyond the trees.

"Oh, thank the suns," I breathe, hugging my arms around myself.

I've made it out.

Beyond the trees, the sky is painted in beautiful streaks of pastel. The suns shine above rolling hills, where emerald green grass shimmers with early morning dew. A well-traveled dirt road cuts through the hills, leading to a city.

Placing my hand against the rough bark of the ancient oak beside me, I drink in the sight. This must be the city my brothers were talking about.

Two massive mountains rise on either side of a large valley, dipping into smaller ranges beyond that stretch as far as my eyes can see. Snowcapped tips vanish into the clouds, reaching for the heavens. The river I've been following widens as it leaves the forest, happily running alongside the mountains before disappearing out of sight.

Set in the valley, as though the mountains are watching over it, is the largest city I've ever seen. It must be at least twenty times the size of Grenbloom. A massive stone wall stretches between the mountains, and black blobs that are likely either Watchers or Enforcers patrol the top. Like the Hunters, they're the king's soldiers, and they exist to do his bidding.

Chills race down my back at the thought of them, and I pull my hand away from the bark, rubbing my arms.

Four towers rise above the city wall, one on each end and two in the middle. At the base of the wall is an imposing iron gate the height of four men standing on top of one another. Despite the early hour, dozens of people and animals trudge down the winding dirt road towards the metropolis, along with several wagons and carriages.

I clutch at my arms, pacing back and forth in the grove of trees as I decide what to do. I had been planning on walking around the city, if I ever found it, but now I see that isn't possible.

Logically, I could circumvent the city altogether and try to climb the mountains. That doesn't seem like a great idea, though. For one, my resources are dangerously low. For another, I've never climbed anything taller than a tree. It seems foolish to attempt something like that for the first time while I'm running for my life.

Not only that, but the Hunter is probably expecting me to avoid people at all costs. That would be the smart thing to do in my situation.

After all, I'm a gods-blessed with a glowing Mark, and I'm not wearing my customary garments. I don't belong in a city crawling with people who could turn me in.

"Going in there would be the height of stupidity, Wren," I mumble, trying to warn myself away from the dangerous plan forming in my mind.

The problem is, even though this plan—if I could even call it that—is risky, it's also unexpected. It could give me an advantage over the Hunter. The faster I can get to the Sapphire Coast, the better.

I glance at the bracelet hanging off my wrist, running my fingers over the solitary sun.

Live, Birdie, Amelia whispers in my mind.

Her voice sounds so real that, for a moment, I wonder if she's really there. I look all around me, but there's nothing but trees and the city in the distance.

"Wow, Wren. That's a new low." Now I'm hearing my dead best friend's voice? This is probably a sign that I'm losing my mind. It's definitely a sign that I've been on my own for too long.

She's right, though. I need to live, and if this gets me out of here, then it's worth the risk.

I rearrange my curls over my forehead, adjusting the placement of my hood before emerging from the forest. Thank the suns, the impending winter means my cloak and hood shouldn't seem out of place.

As I walk, I work on my plan. The city seems to stretch the length of the valley, which hopefully means there's an exit on the other side. I'll pass through the city, and with any luck, I'll find a map vendor while I'm there.

The thought of knowing exactly where I am and where I'm going brings a smile to my face. It remains there as I keep my head down, joining the throng of people headed towards the city.

I can do this.

Burning suns, I can't do this.

My confidence has all but melted away by the time the suns have reached the midday point. I'm still in line, waiting to get into the city, and I've been questioning all my life choices for the past hour.

Rivulets of sweat trickle down my back, my thighs are clammy beneath my dress, and the day is unseasonably hot. I shuffle along with the crowd, keeping my cloak wrapped around me as the looming city slowly draws closer.

The heat is unexpected, but it isn't to blame for my rising panic. No, I have the people all around me to thank for that. I never used to have a problem with crowds, but that's no longer the case. It must be a side effect of my new status as an outlaw.

My heart is a galloping horse, desperate to race out of my chest, sweat is gathering on my face, and my lungs are so tight that breathing is nearly impossible.

Someone up ahead shouts, their indistinguishable words lost to the wind. It doesn't matter that I can't hear them. It feels like they're yelling at me. My body is so tense that walking forward is nearly impossible. But I do, because the Hunter is coming for me.

A few minutes later, an older woman with grey hair driving a donkey and cart ahead of me looks over her shoulder in my direction. Her gaze lands on me for a mere second, but in that moment, it feels like she's ready to scream my secret to the world.

Not long after that, a man around my age bumps into my elbow as he passes me by, walking quickly towards the gate.

"Watch it, woman," he grumbles under his breath, as if he isn't the one who just ran into me.

Cold sweat gathers on the back of my neck, and my chest tightens as if he just cursed me to spend an eternity with Adros, god of the Underworld. It takes me far too long to calm down enough to realize that the man is just an ass and he isn't going to turn me in to the soldiers.

Even so, I don't like the way he made me feel. Falling back, I settle beside a pair of young merchants and their entourage.

The merchants have dark skin, like my sister-in-law Yvette, and the fine cut of their clothing is unlike anything I've ever seen. The men are beautiful, almost painfully so, and they speak to one another in hushed tones. Their ears are pointed, unlike my curved ones, and when one of them lifts his voice to direct a servant, the long, drawn-out way he pronounces his vowels catches my attention.

They don't seem to care that I'm walking beside them, and I stay there until the individual bars of the iron gate come into view. My chest tightens. The soldiers aren't just patrolling the top of the city wall. They're guarding the city entrance, as well.

Four soldiers stand out front, stopping everyone walking in and asking them questions. Oh, suns. This isn't just bad—this could be the end of my journey. Forget about making it to the Sapphire Coast. I don't even know if I'll make it through the gate.

My throat constricts, and alarm floods my veins. As if mocking my predicament, a familiar heat starts in my temples. Fucking hell, why is this happening now? The Mark only seems to burn when I'm dealing with a lot of emotions, which is gods-damned inconvenient. I don't have time to dig deeper into it. The line is shuffling forward, and my mind is whirling, trying to think of what to do.

Why did I ever think coming here was the right move? This might be the worst idea I've ever had, which says a lot.

A rushing wind fills my ears, and I drop my gaze to my feet, trying desperately to think of a way out of this situation. There must be something that will save me from having to speak with the guards. But no matter how hard I try, I can't come up with a single thing that will get me out of this situation.

I fall back behind the merchants and their servants. Anything to buy myself a few minutes.

My fingers twitch at my sides as they stop at the gates. I'm close enough to hear the tallest guard, a slim man with blond hair, ask where they're from.

"The fae courts," says the merchant on the left. "From across . . ."

I don't hear the rest of their answer because the roaring in my ears is crescendoing. They speak with the guard for a few minutes before he steps aside, allowing them through. Their group disappears through the gates, and then the soldier looks up.

"Next," he calls out, sounding like he wishes he were anywhere else.

That makes two of us.

Black spots cloud my vision, but somehow, my feet carry me forward until I'm standing in front of three very intimidating men and one even more intimidating woman. The soldiers are dressed entirely in black, save for the scarlet patches on their chests.

The king's soaring eagle and twin suns seem to mock me as if they know something I don't. I quickly divert my attention away from the sigil, my eyes snagging on the closest guard's baldric. A sword hangs from it, the steel gleaming as the suns hit it just right.

A quick scan confirms that all the guards are armed, and each weapon looks sharper than the last.

Gods help me.

My fingers twitch, and my empty stomach churns as the memory of the head priestess slashing Amelia's throat flashes through my mind. My breath catches, and all I can think about is the crimson pool she landed in.

I'm not sure how much time passes before the blond guard growls, "Miss, I asked you a question."

Shit. I'm not even *inside* the city yet, and I'm already fucking this up.

Biting my lip, I think back to the guard's conversation with the merchants. What was the first question he asked?

A name.

I keep my gaze trained on the ground, willing my hood to stay in place as I give him the first name that comes to my mind. "Amelia Lockheart."

Silence stretches, and I pray that my best friend will forgive me for using her identity. I should probably think of a fake name, since this is the second time this has happened to me, but that's a problem for a later time. If there is a later.

Even though I'm not looking at the guard, I can feel his gaze crawling over me. It's as though he's trying to see into my very soul.

I fight the urge to squirm beneath his attention. Did he look at the merchants this long? I honestly can't remember. I stare at the black tips of his boots, praying to the gods, the suns, and quite frankly, anyone who might listen that he doesn't ask me to pull back my hood.

The longer I wait, the more likely it seems that the guard has figured out my secret. Do the king's soldiers memorize lists of Marked Ones? Do they know Amelia's name? My hands grow clammy. Have I inadvertently revealed myself?

Once again, the unknown is a millstone bearing down on my shoulders. Remaining calm and not letting my panic show takes every ounce of concentration.

Suns help me, this is bad. Worse, possibly, than when Gabriel saw my Mark in the forest. At least then, we were alone. Here, I'm surrounded by people. There's nowhere for me to run, nowhere for me to go.

I'm trapped.

It feels like a century passes before the guard asks his next question. "What business do you have in Mora, Miss Lockheart?"

Mora.

It takes a moment for the name to click in my mind, but when it does, things start making sense. I've inadvertently arrived at Eskana's capital city. Myreth has a capital—Rosebridge—but each province has one as well.

I should've probably made the connection earlier, considering the sheer size of the metropolis, but worry for one's life has a way of making even the simplest facts difficult to process.

I quickly run through the facts I know about the provincial capital. There aren't many, so it doesn't take long. Why bother teaching a human sacrifice about the country where they were born? It's not like I was supposed to be alive long enough to truly experience life.

Mora is the largest textile producer in the Kingdom of Myreth. They import wool and yarn, like the products Alba makes, and export fabrics to be used all over the kingdom and sold abroad.

That information won't be helpful, and I toss it aside. I am many things, but a skilled seamstress is not one of them. I can barely thread a needle without stabbing myself in the process, let alone sew in a straight line. Even James is better with a needle than I am. An ironic fact, Mother always said, since I was the one who often ended up with rips in my clothes, thanks to the many animals I rescued.

Mora is also home to some of the best breweries in the country. Again, it's good to know, but it's not helpful at the moment.

Despair is curling in my stomach, ready to set in, when I remember the third thing the provincial capital is famous for.

"I'm here to see the Moran Gardens," I tell the guard, hoping he buys my lie. "I've heard all about them and can't wait to explore them before the winter sets in."

Keeping my eyes downcast, I smile demurely. Internally, I pray that the guards can't hear the pounding of my heart in my chest. Each beat is a deafening drum in my ears as I wait to see if he bought my lie.

"The Moran Gardens are stunning this time of year." His voice drops, and his boots move closer to me. Why is he advancing? "Are you here alone, Miss Lockheart?"

I nod, because what else can I do? He takes another step towards me, his hand landing on my arm.

He's touching me. *Why* is he touching me? Does he suspect I'm gods-blessed?

My heart seizes, and my breath catches in my throat as the guard leans in close. He smells of musk and sweat, and I fight the urge to wrinkle my nose and yank my arm out of his grip.

His thumb . . . strokes my arm. "If you ever want an escort while you explore the gardens at night, you know where to find me."

Oh. *Oh*.

Bile rises in my throat, and my skin crawls as his meaning sets in. I'm not an untouched virgin who has never enjoyed the company of others. When Amelia and I were eighteen, we asked Felix and Nolen, two boys who attended school with us, to show us the ways of the world before we were Given, but I have no desire for a partner right now.

Do all the single women who pass through the gates on their own get propositioned, or is it just me? Knowing my luck, it's probably the latter.

As much as I want to yank my arm from his hand and make it clear how disinterested I am, I can't risk angering him. The longer I stay here, the higher the chances that he's going to stop me and force me to remove my hood.

No, I need to get through the gate as quickly as possible.

Swallowing my displeasure takes significant effort, but eventually, I calm myself long enough to look up and smile at the soldier from beneath my hood.

"Thank you." I force the smile to remain on my face, even though it feels foreign. "I'll . . . keep that in mind."

It's a blatant lie, but if it gets me through the gates, so be it.

The soldier holds on to my arm for far longer than what is considered appropriate before he releases me and steps back, joining the other soldiers. "Welcome to Mora, Miss Lockheart."

14

BEAUTIFUL CHAOS

Wren

Walking through Mora's gates is like entering another world. The throngs of people arriving to the city were overwhelming, but they were nothing compared to the pandemonium inside the city walls. The gate opens into a large courtyard unlike anything I've ever seen. Even the busiest market day in Grenbloom doesn't compare to the chaos around me.

There are so many people milling about that I can barely sort through them. A young woman with a baby strapped to her chest is gesticulating wildly as she speaks to a man who looks to be her father. To my left, a trio of elderly men are loudly arguing about the weather. Apparently, today's warm weather is an omen. Good or bad, I'm not sure.

People are streaming out of houses and businesses, all of them too preoccupied to notice me. Keeping my cloak wrapped around me, I move away from the gate and press my back against a brick wall.

Gods, this city puts an entirely new perspective on the meaning of the word *busy*. To be honest, I didn't even realize there could be this many people converging in one place at the same time.

I've never felt more like a small-village girl than I do at this very moment. It's not that I didn't know Grenbloom was small and isolated. It's just that, until this moment, I hadn't realized the extent of the isolation.

You need to keep going, a small voice at the back of my head urges me. *The Hunter is coming for you.*

The voice is right. Lingering out in the open is unwise. Just because I made it past the guards at the city entrance doesn't mean I'm in the clear.

Five minutes.

That's how long I'm going to give myself to take in the sights. After that, I'll keep going. It's not long, and I probably shouldn't even give myself that, but I can't help it. Curiosity about the city is stronger than my panic, stronger than my urge to get out of here unseen.

Hoping I'm not making a foolish mistake, I lift my head just enough to take a better look around. There are buildings *everywhere.* They're crammed together, most stretching three stories high, while a few climb even higher. Some are made of colorful bricks, while others are sparkling white with thick brown beams running up the sides. Storefronts occupy the base of most buildings. Even though it's early, merchants are flipping signs from CLOSED to OPEN, organizing displays, and getting ready for the day.

And the sounds. The city is a wonderful cacophony of noise. People are talking, children are screeching, and parents are yelling. Someone is playing the violin on the street corner across from me, and the faint strains of piano chords lilt through the air from an apartment above the bakery to my right.

There's so much life that, for a long moment, all I can do is lean back and appreciate the city.

It's so much. So loud. So busy.

So beautiful.

The panic I felt in the line walking into the city is nowhere to be found, replaced instead by an intense feeling of rightness. I never truly felt at home in Grenbloom. I used to think that my Mark made it so that I didn't belong, but maybe it was the village itself.

The longer I stand here, letting the city seep into my bones, the more I realize that *this* is what I was always meant for. Maybe I was never too much, never too curious. Maybe I was just in the wrong place at the wrong time.

I was meant for this. For a city. For people. For loudness and laughter and life.

I inhale deeply, and the scents of the city wash over me. Notes of freshly baked bread mingle with flowers, covering up the less delightful aromas that come from so many people living in such close quarters. Even the scents that have me wrinkling my nose don't stop me from appreciating the city's beauty.

My gaze snags on a well-dressed woman in a bright blue dress standing on the third-floor balcony of an apartment building. She's smiling, her raven hair braided over one shoulder, as she sips from a mug. I'm not sure how long I spend watching her before someone bumps into my shoulder.

"Move, lady," snarls a man who smells like he's never met a bar of soap before.

Rude. A retort rises to the tip of my tongue, but Esyn must be on my side, at least for the moment, because I miraculously hold it in. The man is probably right. Beautiful chaos or not, I'm still on the run. I can't stay here any longer. My five minutes have surely come and gone.

You're going to get yourself killed if you're not careful, I chide myself as I start moving down the worn cobblestones that replaced the dirt road from outside the city.

I need to work on blending in, which means I can't be a tourist any longer. Acting out of place is precisely the type of behavior that will get me caught.

I have to focus and remember the plan.

Find a map. Get out of Mora. Live.

Those three steps cycle through my mind as I follow the crowd down the street, moving into the city proper. More people stream out of their homes, and soon, my ears are ringing from all the noise.

A far cry from the forest, the atmosphere is chaotic. For a while, I enjoy it. I walk through a commercial area, then a residential one.

But then, when I'm deep inside Mora, my eyes catch on a black shape high above me. My heart races, and I stumble.

Up high, partially hidden by the clotheslines that stretch across the buildings, are men and women dressed in clothes the color of ink. They stand on the rooftops, their stern gazes sweeping over the crowd as we shuffle past.

Watchers.

Swords are sheathed on their backs, the hilts rising above their heads like beacons of death. The soldiers stare at the streets with stern expressions, and auras of violence radiate from them.

Suns help me. My chest tightens, and I trip on a raised cobblestone, barely managing to stay upright. Someone slams into my back. Another person bumps into my elbow.

"Watch where you're fucking going," a guttural voice mutters.

I suck in a sharp breath and drop my head, frantically tugging my hood down. My tongue is heavy, and I trip over my words. "S-s-sorry."

A gruff inhale is the man's only reply as he shoves past me and stomps down the street. His rudeness should bother me, but I don't have the energy to care about it. Not when there are gods-damned Watchers stationed above me.

Have they been there the entire time? The guards at the gate were just a warning—one that I didn't understand until now.

Balling my fists, I force myself to keep moving to avoid attracting unwanted attention. No one has yelled at me to stop, but that doesn't mean I'm in the clear.

Far from it.

My eyes flick from one rooftop to the next, cataloging the soldiers. Now that I've noticed them, they're all I can see. It feels like each of them is staring directly at me. Paranoia is a creeping mist, sweeping over my mind. It pushes out all my other thoughts until the king's soldiers are all that I can think about.

We had Watchers in Grenbloom, of course. They're soldiers whose primary role is to ensure everyone is obeying the king's laws. Watchers are His Majesty's eyes and ears, reporting to the Enforcers if anyone breaks the law.

Like I did when I ran from my Giving.

My chest tightens, and the world warps the longer I remain beneath the Watchers' heavy gazes.

The city's beauty has vanished. Did it ever exist?

The roads are too narrow. Every shoulder that bumps into me feels like a battering ram. The buildings are closing in as if they're about to topple on me. The children's shrieks have become ominous shouts of warning.

They're going to find you.

It's too much. Mora is no longer a sprawling metropolis. The mountains on either side of the city are giant arms reaching for me, ready to snatch me out of thin air and present me to the king's soldiers.

And from there . . .

A stark white temple. Ominous flickering candlelight. Priestesses in crimson robes. A sharp dagger. Prayers. A cackling laugh. And then . . .

Death.

I stumble and gasp for breath, my lungs refusing to draw air. No longer do beauty and peace reside in the chaos. There is only death.

Death and the Watchers. In my mind, they're one and the same.

Oh, gods. I'm going to die here today. Maybe they won't even bother returning me to Grenbloom before they kill me. The suns will shine brightly on me as my blood is spilled.

A fist wraps around my heart and squeezes tightly. Cold sweat trickles down my spine, and my hands are clammy. The sounds of the city vanish, replaced by a panicked hum in my ears. A low moan rises in my throat.

I've made an awful mistake. Lifting my feet is the greatest of struggles, as if I'm dragging my feet through mud. I'm aware of every whisper of fabric, every person who brushes against my cloak, and every eye that falls on me, no matter how briefly.

I want to stop, but I can't risk it.

Death is here, and it's coming for me, just like it came for Amelia.

I glance at the next rooftop, and sure enough, there's another Watcher on patrol. May the gods have mercy on my soul.

The Watchers remain. My panic grows. Time marches on.

It feels like I've been walking beneath the soldiers' gazes for hours, even though it's probably only been a few minutes, before a small alley appears between two buildings up ahead. As I get closer, my eyes water from the unsavory smell coming from the murky yellow stream running down the middle, but there doesn't appear to be a Watcher stationed on the adjacent rooftops.

Breaking away from the crowd, I walk briskly towards the alley. My heart is hammering as I lift my skirts and avoid the nasty liquid, trying hard not to think about what it might be. I make it to the other side of the alley, slipping out onto a less crowded road.

I don't see any Watchers, but now that I'm aware of their presence, there is no peace to be found. I move into a steady jog, desperate to get away from danger as fast as possible. My grumbling stomach quickly reminds me that running without having eaten recently is a bad idea, but at this point, it's my only option.

I'm such a gods-damned idiot. Why did I ever think coming into Mora was a good idea? My foolishness will likely get me killed faster than the iridescent whorl on my forehead, which is a fucking feat in and of itself.

But I'm trapped here, and all I can do is run.

So that's exactly what I do.

Living on the wrong side of the law is exhausting.

The rest of the day passes in a blur of city streets, Watchers, and alleyways. Forget finding a map—right now, all my energy is focused on keeping my head down, literally and figuratively, and staying alive.

I stumble through the streets, trying to find the exit so I can leave this cursed place. Theoretically, it shouldn't be difficult. One would think a city this size would have well-planned streets that were easy to navigate, but since my luck is terrible, that's not the case.

Mora is a gods-damned maze. The streets seem to go in circles, and I can't find the exit.

Even if I could locate the gate I used to enter the city, I don't want to risk running into the same guards as before.

Fear of getting caught has me avoiding everyone, so asking for directions is out of the question. By the time the suns are setting, my stomach is audibly growling as I trudge through the streets. Everything looks the same as it did hours ago, and I'm forced to admit a terrible truth: I'm lost.

As if that isn't bad enough, the warmth of the day has been replaced by a chilly breeze. Weariness is clinging to my bones, and I can't put off sleeping for another night. I'm still human, after all. I need a proper night's rest. I slip my hand into my satchel, feeling the three coins from Alba.

A frown pulls at my lips. I don't want to spend the money yet, but I might not have a choice. If I don't see something soon . . .

My eyes widen, and my thoughts trail off as a splash of green catches my eye. Even in the grey haze of dusk before the moons rise, the color stands out from the rest of the city.

The Moran Gardens.

This feels like a sign. Wrapping my cloak around myself to ward off the chill, I hurry to the gardens. The air is filled with the scent of life, and as I get closer, a sense of awe bubbles up inside me.

No wonder the Moran Gardens are so well known. Even from the outside, they're stunning.

An enormous, moss-covered stone wall separates the green space from the rest of the city. Vines creep along the stones, and beautiful flowers with cerulean teardrop petals hang in clusters from the greenery. The floral scent is pleasantly strong but not overpowering, and it reminds me of the perfume Amelia's mother used to wear on temple days.

Is it a sign?

I crane my neck up, gasping at the flourishing oasis hidden behind the walls. It truly is a wondrous sight. If it weren't for the mountain range rising above the city, I'd think the gardens stretched on forever.

Even now, with the Giving Season coming to a close, the garden is incredibly lush. Almost unimaginably so, although I'm not sure how that would be. I don't know of any royals who live in Mora, so who else could be feeding magic into the land? The richness of the soil must just be a remnant of times past, when magic was plentiful throughout Myreth.

I step closer to the wall, peering through a crack in the stones. Trees that seem tall enough to touch the suns are next to plants with leaves the size of my hand. Bushes grow beside streams, and paths weave through it all. A symphony of birdsong rises, and tiny white squirrels sail across branches.

It's a virtual treasure trove of life, filled with an alluring beauty that is both breathtaking and awe-inspiring. I've never seen anything like this.

For a moment, the beauty of the gardens allows me to forget about my lot in life. Right now, it doesn't matter that I'm a gods-blessed on the run or that the Hunter knows my name. Even the homesickness that has been plaguing me more with each passing day doesn't seem as intense as it did earlier.

If I lived in Mora, I would never leave this place. This is where I'll spend the night, I decide. It seems tranquil, and I'm not ready to leave it yet.

I follow the stone wall to an entrance a few blocks away. An arch constructed from green and blue stones stretches across the path, and a vacant guard post sits on one side. The gate is open, and I hurry through it. When I don't see anyone else around, I exhale.

"Praise Esyn," I murmur under my breath, hurrying up the path.

The moment the prayer hits my ears, I freeze. Wait one gods-damned moment. Why am I praising Esyn after everything that has happened?

Fuck that. She doesn't deserve my praise. The Mother is the reason Amelia died, the reason I'm Marked, and the reason I'm being hunted.

Suddenly, all the problems I momentarily ignored when I stumbled upon the garden come flooding back with increased clarity.

Fuck Esyn.

Fuck the gods and the temples and the murderous priestesses.

Fuck this damned swirl on my forehead.

Fuck it all.

I kick a rock on impulse, and a shooting pain reverberates through my foot.

"Suns fucking help me," I groan. Can't I even have a tantrum in peace? Is that too much to ask?

I don't feel like crying now, nor do I think I'll ever feel like doing that again. Anger is an ember burning deep in my chest. The longer I focus on how extraordinarily awful my life has been of late, the hotter that fire burns.

Soon, a torch lights in the depths of my being.

I never asked for any of this. I didn't want a Mark that glows at the most inconvenient of times, nor did I ask to be destined for an untimely death. Life has thrown me into shitty situations since the day before my Giving Ceremony, and I'm over it.

I stomp down the path, carefully avoiding the other people enjoying the garden during this late hour, until I come across a small waterfall. It's tucked away from the rest of the grounds, and I don't even see the stone walls anymore.

Perfect.

Kneeling on the damp grass, I cup my hands and taste the water. It's slightly sweet, cool, and refreshing. I quench my thirst before filling my canteen. Only then do I sit back and look around.

This part of the garden is so thick that it's practically a forest. If I hadn't come from the city, I would never have believed one existed nearby. I'm surrounded by wilderness. Vines hang in thick canopies from trees, moss-covered stones are scattered about, flowers bloom in clusters, and tall bushes line the paths.

A chittering comes from above me, and I tilt up my head. My lips tug up into a smile at the small white creature balancing on a branch above my head. Its coat shimmers in the silver moonlight, and two tiny black eyes seem to follow me as I tilt my head.

"Hi," I whisper. "Is this your waterfall?"

The creature stares at me solemnly, turning an acorn around in its paws.

"I'm just going to sleep here tonight if that's okay with you," I say.

Two minuscule, fluffy ears twitch.

"I know you can't understand me." I smile sadly, wishing Truffle was here so I could cuddle her. "But it's nice to have someone to talk to."

A long moment passes before the creature chitters again and leaps away. So much for our conversation. Even the garden's tiniest inhabitants want nothing to do with me.

My stomach gnaws at me, reminding me that I still haven't eaten, but it's too dark to try and forage for something now. With my luck, I'd pick something poisonous and make myself violently ill or die.

No, the water will have to be enough for tonight.

Hunger is my companion as I crawl beneath a large bush. The night is cold, and I try to imagine that Alba's fire is nearby, warming me. I'm a bad liar, though, and I can't stop myself from shivering. Keeping my cloak around myself, I curl into a ball and pull out Father's knife. I clutch it to my chest, shutting my eyes and praying for sleep to claim me quickly.

I'm going to rest for a few hours, and when I wake, I'll find some food, get a map, and be on my way.

My last thought before my nightmares claim me is that I hope the Hunter isn't nearby.

15

THE HUNTER IS COMING

Wren

The Hunter is coming for me. His green eyes follow me in my sleep, watching me. Calling me. Taunting me.

His warning follows me, even now.

Run, little bird.

His voice echoes through my never-ending nightmares. Even in sleep, I'm not safe. I'll never be safe again.

I wake with a sense of unease coating me like a second skin. My mind feels too far from my body, a discombobulated sensation that gets worse as I try to wiggle my fingers. They're stiff around Father's knife, and I keep my eyes closed while I carefully peel my fingers away from the hilt. It's a suns-damned miracle that I didn't cut myself in my sleep.

Breathing in deeply, I try to settle my racing heart. I'm here, I'm alive, and most importantly, I'm still free. Even though he chased me in my nightmares, the Hunter hasn't caught me yet. If I have anything to say about it, he will never catch me. I'll make it to the Sapphire Coast and leave this gods-damned country and the Hunters behind for good.

Maybe one day I'll even laugh about the ridiculousness of this entire situation. Wouldn't that be something? Laughing about this nightmare? I can barely smile, let alone laugh.

But someone . . .

Someone *is* laughing.

The joyous sound fills the air, discordant against the unease brought on by my nightmares. I shudder. Who in their right mind has cause to be happy? Certainly not me.

Despite my earlier thoughts, I'm not sure I'll ever laugh again.

I sit up, pulling open my eyes. The darkness is gone, and somehow, I slept the entire night. Green leaves are inches from my face, and an ant is crawling up my arm. I shake it off and roll out from under the bush. My back aches, reminding me that sleeping on the ground was yet another poor decision.

I rotate my stiff shoulders, and a burst of pain runs through me. Because, of course, everything hurts. At this point, I should just expect things to turn out badly. At least then I won't be surprised when they don't go my way.

A baritone chuckle fills the air, breaking me free of my pity party. My head turns towards it, and I frown. That sounds nearly identical to James's laugh. But it can't belong to him—he's at home, far away from me.

My heart twists, and my homesickness returns tenfold. Even though my family followed the rules for the Given and kept me at arm's length during my teenage years, I still love them. Maybe I shouldn't, but I do.

I need to get going, but first I pull open my bag and fish out the necklace my parents gave me. The two suns dangle on the dainty gold chain, and I trace them before clasping the jewelry around my neck. The necklace imbues me with a sense of strength, as though my family is here, encouraging me forward.

Now, I feel ready for the day. I gather my things—a quick affair, since I have very few possessions to my name—and rise to my feet. The suns are bright despite having barely risen, and the sky is blue once again. I scowl, glaring at the cloudless heavens.

What is it with these beautiful days? I hate them.

From now on, gloomy, cloudy days are my favorites. The darker, the better. Fog? Bring it on. Clouds? Perfect. Thunderstorms? Fabulous. Snow falling in blinding sheets, making it impossible to see anything? Fantastic.

They'll more adequately reflect my mood.

Leaves and twigs tangled themselves in the curls that escaped my hood while I slept, and I pick them out, discarding them on the ground. Once that's done, I secure my hood and cloak once more before taking care of my personal needs behind a tree. I wash my hands in the nearby stream and dry them on my dress before getting a drink. I'm replacing the lid on my canteen when the wind carries faint streams of joyous music to my ears.

First, laughter. Now, this. What in the name of all the gods is happening? I'm not sure, but I don't plan on sticking around to find out. Now that I've slept, my desire to find a map and get out of this city is stronger than ever.

Last night, the garden resembled a lush forest. In the daylight, it seems more like a beautiful utopia pulled straight from the storybooks Mother used to read the twins when they were younger.

I don't recognize most of the plants, but a grin spreads across my face when I catch sight of a moonberry bush sitting atop a small hill.

The gods may have forsaken me, but at least the suns are still watching out for me. Their rays light my path as I make my way to the bush. The berries are red and inviting. My stomach lets out a thunderous grumble at the sight.

I pick a moonberry, testing it between my fingers. It's darker than the ones I found in the forest, but it feels ripe. When I pop it into my mouth, a burst of tart, sweet flavor hits my tongue.

It reminds me of home, and for a moment, a wave of longing so strong I can barely stand washes over me. Memories cycle through my mind. Picking berries with Amelia. Making jam with Mother. Eating bowls of berries and cream with my siblings until our stomachs hurt.

Crouching in front of the bush, my fingers roam over the leaves. I toss countless berries into my mouth, focusing on sating the hunger that has been present since I left Alba's.

"Hey," a male voice comes from behind me. "What are you doing?"

I swallow a scream along with my latest berry, which lodges itself in my throat. I half cough, half sputter, slapping my hand over my mouth. Fear is a sheet of pure ice coursing through my veins as I stare at the moonberry bush, my limbs unable to move.

He found me.

Suns, why did I think that stopping in the garden to sleep was a good idea? I should've kept going, even though I was tired. Anything to keep some distance between me and Gabriel.

The Hunter is here. My breath comes in short bursts as I gather the strength to fight back. I won't go willingly. Not now, not ever. Breaking free of my fear, my fingers find the hilt of Father's knife.

I turn around, a snarl rising in my throat. "I'm not going to go— Oh."

The man in front of me isn't Gabriel.

My legs threaten to buckle as relief courses through me. It's short-lived, however. Just because *my* Hunter hasn't found me doesn't mean I'm in the clear. I'm still Marked and on the run.

This man could be just as much of a danger to me as Gabriel.

Tugging my hood further down my forehead in what I hope is an inconspicuous manner, I look over the stranger.

He appears to be a year or two younger than me, but that might just be because he's clean-shaven. He's wearing a black tunic and brown trousers similar to the ones James favors. His brown eyes sparkle with life, his curly black hair is unkempt, and on his tawny neck . . .

I gasp, unable to help myself.

"You're gods-blessed?" The question slips from my lips before I can stop it.

What are the chances that I stumbled across another Marked One in the garden? Wait. Is he on the run, too? His Mark is orange, and it isn't glowing, but maybe he's already learned the truth of what happens in the temples.

Maybe he just wants to get a head start on running for his life. Maybe the gods have shown me favor after all.

For a moment, I feel bad about cursing Esyn yesterday. Could she have sent me this Given as an apology?

Excitement bubbles up within me. We can escape together, this gods-blessed and I. It would make surviving so much easier. We could take shifts sleeping. That way, the Hunters will never catch us unaware. I wonder—

A chuckle interrupts my thoughts. "Just for today."

The strangeness of his words has me jerking my head up. "What?"

I have no idea what he's talking about. Has he lost his mind? A Given . . . for today? That's not possible.

The gods-blessed are born Marked, fated to our positions. No one can be a Given for a day. But he sounds so sure.

My eyes widen further as his fingers find the whorl on his neck, and he lifts it off.

"What the fuck?" I breathe.

He smirks at me, as if he knows this discovery is boggling my mind. Turning it around, he shows me a strange white adhesive on the back. With a smile, he puts the Mark back on his skin, patting it.

And it stays there.

My mind whirls as I try to comprehend what I'm seeing. He's Marked, but the symbol of the gods' blessing came off. It just . . . came off.

I don't . . .

He . . .

What?

My thoughts feel sluggish as I stare at his neck. Before I can ask more questions—like how the fuck is this possible and what the hell is going on—he grabs a handful of moonberries from the bush and strolls down the path towards the entrance. A young man emerges from another path and bumps his shoulder. The two of them laugh, making their way to the street.

So casual. So relaxed.

So *wrong*.

I don't understand. My very first memory is staring into a grimy mirror, studying the blue swirl etched prominently on my forehead. I've memorized the way it looks and feels.

In all my years, my Mark has never shifted, never moved, never done anything at all except start glowing when I turned twenty on the first day of winter last year. Sure, now it burns when I'm emotional, but that's nothing compared to what he just did.

He *lifted* his Mark.

I stumble back, my fingers instinctively rising to my brow. No matter how I scratch at my Mark, it doesn't come off or move or even budge.

Confusion is a swirling pit in me. The berries sour my stomach. I slap my hand over my mouth, swallowing the scream threatening to crawl out of me.

Every single time I think things have gotten as bad as they could possibly get, every single time I think I know what's going on, everything changes. I stare at the empty path for so long, my eyes cross. Only then do I pull my hand from my mouth and start moving again. I need to get out of this gods-damned city.

My footfalls echo in my head, growing louder and louder until they're drums in my ears.

He pulled off his Mark.

I'm so busy mentally dissecting the stranger's movements that I don't watch where I'm going as I head down the path. It isn't until I reach the iron gates leading to the road that I realize the booming drums *aren't* in my head.

By then, it's too late to hide.

The gate is wide open, just like last night, but the cobblestone street is no longer empty. My heart lurches, and instinctively, I yank my hood further over my head as I take in the scene unfolding before me. Yesterday, the city seemed busy, but today, it's brimming with people.

Heavy crowds line both sides of the street. Children hang off their mother's skirts and their father's legs. Teenagers stand in groups, chatting loudly. The elderly are also present—some lean on canes, while others rest in rolling chairs. Vendors stroll down the sidewalks carrying large wooden trays of food and drinks, selling their provisions to the assembled horde.

Everyone seems to be waiting for something, glancing to the left every few seconds. Even though people are crammed onto the sides of the roads, no one is walking in the middle of the street.

The reason for that becomes clear a moment later.

Drumbeats so loud I can barely hear myself think come from the left, announcing the arrival of six drummers. They wear matching uniforms. Sky-blue tunics, black pants, and leather boots that rise to their knees. Black gloves cover their hands. Round drums are strapped to their chests, and each drummer is gripping two mallets, one in each hand. They pound their instruments in perfect synchrony.

Boom.

Boom.

Boom.

The drums are loud, but what comes after them has me pressing my back against the garden's stone wall.

Dozens of female dancers flood the streets, moving their bodies in time with the drumbeat. Their beautiful garments reflect the rainbow, utterly unlike the heavy dresses the women in Grenbloom wear. The fabric barely covers their bodies, accentuating their feminine forms in a way I never knew was possible.

A gorgeous woman with beautiful umber skin dances by me. Shimmering pink fabric is banded around her breasts, matching her flowing slitted skirt and the slippers on her feet. Another dancer with tan skin and silver hair is wearing a similar outfit, but hers is a purple so dark, it's almost black. A third performer with a short cut of bright blue hair and whose flesh is as pale as snow is wearing a teal halter dress that's tight to the waist before it flows out from there.

Every single dancer is jaw-droppingly beautiful, but it's not their outward appearance that has me gasping.

Each of them bears a Mark of the gods. Some have them above their breasts. Others, on their necks or upper arms. A few have them on their exposed stomachs. And three of them are Marked on their foreheads.

Just. Like. Me.

I've never seen so many gods-blessed in one place before, let alone Markings that look like mine. There's something incredibly beautiful about being in the same space as others who are the same as me. Before I know it, pressure is building behind my eyes.

Damn it. This keeps happening to me at the worst moments. I can't cry right now. I blink away the tears, refusing to pull my gaze away from the performers.

I am not alone.

The thought steals my breath, even though in my heart of hearts, I know this isn't real. It can't be. Though the dancers are Marked, none of their Marks are glowing. That wouldn't be a problem for the younger dancers who appear to be in their early teens, but some of these performers look like they're in their third decade of life.

Everyone knows the gods-blessed are Given the year they turn twenty. It happens without fail.

These dancers are fakes, just like the boy from earlier. Knowing that they aren't truly gods-blessed doesn't seem to matter, though. A fracture I didn't even know existed deep in my soul heals at the sight of them.

I've been so alone since Amelia's Giving, but it's not like my loneliness started there. I've been different from the moment of my birth, standing out even from other Marked Ones. The blue swirl on my forehead prohibited me from pretending I was like everyone else, even for a moment.

"Look at Wren's Mark," Gavin, one of the village boys, sneers in the schoolyard. He points at my forehead, and a cluster of children laugh behind him. He's a year older than my ten, and he's been a bully for as long as I can remember. "It's so ugly."

I lift my hands to my face, trying to cover the blue swirl that's always been there. "I can't get rid of it."

There's no hiding the desperation in my voice or the tear that slides down my cheek. Why does Gavin always have to do this? It feels like every week, he has some new way to tease me.

One would think I'd be okay with it by now—it's been happening for years—but it never gets any easier. James and Markus aren't here today—they're hunting with Father—so the bullies decided I was easy prey.

It isn't fair. I want to be like the other kids, but I can't change who I am.

"No one is ever going to want to marry you, Wren," Soral, Gavin's second in command, interjects cruelly. "Not when you look like that."

I try to steel my heart against his cruel words, but they still sting.

"Marry her?" Gavin shoves his friend. "No one wants her at all."

"That's not true," I tell them, lifting my hands away from my face. "I know it isn't."

The gods want me. That's why I'm Marked. Right?

Gavin and Soral elbow each other and laugh, the other children quickly following suit. Their mean words continue. I ball my fists, glaring at them, but no one makes an effort to leave.

A shout comes from behind me.

"Shut up, Soral." Amelia runs up next to me. Her blond braids fly behind her, showing off the pink Mark on her neck. "You're a pig and a bully."

"And you're a Given," Gavin jeers, sticking out his tongue in her direction.

"Yes, we are." Amelia squares her shoulders and glares at the bullies. Her pinky finger brushes mine.

It's a small touch, but her meaning is clear: The Given stick together.

I needed that today. The problem is, as much as I want to believe that Gavin and Soral are wrong, there's a part of me that yearns for the normalcy the other children have. Why can't I be like them, just for one day? Even Amelia can hide her Mark. Not me.

Mistress Fyona rings the bell, and with another set of cruel words, the bullies head inside.

Amelia puts her hand on mine, and I look over at her.

"You know they're wrong, don't you, Birdie?" Her smile is bright. "They're just jealous of how special you are."

Amelia was a good friend that day, but the bullies were right. We *were* different. As much as having Amelia around helped, nothing could change the fact that we were two girls set apart from birth. Fated for the gods.

Cursed from the moment we were formed in our mothers' wombs.

But this . . .

The dancers are beautiful, and my heart sings at being in the presence of so many gods-blessed in one place. There must be over a hundred performers, all moving in beautiful synchrony.

The sight is mesmerizing, and slowly, I move away from the stone wall. No one seems to notice me drifting towards the street. Laughter and conversation rise, but I don't pay attention to their words.

The dancers are entrancing, and a growing stream of people follow behind them. Captivated by the Marked women, I follow them.

The procession continues through the streets of Mora. More and more people melt out of the crowd, joining the parade. Most of them are Marked, too. Some of their Marks are obviously fake and peeling off, but others are so real that they make me do a double take.

What's going on?

Eventually, I can't bear not knowing what's happening. I turn to the older woman on my right. A rosy Mark rests behind her ear, partially covered by her greying hair. She's swaying her hips, humming under her breath.

I touch her arm, the current of the crowd pulling us along with it.

"Excuse me, ma'am?" I say, keeping stride with her. I have to shout to have my voice heard over the drums.

She glances at me, her lips tugging up into a smile. Kindness shimmers in her blue eyes, and I'm glad I picked her to ask my question. "Yes, child?"

"What's going on?" I gesture to the group all around us.

The parade has grown, the crowds on either side of the street are even larger, and the air is practically vibrating with excitement. Everyone else seems to know what this is about, and I feel left out, just like when I was a child.

The woman's eyes widen, and she looks at me with shock. "Why, don't you know? It's the Giving Festival!"

The *what*?

Ice floods my veins. The sense of peace that had been settling in my soul disappears. The music is replaced by a roaring in my ears, and my feet refuse to move. I become a statue. People shout as they avoid me, but their words don't register.

I knew darkness existed in Myreth, even before I learned the truth of the Giving Ceremonies. King Andreas is renowned for his quick temper, iron fist, and penchant for blood. I've heard it said that in Rosebridge, the capital city, public executions happen on a weekly basis.

And yet, this seems *worse* than that.

My limbs turn to lead, and any joy I'd previously felt vanishes into thin air. My head pounds, and each breath feels like I'm inhaling poison.

The Giving Festival.

Somehow, my feet manage to remember how to move long enough to get me off the road before I get crushed. Wouldn't that be an ironic turn of events?

The parade continues by me as my vision blurs, and my heartbeat is erratic at best. Oh, gods. I was wrong earlier when I said that the Mother might have changed her mind about me. So, so wrong.

The Marks, the drums, the dancers, the vendors, the laughter and music . . .

My shoulder slams into the side of a building, and I double over, gasping for breath. Amelia's scream and the priestesses' laughter run through my mind, a continuous cycle that has me clutching my hood and wishing I was anywhere else.

The citizens of Mora aren't celebrating something joyful. The dancers aren't simply showing off their skills.

They're all unknowingly celebrating death.

My death.

16

I WILL NEVER STOP

Gabriel

Earlier That Day

"You need to stay here." Crouching, I meet Mist's silver eyes.

My panther returned to me three days ago, covered in blood. I searched her for a sign of injury, but she didn't seem hurt. I pitied whatever creature she'd come across, though. No person or animal could lose that much blood and live.

I took her to a stream to wash the parts of herself she couldn't reach on her own, which went over as well as could be expected when introducing a giant cat to water. We both made it through alive and relatively unscathed. She's been by my side ever since.

Together, we picked up Birdie's trail. I tracked the gods-blessed to a cottage where a woman and her chatty daughter lived. I interrogated them, but they claimed not to know who I was talking about.

They were lying. Traces of Birdie's jasmine and vanilla scent were all over that cottage. Even if my olfactory senses had been obliterated, I noticed a jar of blessed salve on the woman's windowsill. She could lie all she wanted, but that was all the proof I needed. The little bird had been there, I was certain.

I didn't arrest the woman, instead leaving her with a warning. I would've been well within my rights to take her into custody for lying to a Hunter, but it would've meant losing the Given's trail, and I couldn't afford any more delays. Not when my bond with Mist was on the line.

It isn't that I no longer want my promotion, but losing my familiar would be a fate worse than death. Before her, I was alone. My family situation has been difficult for my entire life. Mist saved me, and she knows me in a way that no one else does.

My panther stares up at me, blinking owlishly. She understands me, even though she's pretending otherwise.

I point to the city in the valley, nestled between the Black Mountains on the left and the Celestial Mountains on the right.

"I'm going in there, but I don't want any extra eyes on me." I don't want to risk alerting my prey to my presence too early.

Mist cants her head and lifts a paw, studying her sharp nails as if they're the most fascinating thing in the entire world.

"The little bird is in the city," I tell her.

She places her paw on the ground and looks up at me. Our bond hums, and I feel her question. *Are you sure?*

"Yes," I reply.

My gut tells me that the Given has chosen to go through the city. Over the years, I've learned to always trust it. My instincts are strong, and they've never led me astray. Besides, she was wearing a long dress. There's no way she climbed the mountains in that outfit.

Mist studies me, her silver eyes gleaming. I reach out and scratch her behind the ears. "I won't be long."

Of all my hunts, this one is proving to be the most difficult. Usually, they last for a day or two.

I'm not sure whether I'm annoyed or impressed by the Given's ability to stay out of reach, but it doesn't matter. I'll find the gods-blessed, tie her up, and return her to her home temple. Then she'll be the gods' problem. She'll be Given, probably sent to work in a temple bordering the northern coast for all the trouble she's caused.

My hunt will be over, and I'll return to Rosebridge victorious. I'll achieve the position of Master Hunter, and I'll be able to breathe more easily, firm in the knowledge that the king won't strip me of my position or my bond.

Sighing, I press my forehead against Mist's. She chuffs and rubs against me, warmth flooding my chest. It's comforting in a way that not much else has been in my life, and for a moment, I sit in the peace of our humming connection.

When I was younger, Grandmother used to tell me about a time when magic was found everywhere in Myreth. There were other types of bonds, she once told me. Fated ones, blessed by the gods themselves, that connected people in soul-deep ways. The magic was ancient and untouchable. Fated bonds were stronger than anything else, surpassing forged bonds in every circumstance.

My bond with Mist isn't like that. Crafted by the king's magic, it doesn't allow us to speak with each other beyond feelings and warmth. But it's still mine.

Calm floods through me, shaking some of the unease that has clung to me for days.

It's the nightmares. Every time I fall asleep, I'm haunted by the same one, albeit with slight variations. Sometimes, the king breaks the bond in the throne room. Other times, he drags us outside and puts on a show for the entire capital to watch.

The audience doesn't matter, though, because every time, my bond is severed. Without fail, I wake up covered in sweat and screaming, my voice hoarse.

I'm becoming increasingly convinced that these nightmares are warnings from the king.

"Go and find some food," I order the panther. "I'll tug on the bond when I'm leaving. Once for this gate and twice for the northern one."

There are passages through the Celestial Mountains that she can take if I need her to meet me on the other side. The crossings are treacherous for people, but even though we're bonded, Mist is still a wild animal. She will have no problem with them.

My familiar blinks again, and our bond thrums with something akin to agreement. I give her one last scratch behind her ears and stand. With a feline meow, Mist stretches, arches her back, and bounds off into the forest. She's a black blur as enthusiasm fills our bond.

My lips tug up into a smile as I turn, approaching Mora's gated entrance. Today's the day. I can feel it in my bones.

I'm going to catch the little bird.

* * *

Tarna, the goddess of humor and frivolity, must be amusing herself by playing with my life.

Booming drums welcome me to Eskana's capital city. They accompany countless peals of laughter and streams of boisterous music as Mora loses itself in the Giving Festival. The provincial holiday is celebrated yearly, and it looks like the entire population has descended upon the cobblestone streets to join the festivities.

Marked Ones surround me, laughing and enjoying the seemingly infinite flow of alcohol. Dozens of vendors and merchants line the streets. The presence of so many people will make my task more difficult, but not impossible.

First things first, I require provisions. I've made it this far without my sword, but now that I'm in a city, there are options at my disposal. I navigate Mora's streets with ease, even with the added crowds, and quickly arrive at my first destination.

A wooden sign hangs above the door, setting the building apart from the otherwise identical ones on either side. The three-story, whitewashed buildings with wooden shingles make up the majority of Mora's commercial districts. The sign features the image of an open book next to a quill and an ink pot on its side. The paint is flaking, but the text displaying MIKAL'S PRINT SHOP is unmistakable.

I push open the door. A jingling bell above my head announces my arrival. The door falls shut behind me, muting the noise from the city's celebrations.

Sunlight streams in through the front windows, and my eyes adjust to the space. Printed flyers cover every available inch of the wooden walls, overlapping one another in places. Books are stacked in piles on counters and shelves. The distinct aroma of ink and parchment fills the air.

I cross the space, my footsteps echoing on the wooden floors. The planks creak as I move, a testament to the age of this historical building. The city of Mora is over a thousand years old, and this building has been standing for over half that time.

Footsteps pound on a staircase, and a door opens to my right as I reach the wooden counter that stretches across the length of the room.

"Sorry about that," a booming voice calls out. "I thought the festival would buy me some time— Oh, Gabe. It's you."

My smile widens. A muscular man a few years older than me kicks the door shut, coming to join me. Messy black curls reach below his ears, and a splash of ink decorates his sepia skin. A leather apron covers his tunic and trousers. His sleeves are rolled to his elbows, and he's carrying a stack of flyers. He drops them on the counter and turns to me, grinning.

"Good to see you, Mikal." I step forward and clap him on the back, my chest warming at the sight of my old friend.

"It's been what, two years?" He chuckles, slapping me on the back.

Stepping back, I rake a hand through my hair. "Three, I think."

The last time I came through Mora, I'd just finished a hunt. That one hadn't been nearly as troublesome as this one is turning out to be.

"Too long." He leans his hip on the counter.

I agree, adding, "How are you?"

Mikal beams brightly, as if the suns have infused his cheeks. "Good. The gods have blessed us. Alara is heavy with child, and she's glowing."

My chest warms, and I shake his hand. "Congratulations, old friend."

I know how hard they've been trying. Throughout their decade-long marriage, they've made hundreds of offerings to Dehena, the goddess of fertility, to bless Alara's womb.

"Thank you. We are walking in the gods' light and couldn't be happier." Mikal makes a religious gesture over his chest before looking me over. "Now, I'm sure you didn't come to Mora just to check up on me and my wife, especially not on the day of the Giving Festival." A black brow lifts. "Unless you've given up hunting and you're searching for a wife of your own?"

I scoff. "Never."

At least, not if I can help it. The king will have to pry this position out of my cold, dead hands.

Hunting is more than just my job. It's become my life. It's my ticket to freedom from the binds I was born into, a way out of the hell that was my childhood. My bond with Mist thrums steadily in my chest, a reminder of all the benefits of my position.

I'll never stop, never give it up.

Mikal nods, making his way behind the counter. "That's what I thought." He leans forward on his elbows. "What do you need?"

Always quick to cut to the chase. That's one of the reasons I came here. I knew my friend would be able to help, and I wouldn't waste all day trying to round up what I needed.

I count on my fingers. "Money, a change of clothes, and a sword if you have one."

I've been able to hide my torn tunic beneath my cloak thus far, but I'd rather not have to worry about it any longer.

Mikal's brows hit his hairline, and he studies me for a long moment. Perhaps he wasn't expecting such an extensive list.

"I see," he says slowly.

"I'll repay you," I assure him, laying my palms flat on the counter. "Whatever you give me, I'll double it once I get my reward."

Hunters receive an annual stipend from the Crown, but the real opportunity for riches comes from catching escaped prisoners and runaway Marked Ones. The Given don't run that often—there are usually one or two a year, but they pay the most. Once I retrieve the little bird and return her, I'll receive a handsome reward from the Ruby Crown.

Mikal's eyes widen at the mention of money. "Double?"

I nod, and he whistles through his teeth. "Damn. This person you're hunting must be important." He tilts his head. "Do I want to know who it is?"

Even though all the Hunters in the land would've received messages via enchanted falcons about Wren's disappearance, the public doesn't know there's an escaped Given. After all, it wouldn't be good for the king's image if people knew some of the Given were fleeing their fates. It's the same reason he squashes the resistance with a crimson fist whenever it pops up.

"It's better if you don't."

"Understood." Mikal raps his knuckles on the counter, looking deep in thought. "How much money do you need?"

I name an amount that should be more than sufficient, and my friend blows out a long breath. He runs a hand through his hair, studying the ceiling.

In the silence, the laughter, shrieks of joy, and music grow louder. The Giving Festival is well underway. Is Wren among them, dancing and drinking the day away, not realizing that I'm here, hunting her?

A thrill races down my spine at the thought of catching my prey. Of the rush that comes from completing a hunt.

After several beats, Mikal nods.

"All right. Come with me." He turns towards another staircase that leads to the lower level of the print shop where his office is located. "I'll get you situated."

I follow him down the wooden steps, and he catches me up on his life as we head into his workspace. His wife has been experiencing horrible morning sickness, and she's been visiting Eses's and Dehena's temples daily to pray for strength for her and the baby. Even so, they're thrilled to begin this new stage of life. They have a name picked out, although they're not sharing.

Something within me twinges at the thought of a baby. I've never considered children—my own upbringing was gods-damned awful, and the life of a Hunter isn't conducive to family life—but I am delighted for Mikal and Alara. He will be an incredible father; I can already tell.

By the time I leave the print shop, I'm ready to complete my hunt. A sword hangs from a leather baldric that crosses my chest, I've exchanged my torn tunic for a fresh one, and my pockets jingle with coin. My steps are light as I head back outside. Energy is coursing through my veins.

Hunting has always invigorated me, but chasing Birdie feels different.

It makes me feel *alive*.

I'm nearing the White Market, Mora's main marketplace, when my skin starts tingling. An awareness sweeps over me, and my pace quickens. Wren is there, I'm sure of it. The White Market seems like a foolish place to go when trying to avoid being seen, but who am I to judge my prey's choice of hiding places?

There are people *everywhere*.

Dancers fill the streets, commoners are dressed in their temple-best, and children run every which way, fueled by the copious amounts of sweets available on festival days. Parents race after their young ones, darting around merchants trying to sell their wares.

There are artisans and bakers, weavers and artists. The taverns have erected wooden tables outside their establishments. They're selling mugs of ale, small loaves of bread, and portions of roasted meat to anyone with coin.

And then, there are the Watchers. My brethren in black line the streets and rooftops, their watchful gazes trained on the celebratory crowds.

I'm not wearing anything that would mark me as a Hunter, but several soldiers must recognize me from my last visit to the city because they dip their heads in my direction. Each time, I press my closed fist against my chest and briefly nod in greeting.

The market's entrance, a large white arch, is in sight when a hand lands on my sleeve.

"Are you thirsty, sir?" a honeyed voice asks on my right.

I look over to the barmaid wearing a white apron over her cream dress, her garments cut to accentuate her ample cleavage. She smiles up at me, a gap in her teeth. Her brown hair is escaping its bun, and there's a rosy tint to her cheeks. She's balancing a tray bearing several mugs of frothing ale on her outstretched fingers.

"Ah, no." I pull my arm away. She frowns, and I hurriedly add, "Thank you, though."

I don't have time for refreshments right now—I need to find the Given. It's all I can think about, all I can focus on.

Disappointment flashes across the barmaid's face, but it's gone moments later as she addresses the people behind me. "Care for a cool beverage to tame the heat on this hot day, ma'am?"

I don't hear the rest of the exchange as I continue through the crowd. It feels as though every single citizen has descended upon Mora's streets. Despite my desire to get to the White Market quickly, the number of people has me moving at a slow pace.

"Bread! Get your delicious, fresh bread!" a portly man calls from my left. His apron and balding head are both covered in flour.

Two young boys with wavy brown hair and bright blue eyes stand at his feet, equally covered in white dust. The children are holding large woven baskets overflowing with rolls, and my stomach grumbles at the sight. This time, I can't help myself.

I fish a coin out of my pocket, and I make my way over. When I reach the baker and his family, I crouch in front of the younger boy. He can't be more than four, and he's scrawnier than his brother and father.

The boy looks at me with wide eyes that seem too big for his face, and my heart contorts. He reminds me of a younger version of myself. Suddenly, the Moran streets slip away as a decades-old memory takes hold of my mind.

Boots click on marble tiles, the steady sound of footsteps outside my hiding place matching the beat of my booming heart. I hug my knees to my chest, squeezing tightly as I try to make myself as small as possible.

"I know you're in here, Gabriel." The voice sends skitters down my spine, and a sob threatens to rip out of my chest.

No, no, no.

No sounds. Even at four years of age, I know that making noise is the last thing I should be doing right now. I can't let him find me.

I clamp my mouth shut, nearly biting my tongue as I try to hold still.

Maybe he won't find me. Maybe he'll leave. Maybe this day won't be as bad as yesterday, or the day before, or the day before.

Maybe, maybe, maybe.

The sides of the white tablecloth hiding me from sight flutter as the breeze blows in through the open window. The summer heat is warm, but nothing chases away the chill in my bones.

He's here, and he's out for blood. I can hear it in the way he walks, feel it in the hatred emanating from him. He sings my name teasingly, tauntingly. I quiver as he circles my hiding space.

"Come out, child."

I shake my head, muffling my cries against the soft fabric of my pants. I need to be quiet for a little bit longer. Maybe, if I am, he'll leave and—

"Aha!" A hand darts under the tablecloth and grabs my arm, yanking me out. "I found you."

My vision blurs as I kick and scream, but there's nothing I can do. Not against him. I'm just a child, and my father's wrath is never-ending.

What did I do to deserve his hatred?

With a gasping breath, I'm thrown back to the present. My father isn't here, and I'm not that weak, powerless child any longer. Shoving thoughts of my childhood and the abusive piece of shit who fathered me far, far away, I smile at the boy. "Excuse me, young man, but did I hear you have some bread for sale?"

The child's eyes widen as he realizes I'm speaking to him. He throws back his shoulders and stands as tall as he can, nodding eagerly.

"Yes, sir!" he says proudly. "Ours is the best bread in the entire city."

"I don't doubt that for a moment, with someone like yourself at the helm." He beams at the praise, and I hand him the coin in exchange for an oval sourdough loaf the size of my palm. It smells heavenly, and my mouth waters as I thank him.

The boy is practically vibrating from excitement as he grins. "You're welcome, sir!"

I stand, thanking the baker and his older son before slipping back into the crowd. As I'm leaving, the boy yells, "Did you see that, Papa?"

"I sure did, Justice," the baker replies kindly. "You did so well . . ."

The hum of the crowd swallows his voice, and I turn my attention to the loaf. A swirl is cut into the top, a replica of a Mark. I bite into the bread and groan. It's as delicious as the baker promised. I reduce it to nothing but crumbs while strolling towards the White Market.

By the time I cross beneath the enormous arch marking the entrance of the marketplace, my tunic is sticking to my back. The heat from the suns coupled with the swelling crowd is making for an unusually hot day. Maybe I should've grabbed the ale when I had the chance.

I duck under a canopy, finding refuge in the shade. Pulling the collar of my tunic away from my neck, I exhale as a breeze blows through the White Market. Taking advantage of the cooler temperature, I assess the marketplace like the soldier I am.

If the Moran streets were rivers teeming with people, the White Market is a vast ocean.

Countless stalls with colorful cloth roofs line the edges of the square. Vendors selling every ware imaginable occupy the stalls, and even more make their way through the crowd on foot.

The White Market is loud and boisterous. The air is humming with excitement. Musicians play from a stage erected in the middle of the square. Their bows fly over strings, producing an upbeat melody that underlies the laughter and chatter.

"Marks! Get your Marks!" a woman calls from my left as she ambles through the crowd. Despite the sheer number of people, she seems to move unencumbered. "Experience the day as a gods-blessed! Favored by the Mother, fated to serve the land!"

The woman looks up, smiling as her eyes meet mine. Silver hair flows to her waist, and she's wearing an emerald dress that shimmers in the sunlight. A child runs up to her, holding up a golden coin, and the woman trades him a Mark for his money.

The exchange is over in moments, and then she's striding towards me, her movements filled with purpose. There's something about her that I can't quite put my finger on, a power in her aura that demands attention. Her floral perfume is strong, the scent becoming nearly overwhelming as she steps into my space.

"Care for a Mark, sir?" She tilts her head, her eyes sweeping over me. I can't help but feel like somehow, even though I'm certain I've never seen her before, she knows who I am.

I glance down at her wares. She has an array of Marks for sale. Glistening grass-green ovals sit next to violet swirls and aquamarine squares. Each Mark is subtly different, reflecting the uniqueness of the ones the gods-blessed are born with.

I shake my head. "No, thank you."

I take a step around her, intent on leaving this conversation, but she grabs my wrist. Her grip is remarkably firm, and I look at her, raising a brow. "Ma'am?"

"Sir, you *need* a Mark." Her voice is sharp, and I angle my head, studying her more closely.

Need? I don't need anything except to complete this hunt.

Her grip loosens on my arm, and she softens her voice, but she doesn't step away. "It is the Giving Festival, after all."

I'm not sure why this is important to her, but she's wrong. I don't need a Mark.

"Thank you, but no," I repeat more forcefully this time, tugging on my arm.

She doesn't take the hint, instead tightening her hold on me.

"Ma'am," I bite out, losing my patience, "I'm not interested."

I was raised to be polite around my elders, but this is a bit much.

The insistent woman purses her lips, and something flashes through her eyes. It's gone as quickly as it appears, but then she reaches her free hand into the box. Her fingers sift through the Marks, even as her gaze remains locked on mine. Finally, she seems to find whatever she's looking for because she pulls it out and tucks it between my fingers.

"Take it, sir." Before I can protest, she wraps my hand around it. "It's a gift. No one should be unmarked during the festival."

I stare at her, slack-jawed, as she steps back, slipping into the crowd. Curiosity nibbles at me, and I turn my hand around. My brows rise. A brilliant blue swirl that's eerily similar to the Mark on Wren's forehead sits in the palm of my hand.

Goosebumps explode on my arms, and I stand on my tiptoes, searching through the crowd. "Wait! How did you . . ."

The woman in the emerald dress is gone. Vanished without a trace.

I drop back down, running my fingers over the sticker. How did she know? I raise my gaze once again, determined to find the woman, when my stomach twinges.

Wren Nightingale is here. I'm sure of it. I don't see her in the massive crowd, but it doesn't matter.

My gut is always right.

Shoving the Mark into my pocket, I promptly forget all about it. I stride forward, run my fingers over the hilt of my sword, and smile.

"I'm coming, little bird."

17

BLESSED ARE THE GIVEN

Wren

This city is a literal nightmare.

That thought has been running through my mind ever since I learned what this festival was truly about. It kept me company as my feet carried me through the streets, following the dancers. Swarms of people joined us, all laughing and giggling as they celebrated the Given.

Not. Me.

My heart has been racing nonstop, and that roaring remains in my ears. I don't have it in me to care that the heat is making my clothes stick to my body or that my meager breakfast of berries has long since worn off.

All that matters is that these people are celebrating *death*.

My death.

It's so fucking macabre that I can barely stand it. I want to climb onto the rooftops and scream that they've all been fooled, that they're celebrating murder. The Giving is a gods-damned lie, and very few people know what's really happening. My fingers twitch with the desire to rip off every Mark I see, throw them to the ground, and trample them beneath my feet.

Every giggle makes the angry fire inside me burn brighter. Every laugh makes me want to bellow my rage and horror.

If the Watchers weren't here, I would do that. They're not Hunters, but they're still dangerous.

The soldiers are everywhere. I don't know how I didn't notice them the moment I arrived in the city yesterday because, for every few jovial citizens partaking in the festivities, there's a guard looking down on them. Watching. Waiting.

"Fucking great."

I must say the last part out loud because an elderly woman nearby turns and frowns. "Language, young lady."

Before I can reply that I'm not a young lady, and who the fuck cares about language when I'm supposed to be dead right now, she disappears into the moving crowd.

It's probably for the best. I shouldn't be picking a fight. I'm supposed to be staying out of sight, getting a map, and fleeing this suns-forsaken kingdom. That's more imperative now than ever.

Besides, I hate to admit it, but the woman is right. Mother would be ashamed of the language I've used over the past few days.

Swearing is undignified, Birdie, she told me the first time she heard me testing out the word *fuck* after I picked it up from my brothers. *People who swear do so because they can't think of more eloquent ways to express themselves. You've been blessed by the gods—your language should reflect that.*

Well, I'm very sorry to break it to you, Mother, but I'm fresh out of eloquent turns of phrase right now.

It's not that I'm exactly proud of the vulgar language I've been using recently, but apparently, when you watch your best friend's throat get slit and your entire world gets flipped upside down, you curse more often. Who knew?

The future I had envisioned as a healer is gone now. Everything I'd ever hoped for is a lie. This is how I'm dealing with that.

I'm starting to realize that this is the way the world works. Things happen. Plans get fucked up. People get murdered. Hunters with twisted senses of humor give already desperate women one day's head start.

It's a lot to deal with, and if swearing helps, then I'm going to do it.

I need to get out of Mora, but my grumbling stomach reminds me that my human needs will start causing me problems if I don't take care of them. I desperately need food and water. My body still aches from sleeping in the garden, and my neck feels like it's one uncomfortable sleeping position away from never fully straightening again.

The only good thing about this gods-damned Giving Festival is that all the fake Marks mean my real one shouldn't stand out too much.

I'm using the term *good* extremely loosely since I've learned over the past few days that my judgment isn't exactly sound. First, I saved the Hunter. That obviously didn't turn out well. Then, I entered this city that is celebrating death.

Clearly, I've had a bad run of things.

Maybe instead of thinking of what *I* would do, since that's not a good idea, I should try thinking like Amelia. She was studious and successful in every avenue she pursued in life. When we decided to make the most of our time before being Given by finding a couple boys to explore the more delicate, passionate part of human nature with, Amelia put together a list of pros and cons for all our possible choices—not that there were many.

We went over them with a fine-tooth comb before settling on Felix for her and Nolen for me. He was fine for a first lover—kind, if not a bit awkward—and he didn't hurt me, which was the important part.

I bet if Amelia were in my position, she would've been a fantastic outlaw. She wouldn't be swearing and trying to keep her head down as she waded through the streets, avoiding attention. She'd use the Giving Festival as an opportunity to get what she needed before leaving Mora for good.

Be like Amelia.

That's not a bad idea. In fact, it might be one of the best ideas I've had in several days.

I don't give myself time to talk myself out of this plan. Instead, I take a deep breath, hold my head up high, and push back my hood. My Mark burns on my forehead as I expose it to the midday suns for the first time since before I left Grenbloom.

Long moments go by as I brace myself for one of the Watchers to catch sight of me. All it will take is for one soldier to realize my Mark looks too real, and everything will be over.

Except, no one notices me. No one yells at me.

I feel eyes on me, and I look up to see a Watcher gazing directly at me. My chest tightens, and I don't breathe, but his gaze moves on after a heartbeat.

It worked. Suns save me, but it *worked.*

I exhale, my shoulders loosening as the breeze plays with my hair for the first time in days. Okay. Maybe this festival isn't so bad. Maybe, in a roundabout way, this is a good thing.

I cough, stopping that thought before it gets any further. Gods above, that's taking things too far. The memory of Amelia's blood is too fresh.

But now that I'm walking around without my hood on and the wind is gently lifting my curls, kissing the sides of my neck, I feel like I can breathe for the first time since the Hunter discovered my identity.

And just in time.

I pass beneath a white arch, and the street widens into a massive cobblestone square. It's chaotic, as I've come to expect the city to be. I turn in a slow circle, taking it all in. I barely know where to look first.

The square is filled with more market stalls and people than I've ever seen. There's a wooden platform in the middle where musicians are playing stringed instruments.

The wind carries the scent of roasted meat and spices towards me, and my stomach rumbles.

Suns, I'm so hungry. I reach into my satchel, turning Alba's three coins over in my hand. No one is looking at me, not even the Watchers stationed throughout the square.

The Giving Festival is dark, dangerous, and morbid, but I might be able to use it to my advantage and get what I need. I walk past a bookseller stationed next to an artist painting a lush landscape. The painter has several canvases for sale, each more beautiful than the last.

To their right is a baker whose table is laden with cakes. Some are small and could be devoured in two bites, while others would be big enough for my whole family and our neighbors to enjoy. All the cakes are frosted, and a few are even decorated with colorful, glassy shards of sugar.

If the twins were here, they'd dive right in. Marie and Violet have the biggest sweet tooths I've ever seen. My chest tightens at the thought of my sisters, and for a moment, a wave of homesickness so strong I can barely breathe bowls into me.

Blessed suns, I hope the girls are okay. I hope they're at home, getting ready to go to school and learn and do all the things that normal, unmarked teenagers get to do. Thanks to my status as a gods-blessed, the twins were sent to school even though it isn't the norm for females in my village.

"Would you like a piece of cake?" a young woman asks from the other side of the table. Her hair is a vibrant shade of green that somehow works with her very pale skin.

I must've wandered closer while I was caught in my thoughts.

She looks friendly, and for a moment, I consider her offer. I'm sure her cakes are delicious, and my mouth waters at the thought of eating something sweet after being on the run for so long. Before I can pay her, though, common sense kicks in. My funds are limited, and gorging myself on sugar won't help me in the long run.

Pressing my lips together, I grimace. "They look delicious, but I can't. Thank you, though."

Forcing myself to step away from the sweet-laden table takes every ounce of self-control I possess.

I pass a stall filled with colorful bolts of fabric and another brimming with skeins of yarn. Beside them is a seamstress who is hand-sewing an elaborate gown. She seems engrossed in her work, and she doesn't look up as I pass her by. She doesn't even seem bothered by the Watcher stationed to the right of her stall.

"Hand pies!" someone calls from my left. "Fresh meat pies, baked this morning!"

At the same moment, the wind blows, bringing me traces of fried dough and spiced meats. My stomach grumbles, and this time, I can't ignore its call. I follow my nose to the source of the delicious scent.

The moment I see the pies, I know I've made the right decision in coming here. The golden pastries are brown around the edges, and the air smells like a warm hug.

There are a few people lingering near the stall, and I wait for them to clear before approaching the chef. She looks to be around Mother's age, with tawny skin and turquoise hair in tight braids that fall midway down her chest. I place my order, handing over one of my three precious coins in exchange for a pie off her cooling rack.

She slides it over to me with some change, leaning across her stand.

"Your Mark is beautiful." Her admiring gaze is locked on my forehead. "How did you get it to glow so realistically?"

My eyes widen, and my next breath is a strangled gasp. Clutching the still-warm pie to my chest, as if that will help get me out of this situation, I swallow.

Fuck. Why didn't I pull up my hood before I came over?

"I . . . uh . . . I bought it from another vendor."

"Did you? It looks so realistic." She reaches out to touch my Mark, and internally, I cry out in alarm. This is the last thing I need.

I can't let my panic show, though. Cognizant of the nearby Watchers, I force myself to remain calm and smile politely at the inquisitive woman as I take what I hope is a casual step back.

"Doesn't it? There are some very skilled artisans here."

My words ring with truth, even though I'm lying about the origin of my Mark.

Please, please, please, stop asking me questions, I silently beg her.

Since luck isn't on my side, she doesn't look away.

"Yes, there are." Something about her expression has alarm bells ringing in my head.

Burning suns, save me. My skin feels too tight for its frame, and my breaths come in short bursts. I take another step back. I need to get out of here.

"Thank you for this." I nibble the corner of the hand pie, and spices flood my mouth. I don't fake the moan that slips from my lips. "Have a nice day, ma'am."

Turning around before things can get even worse, I hurry through the crowd. The knowledge that she could call the Watchers at any moment is sharp in my mind.

Resisting the urge to pull my hood over my head in case the woman is still watching me, I keep my head down and walk towards the thickest part of the crowd. I finish my food quickly, the spiced meat tasting like ash as I dissect every one of the woman's comments.

Does she know?

If she alerts the Watchers to my presence, everything will fall apart. My stomach churns, and I hug my arms around my middle, forcing myself to keep my food down. My body needs this nourishment.

Stupid, stupid, stupid.

So much for being like Amelia. Getting out of this square as quickly as possible is now my main priority.

I'm so preoccupied with putting space between me and the curious vendor that I lose track of my surroundings. The people, the drums, the laughter, and even the burning heat fade away.

I don't notice the shift in the air at first. The laughter dies down. The music quiets, then stops. The citizens who were milling about now stand in one place.

Now that everyone has stopped, I'm forced to freeze as well. Even in the midst of my panicked haze, I recognize that being the only person moving against a crowd will draw attention.

What's going on?

There are so many people that it's difficult to see what everyone is looking at. I rise onto my tiptoes, peering over the shoulders of the people in front of me. The crowd is so vast that it takes a moment for me to see what they're all looking at, but once I do . . .

A scream crawls up my throat. My heart booms, and that rushing sound is back in my ears.

Or maybe it never left. It stayed there, hiding in the shadows, waiting until it could return.

The musicians have vacated the wooden platform, but the space isn't empty. Instead, pairs of Watchers occupy each of the four corners, looking over the crowd. They're joined by five priests and priestesses, whose crimson robes are a shock against the brilliant blue sky. I don't recognize four of them, but the fifth . . .

My stomach churns, and my head spins. I'm not sure whether to scream or cry or run away, so instead, I stare at the stage.

The same head priestess who presided over Amelia's murder is here. The breeze lifts her lavender hair, and the hands that slashed the blade across Amelia's throat are waving to the crowd as if she's a popular noblewoman and not a fucking murderer.

My eyes narrow on the red Mark on the back of her hand, and blood drains from my face. I saw it the day Amelia was Given, and I didn't think twice about it. But now . . .

Now I know what happens. The Given die, so how is she Marked?

The answer appears in my mind a heartbeat later as I realize that the Mark is further up on her hand than it was during Amelia's Giving.

It's not real.

I've been trying to figure out why she wasn't Given, but it turns out, she's a fake. An imposter. Her Mark is nothing but a sticker.

It's nearly a perfect replica, but it's just that—a replica.

A chill sweeps over me. Every time I think I understand how evil the Giving Ceremonies truly are, another layer peels back and reveals more darkness.

The depth of this deception is astounding. These lies are like roots, digging into every single part of our society. Where do they end? Who started them?

The head priestess's mouth is moving, but none of her words register. Suns save me, how long have they been here? I was so worried about avoiding the Hunter, but I didn't even consider the fact that there might be priests and priestesses here.

And then, as if things aren't bad enough, the head priestess waves her hand in the air. It must be a signal because the Watchers descend from the platform.

It's then that I realize that everything I've witnessed today—the drums, the dancers, the laughter and music, the food and drinks, the frivolities of a city celebrating death—have been nothing but a gruesome lead-up to the main event.

Sitting on an elevated bench so everyone can see them, wearing garments that are so close to white they're barely green, are three beaming gods-blessed.

As soon as I see them, everything else fades away. The weight of Amelia's bracelet on my wrist is the only thing grounding me. I grab the remaining sun, squeezing it tightly as I stare at the stage. It's rude, but I can't help myself.

The Given stick together.

There is no doubt in my mind—this trio is gods-blessed, just like me. How could I ever have mistaken the young man who peeled off his Mark for a Given? Even the priestess's sticker doesn't compare to the real, glowing Marks adorning the three gods-blessed on the platform.

I wish I could pull up my hood to hide, but there are too many people around me. Instead, I commit the trio's faces to memory as I draw my curls over my own Mark, hiding it from sight as best I can.

On the far left, furthest from me, is a gangly man. His Giving Mark is a glowing orange flame sitting on his collarbone, peeking out from beneath his tunic. The color of his Mark is a stark contrast to his raven hair and olive skin. Freckles dot the bridge of his nose, and his eyes crinkle as he looks over the crowd and smiles. His hands are folded in his lap, and he looks relaxed.

I've never related less to someone in my entire life.

Next to him is a stunning young woman with ebony skin. Her wide eyes are filled with a spark of excitement, and her hair is a brilliant blue, like crystal-clear water on a perfectly sunny day. It tumbles down her shoulders in soft waves, ending above her breasts.

Her gown is a tailored version of the homespun dresses Amelia and I used to wear. Instead of sleeves that taper at her wrists, hers are tight to her elbows and then expand into bells. She's twisting her fingers in her lap, and a golden glow comes from the brilliant yellow swirl on the inside of her left wrist.

Lucky.

It would be so much easier to avoid attention if my Mark was in a spot like that. I could throw on a pair of gloves, and no one would be any wiser about my status as a gods-blessed.

Of course, since luck has never been on my side, my extremely inconveniently placed Mark starts burning. Why does this keep happening?

Discreetly adjusting my curls so they cover my forehead a bit better, I eye the third gods-blessed. His hair is a silky brown sheet that brushes his shoulders, his skin is pale, and unlike the other two, his eyes are hard as they look over the crowd. Tension radiates off the man. The dark green swirl on his neck pulses as he clenches his jaw.

Does he know the Giving is a lie? That instead of serving the gods, he's sentenced to die?

Wait.

My blood chills as I rip my gaze from the Given and reevaluate the head priestess. Is this . . . Does everyone in Mora know what happens to the gods-blessed? Are they all in on it? Is this festival some kind of sick joke?

Cold sweat breaks out on the back of my neck, and my fingers find the hilt of Father's knife. I don't care that it would be stupid. If they start chanting, I'm going up there.

I'm not sure how I'll get past the Watchers, but I refuse to stand by and bear witness to another murder, let alone three. I can't.

I'm so focused on building up the courage to run into a situation that will expose me that I don't notice the crowd shifting around me. A strong floral perfume reaches my nose, and then someone brushes the back of my hand.

I stiffen, and my heart races as curses barrel through my mind. Has someone found me out?

"You look like you could use an opportunity to relax, my dear," a woman whispers in my ear, folding my fingers around a cold vial. "Take one drop to stop feeling, two to be free, and three . . ."

A tinkling laugh brushes my neck as she pats my hand in an almost maternal fashion. I hitch a breath and turn around, my eyes locking on an older woman with silver hair. Her pupils are blown, and there's a blissful look on her face that tells me she's definitely partaken in *something* today, probably what's in the vial.

"Three?" I say, my gaze sweeping over hers.

"Three is too much." She chuckles breathily, her emerald dress swishing as she sways in front of me. "If you take three, this is the only thing that will save you."

She places something else in my palm. Before I can react, she backs up and is swallowed by the crowd.

She's gone.

My heart is still racing when I drop my gaze to my hand. A small vial the size of my thumb sits in my palm, and it's filled with a crimson liquid. Next to it is a tiny sliver of a red mushroom.

I should drop both items on the cobblestones and forget all about this encounter. What kind of idiot would take something from a stranger? Amelia certainly wouldn't. She would've thrown it away the moment the woman disappeared.

But something niggles in the back of my mind, and before I can think too hard about it, I tuck both items into my bag.

Just in case.

By the time I look back up at the platform, the priests and priestesses have moved. Crimson robes sway in the breeze as they occupy the four corners of the dais, like the Watchers before them. The head priestess stands behind the Given, her hands resting on the men's shoulders.

"People of Mora, we welcome you to the Giving Festival."

A cheer rises from the crowd.

She smiles, the expression serpentine. "Today, we celebrate the Given. Tonight, they will commune with the gods in the Moran Gardens. And tomorrow?" She pauses dramatically. "Tomorrow, they will fulfill their gods-given duties as Marked Ones."

The priests and priestesses hold their hands to the sky. Together, they proclaim, "Blessed are the Given!"

The crowd repeats the prayer, a feverish edge to their words.

Icy beads of sweat trickle down my back, and this time, I don't have it in me to care what anyone thinks. I turn, running from the stage as fast as I can.

I have to get out of here.

18

SHE'S MY PREY

Gabriel

Blessed burning suns, I found her.

Long locks of curls frame her face, her tanned skin is paler than the last time I saw her, and her Mark is glowing an incriminating blue. She's hurrying through the crowd, moving away from me. Her cloak is pulled tight, hiding those curves I'd glimpsed before everything went to hell.

Hundreds of people stand between me and my prey, but now that I've seen her, I won't lose her again. I pull my hood over my head and press my back against the wall to avoid her notice so I don't spook her. The action doesn't seem necessary. She seems distracted, bumping into several people and moving against the crowd.

What could she be so focused on?

Intrigued, I keep my head down and follow her out of the White Market. She's heading east, away from the famous gardens.

Interesting.

Keeping my gaze locked on my mark, I make my way through the crowd. Unlike my prey, I'm careful to move slowly and not attract attention. The last thing I need is for King Andreas to hear that one of his Hunters disrupted Mora's Giving Festival.

Since most of Myreth's villages and hamlets are too small to reliably have a gods-blessed to be Given each year, their Giving Celebrations tend to be much smaller affairs. Dinner with family, sometimes a party in the town square.

This isn't the case in the five provincial capitals or in Rosebridge, where the population size ensures there are multiple gods-blessed prepared to serve the gods each year.

The northern cities of Rosebridge, Moorn, and Van have their Festivals during the first half of the Giving Season. A few weeks later, the southern cities, Mora, Woodmarket, and Tretfall, host their celebrations.

Each city is provided with a stipend from the Crown to help fund their celebration. Once, I heard King Andreas say this was because he believed the festivals helped foster the people's goodwill.

I'm confident that's not the whole truth, since nothing the king says and does can be taken at face value. He always has an ulterior motive, even behind something as innocuous as a yearly celebration. I've been around enough Giving Festivals to know the truth—the king uses them to keep Myreth's population placated.

Give people a day where alcohol flows freely, and they'll forget that most of the time their bellies aren't full. Allow them to party from dawn until dusk, and they're more likely to forgive you when you drag away their brother or sister, mother or father, to be executed for the smallest cause. Play music for them, and they'll be more likely to ignore the fact that surviving is more difficult than ever.

Most people think the king is merely a bloodthirsty monarch, but he's much more than that. He's cunning and spiteful, and he would never do anything without an ulterior motive.

Thinking about the king makes my head pound and my back ache. My fists clench at my sides, and red tinges my vision. Drawing in a deep breath, I force myself to move on. The king isn't here. I'm a Hunter, and I have a job that requires all my focus.

Now that Wren is nearing the edge of the crowd, her movements are slowing. I'm trailing far enough behind her that I don't think she sees me, but I keep my distance nonetheless.

She looks over her shoulder, and I duck beneath an awning, hiding in the shadows. She tenses. Did she see me? I dip my head just in case, but her gaze flies right past me over to the platform in the middle of the White Market.

I follow her line of sight, exhaling when I see what caught her attention. The three gods-blessed have been joined by their families. They're not hugging, since Marked Ones belong to the gods and distance must be kept, but they seem happy.

When I return my gaze to the little bird, I catch a glimpse of a wistful look in her eyes. She wipes a finger under her eye before shuddering and turning away from the crowd, continuing down the street without looking back.

"Where are you going?" I murmur, leaving the shadows once again.

I would've thought she'd run straight for the gates, but that doesn't seem to be the case. I should just push through the crowd, tie her up, and throw her over my shoulder, but I don't. Not yet.

Something about the Given has ensnared my attention. It's not just the fact that she saved my life when she had no reason to do so. Her tenacity and strength have me wanting to know more about her.

To my knowledge, Wren Nightingale is the first Marked One to evade capture for this long in over three decades. Not to mention the bravery—and stupidity—it must have taken to enter Mora during the Giving Season. Most people on the run avoid cities like they're the plague, and here she is, walking around with her Mark on full display.

I can't help but wonder what she plans to do next. Following her around for a few more hours can't hurt. Not now that I've found her.

We leave the White Market behind, and the crowd thins. The air smells less like sweat and unwashed bodies, and soon, tension slips out of the Given's shoulders. She slows to a stroll as she moves past merchants, and I remain a fair distance behind her.

She doesn't seem to notice me stalking her, but then again, she doesn't seem to notice much at all. Several vendors shout, trying to get her attention, but she ignores them until she reaches a stall at the other end of the street.

The merchant is a balding, older man. At first glance, I can't tell what he's selling. She must want whatever he's offering because she reaches into her cloak and produces a coin. He rolls it through his fingers and says something to her before handing her some change along with something else I can't see. She murmurs a reply and then drops down next to his table.

What in Esyn's name is she doing?

I don't want to spook Wren and end up chasing her through the streets, so I browse the stall two tables down from her.

Hundreds of rings are nestled in display cases, sparkling in the afternoon light. Slender silver and gold bands sit next to large rings that bear the weight of glistening gems. Emeralds, sapphires, opals, rubies. They're all here.

"Shopping for a lucky young man or lady?" The shopkeeper, an older woman with navy blue hair tied in a tight bun at her nape, smiles at me. Her eyes twinkle as she gestures to a row of rings. "A handsome fellow such as yourself must have someone special at home."

I shake my head, stuffing my hands into my pockets. By nature of our line of work, the life of a Hunter is one of solitude. Moving around the kingdom chasing runaways isn't conducive to romantic relationships. The first and only time I tried to have something real was several years ago, and it ended very poorly.

Since then, I've realized that I don't need a romantic partner. I'm doing fine on my own. I have Mist for companionship, and on long nights when rising needs are too much to ignore, I have my hand to help me along. It's not perfect, but it's enough to keep me going.

Besides, if there's one thing my lonely childhood taught me, it's that families, especially fathers, aren't all that great.

"No one?" The vendor gasps, placing a hand over her heart dramatically. "You poor thing."

I grimace at the sympathy in her voice but don't bother correcting her. It's not worth my time, and besides, movement flickers in the corner of my eye. Wren stands, thanking the vendor before hurrying down the street.

"Your rings are beautiful," I tell the woman in front of me before following my prey.

I approach the table where Wren had stopped, my brows raising. A painted globe takes up a prominent location on the wooden surface, which must've been blocked by the merchant's body earlier. Several folded pieces of paper sit nearby. A quick glance reveals that they're maps.

My brows raise, and I can't help but be impressed with the little bird's train of thought. It seems she's planning on evading me for quite some time; little does she know, her map won't be of much use to her.

I'm about to pass by the stall when I notice a large golden dog sitting beside the table. Its tail wags furiously, and a pink tongue hangs out of its mouth as it stares at me. Birdie was in such a hurry to flee the White Market, but she stuck around to pet a dog.

Soft-hearted, compassionate woman.

I scratch the dog behind the ears, keeping an eye on Wren. She's almost at the end of the street. Stepping away from the cartographer and his dog, I tap my fingers against my thighs. Wren turns right, slipping down another busy street.

Returning my hands to my pockets, I follow her. It's time for the little bird's last flight. By the end of tonight, I'll have her in possession, and we'll be heading back to Grenbloom.

"What the fuck are you doing here, Birdie?" I mutter, staring up at the wooden sign hanging above the door she entered moments ago. A cup and a pair of dice are etched onto it, right next to the dancing figure of a scantily clad woman.

This isn't the kind of place I would expect a delicate little bird like her to stop for dinner, but if there's one thing I've learned about her after stalking her all day, it's that she's nothing like the others I've hunted.

She stopped a few hours ago to study her map, but instead of leaving the city, she took several side streets, petting any dogs and cats we passed on their heads. She strolled past the Moran Gardens, led me through a few residential streets, and ended up here.

A faint yellow glow filters through the grimy tavern window, and the muted sounds of conversation and music fill the air as I tug on my hood.

I push open the door, the aroma of ale, baked bread, and sweat hitting me all at once. The tavern is packed to the brim, which isn't a surprise on a night like tonight. The air is hazy with smoke from the numerous candles spread throughout the room.

Laughing men sit at wooden tables, sipping from jugs of frothing ale. Women dressed in minimal clothing move around the tables, delivering food and drinks. Most of the building's occupants are wearing fake Marks. A fiddler is in the corner near the blazing hearth, supplying the evening's entertainment.

"Welcome to The Marble Horse, sir," a dark-haired woman with lush terra-cotta skin says, sliding up next to me. Her ample breasts are moments away from tumbling out of her dress, and she bats her dark eyelashes in my direction. "What are you looking for on this fine evening? Food? Drink? Some company, perhaps?"

She twirls a coil of inky hair through her fingers, her meaning clear. What is it with people today? First, the jeweler. Now, her. Gods have mercy on me, I don't have time to deal with this.

"Just a drink," I tell her.

She pouts, her painted lips a stark red in the flickering candlelight. "Well, if you change your mind, you know where to find me."

I assure her I do, even though I already know I won't be using her services. It's not that I have any problem with sex workers—at another time, I likely would've taken her up on the offer.

It's been far too long since I've been with anyone, something my cock is more than happy to remind me of. But this isn't a moment for pleasure. I'm working.

I head to the bar and slip onto a stool, catching the bartender's eye.

"Ale?" he asks.

I nod, and moments later, a frothy tankard is sliding down the wooden counter towards me. I grab it, slapping a coin onto the counter in payment, and lift the mug to my lips. The ale is refreshing, and I drink as I turn in my seat, taking in the tavern.

My eyes find the Given immediately. She's sitting by herself in a booth by the fire. There's only one way into her seat.

Her hood is pulled over her hair, and her cloak is drawn tight around her. She's nibbling on a slice of bread. Those violet eyes are darting around the tavern, and there's a tension in her posture that I hadn't noticed before.

Maybe she isn't as relaxed as I'd initially assumed.

When her gaze drops back to the table, I decide I've played with her long enough. She's tasted freedom, and it's time to bring her home. Whatever reason she has for evading her Giving Ceremony, she's going to have to suck it up and deal with it. The gods demand her service, whether she wants to give it to them or not.

Standing, I drain my tankard before crossing the tavern. Every table is occupied, and there's barely any room to move. It takes some time to make my way through the crowd.

A woman is grinding on a man's lap, and based on the placement of his hand, I'd say he's far more interested in her than the cards he's holding. At the next table, an older gentleman is blowing thick rings of smoke out of his pipe while his two male companions explore each other's mouths with their tongues. Across from them, a woman is laughing as her partner slips his hand beneath the hem of her dress, his fingers dancing up her thigh.

I ignore them all, keeping my gaze locked on my prey. I slide into her booth, block her exit with my body, and set my empty tankard down with a resounding boom.

"Found you."

19

THE HUNTER IS HERE

Wren

Oh suns, oh suns, oh suns.

My lungs squeeze desperately in my chest, attempting to draw breath, but my throat is closing up. My fingers clench around nothing, and my entire body seizes.

Of all the times for me to decide that cursing the gods is a useless waste of time, why did I have to choose now? This seems like the perfect moment to curse Esyn and her fucking godly minions to the Underworld.

A tight fist is compressing my lungs. My heart has stalled in my chest, refusing to beat. The tavern walls are crashing in on me, and panic has my stomach in knots.

The music is too loud, the smoke is too thick, the laughter is too jarring, and the Hunter . . .

The suns and moons and everything else I've ever held dear have failed me, because the Hunter is here. He's here, and he's blocking my only exit with the same suns-damned body that has been haunting my nightmares.

Why, why, why did I come here tonight? Why did I think this would be a good idea? I became complacent earlier, walking around with my hood off. It seemed like a good idea at the time, but clearly, I was mistaken.

I needed somewhere to think about the gods-blessed I saw earlier, which is why I came here. They've been on my mind all day, and while I don't want to leave them, I'm not entirely sure what I can do to help them. I hoped to come up with a plan while I ate, but that no longer matters.

I made a mistake, and the Hunter caught me.

Gripping the edge of the worn wooden table, I look around the tavern desperately, searching for an escape route. Only there isn't one. The tavern is packed, and the Hunter is blocking my only exit.

My Mark is a blazing fire on my forehead, echoing my panic. I don't touch it. I gnaw on my lip, my gaze locking on the bartender. He's wiping down the counter. Maybe if I get his attention—

A hand clamps down on mine, and I barely hold in a scream as the touch yanks me out of my panicked thoughts. The Hunter's hand is warm, as if a furnace smolders beneath his skin. I drop my eyes to where he's gripping me.

Callouses line Gabriel's rough hand, and his fingers engulf mine. Gods, he's big.

My heart chooses this moment to remember it hasn't been beating, and it hammers in my chest. That same spark comes to life in my hand, a reminder of the last time the Hunter and I touched before he saw my Mark. His warmth calls to me in a gods-damned absurd way.

This is about as bad as things could get, and I don't know how to get out of this.

I try to jerk my hand out of his, but those damned fingers curl around my wrist. He could break me without a second thought. One snap, and my bones would be brittle twigs in his hand.

And then Gabriel's fingers shift, and he's touching Amelia's bracelet. My breath catches in a wheeze, and I choke. How dare he?

"Hello, Birdie." He slides down the bench, spitting my nickname between us as though it's a curse. I've never hated the sound of that moniker more than I do at this very moment. "Did you enjoy your taste of freedom?"

Stupid, handsome man. I hate him so much.

His fingers tighten around my wrist, and I drag my eyes up from the table, meeting his gaze for the first time. The air seems to disappear, and for the longest moment, all I can do is stare at him.

One look, and he's ensnared me like an animal in a trap.

Like me, Gabriel is wearing a cloak. Shadows shroud his face from sight.

They don't stop me from noticing the anger flashing through his green eyes, the sharp cut of his jaw, or the stubble on his chin, though.

The Hunter is rugged and rough and stupidly handsome, which only makes me hate him more.

My lips curl into a sneer. I try to yank my elbow back in an attempt to break his grip. Unfortunately, in addition to being ridiculously handsome and the reason for my nightmares, the Hunter is also far stronger than me.

I snarl, "Fuck you."

He tightens his grip on my wrist, and I'm sure it will bruise tomorrow. But honestly, who cares about another mark on my skin?

"No, thanks. I'm not interested," he replies calmly, those infuriating green eyes drilling into mine.

I rear back, shaking my head.

"As if I would *ever* let you touch me like that." Sure, we may have joked about him biting me when he first woke up, but that was before I knew he was gods-damn *hunting* me. "I have values, you know. I will never stoop that low."

He huffs a breathy chuckle, and his infuriatingly handsome gaze darkens. "Did I touch a nerve, little bird?"

"Don't call me that!" I whisper-yell, trying to yank my arm away from his. I hate that he's still touching me, hate that my body reacts so much to his warmth, hate that an insane part of me wants me to shift closer to him. I hate all of this. "Just let me go."

The fiddler glances over at us, his bow pausing over the strings, but Gabriel scowls at him. The musician looks away, the music resuming once again.

Burning suns. Will no one help me?

The Hunter's nostrils flare, and he shakes his head.

"Never." He adjusts his grip on my wrist, his thumb pressing down on my pulse point. His breath warms my ear, and my core twists at his closeness. My treacherous body doesn't understand that we despise him. "I gave you one day's head start, Birdie. You squandered my gift, and now, we're on equal footing. I caught you, fair and square."

Gift. *Gift?*

Does he honestly believe he did something helpful?

I wish he'd never given me the head start. It's almost worse, knowing I'm fated to die now that I've tasted freedom.

Sure, being on the run has been painful and exhausting and not at all delightful, but I'm still alive, and that counts for something.

My hatred for him grows with every word that comes out of his stupidly well-formed lips. I hate the way he's looking at me and the way my body reacts.

I hate it all.

"One day's head start is *not* a gift," I hiss, twisting my hand in his and digging my nails into his skin. "It's a fucking joke."

The Hunter doesn't even flinch as I do my best to scratch him and draw blood. Is this damn man made of fucking stone?

The corner of his mouth curls, but before he can speak, a shadow darkens the table. I look up, my eyes widening at the barmaid standing before us. She can't be older than fifteen, and even though weariness is etched onto her face, no doubt from working in this bustling tavern, she's beautiful. Her blue eyes dart between me and the Hunter, and she's gripping a tray with white knuckles.

"Your order is ready, miss," she says.

In the commotion of the Hunter's arrival, I'd completely forgotten that I'd ordered food.

I stare at the barmaid pleadingly, widening my eyes and trying to let her know I need help. Her face pales as her gaze lands on Gabriel's hand covering mine. She gingerly places the bowl of steaming stew on the table, gnawing on her lip.

"Forgive me for asking, but is everything all right?"

I open my mouth, a desperate plea rising in my throat. Before I can speak, the Hunter tightens his grip on my fingers. He subtly shifts, moving his cloak to the side and revealing the hilt of a sword hanging from his baldric.

Fuck.

I swallow my words, my hope for rescue vanishing. My heart drops, and I wilt in on myself. I can't risk bringing harm upon this young woman. There's a softness about the barmaid that reminds me of my sisters.

My voice is rough as I whisper, "It's fine."

This time, tears don't prick my eyes, and dread doesn't coil in my gut. Instead, cold spreads through me like ice on a lake as I'm thrown back to the day before my Giving.

A sharp silver blade. Amelia's muffled scream. The head priestess's hood falling back. A fountain of crimson. A flash of pink. My best friend's body tumbling to the floor.

I've been living on borrowed time ever since Amelia was killed.

The Hunter's head start was more of a punishment than anything else. It allowed me to fool myself into thinking that maybe I had a chance. Maybe I could get to the Sapphire Coast. Maybe I could live.

But now, I know the truth.

The Given stick together.

Amelia was right all those years ago. We do stick together—even in death.

Just like everything else I've been told since the moment of my birth, the whisper of freedom I experienced was a lie. I'm never going to be free, never going to truly experience anything this world has to offer.

I was born with a Mark branding me for death, and I was a fool to think I could ever escape my fate. I still don't know why they sacrifice the Given, but it doesn't matter. Nothing matters anymore.

I'm so lost in the depths of my despair that I barely hear the Hunter speaking to the barmaid. He thanks her, for what I don't know or care, and then he asks for a refill. Reaching into his pocket with his free hand, he pulls out a coin and hands it to her. She slides it into her apron and nods, hurrying to the bar.

When she's gone, he turns to me, lifting his hand from mine. Locks of dark blue, almost black hair fall in front of his eyes, and I clench my fists to avoid touching them.

What's wrong with me? This man is *hunting* me. I shouldn't want to touch him at all.

"That was wise," he says, his voice gruff.

Was it, though? Because right now, it seems like I allowed my only chance at freedom to slip through my fingers. But maybe this is how it was always meant to be. Maybe this is how everything was meant to end.

After all, the Given were always meant to be returned to the gods.

Bile rises in my throat as I imagine the cool press of steel against my neck, and my fingers spasm on the table.

The part of me that was raised to worship the gods wants to beg for my soul, but I don't think it will do anything.

No, death is coming for me. Will it be cold as it draws me into its embrace? Will I scream as the knife slides across my throat, or will I stand frozen in shock as my blood leaves my body, coating the temple floor?

I'm not ready to die, and yet, I don't know what else to do.

A scratching sound comes from the table as Gabriel draws the bowl closer to me. The stew is thick, and chunks of brown meat float alongside slices of carrots and potatoes. It's peppery, the scent tickling my nose when it reaches me.

I ordered the meal thinking I'd need sustenance to survive the next leg of my trek, but now . . .

Cold steel. Pain. Blood everywhere. Death.

"Eat," the Hunter says brusquely, unaware of the dark direction of my thoughts.

I pull my gaze from the bowl up to his.

"Why?" I ask flatly. "What's the point?"

The man arches a brow, the expression bordering on incredulous. As if my question is ridiculous. "You need your strength."

Well, that's laughable. Does he honestly believe that?

I flatten my hands on the table. Tiny grooves are cut into the otherwise smooth wood, likely from years of use. "Strength so I can be *Given.*"

The word *Given* sounds like *murdered* as it clangs around my mind like a resounding gong, as loud as the temple bells.

A vein feathers in Gabriel's jaw. "Yes."

Bastard. I hate him so much, I want to scream.

The barmaid chooses that moment to return with the Hunter's drink. I grit my teeth as she swaps out his empty glass for a full one.

I haven't moved towards the bowl, and I won't.

"Eat," he repeats once the barmaid has left, moving the stew closer to me.

I ignore the savory aroma that makes my empty stomach grumble and shake my head, pressing my shoulder against the tavern wall.

Between the log wall on my right and the Hunter on the left, I'm well and truly trapped. My heart races in my chest, and a cold sweat breaks out on the back of my neck.

Gabriel is as intimidating as he is gods-damned handsome, but I won't let him boss me around.

Gripping my bracelet, I draw strength from Amelia's gift.

"I will not," I snarl. I may be destined for death, but I'm not some animal to be fattened up for the slaughter.

The Hunter's nostrils flare, and his eyes narrow. If looks could force someone to act, I'd be drowning in that bowl of stew. Luckily, they can't, so after the longest, most uncomfortable staring contest of my entire life, Gabriel huffs and pulls the bowl towards him.

"Fine," the infuriating man says, picking up the wooden spoon. "But I guarantee you'll regret this when you're walking back to Grenbloom on an empty stomach."

"I don't care," I lie stubbornly, crossing my arms and glaring up at him. "And if you think for one second that I'm going to follow you back to my village like a docile little lamb so you can hand me over to the temple, you're out of your gods-damned mind."

The spoon freezes halfway to his lips, and Gabriel slowly turns his head towards me. Even with the shadows from his hood, I can see his eyes perfectly. They spark with interest, and his lips quirk up into a smile.

Why the fuck is he smiling? *Nothing* about this is funny.

"Kick up all the fuss you want, Birdie." He leans in, his eyes twinkling. His obvious amusement makes me want to punch him in his stupidly attractive face. "I assure you, I can take it."

I fucking hate that I gave this man my nickname. Hearing it come out of his mouth is awful, and I want to scream.

My fingers itch to grab Father's knife and slam it into his hand, pinning it to the table, but something tells me that wouldn't go over well.

Gabriel makes a show of lifting the spoon to his lips and eating slowly. He takes his suns-damned time finishing *my* dinner. My hatred grows with each passing moment. I don't speak again until the stew is gone and he's exchanged the bowl for his mug.

"You know, you don't have to do this," I say.

I begged before, and it didn't go over well, but I'm not too proud to admit that I'd do just about anything to avoid being Given.

He pauses mid-sip, shifting in his seat to look at me. Gods, I have no idea how I ever thought he wasn't a threat because predatory grace radiates from his every movement. "What did you say?"

There's no way he didn't hear me. Even though the tavern has gotten louder now that night has truly fallen, he's practically sitting in my lap. Besides, I've been able to hear every little thing he says and does. It's like my body is frustratingly attuned to his. But as several long moments pass in silence, I realize he's going to make me say it again.

Damn it. Damn him. Damn this entire situation.

"You don't have to take me in." I meet the Hunter's green gaze and wonder if there's an ounce of kindness in his well-built body. "You could let me go and pretend like this never happened."

He hasn't replied, so I take his silence as leave to continue.

"I'm not staying in Myreth, you know. I will get on a ship and leave, never looking back. No one would ever know you did this."

And then I'll still be alive.

His brows furrow, and he shakes his head. "Impossible."

My heart drops to the pit of my stomach, but I can't give up. I won't.

"It's not," I insist, gesturing to the packed tavern. "Look around us. Most people here are drunk." Those who aren't will be soon. "Let me go, and you'll never have to see me again. I promise."

I hate that I have to plead my case to this man while staring into his green eyes, searching for something to give me even a spark of hope. Doesn't he realize how much asking him this is costing me? But I'd rather lose my pride than my life.

He crushes my dreams before they can take root. "I can't."

"I saved your life," I tell him, unwilling to give up. Growing up the middle of five children taught me how to be stubborn. "Back in the forest. You'd be dead right now if it weren't for me."

My foolish, compassionate heart twinges at the thought of his death, but I ignore it. Clearly, my body doesn't understand why we hate the Hunter.

"I know," he says. "And I repaid my life debt."

This again. Seriously?

"It wasn't a gift," I hiss.

"Maybe not," he concedes. "But you squandered it, nonetheless."

This man. How can he be so gods-damned vexing and good-looking at the same time?

Frustration bubbles up inside me, and I ball my fist, slamming it on the table. The empty bowl and spoon shake.

No one even glances in our direction, the noises of the tavern drowning out the sound of my anger.

"I did not squander anything." My nostrils flare, and I glare at his stupidly rugged face. "I ran as fast as I could."

I tried so fucking hard to get away from this man, only for him to find me again.

"And you did a good job," he says. "You got far."

"Not far enough." I curl my fists. "Not nearly far enough."

The Sapphire Coast feels further away now than ever before. It's nothing more than a dream at this point, one I'll never see to fruition.

He stares at me for a long moment, his eyes sweeping over me before he dips his chin. "No. Not far enough."

I hate this. I hate that we're still having this conversation. I hate that the handsome Hunter is here. I hate that his green eyes are drilling into me beneath the shadows of his hood.

I hate it all.

"Let me go," I say again, louder than before.

"No." His voice is firm. "King Andreas would know."

It's my turn to furrow my brows. The king is in Rosebridge, which is nowhere near here. According to my newly acquired map, it would take days to travel there.

"How would he know?" The question slips from my lips before I remember who I'm speaking with.

Why am I bothering to ask this man questions? He's already proven that his heart is made of stone.

Gabriel's eyes darken. If they were emeralds before, now they're mossy and filled with shadows and darkness.

No. Bad Wren. Stop thinking about the rugged Hunter's pretty eyes.

"Magic." The word is ominous as it leaves his lips, and he shivers. "King Andreas's power is vast, and he has ways of finding things out that no one else knows."

Cold snakes down my spine, and I fight the urge to draw my arms around myself. How would the king know if I left? What kind of magic does he possess?

Questions for a later time. Desperately, I try the last option in my arsenal.

"I'll do anything you want. *Anything*." I bat my lashes at him, hating myself for even offering this. Not that I'll let him touch me—the moment he stands, I'll run—but still. "Whatever you want."

He scoffs, as if the thought of using me in that way disgusts him, and he shakes his head. "You're not the first person I've hunted to make me such an offer, but I'm afraid I'll have to refuse." His voice hardens. "I do not touch my prey."

His rejection shouldn't sting, but it does.

"Do you want money? I'll find some." At this point, I'd rob the king himself if it meant I could be free.

I don't even have it in me to worry about the king's magic, as much as Gabriel is clearly concerned about it. I need to get out of here so I can survive.

"No. I don't need money." He shoots me down with such ease, as if my offer isn't even worth thinking about.

His eyes drop back to his cup. Clearly, this conversation is over. At least for him.

Maybe he's right. Maybe I should give up and let him take me back to the temple. Maybe accepting my fate would be easier.

My fingers slide off the table, finding my satchel. The bag is much lighter than it was when I first left Grenbloom, since my book was destroyed after the waterfall, and I left the full jar of ointment with Alba.

Slipping my hand inside, I feel the array of the objects I still have in my possession. The sharp edge of my quill pokes my finger, but I ignore the sting of pain. I run my fingers over my remaining jar of blessed salve, then trace the rough parchment of the map I purchased earlier.

None of these will save me from the Hunter. I'm about to give up entirely and accept my fate when the pads of my fingers brush up against something smooth and cold.

The vial from the Giving Festival.

My breath catches, and I curl my fingers around the glass container as I try to remember the woman's whispered words. It was hours ago, but it feels like days have passed since then.

Take one drop to stop feeling, two to be free, and three . . . three is too much.

I tighten my grip around the vial, lifting it out of my bag and into my lap.

The Hunter's tankard is on the table, and his back is partially to me as he gazes into the dimly lit tavern. He seems deep in thought, and if he were anyone else, I'd wonder what he's thinking about so deeply. I don't, though, since he's literally planning on dragging me to my death.

I turn the vial around in my hand, pursing my lips. This might be the only thing that provides me with the freedom I so desperately seek. But is this me? Am I seriously considering giving Gabriel a mysterious substance that a woman slipped me on the street? Judging by the look that had been in her eyes, it's a drug of some kind.

It's one thing to hate the Hunter for doing his job, even if it's despicable, but it's another thing entirely to give him something against his will.

Honestly, I can't believe I'm even considering this. I don't love the idea of harming another person, even the man who has actively made my life a living hell since I saved him.

The problem is, I don't see another way out of this situation.

I stare at the bracelet around my wrist. The sun is resting against the table, and I can't help but think of Amelia. She would've smashed the vial the moment she got it.

She was always good. Always kind. Always morally in the right.

I used to think I was the same. The old Wren would never even consider doing this. She would've been shocked that I was even thinking about it.

But the problem is, the old me is dead. She bled out with Amelia and disappeared along with the matching sun on my bracelet.

I wasn't lying to Gabriel. I won't go back to Grenbloom willingly. I'm going to fight him every gods-damned step of the way.

But this . . .

Drawing my bottom lip through my teeth, I stare at his back. Am I willing to actively throw my morals out the window to save myself?

Wren Nightingale: gods-blessed, outlaw, and now . . . potential poisoner?

I'm not stupid. Some substances taken in small doses can make people feel good. The ale flowing around me is a great example of that. But when they're taken in larger quantities, they can be dangerous. Deadly even.

A shiver runs down my spine, and I inhale deeply. I don't like the idea one bit, but the problem is that as much as I don't like it, I hate the idea of dying even more.

I just want to live.

The Hunter looks over his shoulder at me.

"We're leaving soon, Birdie." His eyes narrow as he studies me. "Prepare yourself."

What the fuck does he mean by that? *Prepare myself.*

Does he want me to get on my knees and pray to the gods for deliverance? I won't do that. The gods, like everyone else, have abandoned me.

"Leave me here," I beg Gabriel again. One last time. Maybe he'll change his mind. "Please. I'll do anything you want. I can't go back. I don't want to be Given."

He doesn't even turn around. "No."

"I won't go willingly," I remind him.

He peers over his shoulder, his lips creaking up into a smile. That expression has no right to be so handsome or to heat my core so intensely.

"Good, I hope you don't," he says.

I sputter. "Wh-what?"

He lifts his shoulder. "You've made my job interesting, and I've had fun chasing you."

I clench my fists and fume. *Fun*. How dare he speak to me in such a manner? Here I am, trying to survive, and he's amusing himself.

I hate this Hunter, with his beautiful green eyes, sharp cheekbones, and blue-black hair that falls in wisps around his face.

I hate that he's so much bigger than me and that his muscles are so well-fucking-defined that it's clear he trains for hours every day.

Most of all, I hate that there's a twinkle in his gaze when he talks about hunting.

I hate him so much that the next time he turns his burly shoulder to me, I pop the vial's tiny cork.

I'm not Amelia, and I'm not even sure I'm *good.* All I know is that

I'm Wren, and I'm not ready to stop living. I'm not ready to be Given, so I have to do everything I can to stay away from the Hunter.

By the time he places the tankard back on the table, I've made up my mind. I'm just going to give him enough to make it easier for me to run away. I edge my hand over to his glass and tip the vial.

One drop, two . . .

Damn it, he's turning back around. My fingers slip, and the vial empties into his glass.

Fuck.

That can't be good. My heart is racing as I panic, pulling my fingers back and dropping the empty vial in my lap.

A second later, green eyes meet mine again. "Time to leave, little bird."

Can he sense my panic? Can he hear my heart racing in my chest?

I stare at him as he picks up the tankard, lifting it to his lips. His throat bobs as he drains the rest of the cup in one go.

The empty cup hits the table with a thud, and he rises. The vial is the heaviest of weights in my lap as seconds tick by, and I watch Gabriel expectantly.

What's going to happen? Will his words slur? Will he fall over and die? Maybe his lungs will stop working. Will it hit all at once or slowly over time?

Suns, I have no idea what to expect, but my imagination is happy to provide me with a plethora of ways the unknown substance might affect him.

Except, in an upsetting turn of events, the Hunter doesn't die.

He doesn't keel over or cry out in pain as his stomach twists into painful knots. He doesn't seem affected at all.

His emerald eyes are crystal clear as he glares down at me. His size is so much more imposing now that he's back to looming over me, and my lip quivers. It didn't work. My last chance at freedom is empty in my lap, and now, I have no other options.

Gabriel pins me with his emerald gaze, and he holds out a hand towards me. "Let's go."

20

LET ME GO

Gabriel

The Given is still in the booth, staring up at me. Her violet gaze is sharp, even in the dim tavern, and it feels like she's waiting for something to happen. I have no idea what it is, nor do I really care. She can't delay the inevitable.

I've wasted enough time on this hunt. We need to leave.

"Come on." Frustration edges my tone, even as I work to keep my voice low. I want to get out of Mora as quickly as possible because Mist is waiting for me on the other side of the city walls.

Eventually, with a jerk of her chin and an irritated huff, Wren stands. She balls her fists at her sides, and I can't help but smile when I notice them. Her anger at being caught is almost adorable.

I'm not sure why she's so against serving the gods, but it's not my place to pry. Maybe she's an atheist, or maybe she doesn't want to live a life of servitude. Unfortunately for her, the Mark on her forehead means she doesn't have a choice in the matter.

There's a part of me that feels bad for her. After all, I, more than most, understand the binds one's societal position can place on them. However, I can't let those feelings get in the way of my job. The thrumming connection I have with my panther is a reminder of exactly why we need to leave.

I'm coming, Mist. I send the message through the bond.

A burst of calm comes through the connection a moment later, and I relax. Mist is okay, and we will be reunited shortly. I'll get my promotion, and this hunt and the awful nightmares will soon be nothing but distant memories.

The little bird's violet eyes are hatred-filled daggers stabbing into me. If looks could kill, I'd be a dead man right now. But they can't, so I take the opportunity to study her in return.

It's not a hardship. She's gorgeous, with her captivating curls that I'd love to twist around my finger, and curves that seem to go on forever. The tavern's dim candlelight accentuates her ample, luscious curves and her beautiful full body.

Had we met under any other circumstance, I would've found great enjoyment in spending the night with her before going our separate ways. I'd be lying if I said I hadn't imagined what bedding her would be like when I first woke, before I realized who she was.

But then, like now, I had to put a stop to those thoughts.

Wren and I aren't two random people. I'm a Hunter, and not only is she gods-blessed, but she's an outlaw. The very person I'm obligated to chase.

No matter how drawn I am to her or how attractive I find her, we are naturally at odds. It's more than just a bad idea. Getting involved with her is forbidden.

I told her the truth earlier. It's not uncommon for those I'm hunting to throw themselves at me as a bargaining chip.

Getting propositioned by our prey is practically a rite of passage for a Hunter. Unlike some of my less savory brethren, I've never taken advantage of the ones I've hunted.

No. I can't have her like that, no matter how good she looks or how I once desired to taste her lips.

The thought further sours my mood, and I reach out, taking her arm. She stiffens beneath my touch, cursing under her breath as I tug her out of the booth. Something drops on the ground as she grabs her bag. She clutches it to her chest as if it contains her entire world.

"Don't do this," she whispers, her voice cracking as she comes to stand next to me.

The plea in her voice has me sucking in a breath, and for a moment, I think about doing as she asks and letting her go.

Turning my back and forgetting I found her. Leaving Mora without her.

My chest tightens, and memories of my nightmares flash through my mind. The pain of losing my bond. The emptiness. The absolute agony of having my soul ripped in two, night after night. Premonition, warning, or bad dream, it doesn't matter. Not really.

Mist is under my protection, and I can't let harm come to her. Even my promotion pales in comparison to that.

I can't do as she asks.

"I'm sorry, but I'm bringing you back." Gripping Wren's arm, I start leading her through the tavern.

A few tables down, a man with glassy eyes stands on wobbly legs and lifts his tankard in the air.

"To the Given!" he yells.

"May the gods bless Myreth this Giving Season!" a woman adds.

"Hear! Hear!"

"To the Given!"

"Praise Esyn!"

Cheers fill the air, masking the curse Wren hisses under her breath as we finally reach the door. Between the smoke and the loudness of the tavern, my head is starting to pound. I can't wait to get outside.

Shoving open the door, I step into the night, pulling my prey behind me. Cool air slams into me, a brisk wind carrying hints of impending frost. A reminder that soon, the Giving Season will be over and winter will be here. By that time, this hunt will be a memory, and I'll be back in Rosebridge.

The door slams shut behind me. A heartbeat later, a foot connects with the back of my leg. It's little more than an inconvenience, but a part of me can't believe she actually kicked me.

"Let me go, you bastard!" Wren tries to yank her hand out of mine.

The breath is knocked from my lungs at the curse, and I stumble before I can stop myself.

She takes advantage of my slip-up, kicking me twice more. *Now*, it's annoying. I regain my composure, grunting as I glare at her over my shoulder.

Her eyes are wide beneath her hood, a faint blue glow emanating from her swirl. There's a fierceness beneath her fear that calls to me, even now.

I know she meant what she said earlier—she won't go willingly. That's fine. I meant what I said, too. I will enjoy every single second of bringing her to heel.

"No," I snarl, tightening my grip on her wrist.

She kicks me again, but even though there's some weight behind the attack, a few bruises won't stop me from doing my job.

I hold her wrists tightly and reorient myself. To our right are residential streets that, if my memory serves me correctly, lead to the gardens. To the left are several other taverns and businesses, all with people pouring out of them. Either direction should take us to the gates, but my gut feeling is that the left would take longer.

Right it is, then.

Mind made up, I start down the road. Or at least, I try to. In reality, I take two steps and groan. Wren has stopped kicking, but rather than coming along nicely, she's hanging limply from my arm. I try to move again, but her dead weight pulls down on me. Her hood is covering her head, so I can't see her eyes.

"That's how you want to play this?" I ask, trying to tug her back to her feet. "You want me to drag you out of the city?"

Her head rears up, giving me a glimpse of her Mark before her hood settles over it again.

"No, I want you to release me," she snaps.

This woman. Her fire is as intriguing as it is frustrating.

"Not going to happen."

She groans, her body weight getting even heavier.

Huffing, I pull her upright. The pounding in my head intensifies, making this annoying situation worse. I drag her closer, until her face is inches away from mine. Her chest is heaving, and her wide eyes meet mine.

My breath catches, and for a long moment, her stubborn glare ensnares me. This woman is beautiful and fierce, and something stirs deep within me as we share the same air.

It's strange. Time is dragging on, but I can't look away. Her violet gaze is a whirlpool, drawing me closer. There's a stirring in my soul, a depth that I don't quite understand, and it grows stronger with every passing second.

She opens her mouth, and my eyes drop to her lips. Lush and plump, they call to me. Her tongue darts out, wetting them.

Gods save me, but heat rushes through me at the sight. Of all the women in Myreth, why am I attracted to the one I can't have?

The space between us feels like far too much and not nearly enough. I want to draw her close. I want to push her away. The desires are warring within me, fighting for my attention.

The little bird is my prey, but that doesn't stop me from wanting to kiss her or wondering what she tastes like.

She steps even closer, and my heart pounds.

"Let me go, Gabriel," she whispers, my name sounding far too good on her tongue. "I saved your life. Can't you do this for me?"

I can hear the hope in her voice. The desperation. She'd run if I let her, there's no doubt in my mind. Between her map and her tenacity, she might even make it out of the kingdom.

Before I can give her request more than a moment's consideration, the king's voice echoes in my mind, a memory from those haunting nightmares.

You failed me.

Sometimes, in those nightmares that feel like warnings from the king, he decides that splitting my soul in two isn't enough punishment. After severing my bond, he drags me out to the whipping yard.

On those days, I wake with tears streaming down my face, and my back aching with phantom pains. On those days, the ghost of the crimson barbs that decorate the tip of the king's favorite whip haunt me long after I wake.

Wren must see something on my face, because desperation and sadness flood her gaze. Her eyelids shutter. "You won't, will you?"

"No, I won't." I can't.

My heart aches at her devastation. I'm filled with an irrational need to soothe her pain, which is ridiculous, since I'm causing it.

Her shoulders fall, and she seems to wilt like a flower during an early snow. Her gaze drops to where I'm still holding her wrist. The longest moment passes before she drags her eyes back up to mine. She scans my features, again seeming to search for something, before sighing. The sound echoes deep in my soul.

"You're not going to let me go, are you?" It's a question, but she already knows the answer. We both do.

"No."

"Never?" She tugs on her arm, trying to get free. The effort has less force behind it than before.

My grip tightens. "No."

Turning her in will protect my bond with Mist and give me the promotion I long for. I can already see the ceremony where the king honors me in front of all my brethren. A twisted part of my soul delights in the fact that, for once, the king will have to show me honor. For once, he will have to be kind to me in front of the court.

I need this, I remind myself, hardening my heart. I can't let Wren get to me—I have a job to do.

With that thought in mind, I start moving again. Wren follows, her gaze still sweeping over mine as if she's looking for something.

"See something you like, little bird?"

She huffs, but her eyes remain on me. "No, I was just wondering how you're feeling."

What a gods-damned strange question.

"I feel fine," I tell her, although that's a lie. My head is still pounding, and it feels like it's getting worse.

"Pity," she grumbles. She continues to curse me under her breath for several blocks, but she's no longer kicking me.

I'm not entirely sure what brought on the change in her demeanor, but the shift is so sudden that it puts me on edge. I keep glancing down at Wren, but other than the way her eyes sweep over me every so often, she doesn't interact with me.

It's almost as if she's . . . waiting for something. But what?

Our surroundings slowly shift as we move through Mora. The loud tavern district gives way to the sleeping city. The moons shine above us, lighting our path. There are fewer Watchers out now as the world slips off to sleep. However, even in the stillness of the night, echoes of life remain.

We pass a couple standing outside their home, screaming profanities at each other. They don't even look our way. The next street down, a young man is leaning against the balcony railing of his second-story bedroom, bouncing a wailing baby on his hip.

Interspersed with all that are moans floating through open windows as lovers indulge in the secrecy provided by the late hour. Two women laugh as they stumble past us, their hands roaming beneath clothing as they slip through an open doorway. A little further down the block, we pass a home where flickering candlelight casts shadows on the wall of three intimately entangled people.

No one looks twice at Wren and me as we walk down the street, and for that, I'm grateful. This damned headache seems to be getting worse, not better. My brain has become a mallet, hammering against my skull.

By the time we pass the gardens, my mind has taken on a pulse of its own. It's a throbbing mass. I wince with each step as the pain worsens. Every so often, Wren yanks on her wrist, and keeping my grip firm is increasingly difficult.

What's happening to me?

Lanterns light up the city gates, a beacon in the night. Usually, I'd find them comforting. Now, the bright lights cause my headache to worsen.

"Fuck," I breathe, stumbling down the streets.

Wren hitches a breath, and for what feels like the hundredth time since we left the tavern, her eyes search mine. Is that a flicker of excitement in her gaze? I try to focus on it, but I can't. I can't focus on anything.

Something's wrong. My heart is a galloping horse, racing to escape my chest. Sweat is dripping down my back, and my vision has grown steadily blurrier since we left the tavern.

Everything feels strange. Even my bond with Mist doesn't feel entirely right. I poke at it, wondering what's going on.

This isn't just the effects of a second mug of ale. I've been drunk enough times in my life to know the difference between the hurt brought on by too much alcohol and this.

Is this why Wren stopped fighting me? Did she do something to me?

The last question flits through my mind, but it's gone as quickly as it appeared, replaced by my headache. Thank the gods, we've reached the gates. The soldiers on duty recognize me, and they allow us through without question.

Getting to the other side of the city walls does nothing for my headache. If anything, I'm feeling worse than before.

This morning, the distance between Mora and the forest felt so short, but now, it feels like we'll never reach the woods. The trees swim in my vision as I drag Wren towards them. No matter how many times I blink, my eyes don't focus.

What's going on? Thinking is the most laborious of tasks. Putting one foot in front of the other takes all my concentration, and sweat pours down my face within minutes.

We're halfway to the forest when a shooting pain erupts in my abdomen.

It starts in my stomach, a blaze devouring me from the inside out. Within seconds, it's spread until my entire body feels like it's on fire.

My steps falter, and my grip on the little bird loosens. She tugs her wrist again, and this time, I'm unable to stop her.

I fall to my knees. The damp grass is cold beneath my palms as I grapple for something to hold on to to lessen the pain, but nothing's working.

Bricks are being dropped inside my skull. My lungs refuse to draw breath. My heart slams against my ribs. And the fire?

It *burns*. Once, when I was a young boy, I ran my finger through the flame of a candle to see what it felt like. That hurt, but it was nothing like this. Even my abusive father's punishments never brought on such all-consuming pain.

Fabric rustles in front of me, and I look up. The Marked One is crouched in front of me, her violet eyes wide as she stares at me.

"I'm sorry," she whispers.

Sorry?

It takes a moment for her words to register. Fucking suns. This is her doing. I don't know how, but she did this to me. Now I know why she went with me so easily, why she was looking at me, why she asked how I was feeling.

She was just waiting for this to happen.

A flicker of respect flutters to life in my stomach, but it's doused by the fire in my gut.

She continues. "But I told you, I can't go back. I refuse to die."

A crease forms between my brows, and I open my mouth to ask what in the Mother's holy name she's talking about.

Die? She's gods-blessed—a life of serving wherever the gods see fit is all that awaits her.

Unfortunately, I can't form a single word, let alone a coherent sentence.

Panic floods my chest, and not all of it is mine. I can feel Mist trying to figure out what's happening. I reach for our connection, but that rope that binds us keeps slipping through my fingers as though it's coated in oil.

Everything is on fire.

I lift my hand, thinking I'll see flames licking my skin, but it appears normal.

But this isn't normal. None of this is.

And then my world flips. One moment, I'm on my knees. The next, I collapse on my side on the cold, damp ground.

The soldiers patrolling the city walls are nothing but dots against the midnight sky, and the only one around is the little bird. We're alone, and for the first time since I picked up the mantle of Hunter, I don't feel in control.

Fear pulses through me, and everything hurts. Is this what my prey feels the entire time I'm chasing them?

I would ask, but the pain is paralyzing.

Fire sweeps through me, and visions of the past flash through my mind with dizzying clarity. Tea with Grandmother. My first punishment at Father's hands. Running from him, even though I was never fast enough. Laughing with the few friends I had as a child, hiding from the guards. My first hunt.

More, more, more, until past and present blend.

Then I look up. Wren's violet eyes hold mine. It's like she's trying to decipher the secrets of the universe in my gaze.

Endless seconds pass, and the fire worsens, but neither of us looks away.

How ironic is it that *she's* the one to do this to me? The little bird has been the most captivating of all my hunts, and in another life, I would've loved to explore the connection between us.

But here, we're enemies. Pure and simple.

Lines stand between us, barriers that can never be breached. I'm a Hunter, and she's my prey.

What could have been never will be.

My heart breaks, and it's not just because of the flames coursing through me. I stare helplessly as Wren stands and runs her hands down her cloak.

Wait! I try to beg her to help me, but all that comes out of my mouth is an incoherent moan.

Oh, gods. I'm going to die here. Panic squeezes my heart.

Even if Mist manages to find me, my familiar can't save me from whatever is causing this. My blood is lava, bubbling and churning as it courses through my veins.

Black spots fill my vision, and I start shaking uncontrollably. Adros, the god of the Underworld, is calling my name. Soon, I'll join him.

The Given takes one last look at me, and then she steps back. A gurgling moan escapes my throat, and wetness dampens my cheeks.

The tears are for me. For the boy who thought being a Hunter would bring him freedom. For Mist, who will feel my death alongside me. And for the future I'll never get to live.

Death has come for me.

21

I NEVER MEANT FOR THIS TO HAPPEN

Wren

The Hunter is suffering.

I try not to notice his pain as I back away, but that would be like asking me not to notice that the three moons are silver or that the wind is getting steadily colder as the night wears on. Gabriel's moans fill the air, and he's convulsing on the ground.

Even though I hate him for chasing me, my heart is shattering at the sight.

This is my fault.

The words swirl through my mind on a continuous circuit as I put space between the two of us. I shouldn't be standing here. The moment he collapsed, I should've turned and run away as fast as possible. After all, I begged him to free me, and he refused. I shouldn't care that he's hurting . . . but I do.

Gods help me, but my stupid, compassionate heart twists at the sound of his agony. Each moan feels like a dagger striking me in the chest. Why? Why does the sound of the Hunter's pain hurt me so?

Even though I shouldn't, I turn around. Horror grips me as I observe the Hunter. He's in *agony*.

His fingers are clasping at nothing, and tears are running down his cheeks. Tremors have overtaken him. His eyes are wide open, but I don't think he can see me through the veil of pain.

"Fucking leave, Wren," I urge myself. "Get out of here."

My words don't have the intended effect because I can't seem to make my feet move.

"Go," I say.

My voice echoes through the silent night. The moons seem to be laughing at me from their positions in the sky.

Instead of walking away from the Hunter, my feet inch closer to him. This is stupid. I know that. I just . . . I don't know if I can leave him right now. Not when he's clearly hurting. Not when this is my fault.

A curse that would horrify Mother slips from my lips as I return to the Hunter's side. I'm not even sure who I'm cursing. The gods? My soft heart? My inability to leave well enough alone?

All good options.

I don't understand why I'm like this. The man is hunting me, for suns' sakes. I shouldn't even be considering helping him, but for some reason, I am.

I crouch in front of Gabriel, a knot forming in my stomach as I take him in. This is my fault. He's hurting because of me. I'm not sure what was in the vial, but he's obviously in serious pain. Could he die because of this? I don't know, but the longer I stare at him, the more I'm convinced it might be possible.

My heart aches, and something deep within me protests the thought of this man's death. I reach for his face, and his eyes seem to track the movement.

Is he still aware? I stiffen, and his eyes stop moving at the same time. Oh, gods. Even though he's immobilized, I get the sense he still knows what's happening. Somehow, that makes this even worse.

The cold wind claws me out of my stupor, and I touch the Hunter's cheek. His flesh is hot, like picking up an ember from a fire.

Squealing, I yank back my hand. My fingertips are red, as though they've been burned.

He whimpers, and more tears flow down his cheeks. A spark of life remains in his eyes, hidden behind the haze of pain . . .

Pain that I caused.

Suns save me, what have I done? This isn't me. None of it is.

"I'm so sorry," I whisper, as if that will magically cure him. "I never meant for this to happen. I just wanted you to leave me alone."

How was I supposed to know the contents of the vial would do *this*? The woman gave me no indication of that happening. Her skin had been a bit warm, now that I think about it, but it was nothing like the inferno consuming Gabriel.

He doesn't respond, but more tears flow down his cheeks. My stomach twists at the sight, and I have the answer to my question in the tavern.

I might not be good, at least not like Amelia was, but it turns out I'm not built for poisoning. I'm learning something new about myself every day.

Yanking open my satchel, I dig through it frantically in search of the small mushroom the woman gave me. It feels like it takes me an eternity to find it while this man suffers in front of me, but eventually, it's in my hand. The mushroom is slightly spongy, and I pinch it between my index finger and thumb, holding it up to the moonlight.

Even in the darkness, the red tinge is bright. A warning.

Not for consumption.

This is definitely not a blossom mushroom. I should throw it away, but honestly, the Hunter already appears to be on the verge of death. I don't think I can make things worse.

Another moan slips from Gabriel's lips, and a sheen of sweat glistens on his face.

I hold the mushroom between my fingers and meet his glassy gaze. "I'm going to give you this," I tell him. "I'm not sure what it will do, but I think it will help."

The rise and fall of the Hunter's chest is unsteady.

"And if it does, I want you to leave me alone." My voice is firm. "You owe me. Twice now, I'll have saved you. Understand?"

A shudder runs through him as I move my hand closer.

"If this doesn't work, I need you to know that I'm sorry," I confess. "I really didn't mean for you to be in so much pain. That was never part of the plan. I just wanted a chance to live."

He doesn't respond, and that's probably for the better. I've confessed enough for one night. Even though the road is empty for the moment, and the guards are far away, I don't want to risk drawing anyone's attention.

I rip up the mushroom into tiny pieces and reach for the Hunter's lips. They're twin flames, and I swallow a scream as I force his mouth open. If it hurts for me to touch him, how badly is he hurting?

Murmuring repeated apologies, because apparently now that I've started, I can't stop, I carefully drop the morsels into his mouth. Keeping my eyes on him, I grab my canteen and untwist the lid. In a movement that is far too familiar, I lift it to Gabriel's lips and help him drink until all traces of the mushrooms are gone from his mouth.

Sitting back on my heels, I study the Hunter. I don't know how long it will take before the antidote—if that's what it is—kicks in.

Twice, we've been in this position, with him helpless before me. The difference is that this time, not only do I know who he is, but I caused this.

As I stare at this man who is so clearly in pain, I search my heart for remorse. I should feel bad about this, right? I think so.

The problem—if I can call it that—is that I don't feel bad. Not really.

I regret that the Hunter is hurting, but I'm a little surprised to find that I don't regret giving him the contents of the vial.

He was going to drag me back to Grenbloom, and I couldn't let that happen. If time turned back and I had a chance to do this over again, I would still give him the contents of the vial. I'd just be more careful about how many drops I put in.

The sky darkens, and clouds roll in. I shiver, looking over at Gabriel. His whimpers have quieted, and his eyes are still watching me. The green has dimmed, but that flicker of life is still present.

Reaching out, I place the back of my hand on his cheek. He's still hot, but he isn't burning up any longer. I exhale, shaking out my hand.

"I think you're going to live," I tell him softly.

He blinks, and his mouth moves, but no sounds come out.

"I really hope you leave me alone." I stand, drawing my cloak around myself. I don't know if he can understand me or if he'll even remember this conversation, but I have to try. "Please."

My voice cracks, and I hate that I'm showing weakness in front of this man who has caused me so much trouble. "I just want to live in peace. That's all."

My plea hangs in the air between us. The stillness of the night amplifies the desperation of my request. The Hunter hasn't said anything, but as I look into his eyes, the truth slams into me.

He'll never stop chasing me.

The realization steals the breath from my lungs, and I stumble back. Freedom, like a normal life, is something I'll never have.

Not for the first time, I curse this damned Mark on my forehead. I despise all of this. The Giving, the Hunter, the gods, and everything else that has fucked up my life so thoroughly.

I wish I had time to cry and wallow in pity for myself, but I don't. I have things to do and places to be.

I turn, and this time, I don't look back as I run from the Hunter. I haven't slept, and my stomach is quick to remind me that I've eaten very little today, but it doesn't matter.

Once again, I'm fleeing for my life.

The difference is that this time, I know where to find others like me. Gods-blessed who need help. As much as I want to save myself and put as much distance between me and Gabriel, I can't leave yet.

After all, the Given stick together.

Sneaking back through the city gates is so easy that for a few minutes, I wonder if I'm walking into a trap. The guards aren't even paying attention. Huddled together, they're gossiping about recent sexual conquests. I creep past them with my hood up.

Their inattentiveness doesn't stop my heart from hammering, nor does it keep me from constantly looking over my shoulder to see if Gabriel followed me into the city. He didn't, but that doesn't help reduce the tension in my shoulders.

This time, I don't stop to take in the city. I move swiftly, energized by the thought that even though I couldn't save Amelia, I might be able to help the Marked Ones I saw in the square earlier.

I murmur Amelia's mantra, letting it bolster my confidence as Mora's buildings pass in a blur. I don't let myself think too deeply about what I'm about to do, nor do I let doubt take root in my heart.

I might not be a warrior or a scholar or a spy, but I can help these Given. I *have* to help them because when the suns rise tomorrow, they're going to die.

"Not if I can help it," I whisper to myself.

I race through Mora, the streets seeming less complicated now that I've been here before. Before long, I reach my destination.

At first glance, the garden looks the same as it did last night. The stone wall is shrouded in shadows, the tall trees loom above me, and the gate is unguarded.

The difference lies within the stone walls.

Stepping into the shadows, I keep my cloak drawn tightly around myself and consider my options. Unlike yesterday, the Moran Gardens aren't silent or empty. Burning torches form a wide circle not far from the entrance, their red and orange flames licking the night sky.

Six Watchers stand along the perimeter of the torches, their backs to the canvas tent occupying the place of honor in the center of the ring of fire. The structure is large enough for several people, and even though it's nighttime, I can tell it's well made. Three shadows move around inside the tent, and I exhale a sigh of relief.

The gods-blessed are here. I assumed they would be, thanks to the head priestess's remarks earlier, but there had been no way to make sure of that until now. I wish they weren't guarded, though. That's going to make things more difficult.

I suppose the Watchers' presence makes sense, in a twisted way. After all, it would be a shame for a human sacrifice to meet an untimely death the night before they're meant to be killed.

I scowl, cursing Esyn and the priestesses once again as sparks fly off the torches. The embers shoot past leaves, illuminating the dark clouds that are still rolling in.

A storm is coming. Trees sway in the wind, their leaves gently rustling. Faint strains of music come from deep in the city, reminding me of the tavern where Gabriel found me. My night took a detour I hadn't expected, but at least I made it here in time.

I could have left Mora and run away without ever looking back. Honestly, that would've been the smart thing to do. But smart or not, I couldn't leave these gods-blessed to die. Not when I know what happens during a Giving Ceremony. If I left them to their awful fates, I'd be just as complicit in their deaths as the priestesses with their fake Marks or that strange, hooded figure.

Digging my fingers into the stones, I observe the Watchers.

These soldiers don't seem nearly as on edge as the ones from the festival. Gods, it feels like that was years ago, not earlier in the day. They're relaxed, and as a roll of thunder comes from above, the two soldiers closest to me grumble. The pair, a man and a woman, move closer together and engage in a conversation too low for me to hear.

I don't waste time trying to eavesdrop, since they've left a gap in the ring of protection around the tent. The situation is far from perfect, but at least the distracted Watchers are providing me with an opportunity.

Reaching up, I tug my hood as far down over my head as it will go. I slip out of the shadows, sneaking past the gate. The garden is filled with trees, and the tent sits in the middle of large plants with leaves the size of my hands.

Even now, with winter coming, they're a vibrant green. The grass here is long, and if I wasn't wearing boots, it would be tickling my ankles. The trees are as tall as several men stacked on top of one another, and their thick trunks are dark brown. There are many of them, reminiscent of River Bend Forest.

I try to keep my steps light, but despite my best efforts, leaves crunch beneath my feet.

I'll add being stealthy to the list of things I was never taught. My brothers and the twins all went hunting with Father, but I wasn't allowed to join them.

I was eight the last time I begged him to let me come.

Father looks up from the bench by the front door, where he's lacing his boots. I'm standing in the doorway, and I just asked if I could go with him.

"I know you want to join me, Birdie, but you can't."

"Why?" I stomp my foot and cross my arms, pouting. "James gets to go, and he's only a year older than me."

My brothers get to do a lot of things that I don't get to do. It's not fair.

I say as much to Father, who nods and pats the bench beside him. I sit, my feet dangling over the ground. He slings his arm over my shoulder, drawing me close.

"You know why you can't come, Birdie," he says gently.

I scowl. "The Mark?"

Everything always comes down to the blue swirl on my forehead. I wish I had been born without a Mark, like the rest of my family. Life would be so much easier if that were the case.

"You're gods-blessed, my child," he says softly, nodding. "The Given don't need to know how to hunt because the gods will look after you."

"But, Father—"

He kisses my forehead and sighs. "No, Birdie." His voice is soft but firm, and I know there will be no arguing with him. "I'm sorry, but it would be frowned upon."

The rest of the conversation is lost to the recesses of my mind, but I'll never forget standing in the doorway, watching as Father disappeared into the woods with my brothers that day. I stayed there long after they left, Father's words echoing through my mind.

The Given don't need to know how to hunt.

Once again, the way I was born has disadvantaged me. How many more times will this happen?

I'm nearly at the tent when my toe lands on a brittle branch. It snaps, the sound pulling me out of the past. My fingers clench around nothing but air, and my chest heaves. I can't see the Watchers around the tree trunk, but I know they're there.

"Do you hear that?" asks a voice on my right. "Someone's here."

Fuck, fuck, fuck.

I wish I could think of something more eloquent, but I can barely breathe, let alone come up with creative curses. I slowly ease my foot off the offending twig and force my frozen fingers to find the blade sheathed at my hip. Thank the suns, Gabriel didn't take it from me.

He probably didn't think I presented much of a threat. Well, I showed him.

Sort of.

Remembering my task at hand, I slowly pull out my knife, clasping the hilt tightly.

Every second feels like an eternity before a gruff laugh comes from my left.

"Esyn's tits, you're losing your mind, Andre. We're in a fucking garden surrounded by animals. Of course you're hearing things. It's probably a raccoon."

A pause, then, "I don't know, Silas."

There's a sound like a hand slapping a back, then a deep male chuckle. "Relax, man. Let's grab a drink. I'm sure it was nothing."

A raindrop falls onto my cheek, but I don't move to wipe it away. I'm focused entirely on the Watchers' conversation.

Andre protests, "But the Given—"

"Aren't going anywhere," says Silas. "You know as well as I do, this job is a joke. Watching over the gods-blessed as they commune with nature the night before their Giving Ceremonies is a ridiculous task. Nothing has ever happened in my twenty years as a Watcher, and it won't tonight. Relax."

I peer around the tree, holding my breath as the two men turn and walk away from the group. There's no one watching the tent entrance right now.

I don't abandon my hiding spot yet. Instead, I grip the bark as Andre and Silas chat with a third Watcher, passing around a silver flask. One of the guards still appears to be doing his job, but he's located on the far side of the tent.

The entrance remains unguarded. This is my chance. If I'm going to do this, it needs to be now.

Torches sizzle as the rain picks up, and I inhale deeply, steeling my nerves. Hoping I'm not making the worst suns-damned mistake of my entire life, I keep my head down and my knife clenched in my hand as I dash towards the tent.

I shove open the flap, dart inside, and gasp for breath.

22

DEAD PEOPLE WALKING

Wren

Three sets of wide eyes meet mine as the tent flap flutters behind me. The Given stare at me, and before any of them can scream, I shove Father's knife into its sheath and hold up my hands in the universal *I mean you no harm* signal.

Blankets and pillows are piled in the corners, and three cots line the walls. Prayer booklets are stacked on a wooden nightstand. A two-foot-high black marble statue of Esyn's naked form sits beside them.

Even here, the Mother Goddess watches over the Given. Before I knew the truth, I would've found the sight of her comforting. Now, I can't stop a shiver from running through me.

I drag my eyes away from Esyn's statue and look over the gods-blessed, who are still staring at me. Dressed in the palest of greens, with their glowing Marks proudly on display, the trio reminds me of myself and Amelia the night before her Giving Ceremony.

Alive. Happy. *Excited.*

The young man with the flame as a Mark is perched on a wooden crate. He's holding a glass bottle filled with amber liquid, and his hand is frozen halfway to his lips.

A lantern is on the crate next to him, casting flickering light on the woman sitting cross-legged on the mat in front of me. She looks younger now than she did earlier, with her blue hair pulled into a high ponytail. Her dark skin looks like the night has wrapped itself around her. She, too, is unmoving.

Next to them, crouched with his hands curled into fists, is the third Given. He still seems to be carrying the tension from earlier, and the Mark on his neck pulses a dark forest green.

Like Gabriel's eyes when he's angry.

Fuck, where did that thought come from? I can't be thinking about the Hunter or the color of his eyes. I have people to save.

"Who the fuck are you, and what are you doing here?" The growled question comes from the angry Given with the green Mark. His eyes flash with emotion, but it's gone too quickly for me to decipher what he's feeling.

All three Given are staring at me, and sweat drips down my neck as I try to figure out how to answer. Damn it.

I should've spent some time thinking about what I would say to these three when I found them because right now, words are escaping me. How do I explain to them that their entire lives have been lies and that they're going to die in a few hours?

Not easily, that's for damn sure.

Think, Wren.

The words bounce around in my mind as I try to come up with something to say. Time is ticking, but the pressure is making it harder to think. I have to get out of here before the Watchers turn around and see a fourth shadow in the tent.

The only thing working for me is the weather—the rain has picked up, and the blowing wind should muffle the sound of our voices.

It's not often these days that I think anyone is on my side, but it seems like someone might be looking out for me.

Amelia's mantra echoes in my mind, giving me strength. I look each of the gods-blessed in the eyes. "My name is Wren, and I'm here to talk to you."

They deserve something Amelia never got: a choice. A choice to leave, a choice to live.

No one else has said anything, so I add, "I'm here to save you."

Maybe that was the wrong thing to say.

There's a beat of silence before an incredulous laugh bursts out of the woman. She leans back on her hands and tilts her head. "Save us? From what?"

The man on her right looks like he's about to smile, while the tense gods-blessed is staring blankly at me. I don't know who to look at, so I move my eyes from one to the next.

Slowly, so as not to spook them, I tug back my hood. The blue glow illuminates the sides of the tent, and I pull the hood halfway on to dim the glow.

The three gods-blessed lean closer and take in my Mark. If this wasn't such a tense situation, and I wasn't being actively hunted, I would've found their reaction amusing.

"The Giving is a lie." I choke on the words as I say them, my lungs tightening as the memory of Amelia's blood pouring from her neck flashes through my mind.

A tense heartbeat passes, and then the blue-haired woman rears back. "What?"

"It's true." I wish I weren't the one delivering this news, but it's better they learn it now than tomorrow at the altar. "You're not going to be sent to serve the gods tomorrow."

Three pairs of eyes look at me incredulously as if I just told them I were the king.

"I know this is a lot," I say, picking my words carefully. "You're not going to work in the temples. They're going to kill you."

The air thickens, and all three of them inhale deeply at the same time.

None of them are speaking. Why aren't they speaking?

Almost desperately, I continue, "You have to believe me, please. I'm telling the truth."

Every second feels like an eternity as my words settle upon the trio. I don't move, waiting for one of them to react. A dozen scenarios about what they might do run through my mind, but none of them prepare me for what happens.

The man with the flaming Mark scoffs, lifting his bottle to his lips. He takes a long drink, wiping his mouth with the back of his hand when he's done.

"A lie?" he sneers, disbelief etched on his face. "You show up here out of the blue and want us to believe that our whole lives have been falsehoods? No. You're just jealous that we're going to be Given tomorrow."

Jealousy is the last thing I'm feeling.

"I'm not lying," I protest, widening my eyes and trying to infuse as much sincerity into my gaze as possible.

"Really?" His brows lift. "I've never even seen you before. Have you seen her, Mirabelle?"

The woman angles her head. Her blue eyes are as bright as her hair, and they sweep over me.

"Nope." Her lips twist into a sneer. "I've never seen her before, Joshua. Have you seen her, Kadyn?"

The tense man with the dark green Mark shakes his head. "No, I haven't."

None of them take their eyes off me, and the air in the tent is growing thick and uncomfortable. Regret is blooming in my stomach, and my fingers twitch at my sides.

Have I made yet another mistake in coming here? How many mistakes can someone make before their luck runs out? I have to be getting close to the limit.

"Please, you have to believe me. I risked so much to come here." I put *everything* on the line for them. To give them a chance to live.

"We don't even know where you came from, Wren." Joshua crosses his arms, his tunic straining against his muscles. "Or if that's even your name."

The cruelty in his voice makes me want to turn around and leave. How dare he be so rude? I'm just trying to help.

There is a part of me—a rather large one, if I'm being honest—that wants to leave these three to their own devices. And maybe I would have, if I didn't notice the leather-bound book beside Esyn's statue. Tucked beneath a stack of prayer booklets, the novel's spine is covered with flowers that are wreathed in flames. Even though the book is cast in shadows, I would recognize it anywhere.

A Flame So Deep.

My heart twists, and a tear runs down my cheek before I can stop it. How many times did Amelia and I sit together in my room, poring over a worn copy of the exact same book? *A Flame So Deep* is a romance, but that's not all it is.

It's an epic tale of love and loss, of darkness and light, of mythical creatures, fated mates, and battles of good and evil. It was my best friend's favorite story, and seeing it here feels like a sign.

Once again, Amelia's mantra echoes through my mind, reminding me of my purpose.

You have to give them grace, Wren, she adds calmly. *You wouldn't have believed this, either, if you didn't see it.*

Even from beyond the grave, Amelia is being logical. She's right. I can't blame this trio for not believing me, not when we just met. I can't give up on them yet. Amelia wouldn't want me to.

"I know this is a lot, but I'm telling you the truth. I don't know why they're doing it, but they're killing all of us." I open my hands in supplication, letting my horror, grief, and sadness leak into my words. "Go ahead. Ask me questions if you want. Touch my Mark if you need to."

Just believe me, I silently add. *Please.*

The man with the Mark on his neck, Kadyn, is the first to move. He reaches for me, and it takes everything I have not to flinch as he touches my forehead. His hand is warm, and there's a sense of wonderment in his gaze as he traces the swirl etched into my skin.

"She's right; it's real," he proclaims, pulling back his hand and sitting on his haunches.

"Of course it's real." Why would I lie about that? "I'm telling you, I'm just like you. I come from a village named Grenbloom, and I was supposed to be Given earlier this month."

"Supposed to be," Joshua echoes, his voice less harsh than before.

Are they starting to believe me? Hope sparks in my stomach. All might not be lost.

"Why weren't you Given?" Mirabelle asks, leaning closer to me.

Uncertainty is still present in her tone, but at least she's no longer sneering at me. Since the trio hasn't alerted the Watchers of my presence, it seems like we might be moving in the right direction.

"I ran away. My best friend . . ." Crimson flashes before my eyes, and I shudder.

I can't stop now, though. My nails bite into my palms, and I take a deep breath, forcing myself to continue.

"My best friend was Given the day before me. I snuck in and watched as they . . . as she . . . they killed her." A silver blade. A scream. Blood everywhere. A pink flash. The priestesses, laughing. "I saw it, and I couldn't stay."

Mirabelle gasps, and Joshua's eyes harden. He sets down his bottle and stares at me. "The time for your ceremony has passed?"

I nod, pinching my lips together.

"And you didn't go?"

"Obviously," I say, gesturing to myself.

"So, you're being hunted." Mirabelle's voice is a hushed whisper, filled with awe and horror.

My stomach twists, and Gabriel's green eyes flash through my mind. I'm sure there are other Hunters after me, but Gabriel and I . . . Whatever's between us feels personal.

As if there's something more to our relationship than just our statuses as predator and prey.

It must be the connection we'd begun building before he found out who I was. There's no other explanation that I can think of.

"Yes, I am," I admit. "I'm on the run, but when I saw you three, I knew I couldn't leave. Not without making sure you knew the truth. If you come with me—"

"Come with you?" Mirabelle jerks away from me, making a religious gesture across her chest. "Why in Esyn's holy name would we do that?"

A cough comes from outside the tent, breaking past the steady pitter-patter of rain, and ice floods my veins. The four of us freeze. My heartbeat sounds like drums in my ears as I stare at the canvas walls.

Oh, suns, this is it. The Watchers will come inside and realize there's a fourth Given present. There's nowhere for me to go, nowhere for me to hide.

I'm going to get caught.

The tent feels too tight, and the air is too thick. Several seconds pass, but even after the Watchers start talking to one another, I don't relax. I can't waste any more time trying to convince this trio to believe me. Either they do, or they don't.

"You're not going to be assigned to a temple tomorrow." I drop my voice, wishing there was an easier way to say this. I tighten my fists, my nails slicing into my palms. "The Given all die."

"What about the Marks the temple workers wear?" Joshua asks. "I saw one on the head priestess."

My stomach lurches. "Fake. Hers doesn't glow. Not like ours."

And it wasn't in the same place today as when I saw her at Amelia's Giving.

A beat of silence passes, and then Mirabelle whispers incredulously, "You think they're *stickers*?"

"They have to be." I'm pleading with them now, but I don't care. "You need to trust me. I saw my friend die, and the priestesses *laughed*."

Thunder booms outside as if accentuating my point. There's a heavy silence that seems to stretch for several lifetimes.

"I don't understand," Mirabelle murmurs. Joshua places his hand on her shoulder while Kadyn is unmoving.

"It's true," I whisper. "I saw it with my own eyes."

This is my last chance to convince them. I can feel time slipping away from me, so I don't hold back. I tell them everything. Sneaking into the temple, being excited for Amelia, and then watching her die. I tell them about the priestesses gossiping as my best friend bled out, the pink flash, and the strange person dressed in black. I keep going until I've recounted the entire tale, and when I'm done, I clasp my hands in front of me.

"I know this sounds crazy, but you must believe me. *Everything* we've been told is a lie."

It feels like I'm breathing in gobs of mud as I wait for them to speak. Every raindrop hitting the canvas tent sounds like the boom of an executioner's drum, reminding me that the Hunter will be coming for me.

Has he already gotten up? Is he pursuing me again?

It feels like hours pass before Mirabelle exhales.

"I'm sorry." She rubs her temples. "Clearly, you've risked a lot in coming here, but I'm not leaving."

"What?" I blink, the unexpected response taking me by surprise. "Did you hear what I said? They *kill* the gods-blessed." Keeping my voice down is incredibly difficult, and my last words are little more than gasps. "They're going to kill you tomorrow."

What doesn't she understand?

"I heard you, and I believe you think that will happen." Mirabelle looks at me with pity in her eyes as she reaches behind her, grabbing the Mother's statue and cradling it lovingly in her arms. "I don't think Esyn would do that to us. She's the goddess of life, the Mother, the reason this world exists. Myreth is blessed because of her. Why would she do this?"

That's the question I've been asking myself.

"I don't know, but I don't think Esyn is kind at all. At least not the way we were taught. Why would she allow sacrifices to happen in her temple if that were the case?" I clench my fists at my sides. "Esyn is fucking cruel, if you ask me."

"Don't curse at her." Mirabelle hugs the statue closer. "I told you, I don't believe you."

"Neither do I," says Joshua, squeezing her shoulder.

Disbelief is acidic at the back of my tongue. I never saw this coming when I snuck back into Mora.

Stupidly, I thought they'd believe me. Stupidly, I thought that even though I couldn't save Amelia, I could help these three.

My chest aches, and I know this is my last chance. Despair tinges my words as I hold their gazes and beg them to believe me. My words pour out of me as I ask them to trust me. To come with me so they can live.

By the time I finish speaking, I'm physically and emotionally exhausted. I've laid it all out for them.

Joshua and Mirabelle share a long look before he looks back at me.

"I'm sorry, but no." A vein pulses in his jaw. "We don't believe you. Even if we did, we'd be running for the rest of our lives."

"The Hunters will chase us as much as they are you," she adds quietly.

There's a finality in her tone that takes my breath away. I'm really not going to get through to them.

I thought the Giving Festival was bad, but that had nothing on the sinking pit that is my stomach.

I'm looking at dead people walking, and I can't stop silver from lining my eyes. This feels worse than when I realized what would happen to me if I stuck around to be Given.

At least then, I was able to escape and save myself. But these three are their own people. I can't force them to come with me. They need to be willing, and they're not.

I failed them. I'm not sure what I could've done differently, but it doesn't matter, because they don't want to come with me.

My fingers are trembling as my gaze swings from Mirabelle to Joshua. "So, you won't . . ."

"I'm coming with you," Kadyn announces, his deep voice interrupting mine. I fling my head in his direction, and my eyes widen.

"What?" Mirabelle exclaims, her hand flying over her heart. "Kadyn, you will abandon Esyn?"

No longer crouched on the ground, he's on his feet, grabbing a cloak from the pile in the corner. He flings it over his shoulders.

"I don't think Esyn is all that kind, Mira," he says softly. Then, to me, he adds, "I believe you."

Three simple words have never meant so much.

"Really?" I breathe. "You do?"

He rakes a hand through his hair, his neck muscles tensing. "Yes."

"Why?" I can't stop myself from asking. The others don't believe me, so why him?

"I'm not the first one in my family to be born with a Mark."

My eyes widen. As rare as it was for Amelia and me to be born in neighboring villages the same year, it's even rarer for one family to have two children bearing the Mark of the gods. I can't even think of the last time something like this happened.

"My brother was Given a decade ago. And I've always thought something was off. My mother and I sought him out in the temples after his Giving, and we never found him. Never caught a glimpse of him. No one I asked had even heard of him." Kadyn's Mark pulses on his neck, and he clenches his fists. "I've already said goodbye to my family, and with my brother gone, I have nothing left. I'm coming with you."

He believes me.

Warmth suffuses my chest, and if I wasn't already sitting, my limbs would go weak from relief. Thank the suns, it wasn't a waste.

Emotion thickens my throat, and I dip my head in Kadyn's direction. "Thank you."

Such small words, but they carry so much meaning.

Thank you for believing in me. Thank you for coming with me.

Kadyn turns to the other two as he pulls on his hood, covering his Mark. "Are you sure?"

The pair shares a look for a long moment. "We're sure," Mirabelle confirms. "Esyn will look after us. I'm confident."

I'm not. I won't lie and say I understand their reasoning, but at least Kadyn is coming with me. Saving one person is better than saving none.

Kadyn makes a religious gesture across his chest. "May the rising suns bless you both."

"And may you forever remain in their undying light," Joshua replies.

The blessing is familiar. A few weeks ago, I would've repeated it.

Now, I don't bother. The suns haven't personally harmed me—that I know of—but based on my rapidly devolving relationship with the gods, I wouldn't put it past the suns to abandon me next.

Besides, we can't waste any more time. There's an itch under my skin that's getting worse with each passing moment. I have a feeling it won't subside until I get out of this gods-damned country.

According to my map, several cities stand between me and the Sapphire Coast. At least now, unlike this morning, I know where I'm going.

I approach the tent flap, pressing my ear against the canvas. Quiet conversations reach me, but it doesn't sound like the Watchers are on high alert. The rain has quieted, and the storm seems to be passing.

When I turn around, Kadyn is standing with his friends. Their heads are bent, and they're murmuring quietly. Kadyn asks them to cause a distraction with the guards, and they agree. The trio speaks for a few minutes, and Mirabelle and Joshua pray over their friend before they break apart.

Mirabelle steps forward, taking my hand in hers. "If what you say is true—"

"It is." I would never lie about this.

She nods. "If it is, please keep Kadyn safe. He's a good friend of ours, and he's already been through so much."

The three gods-blessed exchange a warm look, one that I recognize because I shared it so often with my best friend. They're close, like Amelia and I were close. It makes it even worse that they're not all coming with me.

"I'll do my best," I tell her. It's all I can do.

Mirabelle releases my hand, picking up Esyn's statue. She kisses the Mother's forehead and murmurs a few quiet words before slipping out of the tent.

A moment later, a booming voice fills the air.

"Hey, what are you doing?"

A feminine laugh. "Now that the rain's dying down, I wanted to come and say hi," Mirabelle purrs. "Is that allowed?"

Another Watcher rumbles a reply, and then faint conversations come from the back of the tent.

Joshua pops his head out, looking both ways, before returning inside. "The coast is clear." He throws his arms around Kadyn. "Be safe, brother."

The two men hug, and when Kadyn steps back, he looks at me. "We're leaving Myreth, right?"

I nod. "I'd like to get to the Sapphire Coast. Once we're there . . ."

"We can escape." He exhales, and a spark of hope enters his eyes. "We can live."

He understands. Thank all the suns, he *understands.*

My chest warms. I'm no longer alone, no longer the only Given escaping their fate.

"Yes, that's right."

"I can get us out of the city unseen," Kadyn says as another peal of laughter comes from outside the tent. "I'll explain on the way."

And as we dart out of the tent and into the garden, avoiding the Watchers' gazes, more hope sparks deep within me.

Maybe tonight was a sign. Maybe, even with the Hunter pursuing me and the damned swirl on my forehead, everything will be okay.

23

THIS ISN'T FAIR

Wren

Kadyn is a silent guide leading me through Mora's streets. We move swiftly, sticking to dark alleys and roads cast in shadows. A few times, we see some people up ahead. Ducking onto side streets, we wait for them to pass.

Even though Kadyn has a cloak, which hides his tunic, marking him as a Given, I can't help but worry about getting caught. I don't think I'll ever stop looking over my shoulder. Not after everything I've already survived.

The rain has slowed to a faint mist, and puddles line the cobblestone streets where dancers were performing hours before. It feels like years have passed since I first woke up in the Moran Gardens, and I'm more desperate than ever to get out of this city.

Thank the suns, the winding streets are much easier to navigate with someone who knows where they're going. The moons are still high, but judging by the absolute exhaustion in my bones and the streaks of light pushing back the darkness, dawn can't be far off.

The scent of manure fills the air as Kadyn leads me down a dark alleyway, and a horse whinnies.

Panic squeezes my chest at the sound. *This* is his plan? Oh, suns. We should've talked about this beforehand.

I stumble to a stop, shaking my head. "Wait."

He turns, eyes wide as he scans the street behind me. "What's wrong?"

"I don't know how to ride. I've never even been within five feet of a horse."

Like hunting, riding is something no one ever bothered to teach me. Perhaps if I'd grown up on a farm, I would've learned how to do it even though I'm Marked, but that's a moot point now.

If this is Kadyn's plan, it won't work. We don't have time to learn new skills, especially ones as involved as riding horses.

Burning fucking suns. My feet ache at the realization that running is back on the table.

"Don't worry," Kadyn assures me from beneath the shadows of his hood. "We aren't riding."

He takes my hand, and I jump at the sudden contact. But there's nothing in our touch. Just his warm hand on mine, as if I were touching one of my brothers. No spark or jolt or awareness pulsing through me, demanding my attention.

My mind automatically flies back to Gabriel and his hand on mine earlier tonight. *That* touch sent fire running through me. It made my heart pound, my core heat, and every part of me yearn for him, even though I hate him.

Gods. What kind of person *yearns* for the man who is hunting them? Obviously, the Mark on my forehead sentencing me to death isn't my only problem.

"If we're not riding, what's the plan?" I ask, hoping to take my mind off the handsome Hunter I have no business thinking about.

"I'll show you," Kadyn replies in a hushed whisper, lifting his finger to his lips in a sign to be quiet.

I nod my understanding. He leads me further into the alley and through an unlocked wooden door I didn't notice before. The door leads to a storage space with abysmal lighting.

Faint streams of moonlight filter through two frosty windows, partially illuminating twelve wagons and carriages sitting in two even rows. Some are small, just big enough to hold a driver and a few boxes, while the bigger ones are meant for transporting large amounts of goods over long distances.

Kadyn slips his hand from mine and walks over to the far wall. I follow close behind him, moving cautiously and holding my cloak close so it doesn't get caught on a stray nail.

Unlike me, Kadyn walks through the dimly lit room with the familiarity of someone who knows exactly where they're going, grabbing a clipboard hanging from a nail. Running his finger down it, he taps it twice before returning it to the wall.

"This way." He jerks his head to the left, and I follow him to a long wooden wagon. He taps the railing running along the side. "This wagon is scheduled to leave through the Stone Gate today. They're taking a shipment of fabric to Mivat."

My brows furrow. I remember seeing Mivat on my map—it's a day's ride away from here. The city is one of three standing between us and the Sapphire Coast.

"Okay . . ." I'm not sure I understand Kadyn's plan. The vehicle has a rectangular box at the back, with enough space up front for two people, but where does he think we'll go? "We can't be seen leaving Mora. There will be Watchers everywhere."

Did he miss the glowing swirl on my forehead? It's far more prominent than the green Mark on his neck.

"Don't worry, we won't be." He walks to the back, and after a moment's pause, I go with him. Curiosity nibbles at my insides as he runs his hands down what appears to be solid wood, his brows furrowed in concentration. "It should be right . . ."

His voice trails off as he presses down. There's a hiss, and then the back of the wagon shifts. The top rises a few inches, revealing . . .

"It's hollow," I whisper to myself, staring into the hidden compartment. My chest tightens. The space is small—maybe a foot and a half high at most, but it stretches the length of the wagon.

Kadyn nods, patting the top. "My family builds these. Sometimes, they get requests for hidden compartments like this."

It's like there are ropes around my chest, and someone is drawing them tighter. I grip the edge, staring into the hollow space. "So, we're going to . . ."

"Climb in." He points to the side, where I can barely make out a lever. "When we reach our destination, I'll pull that, and we'll be able to get out. Pa puts a safety feature in all of these."

"I see." To be honest, the presence of the so-called safety feature doesn't instill in me much confidence. The fact that it exists means that at some point, someone was stuck in one of these wagons, and they were unable to get out.

A frown tugs at my lips as I shudder, drawing my arms around myself. "It's so . . . small."

I'm not a tiny woman, a fact that has never bothered me before. I've always loved my curves and the way they make me look. But this space is so tight that it will feel like going into a coffin.

"I know." Kadyn glances over to me, and his lips slant into a frown. "Look, Wren, we can run, but . . ."

"We wouldn't get far," I whisper.

He nods, and I hug myself tighter as I consider our options. Not only are my feet aching at the thought of running again, but I've been awake for nearly an entire day. I've been pushing my body to its limits since escaping Grenbloom, and I don't know how much longer I can go without collapsing.

On top of all that, there's the matter of speed. Riding in this wagon would allow us to get out of this country faster. Maybe . . . maybe we could even make it out of Myreth before my birthday on the first day of winter?

I want the freedom that comes from fleeing this kingdom more than anything. Real freedom, not the taste I got from the Hunter's head start. If I get in here and we survive, we'll be much closer to our goal. That's the thought that has me considering the compartment more closely. One thing is niggling at the back of my mind, though.

"Why should I trust you?" The question is out of my mouth before I can try to word it in a way that might not be considered extremely insulting, and I wince. Suns, I'm so awkward. "I mean—"

"It's okay. That's a fair question." Kadyn steps towards me. I wait to feel something for this man, but there's nothing. "I know you don't trust me, but I have no reason to lie or pull anything over on you. My family . . ." He pauses, seeming to consider his words. "I'm my parents' last child, and I was going to be Given today. We've already said our goodbyes, and I've already resigned myself to a life in the temples."

One word stands out to me. "Resigned?"

"I never asked to be Given," Kadyn says firmly. "This fate was forced upon me, but I never chose it. I never wanted it."

"I did," I confess, remembering how excited I was for my Giving. "Right up until I realized what it truly meant."

Sharp steel. Amelia's muffled scream. Crimson rivers.

Kadyn nods gravely, as if he understands the direction my thoughts have taken. And maybe he does. "Hours ago, I had no hope. Now, you've given me a chance to live. I'm just trying to repay the favor."

I sweep my eyes over his shadowy, cloaked form. Trust is hard to come by, yet nothing is warning me away from this man. No sense of unease or niggling awareness that I should be careful. Besides, I asked him to trust me not long ago—it would be hypocritical of me not to do the same now.

Maybe it's the Mark faintly glowing on his neck. Maybe it's the fact that the sun is rising and we're running out of time. Either way, my head dips, and I agree to his plan.

I half climb, half slide into the compartment at the back of the wagon. I shimmy down, wrapping my cloak tightly around myself, but I make it.

My back protests the wooden slats, which were definitely not made for comfort. By the time Kadyn slides in next to me, I'm doubting whether this is a good idea. This compartment clearly wasn't built for more than one person.

I twist my fingers together and gnaw on my bottom lip. "On second thought, this might be a bad idea. Perhaps we should—"

A horse whinnies, cutting me off. Footsteps ring out. Someone nearby says, "Getting ready for the day, George?"

Gods-damn it. We're out of time.

A masculine huff that sounds far too close for comfort comes from my right. "You know it. I had to drag myself out of bed this morning."

"Drank too much?"

George laughs, and my stomach somersaults. "Just enough, my friend. Just enough."

Kadyn reaches for the lever, pulling it shut before lying down beside me. The top descends, seeming to take an eternity and a few seconds. It leaves us blanketed in darkness as thick as a starless night.

"Fuck," I breathe, my palms growing sweaty around my cloak.

Suns save me, but I think tight spaces might be as bad as heights. I try to draw deep breaths to steady myself, but it's not working. Each heartbeat isn't strong enough, and each breath is too shallow.

The voices outside are getting louder. George and his friend hook up horses to the wagon, chatting about the Giving Festival while they work.

I turn my head, and the wall is right there. My nose could brush against it. I look back up, where wooden slats greet me. Sitting up isn't an option. Panic squeezes my chest, and those ropes from before constrict tighter, tighter, tighter.

What if something happens? What if I need to move? What if—

Kadyn's hand brushes against mine, and I hitch a breath.

"Sorry," he whispers, his words little more than air. "It's tight."

I huff an incredulous laugh, his words drawing me out of the panic spiral I was falling into. He's wrong, though.

Tight is when my whole family gathers around the kitchen table after Mother forgets to put in the extender. This isn't tight. It's godsdamned suffocating.

Forget worrying about Gabriel finding me—right now, my only thoughts are about this coffin I willingly entered. What will we do if we're discovered? Scream? Kick? Neither of those options seems like they'll truly help us.

A thousand curses race through my mind. I ease my hand up my hip, sliding Father's knife out of its sheath. Gripping the hilt, I hold it against my chest and try to breathe.

I remind myself that I'm armed, which means we at least have a chance if someone finds us. Not a big one, but a chance is still a chance.

A series of bangs and thuds come from above us, and the wooden slats shudder as heavy objects are loaded onto the wagon. Every movement is louder than the last, until it sounds like we're back in the middle of the storm.

Only this time, all it would take is one wrong move, and everything will be ruined. They'll drag Kadyn back to the temple for his Giving, and I'll be held until a Hunter can return me to Grenbloom.

Then we'll both be dead. The knife grows slippery in my palm as memories of Amelia's Giving mingle with thoughts of what my own might entail. There's no excitement, no joy. Just pure, cold dread.

Time seems to play games as the wagon is loaded. It could be seconds or minutes before a muted, "Safe travels, George," comes from outside.

I hold my breath as the wagon dips.

"Thank you, Ky," the driver calls out. "The ride to Mivat takes most of the day, so I won't be back until tomorrow."

My nails dig into my palms as I hold my breath. Have we done it?

"Suns be with you," Ky responds.

"And also with you." George clicks his tongue and murmurs a low command to the horses.

I exhale a long breath when the wagon starts moving. It feels like it takes forever for us to make it through Mora. The sounds of early morning life are far more subdued than yesterday.

The driver stops at the gate and speaks with the guards. Thank the suns and moons, they don't inspect the wagon.

After that, we're bumbling down the road. Once dirt and stones crunch beneath the wagon wheels, I take my first full breath.

We did it.

I can scarcely believe this worked. So much can change in a day. Yesterday, I woke up in Mora's garden, and now I have a new travel companion and a ride.

By the time we stop tonight, we'll be well on our way to the Sapphire Coast.

Thank the blessed, burning suns. Gratitude warms my chest as the suns rise, chasing away the night's chill. Slivers of light make it through the slats in the roof, welcoming us to another day. I'm still here. Still alive.

I tilt my head, looking over at Kadyn. His hands are folded over his chest, and his green Mark is a leafy squiggle on his neck. It's glowing faintly as he stares above us, but he notices my attention and tilts his head towards me.

Thankfulness shines in his eyes, and a knowing settles in my gut. I did the right thing, sneaking back into Mora. Not just because Kadyn's still alive but because whether the head priestess knows it or not, I'm sending her a message by saving him.

Fuck her and her fake Mark.

Fuck the Giving.

Fuck it all.

Together, Kadyn and I will defy all the odds, escape our fated deaths, and flee this country, never looking back.

The Given stick together.

Amelia's words echo in my mind, becoming a silent vow that dances across my lips until, finally, I give in to sleep's call.

24

THIS IS THE REAL NIGHTMARE

Wren

I wake with a scream. The only thing keeping me from giving away our position is Kadyn's warm hand slapped over my mouth.

My heart is racing, and cold sweat is dripping down my neck and arms. My breaths come in gasps, and I tighten my grip on my knife. The hilt digs into my hand, proof that I'm awake.

It was a nightmare, I think, staring at the wooden slats as if they could help me ground myself. *Just a bad dream.*

The words aren't comforting. The nightmare was the worst I've ever had. Never has a dream felt so real or so gods-damned terrifying.

Even now, it feels like the wisps of the dream remain in my mind. Haunting me. I'll never forget it for as long as I live.

I woke in a dark room with no ceiling and walls made of the night sky. Naked and strapped to a stone altar, I tried to scream, only to find out that my voice had been stolen. I was unable to make a single sound as the head priestess and the strange, cloaked figure from Amelia's Giving approached me.

Tears ran down my cheek as the head priestess placed a crimson candle on the altar next to me. She stood over me, speaking of strange things. Of Harvests and Givings and people she referred to as Blessed and Inherited.

I didn't understand what she was talking about. Coming from anyone else, I would've put them off as the ramblings of a mad woman. But there was something about the gleam in her eye that told me that, at the very least, *she* believed what she was saying.

As if that weren't bad enough, when the head priestess's ramblings ended, the cloaked person began chanting.

Amelia's murderer leaned in close, her breath brushing my cheek, and she whispered, "You've been a very bad Given, Wren Nightingale."

Her words swirled around me as she raised a silver dagger and brushed it against my cheek. I tried to move, to escape her wrath, but the invisible binds were holding me down.

Silent screams echoed in my head.

The cloaked person put their hands on my bare chest, their nails digging into me like claws. The head priestess slammed her dagger into my shoulder.

Time grew hazy, but everything came into focus when she laughed and yanked out the dagger.

I watched through a veil of tears and pain as she stabbed me repeatedly, using me as a pincushion. My stomach. My arms and legs. My chest, although she was careful never to get too close to my heart or my neck. She kept going until black spots overtook my vision and every single breath felt like it would be my last.

The last time, she grazed the side of my neck with her blade. I screamed and screamed, the silent sound echoing in my mind.

Only then did the nightmare finally release me from its grip.

If it was a nightmare. My body still aches with phantom pains, and I can still hear the cloaked person's chanting in my mind.

After a long moment, Kadyn slowly removes his hand.

"Thanks," I whisper, pressing my palm that isn't holding Father's knife flat against my chest and willing my heart to slow. It's beating so hard that I'm afraid it's going to break my ribs.

Thank goodness for Kadyn's quick thinking. If he hadn't muffled my cry . . .

I shiver, my stomach cramping. It *was* a nightmare, right? It had to be.

But something warm is trickling down the side of my neck, and there's a niggling in the back of my mind telling me to pay attention. Slipping the knife into its sheath, I lift my hand to my skin.

My fingers come away warm and bloody.

I stare at the blood for so long that my vision blurs. Was it real? Were all the things the head priestess said true? If that's the case, who are the Blessed and Inherited she spoke about? What is a Harvest?

Confusion swirls in my stomach, and long minutes pass without any answers. Either I scratched my neck, or the nightmare was real. A premonition? A warning? I'm not sure.

Eventually, I wipe my hands on my cloak and shudder. Nightmare or not, it has convinced me that we need to get out of this gods-damned country as quickly as possible.

Needing to get my mind off the head priestess and her strange words, I tilt my head to the side. "How long was I out?"

"Hours," Kadyn replies.

Considering how tired I was, that's not a surprise. Even now, bone-deep exhaustion pulls at me. It doesn't matter how tired I am; I won't fall asleep again. Not now, when that nightmare is still present in the recesses of my mind.

Eventually, Kadyn succumbs to the wagon's steady rocking. His eyes droop, and I tell him to rest, promising that I'll keep watch. He sleepily nods, and soon, he's out cold.

This is what I've been missing—a companion on my trek, someone with whom I can share the burden of being on the run. Kadyn and I can look out for each other, protect each other, and keep each other safe.

Hours pass, and it doesn't take long to remember how boring waiting can be.

I count the slats above me, and when that gets tiresome, I wiggle my entire body. I start with my toes, working my way up to my head. After having been immobilized in my nightmare, being able to move is a relief.

When that grows tiresome, my mind wanders back to the Hunter. I'm not entirely sure what it is about Gabriel, but I can't seem to stop thinking about him.

Chances are, he's awake and better now.

Someone else might hope that, since they saved the man's life not once but twice, he'd leave them alone, but I know better. If Gabriel still lives, he'll resume his hunt. I know it's true, just like I know winter follows the Giving Season.

The Hunter will never let me go.

Even though we seemed to have a natural connection before he found out who I was, he will not forget about me. It doesn't matter that I'm drawn to his handsome face, chiseled jaw, and emerald eyes or that sparks jump between us like embers in a crackling fire when we touch.

None of it matters because his job is literally to hunt people like me. I would do well to remember that.

I'm so focused on banishing thoughts of the Hunter that the slowing of the wagon doesn't register at first. The wheels, which have been churning steadily beneath us, turn less frequently. Fewer rocks fly up and hit the bottom.

And then the air shifts.

It was already stale, but now . . .

The hairs on the back of my neck prickle, and goosebumps pepper my arms. My Mark burns. Awareness slithers over me like a snake.

Something is happening.

If I could sit up, I would. As it is, I take out my blade and pass it from one hand to the other, wiping my sweaty palms on my cloak.

Then, the wagon stops completely. The lack of movement is sudden and unwelcome.

Kadyn jolts awake beside me, his eyes flying open as he draws in a deep, gasping breath. His Mark pulses on his neck, dark green filling the space as he turns his head and meets my gaze.

"What's happening?" he mouths.

Wide-eyed, I clutch my knife against my chest and shake my head. "I don't know."

Whatever it is, it can't be good. I don't think we've reached Mivat yet. The suns are still shining, and the silence surrounding us is incongruous with a city.

Footsteps crunch on the ground, simultaneously far too loud and too quiet. My back stiffens, and the urge to flee pulses through my veins.

But I can't run or hide.

We're literally boxed in. All I can do is stare at the ceiling, regretting ever agreeing to get into this moving coffin.

Running doesn't seem so bad now. At least then I was in the forest. Sure, I encountered the panther and the bear, and I nearly drowned, but I was never trapped and waiting helplessly for my death.

"Name and identification, please." The gravelly voice comes from outside the wagon. Even though the wood slightly mutes the voice, I still shiver. There's a warning in the man's voice, an edge of violence I recognize far too well.

I crane my neck, wincing as I unnaturally contort my body so I can peer through the slats behind my head. I can barely make out the driver's shadowy form as he sits perched above us. The brilliant blue sky is a backdrop to his lanky form. He's wearing a cap, and wisps of forest green hair fan out beneath it. He appears to be in his fourth or fifth decade of life.

"George Lovitt, sir," the driver replies, handing something over. I can't see what it is. "I'm headed to Mivat."

"Is that so?" The dangerous man hums, and a pit yawns in my stomach.

I glance at Kadyn. He's as pale as snow. His hood is back over his head, hiding his glowing Mark.

Stones crunch as footsteps circle the wagon.

"Yes, sir." George sounds unperturbed, which is unrelatable. "I'm delivering fabric to Ivanna Bell."

The crunching stops. "The seamstress?"

"The one and only." The driver sounds proud, and his shoulders straighten. "She's been tasked with making a gown for Queen Lucille to wear at the Winter's Eve Ball."

My eyes widen. The ball. How could I have forgotten about that? It was always a topic of discussion at school near the end of the Giving Season.

The first time I learned about it, I was around Nakisha's age.

Mistress Fyona stands in front of our classroom, her hands perched on her hips as she studies our class. Amelia and I are sitting in the front row—her choice, not mine—and the temperature is dropping. It's going to snow soon; I can feel it.

"Who can tell me about the Winter's Eve Ball?" Mistress Fyona asks.

Amelia raises her hand, waving it frantically in the air. "Me, me!"

My best friend loves school, and she's good at it. Honestly, she's good at everything she tries. It doesn't surprise me that she knows the answer.

A smile stretches across Mistress Fyona's face, and she dips her chin. "Go ahead, dear."

Amelia grins, folding her hands on her desk and straightening her back. "The Winter's Eve Ball takes place on the last day of the Giving Season, and it's hosted by the royals every year in Rosebridge."

I've never been to the capital city. No one in my family has. It's so far! I can't imagine traveling to the other side of the country—I've never even been to the other side of River Bend Forest.

"That's correct. What else?"

"There's an honored guest." This comes from my oldest brother, Markus, who is leaning back in his chair several rows behind me.

"Yes, you're right." Mistress Fyona's dress rustles as she strides across the room, and then she picks up a piece of chalk. "The honored guests are different every year. They're chosen to attend the ball because one of their family members was Given to the gods."

"Like Amelia and Wren will be?" The question comes from Yvan, the tailor's son and Markus's best friend.

"That's right." Our teacher beams. "Perhaps one day, when our own gods-blessed are Given, someone in this room will be chosen to go to the capital. Wouldn't that be special?"

At the time, I thought being chosen as an honored guest would be a blessing. That's what it sounded like.

But now?

Now that I know what happens to the gods-blessed, I can't help but think that it isn't an honor, after all. Pity unfurls in my stomach for the people the king selects to go to the ball. They're unknowingly celebrating their family member's death.

There's a pause from outside the wagon and then more footsteps. That fist is back, compressing my lungs as a shadow falls above my head.

A man is leaning against the side of the wagon, his uniform marking him as a Watcher. I clamp my mouth shut, breathe through my nose, and tighten my grip on my knife.

Mere slats of wood separate me from the Watcher. This man could discover us at any moment—all it would take is a too-loud breath or a cough that can't be covered.

And then, as if things can't get any worse, my Mark starts burning.

I want to scream.

No, no, no. Not now.

Why does this keep happening at the worst possible moments? Which god thought it would be funny to make our Marks glow? I'd like to have a word with them.

Reaching up with my free hand, I tug my hood further down. The rustling of fabric sounds like a blustering wind to my panicked ears, mocking my efforts to remain as silent as possible.

And then a woman in Watcher garb steps into my view. Because of course there are two of them. Suns fucking help me, why can't I catch a break?

I wiggle around, moving until I can make out her face. She's scowling at the driver, staring up at him distrustfully. "What do *you* know about the ball, Mr. Lovitt?"

Her derisive tone makes it clear that she doesn't believe a delivery driver could ever know anything about the royal ball. My hackles rise, but George doesn't seem bothered.

"I know all about it, ma'am," he says in a relaxed voice. "You see, my family has been making and delivering fabric for the Winter's Eve Ball for over a century. Moran silk is the best in the land, as I'm sure you know."

His pride is evident, reminiscent of the way Father glows when he speaks about the butcher shop.

The female Watcher nods. "I have heard that, yes."

"Would you like a sample? I have a few spare yards with me, if you're interested."

Even from my awkward position, I can see the spark that enters the soldier's eye.

"I'd love that," she says.

Several minutes pass in silence as George turns around and riffles through a crate. My shoulders are so tense that it feels like they're made of steel.

"Here you are." He hands a roll of purple silk to the Watcher, who smiles and runs her hands over it. He leans over, his arm resting on the back of his seat. "You know, I heard this year's ball is special."

Something about his tone snags my attention, and I roll onto my side. The Watcher leaning against the wagon shifts. "Oh?"

George nods. "For the first time ever, there will be two honored guests who were specially selected to represent the families of this year's Given."

Two guests.

The hairs on the back of my neck prickle, and my stomach twists into tight knots.

Something is wrong, a voice whispers in my mind. *Pay attention.*

I know the voice is right, just like I know that my Mark is a death sentence, the sky is blue, and I was never meant to reach my twenty-first birthday.

The next word out of George's mouth confirms my worst fears. "Twins."

Ice sweeps through me, encasing my chest. If I could draw breath, I'd use it to curse the gods who put me in this fucking position. Except curses won't help me with this situation. Nothing will.

The chances that these twins aren't my sisters are so low that I can't even calculate them. Twins are rare in Myreth—so rare that it was more shocking when Mother gave birth to the girls than when Amelia and I were born in neighboring villages.

George adds, "King Andreas handpicked them himself."

A roaring like a blistering wind fills my ears. A tornado would be quieter.

"Twins," the male soldier muses, his voice barely audible over the roaring. "Fascinating."

"Very," the driver agrees. "They're a blessing from the suns. Esyn is surely smiling down on us."

They continue speaking, the Watchers having apparently decided the driver isn't a threat, but their words don't register.

Horror has me frozen. Why would the king choose the twins?

You've been a very bad Given.

The head priestess's voice echoes through my mind, the answer to my question. More voices join in, repeating the refrain. My parents join in. My sisters. Even Amelia speaks from beyond the grave.

They continue until the awful words are all I can hear. They're shouting at me, reminding me of all the ways I failed.

And then the voices shift.

This is your fault, Wren, Mother says.

The king took the girls because you ran away, Father adds sternly.

James sighs. *What were you thinking, Birdie? You've endangered everyone with your foolish, selfish actions.*

The head priestess laughs. *You thought you had escaped your fate, but you were wrong. The gods-blessed* must *be Given.*

The next voice makes my stomach cramp.

Why did the king take us? Violet asks. She's always been the louder of the twins, more outspoken than Marie. *What's going to happen to us?*

Moisture dampens my cheeks, and I don't know what to say. I don't know how to answer these questions. I don't know anything at all.

The unknowns are millstones, crushing me as I rack my brain for more information about the Winter's Eve Ball. Now that I'm thinking about it, no one ever talked about what happens to the honored guests *after* the Winter's Eve Ball. Are they returned to their families? Or do they disappear, like the Given?

I don't know. All I know is that everything I've been told about being Given is a lie. Our society's foundation is built upon falsehoods and death.

The suns may cast their light upon our kingdom, but darkness is hiding in plain sight. If the Giving Ceremonies are lies, then nothing can be trusted.

What if being an honored guest isn't a blessing but a curse? What if my sisters are in danger?

The Watchers leave, but their absence doesn't ease the panic rooted in my chest. The wagon starts moving again, and the twins' smiling faces flash through my mind. I can still hear their voices, asking me why this is happening to them.

I don't know. A cry rises in my throat, and I shove my fist against my mouth, stifling the sound that threatens to reveal our location.

I could be wrong. Maybe they're not in danger. But Amelia's scream and the phantom ghost of a dagger being shoved into my stomach tell me I'm not.

Several minutes pass before I ease my fist away from my mouth.

Kadyn meets my gaze, concern flickering in his eyes. "What's wrong?"

For a moment, I consider not telling him my suspicions. After all, we don't really know each other. But what would be the point of keeping secrets?

We're both Marked, both on the run, and both in this together. He might as well know what has my heart trying to escape my chest.

"You know the twins the Watchers were talking about?" Just saying the words hurts.

His brows knit beneath his hood. "The king's honored guests?"

I nod, taking a deep breath. "I think . . . I think they're my sisters." I squeeze my eyes shut, but that sick sense of unease remains. "I think the king took them."

Speaking those words out loud and hearing them for the first time has ice wrapping around my heart again.

"That's . . . Fuck," he breathes. "What do you think it means?"

That's the question of the hour, isn't it?

"I don't know, but I have a bad feeling." It's like my gut is coiling in on itself.

Kadyn's eyes widen. "Like a sixth sense?"

I pause, considering the question. "Actually . . . yes. Just like that. But I've never felt anything like this before."

There's no way anyone could forget a sickening feeling like this. It's like my stomach has fallen to my feet. It's twisting in tight knots, a warning so severe that no one could ignore it.

Kadyn hums, and he appears deep in thought for a few minutes. "Has anyone in your family ever had a . . . stronger sense of things?"

The question strikes me as odd.

"No . . ." I start shaking my head when a memory pops into my mind. "Actually, yes. My nana, the suns be with her soul, used to get them all the time before she died." I can't believe I forgot about this. "She'd tell us about them, and I used to think they were an old woman's tales, but now . . ."

Now, I can feel in the depths of my soul that something bad is going to happen to my sisters.

Drawing my arms around myself, I press my back against the wall. Despite the warmth of the day, I can't stop shivering.

Is this how Nana felt when she got her bad feelings? She didn't get them often, at least not that I can recall, but whenever she did, everyone always listened.

If Nana said a storm was coming, it would be devastating. If she gave you tea for your throat, you took it even though you didn't feel sick. She just . . . knew things.

My sisters are the guests of honor at the king's ball . . . but what kind of honor can a man who presides over the yearly slaughter of hundreds possess?

The twins are in danger. I can feel it.

Whether it's a sixth sense, as Kadyn is suggesting, or something else entirely, it doesn't really matter. If the girls are hurt because of something I did, a decision I made . . .

Rough sobs rip out of me. It takes everything I have to remain silent, my fingers gripping my sides as I shake. All the feelings that I've been shoving down and ignoring since I witnessed Amelia's murder come pouring out of me all at once.

A heaving sob is wrenched from my chest, and rivers of hot tears stream down my cheeks.

I shove my fist back over my mouth, biting down on it. I can feel Kadyn's gaze on me, but I squeeze my eyes shut, unable to look at him.

I ran to save my life, but now I'm not sure it was the right thing to do. What good is being alive if my actions hurt others around me? What if the king does something to the twins because I ran from my fate?

The bad dream from earlier seems so far away now. Who cares about phantom pains and stab wounds that feel real but aren't? This is the real nightmare.

My blood chills as another thought enters my mind.

What if the twins are Given instead of me?

Bloody hell. Is that even possible?

They're not Marked, but maybe that doesn't matter. I don't even understand why the Given are being killed in the first place.

What do the Marks really mean? Why do the priestesses pretend to have Marks? Why lie to everyone?

The questions remain answerless, but I can't focus on them any longer. My sisters need me. They're in the king's hands because of me.

As desperate as I am to escape the Kingdom of Myreth and never look back, I can't go yet. I need to find the twins and save them, which means the Sapphire Coast will have to wait.

I have a ball to attend.

25

DEATH'S COLD EMBRACE

Gabriel

Pain has infiltrated every part of my being. The fire has its own heartbeat as it pulses through me. There isn't a single part of me that doesn't fucking hurt.

Whatever the little bird gave me was potent, and even now, its lingering effects are still running through my system.

My chest aches, and my legs feel like they're twigs, one harsh kick away from snapping in two. The jostling of the horse beneath me isn't helping ease the pain at all, but it's a necessary evil.

As soon as I regained enough strength to walk, I returned to Mora with the sole intent of purchasing a horse. The city guards had been in an uproar, talking about how a Given had gone missing overnight.

Another one.

There is no doubt in my mind: this is the little bird's doing. I'm not sure why she didn't run—after all, she's an outlaw, and she knows I'm here, chasing her—but I know she has something to do with the missing gods-blessed.

I can't get her eyes out of my head. They've been haunting me ever since she left. My memories of last night are hazy. I know she was talking, but I can't remember what was said.

I have to find her and finish this hunt.

This isn't because of my promotion or my bond with Mist anymore. Wren poisoned me, and now, this feels personal.

I need to see this through.

That thought has me leaning forward in my saddle and whispering in Steadfast's ear, encouraging her to move faster. The chestnut mare was the fastest the stable had available, and I've been riding for several hours.

True to her name, Steadfast hasn't faltered once, galloping down the Stone Road like she was made for this.

Two gates lead out of Mora: the Iron Gate and the Stone Gate. Mist was watching the former, having arrived minutes after Wren left, licking my face and waiting for me to heal. I know the little bird didn't go that way. Mist would've scented her. Which leaves the Stone Gate, and therefore, the Stone Road.

For hours, Steadfast gallops, leaving a trail of dust behind us. I'm curved over the saddle, and the rising suns are warming my back when a smattering of paws catches my attention. I look to my right, my lips creaking up into a smile.

Mist bounds down the road towards me. Our bond hums with delight, and I send waves of warmth towards her.

I'm glad to see you, I tell her. Once I was strong enough to get up this morning, Mist left to cross the mountain passage and meet me on the other side of Mora. Our forged bond gives her strength and speed, which allows her to move quickly.

My panther keeps her distance, careful not to spook Steadfast. Even so, our connection thrums steadily with her nearness. Tension seeps out of me, and strength returns to me more quickly now that my bonded familiar is nearby. I'm not sure what magic the bond contains, but I've always healed more quickly when Mist is close by. Today is no exception.

The Stone Road is well traveled. It connects Mora to Mivat and Saltwater, before heading further north and eventually leading to Rosebridge. Every time we pass another rider or merchant carting goods, Mist darts into the woods. Occasionally, she's gone for a few minutes, while other times, she disappears for longer.

Our bond hums, the connection never faltering. By the time the suns are high in the sky, I'm feeling much better.

That is, until an eagle's cry shatters the stillness of the afternoon.

The leather reins cut into my hands as I clutch them with white-knuckled fingers. A tremor courses along my back, and my breath comes in short bursts.

I lift my gaze, scanning the horizon.

At first, I don't see anything amiss.

The sky is blue, as it often is near the end of the Giving Season. A final gift from the gods before the winter brings snow and ice. Even the twin suns can't stave off the bitter cold of those months.

A few clouds dot the sky, but they don't stop the suns from shining their brilliant light upon the land.

Then I see it. A black speck is careening straight towards me, a dark stain on the horizon rapidly growing larger.

The eagle opens its beak, and another cry reaches my ears. A predator's call. A warning.

"Gods-damn it," I groan.

I'd known this was a possibility, but I'd hoped to have Wren firmly in my grasp before it happened. Vile curses slip from my tongue as I quickly lead Steadfast off the road.

My usually smooth dismount is rough, my foot catching in the stirrup as nerves race through me. I wobble like a child learning how to ride for the first time, swearing as I struggle to free myself. It takes far more effort than it should.

Once I'm back on two feet, I slip Steadfast's reins over a nearby branch. Wiping my sweaty palms on my trousers, I move away from the horse. When the Stone Road is barely visible through the trees, I stop.

No one else is around, which is good. There will be no witnesses.

My stomach twists in knots, and the strength that I've regained doesn't feel like enough to handle what's coming next.

I hate this. The nerves coursing through me. The helplessness. The memories of my childhood that I'd worked so hard to suppress. I hate it all.

A nose bumps against my left leg, and I look down. Mist is sitting next to me, her silver eyes sweeping through the forest. My familiar's head reaches my hand in this position, and I scratch behind her ears as the eagle descends.

You cannot show fear, I remind myself.

My body bears the reminders of what happens if I do.

Drawing my shoulders back, I inhale deeply and straighten as the eagle lands on a branch above my head. The creature is as deadly as it is violently beautiful. This close, its crimson eyes are like blood rubies, drilling into mine. The eagle spreads its majestic wings and caws three times, never breaking eye contact with me.

My blood chills, and I can hear my heartbeat echoing in my ears. The rhythm is loud and erratic, betraying my nerves. I don't draw my sword because that will end poorly. Instead, I dig my fingers into Mist's fur and let her ground me as we wait for what feels like an eternity.

Then I see them.

Crimson sparks dance on the ground in front of me. At first, there are just a few. Each ember bears a promise of power and pain. They multiply quickly, and inadvertently, I take a step back as they morph into red smoke.

I flatten my hands on my sides, keeping my sword within easy reach, even though drawing it now would be futile, and force myself to breathe. Despite my desire to show no fear, my back aches with phantom pains. Another tremor runs through me.

Mist stiffens, growling as the crimson-tinged smoke swirls in front of us. Layers of dark red ribbons stack on top of one another until they form the rough shape of a being an inch shorter than me.

The smoke solidifies.

Leather boots that seem to absorb the light of the midday suns appear. Two legs clad in black form. A torso. Clenched fists. Finally, an entire body that glows a muted crimson.

A reminder of his power. His strength.

And my weakness.

There's no time to wallow in it, though. The smoke hardens, and I get a good look at the man in front of me. Pale skin, black hair, and malice-filled eyes that lack all traces of kindness. A black crown inlaid with rubies rests on his brow. The ruby crown is a marker of his power and position, as if the blatant show of power weren't enough of a sign.

My heart races. I clench my right hand, place my fist over the pounding organ, and drop to my knees.

"Your Majesty," I say, staring at the tip of his boots.

Gods, I hate those boots. The number of times I've seen them painted in my own blood is enough to make anyone quake in fear. I don't, though. I hold still, remaining on my knees as the king's gaze bores into the back of my neck.

Minutes pass.

The forest is eerily silent, save for the sound of someone riding by on the Stone Road. They don't stop.

That's probably for the best.

"I thought you understood the importance of the Giving Season." The king's voice is darkness and death and everything wrong with this world. Leaves crunch as he circles me slowly, and I stare at the spot he vacated. "I thought you knew that each gods-blessed bearing a glowing Mark *must* be returned to the gods during their twentieth year."

Of course, I know that. Who doesn't?

Our entire country is built on the foundation of the Giving. Everything we do, every custom we hold sacred, revolves around the gods-blessed.

The Given are the reason Myreth exists as it does today.

Silence stretches as the king continues circling me. The air thickens, and the rushing in my ears gets louder as I wait for the king to continue. He hasn't given me permission to speak, and I won't dare risk his ire by doing so out of turn. Not now, when my body still carries traces of Wren's drug.

It feels like endless lifetimes pass before the king places his hand on my shoulder. Even through my cloak and tunic, I can feel the ice in his touch. He's never been warm, but now it's like he bathed in the glacial waters of the northern Frozen Sea.

"Do you recall the words you spoke when you took up the mantle of your position?" King Andreas's grip tightens on my shoulder, his nails digging into my skin like claws, and I grunt. "Speak, Hunter Moreau."

There is no peace that comes from hearing the king address me by my title. No calm. No pride. Just frigid fear, settling in my stomach.

My eyes are trained on the ground, but my mind is back on my Bonding Day.

A heavy black cloak had been placed on my shoulders, the fur lining tickling the back of my neck. I knelt before His Majesty with three other initiates, waiting to take our vows and finally become Hunters.

That day, I'd been surrounded by my brothers and sisters in the chase.

Now, I'm alone.

"Yes, Your Majesty," I rasp.

"Remind me of them," he commands.

My voice is rough as I recite the same words I spoke that fateful day. "I, Gabriel Charles Aiden Moreau, vow to keep the suns-blessed Kingdom of Myreth safe at all costs. As a Hunter, I will protect Myreth from those who wish to harm it, and I will hunt those who seek to disrupt the balance. I am a servant of the Crown, a weapon to be wielded. Above all else, I vow my loyalty to the Ruby Thrones and those who sit upon them."

I exhale, remaining still as I close my mouth.

Mist is unmoving next to me, but our bond is filled with discontent. I know she's holding herself back from trying to tear into the king's throat—*trying* being the operative word. She wouldn't get close enough to nick the king, let alone draw blood.

I push waves of calm through our bond, hoping to ease her discomfort and encourage her to stand down. The king and his eagle are too powerful for us to go against, and doing so would spell certain death for Mist.

The longest moment seems to pass before the king lifts his hand from my shoulder. I remain on the ground, even though internally, I'm sighing in relief.

There is little in this world that I hate more than that man's touch.

"I'm surprised you recall those words so well." King Andreas steps back. "I would've thought you'd forgotten them since the woman you've been tasked with hunting is still roaming free."

Wren.

I'm not the only Hunter in the lands, and I'm sure others are searching for her, too. But apparently, I'm the one who is bearing the brunt of the king's displeasure. I'd suspected as much, based on the never-ending nightmares that have been plaguing me.

They were too real, too similar, and too dark to be anything but messages from the king. He's all but confirmed it now.

I drag my gaze upwards and instantly wish I hadn't. The king's eyes are empty black pits flecked with crimson, and they're drilling into me.

"*Why* is she still free, Gabriel?"

The way he says my name makes me want to scream to the heavens. I despise the way he forms the syllables, despise the sneer he adds as he directs the question to me, despise the way I'm instantly reminded of his true feelings for me.

Because she's different.

The answer to the king's question forms in my mind, but since I don't have a death wish, I stop my mouth from forming the words. It doesn't keep me from thinking about her, though.

The little bird is persistent, and her ability to evade capture longer than most is impressive. That's not the only thing that sets her apart from the others I've hunted. She has a compassionate heart and a fire in her that burns brighter each time we meet.

It's more than just the way she saved me in the forest, more than the fire in her eyes when she refused to come easily, more than the fact that she's made things personal now.

I'm drawn to her in a way that I've never been drawn to anyone before.

But I don't tell the king any of that.

"Mist and I are tracking the gods-blessed to Mivat, Your Majesty." I keep my voice steady. "We will catch her and bring her back to the temple before the Giving Season is up."

The king steps towards me, balling his fists at his sides. Each movement is deliberate. A threat. A reminder of his strength.

"There isn't time to return her to Grenbloom, Gabriel," he warns. "She must be Given before the end of the season, and any temple will do."

I stare at him, my brows knitting. I've never heard of a Giving taking place away from the gods-blessed's home temple.

This feels strange. It's more than the king's demand that I catch Wren. It's the way he's pushing for this so hard.

Before I can stop myself and remember who is in front of me, I ask, "Why is it so important that she's Given *this* season? What happens if she isn't apprehended until the new year?"

There are four seasons—winter, spring, summer, and giving—but the ceremonies that return the Marked Ones to the gods only happen during one of them. I've never thought about why that is, but something about the king's insistence on this matter has me paying attention.

King Andreas is moving before I realize what's happening. A swarm of magic bursts from his hands, yanking me off the ground and slamming me into a tree. Wood splinters behind me, and the force of impact steals the breath from my lungs.

The magic has me pinned, helpless as the king's hand finds my throat.

"You dare question me?" he snarls, his fingers digging into my neck. "I am your gods-damned *king*."

I've never hated that fact more than I do right now.

Gasping for breath, I struggle against his hold. It's no use. His magic is strong, and ropes of power wrap around me like crimson snakes. They bind me to the tree, the rough bark digging into my back. The more I struggle, the tighter the ropes become.

Here I am again, trapped and at the king's fucking mercy.

Mist growls and snaps her teeth at the royal. Even though worry and fear pulse through our bond, she won't come closer.

"I just thought—"

He slams my head into the tree twice. My brain shakes in my skull from the impact. I bite my tongue. Copper floods my mouth as black spots appear in my vision. I groan, fighting to stay alert and keep my guard up.

"That's your fucking problem." King Andreas sneers. His skin takes on a red hue that has icy fear coursing through my veins. "Your job isn't to think, Gabriel. If I wanted you to do that, I never would have allowed you to become a Hunter. Your job is to pursue those who have broken the law and return them so they can face their punishments. No more, no less."

Malice is a crimson flame burning bright in the king's eyes. All it does is fuel the bitter hatred at the back of my throat.

King Andreas abhors me, and the feeling is fucking mutual.

The royal's nails dig into my throat, breaking the skin and drawing beads of blood. "I thought I taught you better than that, *son*."

The term drips with so much revulsion that I could drown in it.

The king calls me son, but he's never let me forget that I'm just a bastard. The fruit of his fling with a maid, I was dropped at the foot of his throne the day of my birth.

He took me in and raised me, but he never let me forget that I am here only because of his benevolent grace. He's never considered me his own.

I'm only half royal, and I don't have the same blessings from the gods as my half brother or the king and queen.

Hunting is the only thing I'm good at, the only thing that makes me feel wanted. That's why I've worked so hard to become a Master Hunter. And now, if I don't catch Wren Nightingale by the end of this Giving Season, that will be taken from me.

Who will I be if that happens? The king's bastard, stripped of all his titles. Magicless. Penniless. Bondless.

Fucking *worthless*.

Growing up, I lost count of how many times the king reminded me of my position—or lack thereof. Most of the time, he forgot I existed. But when he didn't, when someone or something reminded him I was there, I always paid the price for his hatred.

I'm nothing in his eyes. Worse than a commoner, I'm a failure on all counts. A *mistake*. Someone who never should've existed, a black smear on the crimson tapestry that is his life.

For a time, I thought I could prove him wrong. I thought that by becoming the youngest Master Hunter the kingdom's ever seen, I could show him I have use.

Suns save me, but even though the king hates me and I hate him, I used to yearn for his love and affection. I would watch as he showered my older brother with all the care in the world while I was told I was nothing.

The perfect prince in every way, Severus is the fucking apple of my father's hatred-filled eyes.

The king's hand still circles my throat, and his curling lip tells me everything I need to know about his feelings.

I wish I'd never been born to him. As a child, I was swept into corners, sneered at by the queen and her ladies, and hated by my father and brother. When my grandmother crossed the Veil, even the small semblances of love she'd given me vanished. I was alone, save for a few friends.

The king's grip tightens, tightens, tightens, until death's embrace brushes against me. This isn't the first time I've been in death's cold presence—my father has a propensity for executions.

Today is different because I'm no longer a spectator. Death is coming for me, and this time, I don't think I can avoid it. I fight against the king's binds, refusing to give up, but his powerful magic presses me harder against the tree.

There's a deep sense of irony in the fact that the man who played a part in bringing me into this world will be the one to end my existence.

My lungs contract, trying desperately to draw breath. Nothing gets past the king's grip on my throat. My fingers claw at the tree, searching for purchase in a desperate attempt to save me from my fate.

I should probably be praying for mercy on my soul, but I don't bother. Death will release me from having to deal with my prick of a father, and maybe that's all I can ask for. Maybe the end of my life will bring me peace.

I'm waiting for death to swallow me whole when the king's hand loosens around my neck. Wordlessly, he releases me. His magic falls away, and I collapse onto all fours.

My lungs burn, guzzling air greedily. Mist is there, licking my face. The rough pad of her tongue is a cool, comforting balm as I gasp for air.

I can feel the king's eyes on me. Watching. Waiting.

It feels like an eternity passes before I muster up the strength to drag my gaze up to his. He's standing over me, his fists clenched as my blood drips from his nails onto the leafy ground.

It's not the first time my blood has decorated his hands, and I have a sick feeling that it won't be the last.

"Did you get my messages?" His glowering stare never wavers.

The nightmares.

"Yes," I choke out.

A long moment passes as the king circles me once again. A true predator, watching his prey. "I've been lenient with you, Gabriel."

That's a fucking lie, and I don't even bother responding.

"You will deliver Wren Nightingale to me personally by the Winter's Eve Ball, or you will never hunt anyone again." The king's voice is filled with the promise of unfathomable levels of violence. "I'll send other Hunters after the foolish Given who escaped Mora today, but I am holding *you* responsible for Wren. If she isn't returned to me, you alone will bear the weight of your failure. Do you understand?"

I have no choice here. I've never had a choice where the king is involved. But what can I say? What can I do?

He has death at his fingertips, and all I have is my sword. I'm well trained with weapons, but steel cannot win against the most powerful magic wielder in the land. I'll never get close enough to hurt him.

"Yes, Your Majesty." The words are rough as I force them out of my dry mouth. "I understand."

"Do not fail me in this task," King Andreas snarls.

The vicious sound echoes through the forest, and Mist growls back. The king's attention snaps to my familiar. A long moment passes as he stares at her, malice painted on his features.

I grab Mist, hugging her to my chest as the king laughs cruelly. He steps back, his eagle cawing. Crimson sparks rise, swirling around him.

"Bring me Wren Nightingale, Gabriel." He holds my gaze as his body returns to smoke, his eyes the last to disappear.

The king vanishes, but his eagle remains. It stares at me through crimson eyes.

As though it knows what its cry does to me, it opens its beak and caws. The sound is deep and unnatural, utterly unlike a regular eagle, and it echoes through my mind. That sound . . .

I've heard it far too many times.

Memories I buried long ago shove their way to the front of my mind. I dig my fingers into Mist's fur as past and present collide.

Hundreds of lashings merge. My back aches at the countless memories of pain and blood and having my skin flayed from my bones. Every time, I bled. Every time, I was healed by the queen's salve, ready to take another beating whenever the king saw fit.

The king's curses race through my mind as though he's still here, shouting at me. Magicless bastard. Weak, like my whore of a mother. Good for nothing.

He has hundreds of ways of making me hurt, and he's called me thousands of names over the years. They all amount to the same thing.

He hates me more than he's ever hated anything else.

For years, I've kept his hatred close. If the king hates me, it means I must be doing something right.

Long ago, I vowed that I would be better than him if it was the last thing I ever did. Becoming a Hunter allowed me to leave Rosebridge and all the memories of my awful childhood behind.

I can't escape him, though. Not entirely. But my vow remains. I will be better than him if it's the last thing I ever do.

After what feels like an eternity, the king's eagle flies away.

I remain crouched on the ground for a long time, my fingers digging into Mist's coat as I hold her close. I'm not sure why the king is so insistent about his timeline, but in the end, it doesn't matter.

Wren Nightingale is my prey. No matter how enticing I find her, I cannot forget that.

And so, when I've wiped away all traces of blood on my neck, I return to Steadfast and remount. Whispering a few commands in her ear, I bend over the saddle as she takes off in a gallop.

There's no time to waste. I have a little bird to hunt.

26

THE RIVER MARKET

Wren

It's fucking cold.

That's the first thought that comes to mind as I wake up. The early morning breeze carries hints of frost and nips at my cheek. For a moment, I don't remember where I am, but then the events of the past few weeks come flooding back all at once.

The Giving is a lie, I'm on the run, a Hunter is pursuing me, and Kadyn and I are headed to the Winter's Eve Ball in Rosebridge.

A few days have passed since I rescued him, and we've fallen into a routine of sorts. Having a partner is nice, but Kadyn's presence isn't enough to ward off the impending winter's chill. Last night was the coldest one yet.

Worry races through me as I groan, wrapping my cloak tighter around myself. As soon as we get the twins, we need to leave this country. I don't want to expose my sisters to the dangerous temperatures winter can bring, especially without a roof over our heads or money to buy food to fill our bellies.

I blink open my eyes, white clouds forming in front of me as I exhale. The alley where we found refuge last night is still dark, although the first traces of dawn streak across the sky. Frost lines the crates we slept behind, a white glimmer foretelling the end of the Giving Season in two weeks.

A snore comes from beside me, where Kadyn is curled into a ball. His head is resting on the brick wall, and his arms are wrapped around him.

I don't know how he can still be sleeping when it's so cold—I tossed and turned all night—but I'll let him get as much rest as he can.

After all, that's the benefit of being on the run with a partner: we can look out for each other. It's more important now than ever, since the numbers of Watchers and Hunters seem to increase with each passing day.

Last night, I overheard two Hunters discussing the missing Marked Ones as they walked past the alley. They hadn't seen us, but that didn't stop me from clutching Father's knife all night long.

They're still searching for us. The continued attention is getting more and more frustrating. Why won't they just let us go?

Every year, dozens of people are Given to the gods. Why does it matter if two of us escaped our fated executions and ran?

I rub my hands together for warmth, and as it has a thousand times since I witnessed her Giving, my mind wanders back to Amelia's ceremony. It feels like every time I think back to that day, I have even more questions.

Why do they do this? What good comes from killing us? Why is it so important the gods-blessed be Given?

I keep thinking about what the head priestess said in my nightmare. The Blessed and the Inherited. Who are they, and what do they have to do with me?

Something isn't adding up, and it feels like everyone else knows something we don't.

Or maybe I'm wrong, everyone's in the dark, and I'm being paranoid. Honestly, I wouldn't be surprised if that were the case. I'm looking over my shoulder more now than ever before. It feels like every time my Mark burns, it's getting hotter than before. It might just be in my mind, though. A side effect from being on edge ever since we heard about the honored guests a few days ago.

After the Watchers stopped the wagon, there were no more interruptions. We reached Mivat that night. Kadyn and I slipped out when it was safe and found an abandoned shed to stay in. We shivered, taking turns keeping watch while the other slept. The next day, we ate some apples we found in the shed before hitching a ride on another wagon—secretly, of course.

The second leg of our journey took us from Mivat to Saltwater. Getting to the riverside city had been an uncomfortable two-day journey.

The second secret compartment made the first one seem palatial in comparison. Kadyn and I had been pressed together, barely able to move. We'd sipped just enough water to avoid dehydration, but no more than that. The journey had been highly unpleasant, but we made it here.

Kadyn shifts beside me, unfurling from his ball. "Morning, Wren," he whispers.

I return the greeting and sheath my knife before tucking my hands beneath my cloak. "How did you sleep?"

He rubs his eyes. "Well enough, I suppose. You?"

"Same." I dreamed of the Hunter, but that's nothing new. His emerald eyes seek me out whenever I rest.

I can't escape him. However, I'll take dreams of the Hunter over ones of the head priestess any day.

Kadyn's stomach grumbles, and I frown. "We need to find some food today."

Not only that, but I'd do just about anything for a bar of soap and a fresh change of clothes. Being on the run isn't conducive to hygienic practices, and my dress is proof of that. Besides, if I'm going to sneak into the Winter's Eve Ball in two weeks—something I haven't entirely figured out yet but can't ignore for much longer—I can't be wearing Mother's old gown.

I mention as much to Kadyn, and he chuckles. "Your dress definitely looks like it's seen better days, that's for sure."

I gasp in mock outrage, elbowing him in the side. We've fallen into a quick friendship, likely sped along by the fact that we're on the run for our lives.

"We should spend the day in Saltwater," Kadyn suggests. "We can get some real food, find some clothes, and then plan our next steps." He draws his hood more firmly over his head. "You're still planning on going to Rosebridge, right?"

"Yes. I can't leave my sisters in the king's hands." Goosebumps erupt on my arms, and I shiver. "I could be wrong, and nothing will happen to them, but I have to be sure." I lean my head back and sigh. The sky is growing lighter, and the city is waking up around us. "I need to be there for them."

That feeling, the one Kadyn called a sixth sense, hasn't gone anywhere. Every time I think of the twins, my stomach twists tighter and tighter, warning that they're in danger.

"I understand." Kadyn rubs his temples, and his voice is heavy. "Family is everything."

Grief is laced through his words, a thread of loss and pain that I'm all too familiar with. I haven't forgotten what Kadyn said before we left Mora—his brother was Given.

"Do you want to talk about it?" I ask quietly. "About your brother?"

He pushes his tongue against the side of his stubble-covered cheek and shakes his head. "Not really."

"I'm here if you change your mind." I place my hand on his. "If you want to talk about anything, let me know."

I can't bring his brother back, but I can do this. Gratitude fills my friend's eyes, and he dips his head in thanks. Silence stretches between us, but it isn't uncomfortable.

Several minutes pass before our stomachs rumble, and we decide to emerge from the alley and start our day.

Even though it's still early in the morning, people are already walking down the cobblestone streets. They all seem to be headed in the same direction, so logically, we follow them.

Two rights and a left later, a large sign reading THE RIVER MARKET leads into a bustling square.

"This must be where Saltwater got its name," Kadyn murmurs beside me.

I nod, drinking in the sights unfolding before us. "It's enormous. Have you ever been here before?"

He shakes his head. "No, but I've heard of the Salt River before."

When I see the body of water, I understand why that is. The Salt River is at least four times the size of the one I fell into earlier, and it's filled with boats of all sizes.

Fishermen and merchants mill around the docks. Early-morning shoppers weave through them, filling wicker baskets that hang on their arms.

Hundreds of voices call to and fro. There's a frantic energy in the salty air. The chaos is reminiscent of Mora, but the atmosphere is decidedly less joyful and more businesslike.

"Excuse me! Pardon me!" A young boy whose navy curls peek out from beneath his blue cap bumps into my arm. He races through the market, running around people before careening down the docks.

He's not the only one in a hurry—everyone here seems to be moving with a purpose.

To my right, a group of fishermen are lugging in this morning's catch. Their nets are brimming with fish whose tails slap on the ground as they valiantly attempt to escape their fate. These aren't the tiny fish my brothers would sometimes pull out of Mud River in Grenbloom. Those were barely the size of my palm. These are massive. A few are as tall as the fishermen and women pulling them out of the water.

Kadyn touches my arm.

"Breakfast is on me," he says quietly, steering me towards a merchant manning a fire nearby. He's rotating skewers on a grate over flames, and as we draw near, he drizzles oil over the fish. "Thank the suns, I had some money in my cloak for my offering when you arrived. I've been saving it until we could spend it without attracting attention."

I bite my lip. This is the closest either of us has come to acknowledging what happened the night of the Giving Festival.

Even though I've tried not to dwell on it, I've been thinking about Mirabelle and Joshua. We left them behind, and if their Giving Ceremonies went as planned, they've met the same fate as Amelia.

I'm not sure if there's anything I could've done differently, but the weight of their deaths is heavy on my shoulders. It's one thing to know the Given are being killed, but it's another to have names and faces to put to them.

Still, we should be careful talking about this in the open. My eyes sweep across the River Market, checking for nearby soldiers. I don't see any, but that doesn't mean they aren't here. These days, Watchers are everywhere.

By the time my gaze has returned to the merchant, Kadyn has placed an order for four skewers, two for each of us. He pays with a silver coin. Once the merchant squeezes lemon over the top, we take our food and find an empty bench overlooking the water.

I'm not the biggest fan of fish, especially for breakfast, but at least it's not jerky. I take a small bite of the roasted fish, pleasantly surprised to find that it's delicious. The fish is strongly spiced, but the lemon complements the flavors perfectly. I gobble it up quickly, my belly delighted by the warm meal.

Neither of us speaks until our skewers are empty. The silence between us isn't heavy, but I can tell Kadyn has something on his mind. When we're done, he leans forward and rests his elbows on his knees. He stares pensively at the water.

"The day my brother, Kaleb, was Given, I woke up with the strongest sense that something was off." Kadyn's pained voice is quiet, and I strain to hear him over the sounds of the morning market. "Like me, he'd been at the Giving Festival the day before, and he spent the night in the garden. Communing with the *gods*."

Kadyn curls his fist, and his chest heaves. Several moments pass in silence before he continues.

"It was wrong, but that morning, I snuck out of my house. Even though I wasn't supposed to, I went to the Moran Gardens. I snuck past the Watchers and crept inside the tent. I spoke to Kaleb before they took him."

He shudders. For a long moment, we sit and listen as the water rhythmically hits the sides of the dock.

"He didn't . . . I told him I felt like something was off and begged him to run away, but he didn't listen to me," Kadyn chokes out. He opens his palms, tracing the lines of his left hand. "He was Given that same day."

My heart constricts at the pain in his words, and I shake my head.

"I'm sorry." The words sound inadequate, even to my own ears, and I place my hand on his arm. "Truly, Kadyn, I wish things had gone differently for you."

I lost Amelia, but he lost his brother.

Kadyn looks up, his eyes shimmering beneath the shadows of his hood. "Being gods-blessed is a curse."

I inhale sharply. "I know."

How many times have I thought that exact same thing? Suns save me, but I know that all too well.

"My parents only had two children, and we were both born with Marks. Everyone in Mora called us blessed, but how can the Mark be a good thing when it stole my mother's sons?"

He drops his head, raking his hands through his hair beneath his hood. His shoulders shake, and my heart cracks at the sight.

"Ma wept for a year after Kaleb was Given," he says, staring at the ground. "Every single day, she sobbed. I had to stand by and watch her cry for the son she would never see again, knowing that in a decade, those same tears would flow for me. That she would weep for me as much as she did him."

His muscles tense beneath my touch, and I shift closer to him. "Kadyn, I—"

He turns to me, his eyes hard. He grits his teeth, and a vein pulses in his jaw. Grief morphs into anger.

"Every time we went to the temples, she searched for him. Every time we traveled to another city, she wondered if he was there, serving the gods. Ma wasted years trying to catch a glimpse of the son she lost, and now . . . now I find out it's all a lie. He's been dead the whole time."

Visions of a pink light followed by blood pouring from Amelia's neck flash through my mind. I draw in a stuttering breath, shaking my head.

"I know." An amorous young couple walks by, trading kisses, and I shut my mouth, waiting for them to pass before I turn back to Kadyn. "I don't know why they do this to the Given."

Why kill everyone with a Mark?

"Neither do I." Kadyn's voice is quiet. Resigned. "But there has to be a reason. Maybe when we save your sisters, we'll learn why they're doing this."

"Maybe," I whisper, twisting Amelia's bracelet around my wrist.

There are so many unknowns. So many things I don't understand. It boggles my mind to think that, not long ago, I thought the Giving was something to look forward to. Now, I can't imagine looking forward to anything ever again.

Life in the market continues around us. A young mother who can't be much older than me walks past with her son, holding his hand as he toddles beside her. A sailor carrying a line full of fish hurries by, calling out into the crowd. Two older men laugh as they hobble past, leaning on canes and smiling as they reminisce about the past.

They're all just living like this is any other day. And to them, it is. They're unmarked, blissfully unaware of the horrors Kadyn and I are running from.

It isn't fucking fair, but if there's one thing I've learned, it's that fairness, like the Giving, is a lie.

Some people are destined to have a nice, easy life. Those people see the light easily. I bet they can laugh at a moment's notice, and they find joy in everything.

Then there are others, like Kadyn and me. People whose lives revolve around darkness.

The Marks we bear mean that we will never know a simple life.

The gods-blessed are doomed to darkness, a life where we are different from the moment we leave the safety of the womb.

The Given may stick together, but ours isn't an easy path.

I'm not sure how long we sit there, the weight of everything that's happening to us pushing us both down, before a flicker of movement in the corner of my eye catches my attention. At first, it's so quick that I'm not sure I see it. But then, it appears again. And this time . . .

This time, I know it's real.

Standing several dozen feet away, looking in the other direction, is a man taller than most others in the market.

It doesn't matter that his back is to me. I'd recognize that hair anywhere. It's been haunting my dreams, and now, my reality.

My chest tightens, and my empty skewers clatter to the ground, forgotten.

"Fuck," I breathe, tugging my hood further over my head. "The Hunter is here."

27

MAY THE SUNS KEEP YOU SAFE

Wren

Kadyn's head whips towards me, his eyes wide beneath his hood. He jolts and jumps to his feet. "What?"

His voice is far too loud, and I shush him.

I knew it. I knew the Hunter was still pursuing me, even after I begged him to leave me alone.

Maybe I should've let Gabriel die.

My Mark seems to pulse on my forehead at the thought, but that can't be right. The glow is nothing new. I've been dealing with it for almost a year, but pulsing? That's never happened before.

My fingers itch with the urge to reach up and trace the swirl, but I clench my hands. Touching my Mark would be far too suspicious. I need to avoid attention, not draw it towards me.

"Over there." Trying to be nonchalant—I'm not sure it's working—I tilt my head in the direction I just saw Gabriel. "We need to leave."

I stand, my skewers long forgotten. That's when I notice that the salty air in the River Market has shifted.

No longer is it light, filled with the hustle and bustle of people living their regular lives. Now, it's tense. Thick.

Dangerous.

Inhaling as deep as I can manage—which isn't much, thanks to the panic squeezing my chest—I slowly scan the area for the source of the shift. The merchants remain at their stalls; the fishermen are still bringing in their loaded nets, but now . . .

Now the Watchers are here. No longer hidden, they're standing out in the open. They're not alone.

I count six Enforcers, the red sigils on their chests marking them as the special brand of the king's soldiers employed to punish lawbreakers.

People like Kadyn and me.

Oh, suns. I sip air, trying to remain calm, but it isn't working. Gabriel is here, and he's brought Watchers and Enforcers with him.

Spending time in the River Market seemed like a good idea before, but now I'm noticing how enclosed it is. With the Salt River on one side and buildings on the other, there aren't many places to run and hide.

Instinctively, I duck my head. Grabbing the edge of Kadyn's cloak, I draw him close. "We need to split up and get out of here."

We're going to draw too much attention if we remain together. The chill from this morning has worn off, and the day is warming up. Our cloaks are bound to stand out. One person wearing a hood on a hot day is odd, but two practically screams *Look at me!*

Thank the suns, Kadyn doesn't argue. He nods and reaches into his cloak, grabbing some coins.

"Take these; you might need them." He presses the money into my palm. "I'll meet you at the stable tonight. You remember how to get back there?"

"Yes." And honestly, even if I didn't, it wouldn't matter. We need to move.

The Watchers and Enforcers worry me, but it's the Hunter's presence that has cold sweat gathering on the back of my neck.

What will Gabriel do if he finds me? How angry is he that I almost killed him? What if . . . what if he returns the favor? What if I never make it to our meeting place because Gabriel gets to me first?

"Wait." My heart hammers as I pull Kadyn in for a hug.

We haven't known each other for long, but between our Marks and everything he shared with me about his family, I feel a kinship with him.

"What's wrong?" he asks, hugging me back.

We don't have much time, but the Hunter's presence has my paranoia rearing its ugly head. Thoughts of dying cloud my mind, but I don't want to split up without saying this.

"If something happens to me and I don't make it to the stables tonight, don't wait for me." My chest tightens. "Run as fast as you can and do whatever it takes to get out of Myreth."

Live.

For me. For Amelia. For his brother. For all of us who are born with a damned Mark fating us to die.

It's not that I don't want to live, too. It's just that I don't know if I'll make it out of this city. Not with Gabriel here.

If he kills me, at least I'll die knowing that I did something good with my freedom. I might not have been able to save the twins, but I saved Kadyn.

That counts for something, right?

Kadyn squeezes me before stepping back and making a religious gesture across his chest. "May the suns light your path and keep you safe, Wren."

Once, a benediction like that would've warmed my soul. Now, it just reminds me of all the ways things have gone wrong.

"And you, as well," I return the benediction. "Be safe, Kadyn."

Assuring me he will do that, he makes me promise to do the same. I give him my word, even though I don't think it's up to me. Someone seems to have it out for me.

Kadyn studies me for another moment before he dips his head and walks away. He passes a pair of Watchers, disappearing into the crowd.

Once he's gone, I turn and walk in the other direction. Keeping Kadyn's coins firmly in my grasp, I head towards the exit.

Be calm. Be relaxed. Be normal.

The words cycle through my mind, and I try to embody them. It doesn't feel like it's working, though. The back of my neck burns, and it feels like everyone is looking at me.

The thing is, as much as I want to be, I'm not normal. My otherness is as much a part of me as my indigo hair or my curves.

It's in every twitch of my fingers, every ragged inhale, every step I take, every glow of the Mark beneath my hood.

This time, I don't notice the shoppers, the vendors, or the fishermen. All I can think about is my freedom and whether the king's soldiers will rip it out of my grasp.

My fingers grow slippery around the coins, and the knots in my stomach tighten to the point of pain.

Don't attract attention.

The words are a reminder to be careful as I leave the River Market behind. The sound of wood creaking fills the air as I turn a corner. My eyes widen at the sight of a decaying body hanging from the gallows next to an empty pillory. The body is unrecognizable where it hangs, swaying gently in the morning wind.

I shudder. Judging by their decaying flesh and the crows feasting on their body, they've been there for a while. A thief's brand is still visible on their neck, a permanent marker of their crime.

I plug my nose, abandoning my slow pace and scurrying past the hanging thief. No one would question why someone doesn't want to linger in the face of death.

The next street is lined with shops on both sides. There are fewer people here, but it's still busy.

I never thought I'd yearn for the emptiness of the endless forests, where it's just me and the countless trees, but here I am. Between this and the Giving Festival in Mora, I'm seriously considering taking up a life of solitude.

Once I save my sisters.

My thoughts are so loud, and my panic is so complete that I only pick up snippets of conversations as I hurry past clusters of people. Some are innocuous, but others have my blood chilling.

"There's a new curfew . . ."

"Jack and the other Watchers are working double shifts from now till the end of the Giving Season. No one knows . . ."

Two women are walking down the steps of a white temple. Larger than the one at home, Esyn's holy space sends shivers down my spine. Not wanting to linger near the goddess who abandoned me and demanded Amelia's lifeblood, I race around the corner.

An old, bearded man wearing rags is standing on a crate in the middle of the street. A small crowd surrounds him.

"Lies!" he shouts. "It's all lies."

The man's voice is hoarse, and he's little more than skin and bones. I press myself against a wall, and my breath catches. Does he . . . does he know the truth?

"The Blessed and the Inherited are being killed! This is why we've lost the gods' favor. Everyone thinks the gods are good, but—"

A pair of hands violently wrench the man down from the square. Horror fills me as a Watcher unsheathes his sword and slams the pommel over the man's head. Blood pours from the wound as he falls silent, and the Watchers drag his limp, unconscious body behind them.

A third soldier stands on the crate.

"Get out of here!" he shouts. "This man is insane, and he will suffer King Andreas's wrath for disturbing the peace."

The crowd disperses, running in every direction. I do the same, racing down the first street on my right. I'm so busy running—again—that I don't pay attention as I take the next corner.

It turns out to be a suns-damned mistake.

Another pair of Watchers are standing on the sidewalk, huddled over a stack of parchment. They're so close that I can see the scruff on the taller one's jaw.

"Wren Nightingale," says the clean-shaven Watcher, slapping what appears to be a poster on the nearby wall. "Suspected to be traveling with another gods-blessed . . ."

My ears start ringing, and the rest of his words don't register. His partner murmurs something inaudible as he studies the portrait—the fucking Wanted ad—with *my* name, sketched likeness, and a damned reward printed on it.

Oh, suns.

It's one thing to be an outlaw because I broke the Giving Agreement, but this? I never imagined it would come to this. At least, not before I left the country.

Now, *everyone* will know who I am. What I am. I won't be able to trust anyone because the reward listed for my return to the temples before the end of the Giving Season is astronomical.

I knew the Hunters were aware of my disappearance since I'd seen Gabriel's piece of paper with my information on it. But this? This is a whole new level of danger.

I don't have time to consider why there's a Wanted ad for me, nor do I have time to think about what it means for my family, because the clean-shaven Watcher looks up. His brown eyes scan the street, and then they rest on me.

It's like the air is sucked out of my lungs. For the longest moment, time seems to stand still.

This is it. The moment of my capture. It feels like I've been running for years, even though it's been less than a month, but it's all about to come to an end now.

Except, this can't be the end. The king has the twins, and I don't know what he wants with them. What will happen to them if I don't help them? They need me.

I don't wait for a flash of recognition to spark in the Watcher's gaze or for him to shout at me to stop moving. Dropping my eyes to the sidewalk, I spin and walk away from the soldiers as nonchalantly as possible.

Panic is on the edge of my mind, but I refuse to let it take hold of me. I need to stay calm.

A shop with a wooden form wearing a dress in the window is on my right, and my eyes widen. Now, more than ever, I need to change into some less recognizable clothing. I push open the door. A bell rings above my head as I step inside, and I sweep my gaze over the shop.

Bolts of colorful fabric line the walls. Several other headless wooden bodies stand near the front door, joining the first one I noticed. They're elegantly dressed, displaying what I'm assuming are the latest women's fashions in Saltwater. There are dresses, loose pants, flowy tunics, and sweaters belted around the middle. There's every color imaginable, as if someone pulled a rainbow out of the sky and infused it into these fabrics.

The shopkeeper is behind a wooden counter, smiling welcomingly at me. Her brilliant red hair is in a bun on top of her head, and her relaxed air has the tiniest bit of tension leaving my shoulders.

"Good morning," she says, straightening some papers on the counter. "How can I help you?"

"I'm just looking for a new outfit." I head over to the closest shelf, doing my best impression of an unmarked shopper as I browse the available goods.

The shopkeeper must not have seen the Watchers' posters yet, because she doesn't seem alarmed by my presence. Thanking the suns for small mercies, I grab a pair of pants and a loose cream tunic. The materials are soft beneath my fingers. Suddenly, all I can think about is getting out of Mother's old dress and into these.

Smiling from beneath my hood, I approach the counter. "I'll take these, please. How much are they?"

She names her price, and I count out the coins. Once I've paid, she directs me to a small, curtained-off area in the back of the shop where I can change. As I head to the back, I notice a pitcher of water and a cloth sitting on a counter. The woman has her back to me, so I grab those and slip into the changing room, rejoicing in my find.

I pull the curtain shut, placing the pitcher on a small table before unclasping my cloak and sliding my satchel over my head. Every second is precious, but I don't want to leave behind one of my only belongings tying me to my family without a memento. Especially not when I don't know if I'll ever see my family again.

Taking the dress off quickly, I grab my knife and slice through the blue fabric with a gentle *rip*, cutting a rough square. The scrap goes in my satchel before I ball Mother's dress up and put it in the waste bin.

I hurriedly pour water into the bowl, using the cloth to wash my body as best I can. Even without soap, I feel infinitely cleaner by the time I pull my new tunic over my head.

It boasts three-quarter sleeves and forest green embellishments along the collar and arms. I tie a belt under my breasts and slide on the pants. They're a little long, but once I roll them around the waist and belt them, they fit.

Lovely. The sensation of being clean cannot be overrated. My lips tug up into a half smile as I attach Father's knife to my belt before grabbing my bag and cloak. I replace my hood, making sure my forehead is covered, before stepping back into my boots and lacing them up. I'm about to pull back the curtain when the bell above the door rings. Beads of sweat form on my forehead as two sets of heavy footsteps enter the shop.

"Greetings, gentlemen," the shopkeeper says. Is she speaking louder than before? "How can I help you today?"

There's a crinkling sound, like a piece of paper being smoothed out, and then a man asks, "Have you seen this woman?"

Shit. I peer out, my eyes widening. The Watchers from the street are here. Gods-damn it.

Changing my plans on the fly, I slip out of the changing space. A thin wall separates it from the rest of the space, and I stay behind it, racing towards the back door.

It leads into an alley, and I slip outside, careful not to let the door slam shut behind me. I turn right, not really paying attention to where I'm going. All I know is that I have to put space between me and the guards.

Several minutes pass as I run through alleys and down side streets. I keep going until I'm sure that I've lost them. My hood is still on, which feels like a miracle, and I don't see anyone.

I slow, taking my first deep breaths since the Watchers walked into the dress shop, and press my hand against my hip. A cramp is starting to form.

Gods above, I fucking hate exercise.

Sagging against a brick wall, I shut my eyes. Wiping a hand across my brow, I breathe in deeply. Okay. That was far too close of a call. I'll need to be more careful for the rest of the day until it's time to meet up with Kadyn again.

Thank the suns, I was able to—

A hand slaps against my mouth, and another grabs my arm painfully.

"What's a pretty little thing like you doing out here?" a low, accented voice growls.

A scream rises in my throat, and my eyes fly open.

Three men who smell of salt and sweat are crowding me against the wall. There's a dark glimmer in their eyes. They aren't here to comment on how lovely my new tunic looks.

Each of the men is armed with long knives that taper off to a very sharp end, like the fishermen at the docks.

I curse, trying to yank my arm out of the constricting grip. The hand holding me gets tighter.

"Aren't we lucky, boys?" the one with his hand against my mouth asks.

I scream into his hand and try to bite him, but he digs his fingers into my cheek.

"Very lucky. Who knew this pretty thing would be waiting for us when we docked today?"

This comes from the man on the left. He steps forward, running his filthy fingers down the side of my face and neck, stopping at the collar of my new tunic. His touch is nothing like Gabriel's. There are no sparks here. No tension. Just pure, frigid terror.

No, no, no.

I fight against their grip, but it just makes things worse. I kick and pull and scream, but nothing is working.

Angry tears prick at my eyes. This can't be happening.

"Thanks be to Nyna for her many gifts," says the third, referencing Esyn's youngest sister, the goddess of the sea. He continues, making a lewd remark I wish I could wash from my mind forever, and the sailors laugh.

Scum. Only the lowest of the low find joy in what these men plan on doing.

They're still laughing, making crude jokes that have bile rising in my throat. They must not think I'm a threat because the hand holding my mouth has loosened a fraction.

Taking advantage of their momentary distraction, I snake my free hand into my cloak. My fingers wrap around the hilt of Father's knife. I draw it out of the sheath, preparing to stab the man in front of me.

I might not know much about weapons, but I've been around my brothers enough to know that if a knee to the balls hurts, a knife has to inflict greater damage.

I just have to—

"Sneaky little bitch, aren't you?" Fingernails grip my jaw, squishing my features together. Cold fingers wrench the knife from my grip.

Horror fills me as my blade clatters on the cobblestones.

Burning suns, no. If there ever was a god who cared about me, this would be their moment to help me.

Please, I pray desperately. *Somebody, help me.*

No one comes. Of course.

The tremors I tried to suppress earlier race through me as the sailors laugh again. Their mirth sounds like darkness personified.

Hands trace my skin above my tunic, dipping lower and lower. I struggle and kick, desperately trying to break their hold. My efforts only seem to act as fuel to their cruel fire.

I never should've left Kadyn's side. I should have stayed out in the open, where things like this don't happen as easily.

But it's too late for regrets, too late for things that I should've done.

Someone grabs a lock of my hair and pulls. I yelp, pain running through my scalp. Another hand reaches up and tugs on my hood before roughly yanking it back.

No.

A ringing fills my ears as the men pause, their gazes locked on my forehead.

Two weeks. That's all that stands between me and the Winter's Eve Ball, marking the end of the Giving Season.

I've stayed hidden for so long, but now . . .

Now my secret is out, and these men are going to . . . They want to . . .

They laugh, their voices mingling together as panic forms a haze over my mind.

"I've never tasted a gods-blessed."

A dark chuckle. "Nyna has blessed us indeed."

"I get her first."

They keep laughing, keep touching me, and I keep struggling against their holds. No matter what I do, I can't seem to break free.

An angry tear slides down my cheek. I've always wondered what fate could be worse than death, and I fear I've discovered it.

The sailor in front of me leans in so close that I can make out the silver scar slashed across his cheek. His eyes shimmer with violence and lust, and my stomach twists.

The evil man's breath brushes over my cheek, and for a moment, I wonder if he'll try to kiss me.

I'll bite his fucking mouth if he does.

"We're going to have so much fun with you, little gods-blessed . . ."

His words end in a bloody gurgle as the life drains from his eyes. I look down in confusion, my eyes widening at the steel sticking out of the sailor's neck.

Then, the blade is gone. The man falls to the ground, dead.

And I'm staring into the Hunter's emerald eyes.

28

THE LITTLE BIRD IS MINE

Gabriel

Death has always come naturally to me. Perhaps it's because of my upbringing, or perhaps it's my father's blood coursing through my veins.

Either way, these sailors are no match for me. It doesn't matter that I've lost the element of surprise, because they'll be dead in minutes.

There's a ring of metal being drawn behind me. I turn around to find the taller of the two remaining seafarers gripping a fisherman's knife in his scarred palm.

I smirk, and my bond with Mist awakens. I feel her curiosity as I tug on our bond three times, a signal we've used many times over the years. Knowing my familiar understands what I'm asking of her, I swing my sword through the air. My blade sings as I meet the sailor's attack head-on. He grunts, and I spin out of the way.

Death is a dance, and this man is not my equal. We spar for a few minutes before I turn on my heels. I slam the tip of my blade through his back. It sinks through skin, bone, and then his heart.

The man falls to the ground with a thump, and I pull my blade from him. A muffled cry comes from my left. The sound calls to me like a rope tugging in my stomach, and I can't ignore it. I snarl, twisting around.

The last sailor is holding the little bird against him, her back to his chest. One of his dirt-covered hands is clasped over Wren's mouth, and the other is digging the tip of his knife into her throat. Her hair is disheveled, and her Mark is a pulsing blue swirl on her forehead.

Wide violet eyes filled with panic meet mine, and her nostrils flare as she trembles.

"Stop moving, bitch." The seafarer must have a death wish because he nicks her throat.

Red beads above the blade, and Wren whimpers. The sight of her blood has my lips curling and my heart thundering in my chest.

Rage courses through me, a wave of anger unlike anything I've ever felt. All-consuming, it's the only thing I can think about.

Why? Why am I reacting like this? Why does every part of me want to roar at the sight of her in danger? Why does it feel like my heart has been ripped out of my chest and is about to be destroyed?

I'm not sure. All I know is I was tracking the little bird after she fled the River Market, and when I found her, three horrid men were pawing at her. Touching her as if they owned her. How fucking dare they?

She was struggling, trying to get away, and they were holding her against her will.

I acted on instinct, drawing my sword and driving it through the first man's throat. He was far too close to my Given, and I couldn't let him touch her.

And now this asshole has his hands on her.

As if she's his. As if he thinks he can do with her as he wishes.

He's dragging her back, his dagger still at her throat.

"Don't come any closer," the soon-to-be-dead man snarls.

I meet his gaze, my stomach twisting at the promise of death glinting back at me. Tightening my grip on my sword, I growl, "Release her."

In direct opposition to my command, he draws her closer to him. She gasps against his hand, the sound an arrow to my heart.

He takes one step back, then another. Wren is forced to move with him lest the knife dig deeper into her neck. Another bead of blood rolls down the column of her throat, and a snarl rumbles through me.

A sense of possessiveness I've never felt urges me forward, and my bond with Mist thrums frantically.

There's no time to question my emotions or wonder why this gods-blessed is making me feel this way.

"She's *mine*," I growl, not taking my eyes off the sailor.

My little bird. My prey.

How dare he try to take her from me? I didn't track her from the forests outside Grenbloom to Saltwater just to watch her die.

Especially not after my unpleasant encounter with the king.

That's probably why I feel unnaturally possessive of her. My father's demands have put me on edge.

He smirks, dragging Wren away. "You come any closer, and I'll slit her lovely throat. She'll bleed out before you get here."

Wren whimpers again, and a tear slides down her cheek. I've never hated the sight of someone else's pain more than I do at this moment.

Comforting words rise to the tip of my tongue, and I want to tell her it'll be all right. I won't leave her with this man who so clearly thinks he's won.

But there's no time. A flash of black further down the alley catches my eye, and the corner of my lips quirks upwards.

"You could try," I tell the dead man walking, needing to distract him for a moment longer. "But you have a slight problem."

He growls. "I don't know what kind of games—"

A feline snarl cuts him off, and I arch a brow. "No games, but I'm afraid you forgot to look behind you."

The sailor's eyes widen, and he follows my gaze over his shoulder. He yelps in surprise, but it's too late.

Mist leaps off a crate, sailing through the air with a vicious snarl. The predatory sound echoes through the alley, a warning to everyone with ears.

Death is here, and she is fierce. Mist lands on the sailor's back, and he screams as her claws dig into his mortal flesh.

Taking advantage of the distraction, I run and grab Wren's arm with my free hand, pulling her away from her attacker.

Thank the gods, Mist came with me into Saltwater. The king's visit spooked me, and now I won't risk going anywhere without my familiar. It's those damned nightmares—my father's "warnings."

Each time I wake, I feel for my bond with Mist, needing to reassure myself it's still there. It is, but the relief I feel is diminishing with each passing day.

A pained yell fills the air as Mist rips open the man's back. The sound is cut off as she turns his throat to ribbons. Perhaps I should feel bad that the asshole is about to die a painful death, but since he was about to hurt my little bird, I find myself hoping he suffers before Mist sends him to the Underworld.

Leaving Mist to her meal, I pull Wren away from the dying man.

"Come," I command.

She's compliant, for once. The action is so far out of character that I know she's in shock from the attack.

That knowledge has me moving faster as I lead Wren around a corner, away from the dead men. This alley is darker than the last, cast in shadows by the tall buildings rising above us, and it's secluded.

Tucked away from the hustle and bustle of Saltwater, I return my attention to the little bird. Her chest is heaving, and her eyes close as she draws deep gulps of air.

"Did they hurt you?" I ask, my voice rough as I look her over, searching for injuries. "Before I . . . Did they touch you?"

This question is all that matters right now, all I can focus on. Spots of blood mar the column of her throat, a reminder of the fate I narrowly saved her from.

Violet eyes open and meet mine, as if she's trying to understand why I'm asking her these questions. Why I care. To be honest, I don't know the answer. All I know is I'm pulled towards her, and I'm too relieved to have found her to keep fighting against it.

Seconds pass, each longer than the last. She still hasn't spoken.

"Did they?" The words escape me on a growl.

Burning suns, if they hurt her, I will find a way to travel to the Underworld and make them pay for what they did. I will rip them apart. They will suffer for an eternity. No amount of pain would be sufficient if they hurt her.

"I . . . they wanted to, but . . . no," she says, her eyes locked on mine.

I wasn't too late.

I stagger back a step, exhaling. Thank Esyn, I got there in time.

My next breath comes more easily, but I still don't let go of Wren. I can't.

Now that I'm touching her again, I'm not sure I'll ever be able to let her go. That strange sense of possessiveness is still coursing through me, and I'm filled with the strangest urge to make sure she stays safe.

Those thoughts are confusing, so I shift my attention to the wrist I'm holding. It's so much smaller than mine. Her skin is unblemished, lacking the scars and callouses I carry on my flesh.

My fingers circle her wrist, and if I wanted to, I could break her easily.

I don't want to, though. In fact, if there's something I learned watching those men handle her so roughly, it's that seeing her broken might break *me.*

What the fuck is happening to me?

I swipe my thumb across her pulse, and it flutters like wings flapping beneath my touch.

So soft. So fragile.

She hitches a breath and tries to take a step back. "Hunter—"

"Don't say it," I breathe, interrupting her.

This moment is like glass—one wrong move, and it will shatter. I'm not ready for that. I don't think I'll ever be ready for that.

I don't want her to tell me to stop any more than I want to look up and see her glowing Mark reminding me that I'm hunting her. I'm not ready to go back to what we were.

Right now, we aren't predator and prey or Hunter and Given.

At this moment, it's just the two of us, and it's *good.* Fear and nightmares and glowing Marks have no place here.

She steps back, but I don't let go. She's caught between me and the brick wall. There is nothing else. Just me, her, and this damn pull that I've felt since we met.

"Gabriel," she tries again, her pulse fluttering beneath me.

Gods. The sound of my name on her lips, the way she forms those syllables, has me closing the distance between us and leaning over her. My breath brushes over her forehead, and my heart pounds with the knowledge that her kissable lips are inches from mine.

I could claim her in a heartbeat.

"No," I whisper. "Not yet. Don't speak yet."

We can't ignore the barriers between us forever, but for now . . .

Holding her gaze, I slide my sword into its sheath before resting my hand on the wall above her head. I'm not gripping her wrist tightly, and she could break my hold if she wanted to, but she doesn't. She stares up at me, her breath catching and her cheeks reddening beneath my gaze.

Everything else seems to fade away. In this singular moment of time, there is nothing in this world but the two of us: the bastard son of the king and the captivatingly beautiful woman he's drawn to.

My eyes sweep over Wren, committing every part of her to memory. Her bright eyes, sharp cheekbones, and brilliant curls that shimmer when she's in the sunlight. She's changed. Her pale blue dress has been replaced by a curve-hugging cream tunic and trousers that make me imagine what bedding her would be like.

My feet draw me closer to her. I can't help it. Asking me not to be in her space right now would be like asking me not to breathe.

Gods-damned impossible.

Her heart rate picks up, her pulse beneath my thumb flapping like wings. She really is a little bird, and one wrong word will have her flying away from me.

My chest tightens at the thought. This moment can't shatter. Not yet. Maybe not ever.

I move even closer, lowering my head. Every movement is slow and controlled, giving her time to react. To yell at me. To say something.

Wren doesn't pull away, though. Her lips part, and she breathes my name.

My heart thunders and every part of me wants to draw her closer. Long, eternal moments pass as we remain frozen and sharing the same air.

I want to kiss her, claim her, and make her mine. I want to take her so thoroughly that no one would ever question who she belonged to.

I want her in ways that don't make sense.

It feels like we've been standing there for hours, although it's likely only been a few seconds. I wish I could freeze this moment and we could stay here forever, but we can't.

Time is no one's friend, least of all mine, and all too soon, a horn is blown somewhere in the city. The call for sailors to return to their boats shatters the moment, and Wren sucks in a breath.

"You . . . you saved me." Her brows furrow, and an insane part of me wants to lift my thumb and press out the crease. "They were going to . . . but you stopped them."

"I did," I say through clenched teeth, the mention of the fate she barely avoided sending fire running through my veins. Thank Esyn, I got here in time.

"The panther . . . It's yours?"

I nod.

"And you saved me." She seems stuck on that. "Why? Why would you do that? Why not let them take what they wanted and kill me?"

Why, indeed? It's a good fucking question, and I don't know the answer.

All I know is that when I saw Wren in the River Market this morning, it felt like a missing piece was settling in my soul. Like I could breathe again now that I'd seen her.

I've never felt this way about anyone before, least of all my prey.

Nothing else had mattered in that moment—not the nightmares about broken bonds and eternal emptiness and not the fact that my father's words have been haunting me since he made his unwelcome appearance.

All that mattered was that she was here and so was I.

I'm not sure what's happening to me. To us. Does she feel the pull, too? I want to ask, but I'm not sure I'm ready for her answer.

Instead, I tell her the truth. "I couldn't let them hurt you."

My voice is quiet, and my words hang in the air between us. Wren's Mark seems to glow brighter on her forehead, drawing my attention.

Gods, that thing is a fucking torch, even in the middle of the day. At night, it must be visible for miles. How has she made it this far without attracting attention?

She must notice the direction of my gaze because she reaches up, pulling her hood over her forehead.

"I see." Her tone makes it clear she doesn't really understand.

Well, that makes two of us.

An eagle caws above us, and my back tightens. I raise my eyes, searching for the king's red-eyed familiar, but there's nothing but blue sky.

When I lower my gaze, clarity has entered Wren's eyes. I hate it almost as much as I hate waking up feeling empty after nightmares from the king.

"Birdie," I murmur, trying to prolong this moment between us. Can't we ignore everything else for a few more minutes?

She stiffens in my grip and tries to pull away.

"You're a Hunter."

I can't deny it. The truth of what I am is as plain as the swirl on her head. "Yes."

The air grows heavier with each passing moment. My heart is a booming drum, echoing in my ears.

She licks her lips. "Are you still hunting me?"

I exhale, squeezing my eyes shut. It's just a moment, but it's long enough for the king's final words to echo through my mind.

Bring me Wren Nightingale, Gabriel.

Even though it pains me, even though it feels like my heart is inexplicably breaking as I open my mouth, I admit, "Yes." I remove my hand from the wall above her head. "But—"

Her face hardens, and I can sense her building walls between us, shutting me out.

"Let me go," she says, shoving my chest. "Just pretend like this didn't happen."

"I can't. The king won't allow it."

An almost frantic look appears in her eyes as she shakes her head. "The king isn't here. He doesn't have to know."

Naïve words from someone who's never met my father or felt the sting of his whip slashing across their back.

"He would know," I say grimly.

Somehow, the king knows nearly everything. I've learned a hard truth over the years: Esyn blessed my father with immeasurable magic. The queen and my half brother both have power, but theirs pale in comparison to his.

I've seen him level buildings with a thought, suffocate a row of convicted felons with a clench of his fist, and ruin lives with the flick of his wrist.

"Please," she whispers, the desperation in her voice a knife to my heart.

I wish I had another answer. I wish I weren't a Hunter. I wish we weren't destined to be enemies.

My next words break my heart. "I can't."

Most people would give up at this point. Suns, most people would've given up days ago, but not her. The little bird is tenacious and stubborn as hell, which is equally gods-damned infuriating and attractive.

"I saved your life," she bargains. "I could've let you die in Mora, but I didn't. I gave you the antidote. Doesn't that mean anything to you?"

"You only had the antidote because you're the one who drugged me in the first place."

Instead of showing remorse, she lifts her chin. "You were asking for it."

"Excuse me?" I sputter, my fingers flexing. "I was just doing my job."

"I told you, I don't want to be Given." Whatever softness had been in her voice has vanished.

This again. I don't understand why she's running. Raking my hand through my hair, I shake my head.

"Why not?" I ask. "Is it really worth all of this? Being hunted for the rest of your days? What's so bad about serving the gods?"

Wren stares at me as if I asked her whether the sky is blue. As if *I'm* the one defying logic by running from my fate.

"Of course it's worth it," she says incredulously. "I don't want to *die.*"

Die?

My brows knit. I have the vaguest recollection of her saying something similar when she drugged me, but I thought I'd dreamed it.

"What the fuck are you talking about, Birdie? You're Marked to the Given. It's not like I'm bringing you to the executioner's block."

At least then, I'd understand why she's fighting me so hard on this.

That violet gaze sharpens, and she stares at me as if I'm a puzzle she's trying hard to solve. Then she does the strangest thing.

She *laughs.*

The melodic sound is like the first birdsong after a long storm, and it stirs deep in my soul. Her laugh is beautiful and entrancing. I want to hear it every day for the rest of my life.

She yanks her arm out of my grasp, and I'm so enthralled by the sound of her laugh, I let her go. She doesn't go far, standing a few feet away from me.

"Suns, have mercy on my soul," she gasps out between heaving laughs, gripping her sides while staring at me in disbelief. "You don't know."

I suck in a breath and hesitate for a moment before asking, "Know what?"

She takes a step back, her gaze never leaving mine. "Of course you don't. It makes so much fucking sense now."

The last part is muttered, as if she's speaking to herself. What is she talking about?

I move towards her. She steps back again.

The distance between us is making my heart ache.

"I'm going to need you to explain what's going on here, Wren."

Her mirth dries up, and something dark flickers through her gaze. "Let me guess, *Gabriel*." This time, when she says my name, there's no warmth. Nothing that draws me to her. Her voice is pure steel. "You think the gods-blessed are sent to work in the temples once they're Given."

The hardness in her voice sets me on edge, and Mist appears in the corner of my vision. I raise a hand, signaling for my familiar to stay back as I stare at Wren.

Even with her hood on, I can make out the faint blue glow of her Mark. She's destined for the gods . . . isn't she? A few minutes ago, I would've said yes, but now . . . now I'm not sure.

"Of course they are. Everyone knows Marked Ones are fated to work for the gods." It's one of the first lessons children are taught.

"No. They're killed," she says matter-of-factly.

"What?" The word bursts out of me. "No."

Has she lost her mind? Is that why she's running so hard?

"Yes." She holds my gaze, and I stare into her violet eyes, searching for a hint that she's lying. There isn't one.

In her mind, this is the truth.

I step towards Wren, trying to reason with her. "That's not true. The priests and priestesses are Marked—"

"Those Marks are fake, Gabriel," she interrupts me, her voice hard. "Stickers."

"I . . . What?" I can barely form words, barely comprehend what she's saying.

"Think, Hunter. Really think about it. When was the last time you saw a glowing Mark on a gods-blessed older than twenty?"

She takes another step back from me, and this time, I don't mirror her movements. I'm too focused on her question, too focused on running every single visit to the temple through my mind. Because . . . what the actual fuck?

She's right.

In all my years and all my journeys through Myreth, I can't recall ever seeing a glowing Mark on a gods-blessed past their second decade of life.

It's odd because even though my father's a bloodthirsty tyrant who rules with an iron fist, he's also strangely obsessed with the deities. I've been in dozens of temples, and even though I've seen the workers' Marks, they've been brief glimpses. None of them have prominent Marks like Wren.

Could they really be fakes?

My stomach spins with the implications of what she's saying, and my mouth dries. "But . . ."

"Think," she urges me, her voice tense. "Have you seen one?"

My lungs tighten, and my fingers twitch at my sides. My bond with Mist strums frantically in my chest, and her concern fills me. I shove it away, desperately trying to understand what Wren is saying.

They're killed.

The little bird's voice echoes through my mind, and I tug on my hair. How can this be?

The Giving Season's existence can be traced back to the foundation of Myreth. The festivals, the honor the gods-blessed receive, and the lore in our culture are all centuries old.

If Wren is telling the truth, this would have to be the most elaborate ruse ever spun. People would have to be in on this, carefully crafting the lies from the inside.

The enormity of this situation is staggering.

Hours go by, or maybe minutes, before Wren pulls back her hood and points to her glowing Mark.

"You haven't seen a real gods-blessed in the temples," she says softly, her voice strangely calm. "The Marks they wear are fakes, just like the ones in the Giving Festival."

She keeps saying that, but how can it be true? "Wren—"

"You know I'm right, Hunter." Pity flickers through her eyes as if she knows she's peeling the truths of my life away, one word at a time. "They're killing us. Giving Ceremonies are nothing but well-planned murders. The gods-blessed are sacrificed."

She says it evenly, as if she's reminding me that Esyn is the Mother Goddess and that she has three sisters, not telling me that everything I've ever been taught is a lie.

If this is true, I'm no better than the man who fathered me.

A tremor starts in my hands, working its way through my body. Bile rises in my throat, and my head spins. Oh, gods.

I search her eyes again for any sign that she might be lying, but all I see is truth. If Wren is lying, she's the best gods-damned liar I've ever met.

Which means . . .

I am my father's son.

The thought slams into me, stealing my breath. And then, while I'm still off-kilter, the little bird continues. She runs her fingers over her bracelet as she recounts an awful tale of sneaking into a temple to watch her best friend's Giving.

When she's done telling me about her friend's murder, all I can do is stare at her. Each breath feels shorter than the last.

All this time, I worked so hard to become a Hunter and be different from the king. I fought and clawed my way to the top, desperate to become a Master of my craft.

And now . . .

Now I find out that every single escaped gods-blessed I caught was *murdered*. That *I* was the one who handed them over to their deaths.

I gasp, the weight of her words threatening to ruin me. I wish she were lying. I wish her words didn't ring with a truth that I can feel in my core.

But they do.

The faces of the gods-blessed I've hunted flash through my mind. The redheaded boy from Woodmarket who escaped his Giving five years ago. The tall gods-blessed with white hair from the province of Etelle, who I peeled off her lover in a cave. Both women had been sobbing as though I were tearing their hearts out of their chests.

I'd thought the women were simply being sentimental, but I was wrong. Esyn help me, but I was so fucking wrong.

A dozen other faces blend together in my mind until all I can see are their glowing Marks shining brightly as I delivered them to their respective temples.

I thought I was doing the right thing. I thought I was serving the gods. I may not have wielded the blades that brought about their deaths, but I played a role in their demises.

My fists clench, and bile continues rising in my throat as the truth settles in my core.

I thought I was a fucking decent man. Not a good one—I've killed enough people that both my hands and soul are covered in blood—but I thought . . .

I thought I was better than him.

It turns out I'm not. I've dragged runaways back to be Given, unknowingly delivering them to be murdered. For fuck's sake, I've chased Wren all around this province for that very purpose.

And it's all a lie.

The more I think about it, the more questions I have. Who is behind all this? Why are they doing this? And what happens to people who learn the truth?

There's no way something this big—this awful—could happen for centuries without *someone* learning what's happening. Does the resistance know? Small groups of dissatisfied citizens pop up occasionally, but my father is quick to silence them by any means necessary.

Have they learned the terrible truth? Is that why they push back on the king's rule despite his bloody attempts to force them down?

I'm not sure how much time goes by as we stand there. The truth is a thousand-pound weight settling on my shoulders. Wren stands a few feet away from me, her hands clenched at her sides. She hasn't looked away, and I know she's trying to figure out what I'm going to do.

I don't fucking know.

I know what I *should* do—I should grab her and bring her to the nearest temple, as the king requested. But this conversation has made it clear there are other things I should've been doing for some time now.

I should have questioned the lack of gods-blessed with glowing Marks in the temples. I should have wondered where the Given went after their ceremonies. I should have asked myself why people were running from their fates in the first place.

There are a multitude of things I should have done. Many people I could have helped instead of bringing them to their deaths.

It's too late for the others, but Wren . . .

She's still here. Still alive.

A man without morals is more monster than man, Gabe.

My grandmother's soft voice runs through my mind, confirming that I'm making the right choice.

My chest heaves as I inhale deeply and step away from the little bird. She tracks my movement as I reach into my cloak, unhooking a bag of coins from my belt. It's one of two that I have—the other is with Steadfast in the stables—and it's heavy in my palm. This should be more than sufficient. I toss it to her, the bag jingling as it flies through the air, and she catches it.

"What—"

"Run," I snarl, repeating my command from the first day we met. "Get out of here, little bird." My chest aches as I take another step away from the woman who has turned my world upside down. "I never want to see you again."

Her mouth falls open, but she isn't moving.

Why isn't she moving? Doesn't she understand what this is costing me?

"Go!" I cry, my chest tightening as though a giant is squeezing me in their fist. "Take the money, buy a ticket on a ship, and get out of Myreth. Just . . . *leave.*"

I can't help the others, but I can save her. This won't wash away my sins, nor will it provide my soul with the absolution I crave, but at least it's something.

I'll be giving a lot up by doing this—my promotion to Master Hunter, my bond with Mist, and whatever else my cruel father has in store for me—but I've done so much harm. Caused so much pain.

This is the least I can do.

Wren is still staring at me with disbelief in her eyes. Isn't this what she wanted? Hasn't she been begging me to let her go from the moment I realized who she was?

"Run, damn it!" I scream, my voice echoing through the alley. "Get out of here!"

And gods help me, she does.

She sucks in a breath, shoves the money into her bag, and runs like she's a rabbit being chased by a wolf. Her cloak flaps behind her as she races away from me, disappearing around the corner.

Only then do I sag against the wall, scrubbing my hand over my face. What in Esyn's holy name have I done?

29

THOSE DAMNED VIOLET EYES

Gabriel

A brilliant light shines through my window, pulling me out of sleep. I crack open an eye, confirm the late morning hour, and my head falls back with a groan.

"Esyn help me," I groan, my cock rock hard beneath the sheets, thanks to Wren.

I've been dreaming of her every night since I let her go two weeks ago.

The dream is always the same. Every night, I wake to the sound of her screaming in our bed after a nightmare. Every night, I hold her close, comforting her. Every night, I remind her that she's mine as I sink my cock into the warmth between her legs.

The dreams aren't the problem; it's what's causing them that has me scratching my head. I don't understand where they're coming from. On the one hand, a sex dream is far better than the nightmares of the king breaking my bond with Mist, but on the other hand, I wake up feeling more disconcerted and out of sorts than before. The dreams feel so real. So right.

And then reality sets in. I'm alone in a cold bed, haunted by the memory of those damned violet eyes.

I thought the dream would stop when I returned to Rosebridge, but evidently, I was wrong. I got here last night when the moons were high and the city was silent.

Instead of returning to my apartment in Rose Palace, I paid for a room at the Red Hound, an inn in a less affluent part of the city. Anything to avoid the king as long as possible.

The Winter's Eve Ball is tonight, and my time is up. When the clock strikes midnight, the Giving Season will be over. A new year will begin, and I'll have officially failed my task.

Even knowing that I'll face the king's rage and likely lose my bond with Mist tonight, I can't help but hope that Wren took my advice and left Myreth.

My chest aches at the thought of never seeing her again, and I *miss* her.

Like the dreams, I don't fucking know where these feelings are coming from. I was hunting Wren, for gods' sakes. These feelings are completely ridiculous. How can I miss someone I barely know?

I throw off my covers with a groan. It's one thing to dream about the little bird but another entirely to think about her while I'm awake.

I can't waste any more time thinking about her piercing stare. I have a ball to attend.

If I had a choice, I'd skip it, but all Hunters are required to be present at the Winter's Eve Ball. When one is invited to a royal function, one does not simply decide not to attend. Doing so would be a ticket to the executioner's block.

Rolling out of bed, I stumble into the adjoining bathing room. I splash cold water on my face, take care of my needs, and get dressed. I strap on my weapons, including Wren's dagger that I picked up in the alley the day I told her to run, before heading out.

Rosebridge has always been a bustling city, but today, the air is practically vibrating with excitement.

The last day of the Giving Season is a kingdom-wide holiday. It's one of the only days the king doesn't hold court. Suns, even the king's executioners get the day off.

Everyone else is excited, but I'm filled with dread. It's growing worse by the hour. Not only have I felt sick ever since learning about the truth of the Givings two weeks ago, but I disobeyed the king's direct orders and let Wren go.

Knowing that he'll be filled with rage, I don't head directly for Rose Palace. Keeping my head down, I avoid the areas my father's spies frequent and go to the central bank. There, I send Mikal the money I borrowed in Mora, which will be delivered by rider next week. I don't want to go into tonight with any debts hanging over my head.

I'm not the only one feeling apprehensive. My bond with Mist has been buzzing since I woke up, and I can feel her anxiety rising as the night draws nearer. She's waiting for me outside the city because I ordered her not to follow me. Maybe if she isn't easily found, King Andreas won't rip apart our bond.

And maybe horses have wings.

Even though it's a long shot, I'm trying to protect Mist as best I can. I roam the streets until the suns are setting, and then I turn towards my childhood home. It's time to face the king.

Rose Palace is impossible to miss, and it's not just because of its blush-pink walls. Three stories tall, the U-shaped building stands behind a fifteen-foot-tall wrought iron fence. The structure is palatial in every sense of the word, from the multiple towers it boasts to the dozens of windows on each level.

The contrast between my father's home and the rest of the city is stark. On one side of the gate are cobblestones and tightly packed buildings. On the other is a sprawling lawn that is still green, even on the last day of the Giving Season, and gardens that are perfectly manicured all year round. Snow never touches Rose Palace; the grounds are enchanted to remain green no matter the time of year.

Such a beautiful, rosy building to house a man whose soul is as black as ink. This place is filled with pain, yet it's the only home I've ever known.

The setting suns paint the expansive lawn in shadows, adding an eerie tone to the king's residence. A few carriages carrying partygoers bumble along the long, curved road leading to the palace entrance. Up ahead, men in their finest silk suits help women wearing splendid ball gowns out of carriages. Following tradition, they're all wearing intricate masks.

I look beyond them to the walls of Rose Palace. Somewhere inside them, the king is waiting for me.

I shake out my shoulders, approaching the guarded gates. Faint streams of music are already lilting through the air. Based on the laughter coming from the carriages around me, alcohol is already flowing freely. No one could say that the people of Myreth don't know how to party when the occasion calls for it.

I give my name to the two Watchers at the gate, and they nod. Wishing me well, they open the gate and let me through.

It won't be a good night, but these soldiers don't need to know that. I thank them, draw a deep breath, and step onto the grounds of Rose Palace.

My skin crawls as I pass through the king's wards. His magic feels like ants creeping over me, and I shiver. He knows I'm here.

Hoping I timed this right, I stuff my hands in my pockets and stride towards the palace entrance.

30

THE WINTER'S EVE BALL

Gabriel

The king's soul may be black, and his fists may be coated in blood, but he knows how to throw a party. Even I cannot deny that.

I lean against a column, the Winter's Eve Ball unfolding around me.

A ten-piece string orchestra is on a raised platform, their bows flying as they fill the ballroom with music. Masked dancers are a study in the rainbow as they swirl across the floor in the arms of their partners. Candles sit in large candelabras, illuminating the festivities. Tables laden with copious amounts of food line two walls.

Across the ballroom from me is a dais where two vacant black thrones sit. The twinkling rubies that give the Ruby Thrones their name stand out among the carved obsidian. I suppose my half brother isn't planning on attending. At least I don't have to face him tonight.

Following Hunter tradition, I'm wearing a mask honoring my familiar—a tribute to the animal I've tied my soul to. Covering my eyes and the bridge of my nose, it leaves the bottom half of my face bare. Usually, I don the panther's mask with pride. Tonight, it's just another reminder that I've failed as a Hunter.

The thought makes my blood run cold. I've tried to mentally prepare for my impending punishment ever since I let Wren go, but it turns out there's no real way to ready oneself to have one's soul ripped in two.

"Would you like some sparkling wine, sir?" A servant wearing crimson livery stops in front of me, balancing a tray of crystal glasses on their fingers.

"I'd love some." Liquid courage will be necessary for dealing with my father.

Taking the glass, I toss back the contents in one go before placing the empty flute on a nearby table. Although I've garnered a few looks, no one has tried to talk to me. Most people know I'm the king's bastard, and the members of the court delight in showing me the same disregard as my father.

Ignoring the nobles, I take in the ballroom. It looks the same as it always has. As a child, I used to love coming in here when it was unoccupied. This was the perfect hiding space, with its massive domed glass roof and dozens of pillars. I would find refuge here for hours, studying the tapestries that line the walls and hiding from the king.

Grabbing another glass of wine, I wander, studying the artwork. *The Gods' War* is the tapestry closest to me.

The black-and-red tapestry depicts a bloody battle between the celestials before mankind was created. It is a tribute to death as much as to the gods' power.

Next to it is *Helios*. The artwork, which celebrates the suns, shimmers in the candlelight. It's like the artist imbued the threads with sunlight.

I sip my drink, strolling past several other tapestries. *Esyn's Lovers, The Making, The Hunter's Moons,* and *Adros's Journey.*

And then I see it.

A new tapestry is hanging to the right of the thrones. I didn't notice it earlier, but now that I've seen it, I can't pull my eyes away.

Kneeling before an altar, wearing a fur-trimmed cloak the color of snow and a lace robe that's a green so pale it's almost white, is a young woman. Even though her hood is up, covering her blond hair, it doesn't hide the faint purple glow emanating from the swirl on her cheek.

A Mark.

The Given's eyes are upturned. Her hands are clasped in front of her, pleading with an unseen being. Emotion radiates from the tapestry—pain and despair and a desire to live.

My chest tightens as I stare at the artwork, questions swirling in my mind. What in Esyn's name is this doing here? Moreover, what does it mean?

The longer I study it, the more questions I have. I'm not sure how much time passes before a hand touches my arm.

"Do my eyes deceive me, or has the Hunter finally returned to Rosebridge?"

The speaker is familiar, and I turn around, a small smile playing on my lips. "Ladybug, it's good to see you."

I place my right hand on my left hip, bowing to the lady in front of me. Maia Villeneuve is a friend—one of the few I have in my father's court.

"No one calls me that but you and Theon, Gabe," she chuckles, waving her hand at me. "Get up."

I do as she asks, my smile widening. "I wager it's because we're the ones who watched you eat a ladybug when you were four." Smirking at her gasp of mock outrage, I ask, "Is your brother here?"

Maia adjusts the sleeve of her gown. "No, Father sent him away on business a few weeks ago. I think he'll be back soon, though."

I nod. Maia and Theon's father, Samir, is the Hand of the King. The three of us spent many hours together as children, since our fathers were often working.

Severus, my half brother, never joined us. Even though he's only five years older than me, he's always made it clear he's above me. Why should he play with me when I'm just a bastard?

I pull my mind from the crown prince. "How's court been?"

Maia frowns, brushing a lock of her wavy black hair over her shoulder. Silver glitter shimmers on her ebony skin, matching the fox mask over her eyes. Her sleeveless gown is exquisitely tailored, and long gloves reach past her elbows. "Exhausting, as always."

"Oh?"

"Every time I come to these, I hate them more. May I?" Before I can answer, she takes my half-empty glass of wine. She drains it before placing the empty flute on the tray of a passing waiter. "Father has decreed that I must find a husband."

I stare at her, trying to figure out how we got from hellos to discussing marriage. "Oh, gods."

She nods solemnly. "I've tried fighting him on it, but I don't think he will forget about it again."

Maia has been trying to avoid marriage for years. She's loved her freedom ever since we were children. Theon has fought for her to have a choice in her husband, but it seems their father has run out of patience.

"I'm sorry," I say, meaning it. No one should be forced to do something they don't want to.

"That makes two of us." She smiles sadly up at me, stepping closer. "In another life, I'd ask you, but you know Father would never allow it since . . ."

I'm a bastard.

"I understand," I say.

This is the story of my life. I might share the king's blood, but I'm not fully royal.

I don't have magic, unlike the king and his "real" family. Therefore, I'm not worth anything. My father, his wife, and their son have all made that perfectly clear to me over the years.

That said, I'm not sure I could marry Maia, even if she was asking for my help. At least, not if she wanted something more than a marriage on paper.

My friend is objectively beautiful, but she isn't the woman who has been haunting my dreams. Wren is a few inches taller than Maia, curvier, and there's a spark in her eyes that I don't see in the brown gaze looking up at me. The Hand's daughter is beautiful, but the little bird is stunning.

Not only that, but Wren has a kind heart. She saved me twice. Her compassionate soul rivals her external beauty . . .

And she's gone.

Fuck, something is definitely wrong with me because there's a pang in my heart at the thought of never seeing Wren again. I shouldn't be thinking of her at all.

Not only has she left the country, but I was hunting her. There will never be anything between us, and thinking of her in this way isn't beneficial at all.

"So, who are the lucky contenders for your hand?" I ask, desperate to get my thoughts away from the one person I can never have.

Maia pinches her lips in a line. "Crusty old men," she says after a moment. "Apparently, that's all I'm good for at the ripe old age of twenty-four."

I open my mouth to reply, but before I can, the door behind the thrones opens. The orchestra music halts, and a herald steps onto the dais. A hush blankets the space as he raises a trumpet to his lips, the resulting sound echoing through the now-silent ballroom.

The king's herald swaps his trumpet for a scroll. "Ladies and gentlemen of Myreth. Welcome to the Winter's Eve Ball."

He pauses, and a smattering of applause fills the ballroom. Maia claps, arching a brow in my direction when she notices I don't follow suit. I'm not here by choice, though, and I won't pretend to be happy. After all, tonight will likely be the worst night of my life.

"It's my pleasure to announce the arrivals of their Majesties, King Andreas, and Queen Lucille, and their honored guests," proclaims the balding man.

It's tradition for the honored guests to join the royals on the stage. They won't be introduced until the clock strikes midnight and the Giving Season officially ends. It's happened this way for as long as I can remember.

The queen is the first to appear, heralded by thunderous applause. She's wearing a crimson gown that's so large she has to turn sideways to make it through the door. A ruby necklace hangs from her throat, and a black tiara sits daintily on her head.

The picture of duty, Queen Lucille smiles and waves at the gathered crowd. After a few moments, she makes her way to the smaller throne and stands in front of it.

The crowd's roar becomes deafening as the king strides through the door. He's dressed in crimson, like the queen, although his outfit is lined in black. A midnight crown embedded with rubies sits atop his raven hair, and his eyes seem angrier than normal.

Or maybe it's my imagination. A product of the fear running through my heart.

Walking behind the king, hands clasped together, are two young women. Identical twins, by the looks of them. They move to stand next to the queen. Like Her Majesty, the twins are unmasked. Unlike the queen, the girls are radiating nerves. Wide-eyed, they're practically trembling as they look over the crowd.

King Andreas steps to the edge of the dais, welcoming Myreth's upper class to the ball. I barely hear him, unable to pull my eyes from the honored guests. There's something strangely familiar about them, but I can't quite put my finger on what it is. I'm sure I've never seen them before.

The king's speech ends, and the royals take their seats. Not the twins, though. They remain standing next to the queen, clutching each other's hands. They seem more nervous than before. No one else seems to notice—or more likely, they don't care—and the orchestra begins playing another set.

My father's eyes narrow, sweeping the room. A chill crawls over me, and I suppress a shiver. He's looking for me. I'm not sure how I know it, but like my gut that is always right, this feeling rings with truth deep within me.

I'm not ready to speak with him yet. Even though it's only delaying the inevitable, I ask Maia to dance. She readily agrees, eager to get away from her ancient suitors—her words, not mine—and we make our way to the middle of the dance floor. Her hand rests on my arm, and my palm is on her back, holding her just close enough that no one should bother us.

Elegant music swells around us. Despite the dread in my heart, I fall easily into the familiar steps.

Dancing, like fighting, has always come naturally to me. The acts are similar—one can dance with a partner as easily as one can spar with a sword.

The only thing I like more than fighting is hunting. Being a Hunter gave me freedom and introduced me to an entire world I'd never known existed. It allowed me to escape the palace and the evil man who fathered me.

It gave me a purpose, and it gave me Mist. And now that I let Wren go, I'll lose all of it.

The thought causes me to stumble, and Maia gasps as I miss a step.

"Sorry, Ladybug," I murmur, tightening my grip around her waist.

She frowns, her knowing gaze sweeping over me. We've shared many dances, and I've never stumbled. "What's wrong?"

Where do I fucking start? I met a woman whose very presence spoke to my soul, only to find out she was gods-blessed and the one I was supposed to be hunting.

I gave her one day's head start, only for her to drug me when I caught up with her. On top of all that—as if that's not fucking enough—the Giving is a gods-damned lie.

"It's too much for right now," I tell her, unable to sort through it all and put it into words. "Maybe another time?"

The music speeds up, and I spin Maia around. When she faces me once more, understanding is in her eyes. "I'm always here if you need me, Gabe. All you need to do is ask."

Perhaps one day, I'll take her up on it. But not tonight.

After that, very few words pass between us. We lose ourselves to song after song, swirling across the ballroom for hours. Before I know it, the clock is striking eleven, and a faint sheen of sweat dots Maia's brow. I'm sure mine looks the same.

I lead her off the dance floor to a table of refreshments, procuring two glasses of water.

"You mentioned your father is requiring you to marry?" I ask as she sips the water.

"Well, you know how it is. He says I'm practically a spinster and a dishonor to his name." Maia laughs, but real pain shines in her dark brown eyes. "He's upset that I turned down the last three proposals, and I'm afraid he's not going to give me even the illusion of a choice this time."

Grimacing, I squeeze her hand. "I'm sorry, Ladybug. I . . ."

My voice trails off as she stiffens, her eyes looking over my shoulder. The hairs on the back of my neck prickle. The moment I spot the vacant throne, I know who's standing behind me.

Maia drops into a low curtsy, her silver gown brushing the floor. "Your Majesty," she murmurs.

"Lady Villeneuve." The king's baritone voice at my back has goosebumps exploding on my flesh. "You are dismissed."

Just like that.

My heart drops to my stomach as Maia rises from her curtsy. Keeping her head down, she brushes past me with a murmured, "Good luck, Gabe."

I don't blame her for leaving me with the king. No one should be subject to his cruelty any longer than necessary.

Long, seemingly never-ending seconds pass in silence as I wait for the king to approach. Using silence to make his opponents uncomfortable is one of the king's favorite tactics. He loves to unsettle people, and gods help me, it's working.

Even though I can't see him, I can feel the king's eyes drilling into my back. The dancers start another waltz before he steps closer. A hand clamps down on my shoulder.

It takes everything I have not to react. My father's touch has always been cold, but now it's entirely devoid of warmth. Even the gold ring on his left hand feels like it's made of ice, the massive ruby inlaid within it glinting in the candlelight.

"Gabriel." His low voice is laced with traces of darkness, and it sends shivers down my spine. "I'm very disappointed in you."

His fingers tighten on my shoulder, forcing me to turn around and face him. I'm sure that to anyone else, this looks like a fatherly embrace. The king, greeting his bastard son who has been gone for months.

I know the truth.

Crimson embers flash in the king's eyes, and he drags me away from the dancers. I follow his lead, keeping my head up high. Hatred seeps off him, and it's bitter at the back of my tongue. My fingers twitch at my sides. The desire to grab my sword and slam it into my father's heart before he can break my bond with Mist is so strong that it's nearly overpowering.

We round a column, and the king waves his hand. His skin glows a muted crimson as he erects a ward around us. The other attendees can see us, but they won't be able to hear a word we say, even if I scream at the top of my lungs.

Fucking fantastic.

The king lifts his hand from my shoulder and glares at me. I remain immobile. I should be relieved that he's no longer touching me. I should be able to breathe more easily. I can't, though. Tension courses through me as I wait, dreading the hellish storm that is about to be rained upon me.

"Where is she?" King Andreas growls, low and menacing.

The hairs on my neck lift, and cold sweat drips down my back. Fucking hell. I hate that even now, as I near my third decade of life, the king is still capable of instilling such great fear in me.

I'm not a helpless child any longer. I shouldn't flinch whenever he speaks to me in that tone that says he knows how dangerous he is. But I fucking do. I may be a Hunter and a trained soldier, but he's the gods-damned king and the one with all the power.

Despite the fear coiling in my stomach, I hold my ground and refuse to cower in the face of my abuser.

I stare at my father's dead eyes. "I couldn't locate her."

The lie slips off my tongue as smooth as silk, like I practiced.

The embers in the king's eyes darken, and the ground trembles. A rumbling starts in the king's chest, and my flesh crawls at the predatory sound. Unmasked malice glimmers in his eyes as he steps towards me.

"I told you to retrieve her," he snaps. "She *must* be Given before the season ends at midnight."

"I understand, Your Majesty, but I couldn't find her."

Lie, lie, lie.

The memory of Wren's violet eyes widening as I shoved the tip of my sword through the sailor's throat flashes through my mind. Thankfully, although the king's magic is vast, he isn't capable of reading minds. It's a small blessing, but I'll take it.

He growls my name in warning.

I lift a shoulder. "She must've left the country."

His hand moves so quickly, I don't even see it before it connects with my cheek. The blow sends me stumbling, and my back slams against a column.

No one looks my way as King Andreas stalks towards me, his fists balled at his sides.

"You failed, Gabriel," he seethes, crimson sparks rising around him. "You had one job. Find the missing girl and bring her in. That's all I asked of you."

My chest tightens, and I brace myself for a blast of his magic. I've experienced this enough in my nightmares to know what's coming next.

Grabbing my bond with Mist, I grip it with all my might.

I'm sorry, I tell my familiar. *Gods above, I'm so fucking sorry.*

We've been together for nearly a decade, but it's all about to come crashing down.

"I should've killed you the moment your whore of a mother dropped you at the foot of my throne." The king makes no effort to moderate his tone as he screams his cruel words. They're for me, and me alone, thanks to his magical ward. "Your whole life, you've been nothing but a fucking failure. A gods-damned disappointment. You call yourself a Hunter?"

His eyes widen, and spittle flies from his mouth as he shouts, "You couldn't even bring in a single girl."

He's conveniently forgotten the forty-nine other hunts I've successfully completed. His hateful rampage continues. I'm not worthy to share even a drop of his blood. I would've been better off never being born. If only he'd stuck his dick somewhere else.

I steel my heart against the king's words, forcing a blank mask over my face. I've heard these things countless times before, and I let his hatred slide over me like water over rocks.

Instead, I gaze into the crowd.

The hour is growing late, and I've been to enough of these parties to know that the longing glances, whispered words, and hands brushing against arms will soon result in countless couples and small groups running out to the gardens to find some privacy. A few more brazen couples embrace on the dance floor, in full sight of everyone.

Maia spins by in the arms of Lord Clearwater, a balding, wrinkled old man nearly three times her age. The King's Hand watches nearby, a calculating grin on his face. Theon would want me to step in and stop this, and I would if I wasn't currently dealing with the king.

Then something stirs deep within me. An awareness. A tug in my gut. A call to pay attention.

The king is still raving, his usual pallor taking on a red tinge as he screams in my face. It won't be long until he punishes me for my failures, but I can't find it in me to care right now. Not when that tug is getting stronger.

My eyes slide through the ballroom with more purpose than before. Left to right, from the orchestra to the thrones, where the twins remain, to . . .

Blessed fucking burning suns.

A stone lodges itself in my stomach, and my breath catches. My eyes widen for a fraction of a second before I remember it's a tell. I force a mask of blankness over my face once more. It's like dragging a blanket of steel over my body, and the act takes far more effort than it should.

It takes me one second too long.

The king stops mid-sentence, his eyes narrowing. "What did you just see?"

I clamp my mouth shut. My actions earn me a stern glare and a muttered, "Useless bastard," before he turns.

"No—"

It's too late.

I can tell the moment he sees the same flash of indigo I did because he curses. I saw the Wanted poster the king commissioned. There's no way he doesn't know who that hair belongs to.

The stone in my stomach sinks as the king waves his hand and dismantles his ward. I should feel relieved that he hasn't broken my bond yet, but I don't. Dread is a curling, icy mist in my veins.

Why is she here? Why didn't she leave?

There's no time for questions because the king pins me with a glare. "We're not done yet, Hunter."

He murmurs a spell and twists his fingers, disappearing in a crimson mist.

When I look up, the little bird has vanished.

31

THE HONORED GUESTS

Wren

Earlier that night

The twins are here. I stare up at them through my black raven's mask, my eyes glued to the dais where they're standing. My fingers curl around the glass of sparkling wine Kadyn handed me a moment before the king and queen entered the ball.

They're actually here. I can barely believe it. My forehead feels like it's on fire as I stare at the stage, and I pray that the raven's feathers covering the swirl block out the glow.

Even if no one else can see it, I know it's there. I always fucking know it's there.

Ever since the Hunter told me to run two weeks ago, the Mark has been burning nearly nonstop. Not only that, but this morning, I woke with a strange tingling in my fingertips.

None of that matters, though, because my sisters are *here*. The knot of unease that has been in my stomach since Kadyn and I arrived in Rosebridge yesterday unfurls a bit.

Thank the suns, this wasn't for nothing.

"Is that them?" Kadyn whispers from beside me as the king starts speaking. We're standing at the back of the crowd, far enough away to hopefully avoid attracting attention.

All I can do is nod as emotion thickens my throat. Kadyn seems to understand because he steps to the side, giving me space to breathe.

He has proven himself to be a good friend over the past two weeks, refusing to leave when I tried to give him Gabriel's money. I saved his life, he told me, and now he would stay and help me with my sisters.

The Given stick together.

I'm not sure I would've gotten this far without his help. There were more Watchers and Hunters than ever before, and even with Gabriel's money, moving through the country undetected was difficult.

We paid an elderly woman who was traveling north to let us ride in the back of her cart for several days, and we walked the rest of the way, trying to conserve our limited funds. Finding ball-appropriate attire this morning was an expensive endeavor, requiring nearly all our remaining money.

But I no longer care about the hardships we endured, because the twins are here.

I pass my glass of wine to my left hand, the beads on my gown rustling. The dress, like the mask covering my eyes and nose, is black. It's easily the most beautiful garment I've ever had the pleasure of wearing.

The fabric is formfitting up top but still easy to move in, thanks to the flare at my hips. The sleeves are tight to my elbows, and boning runs down the length of my chest, acting as a corset. Between that and the scooped neckline, it's extremely flattering. At another time, when I wasn't worried sick about my sisters' wellbeing, I'd feel like a princess.

The king is speaking from the dais, but I don't hear a word he says. I haven't even tasted the wine, although I could probably use a drink to help with my nerves.

I'm just staring at my sisters.

Violet and Marie look as lovely as they did the night I left. Their violet hair hangs in loose curls down their backs. The girls are wearing matching coral gowns, and their hands are clasped together. Unlike the rest of us, they aren't wearing masks. Their wide eyes sweep across the room, and their nerves are palpable.

It takes every ounce of self-preservation I possess to stop myself from ripping off my mask and shouting to get their attention. I still have no idea why the twins are here, but it can't be good.

At some point, the king's speech ends. An orchestra starts playing, and people pair up, heading for the dance floor.

I turn to Kadyn. His mask is black, like mine. Feathers rise around the neckline of his tunic, making an elaborate collar and hiding his Mark from sight.

"I need to get closer to my sisters." The ballroom dividing us feels like an ocean. "Can you search for a way out of here?"

Once I get the twins, we'll need to run as quickly as possible. The sooner we get out of Rosebridge and to the Sapphire Coast, the better. The Watchers lining the walls of the ballroom will make things difficult, but that's been the story of my life lately.

Kadyn nods, melting into the crowd.

The king and queen are seated, their heads bent together as they talk quietly. Marie and Violet haven't moved. Between their nerves and the pink dresses, they look so much younger than fifteen.

That sinking feeling has returned, stronger than ever. I just *know* my sisters are in danger. Keeping them in my sights, I start making my way across the ballroom.

It feels like I'm playing a high-stakes game of hide-and-seek. I stroll around columns and past clusters of partygoers, all the while avoiding the Watchers. It's slow going, but if it helps me avoid capture, I'll move as slowly as needed.

I'm walking past two men kissing behind the privacy of a column when movement on the dais makes me pause. The king rises from his throne, stalking off into the crowd, his skin glowing crimson.

Is that normal? I honestly don't know, but the sight has my skin crawling.

Seconds later, Queen Lucille murmurs something to the twins before she, too, rises and leaves the dais.

This is it. This will be my only chance to get to my sisters. Discarding my untouched glass of wine on the nearest table, I grip my skirt in both hands and pick up my pace.

I'm near the edge of the dance floor when a hand touches my arm. I suck in a breath, exhaling when I lock eyes with Kadyn.

We slip behind a column, standing near a red-and-black tapestry.

"Well?" I ask, my eyes darting between my friend and the dais, where my sisters remain.

"The door behind the thrones leads to the servants' corridors. We should be able to use the passageways to get out of here," he whispers.

"Thank the suns. Did you see any guards?"

Not for the first time, I wish I hadn't lost Father's blade. Kadyn and I stole a set of daggers a few days ago, and one of them is sheathed against my thigh beneath my dress, but it doesn't hold the connection to home that Father's knife did.

Kadyn shakes his head. "None, but . . . are you sure about this, Wren?" He glances at my sisters and chews on the inside of his cheek. "They could be here for innocuous reasons. Maybe the honored guests really are *just* guests."

This isn't the first time we've talked about this over the past two weeks. We've both speculated about what might happen to the honored guests after the Winter's Eve Ball, but in the end, they're just that—speculations.

"I'm sure. They're my sisters, and I can't leave them." I would never be able to live with myself if something happened to them.

Kadyn rakes a hand through his hair, blowing out a long breath. "Okay, I trust you."

We go over the plan, and once I confirm I remember the signal, we split up.

He slips back into the crowd, and I continue on my path towards the dais. The closer I get, the more it seems like everyone is watching me. I reach up, carefully adjusting the raven's feathers over my Mark. Even though I'm certain it's covered, I can't help but feel like I'm a lamb standing in a lion's den.

One wrong move, and everything will be over.

The platform is close when a strange sensation blooms to life in my middle. It's an insistent tug that's so sudden, it has me pausing mid-step.

An awareness crawls over me, and I turn slowly, scanning the ballroom. Dancers swirl, my sisters are still the only ones on the dais, and there's a healthy crowd at the overflowing tables, picking at the feast.

Maybe it is nothing. Maybe being on the run for weeks is getting to me. Maybe—

Oh, suns.

I suck in a sharp breath and freeze. My fingers spasm and release my skirt. A vise clamps around my heart. Mask or no mask, I'd recognize those sweeping locks of blue-black hair anywhere. They've been haunting my dreams and nightmares for weeks.

Run, little bird.

What is he doing here, and why is he talking to the king? I can't hear them, and the royal's back is to me. Even so, there's no mistaking the crown on his head, his rigid shoulders, or the aura of violence surrounding him.

Suns, have mercy on my soul.

Cold sweat gathers at the back of my neck, and the mask feels like it's digging into my skin.

My dress no longer feels like a beautiful garment. Now, it's constricting. The sleeves are too tight. The corset is gouging my skin.

The Hunter is here.

He's here, and even though I need to keep going, I can't move.

Fuck, Gabriel is beautiful. Even now, clean-shaven and dressed in finery, he's still rugged and large and handsome. The mask of a panther covers the top half of his face, which is entirely fitting. He's a predator, through and through. Nice clothes can't disguise the hunter beneath his skin—it's as much a part of him as the emeralds in his eyes.

I hate him. I hate him so much, for his "gift" of a head start, for the way he kept chasing me, and for the way he haunts my dreams.

I hate him, yet he saved my life in Saltwater. Not only that, but he listened to the truth about the Given. He gave me money and tried to get me to leave.

I hate him, but I can't stop thinking about him.

And then, his gaze lifts. His eyes widen as they meet mine. Shock flashes through them.

A second that feels like an eternity passes, and I'm drowning in Gabriel's green gaze. The ballroom melts away, the music fades, and something deep within me sings. My Mark burns hotter than it ever has before, even with the raven's feathers covering it. My feet twitch, desperate to close the distance between us.

And then the Hunter's face shifts. One moment, he's staring at me. The next, he dons a blank, expressionless mask. Before I can ask myself what just happened, the king spins around.

His eyes sweep through the room, much like mine did moments ago, and then he looks directly at me. Recognition flashes through his eyes, and my heart drops to my feet.

Fuck!

The word bounces through my mind, shattering whatever spell had frozen me in place. The king knows I'm here, and for some reason, that scares me more than the Hunter ever did.

A quiver of fear races through me as I turn and run through the crowd. There's no time for stealth, no time to consider what the king was talking to Gabriel about, no time to think about that tug in my gut.

My knot of worry has returned. I need to get my sisters out of here before it's too late.

32

HOPE IS A LIE

Wren

When I look over my shoulder next, both the king and the Hunter have vanished. Fear encases my heart in ice. Where did they go?

Before I can panic, a crash comes from the back of the ballroom. One of the tables that was laden with food is now on its side. Roasted meats, breads, and platters of dainty tarts are now strewn across the floor.

Chaos erupts. People start shouting as a streak of black slips out the back door. The musicians keep playing, even as people yell about ruined clothes and wasted food. Watchers converge on the area. No one is looking at the dais.

"Thank you, Kadyn," I murmur, heading towards the platform.

I hadn't been sure how I'd get the twins' attention, but it turns out I'd been worrying for nothing. The moment I get to the base of the platform, Violet's eyes land on me.

"Birdie?" she gasps.

Marie's head swivels over, a beaming smile on her face. Suns. When was the last time I smiled? She opens her mouth, but I shake my head and lift a finger to my lips.

"Come with me," I whisper urgently. "We don't have much time."

Marie nods, but Violet hisses, "The queen said we have to stay put—"

"I'll explain later, but just . . . please. You have to trust me. We don't have time to waste." We're going to use the last of our money to hire a wagon to get us out of Rosebridge tonight, but in order to do that, we have to get out of this gods-damned ball.

Long seconds pass as the girls stare at each other, seeming to communicate silently before Violet nods. "Okay."

I don't look around as I take the steps onto the dais and hurry behind the thrones. My sisters follow me to the wall, where a door is cut into the stone. I'm sure the girls' absence will be noted quickly, but hopefully, by then, we'll be out of the palace.

I don't let myself think of the king or the Hunter as I hold my breath and push open the door. The hallway beyond is empty, save for a flickering torch. I exhale, ushering the twins inside before letting the door shut behind me.

An iron bar hangs above the handle, and I yank it down, sliding the makeshift lock into place. It probably won't hold for long, but hopefully, it will buy us some time.

Marie breathes, "Wren—"

"Shh," I whisper. "One second."

I draw up my skirt, unsheathing my dagger before letting my dress fall to the ground. Holding the blade with my left hand, I grab the torch with my right.

Arms wrap around me from behind, and I stiffen before realizing Marie's hugging me.

"What are you doing here, Birdie?" she asks, her words muffled in my dress.

Adjusting my grip on the torch so I don't burn her hair, I twist in her arms and smile at her. "I came for you."

Marie squeezes me even tighter, but Violet crosses her arms and studies me. She looks so much like our mother that my heart aches.

"Why weren't you Given?" She purses her lips. "The king's soldiers were at the house searching for you, and you weren't there."

"The priests and priestesses came, too," Marie adds. "They brought Watchers and Enforcers and interrogated everyone for hours. Father had to go with them for questioning."

My heart plummets. "What?"

I had no idea they would take him away.

"He was gone for days, Birdie. Mother thought we couldn't hear her, but she cried every night." Violet glares at me. "He came back, but it was so frightening."

"I'm sorry." I pull away from Marie and look both my sisters in the eyes. "I never meant for that to happen."

I just wanted to survive.

"So, you ran away," Violet says, her voice cold. "You abandoned the gods."

She's only two minutes older than Marie, but right now, she seems to have years on our youngest sister.

"It's not like that," I tell her, desperate to keep moving.

Marie doesn't seem to notice my need to get us out of here. "Then what's it like?"

"Everything is a lie." My gaze swings between the twins. "There's more to it than that, but there isn't enough time to talk about it right now. I had to run because the Giving isn't safe."

"But you didn't leave Myreth?" Marie asks quietly.

"I was going to, but I heard you were here." I look at them pleadingly, the dagger growing slippery in my palm. "I had a bad feeling that something would happen to you."

Violet's brows knit, but Marie nods. "Bad feelings like Nana used to get?"

"Yes. Just like that."

The twins share a look, silently communicating in the way only they seem to be able to. Nana died when they were young, but surely they remembered how her feelings worked.

"Okay," Marie says after a long moment. "We believe you. I didn't get a good feeling about the king, anyway."

That doesn't surprise me. Even from afar, the man feels frightening. Shouts of alarm come from the other side of the wall, and my heart slams against my ribs. The twins' escape has been discovered.

"We need to leave." There will be time for catching up once we're safe. Then I'll tell them the whole story.

I rip off my mask and throw it on the ground. Thank the suns, the girls don't push back again. They fall in line behind me, and we race down the corridor. Flickering torchlight casts shadows on the walls, adding an ominous tone to our escape.

We turn left, dashing down the stone passageways, when another set of footsteps comes from ahead of us. I hold out a hand, and my sisters barrel to a stop behind me. I tighten my grip on my weapon as a high-pitched bird's call comes from down the corridor.

"What's that?" Marie gasps.

The bird's call is repeated twice more, and my shoulders relax. "That's my friend, Kadyn."

I wave for the girls to follow, and we round the bend. Kadyn is waiting for us. He's bent in half, his hands resting on his thighs as he gasps for air. His feathers are askew, the Mark on his neck glowing a deep green. He must have used the light as a guide to find us.

"Were you followed?" he asks between deep breaths.

I shake my head. "No. You?"

"No." He straightens and runs a hand through his hair. "The king's soldiers are coming, though. We need to move."

A pit lodges in my stomach at the urgency in his voice. He's right. Every second we spend standing around is another second the king can find us.

I break out into a sprint, my hatred for the activity shoved aside by our perilous situation.

We turn left, then right, then left thrice more. None of us speak, our breaths the only sound other than our footsteps pounding the stones. The flickering light from my torch provides the only illumination, save for the blue and green glows of Kadyn's and my Marks.

Twice, the faint echoes of shouts come from behind us. They're coming for us. The pit in my stomach grows until it feels like a canyon has taken up residence inside me.

The servants' passage seems to continue forever. It feels like we've been running for hours. Midnight must be drawing near, and with it, my birthday. This is not how I expected to spend the minutes before I turned twenty-one.

We run and run until finally, the corridor ends. A spiral stone staircase is in front of us, so narrow that it seems like an afterthought.

"Up or down?" Marie asks, clutching her side as she pants.

Fuck if I know.

"Down," I decide after a moment.

The ground floor must lead outside, right? That's where we're going. Away from the royals, this gods-forsaken palace, and the Hunter.

I lead the way. The stones are worn and slippery, and muttered curses come from behind me as we navigate the steps. A cool breeze drifts up from below, and goosebumps dot my arms.

Cold is good, right? It must mean we're getting close to getting out.

Hope warms my chest, and I hurry down the steps as quickly as I dare. Maybe this is a good sign. Maybe we're getting close, and soon, we'll get out of the palace.

And maybe that would've been the case if the gods didn't hate me. Maybe if I'd been anyone else, we wouldn't have encountered any more problems. We would've boarded a boat and left Myreth for good, off to live a calm, peaceful life.

But the gods do hate me, and my destiny is one of pain and suffering and death. This is made all too clear to me when I step onto the landing at the base of the stairs and look up.

A whimpered curse escapes my lips, and time slows. My stomach plummets.

It turns out that hope, like the life I thought I would lead once I was Given, is nothing but a fucking lie.

Fanned out at the base of the stairs, in a dark, stone corridor similar to the one we just vacated, are a dozen guards. Their swords are drawn, and their faces are set in deep scowls.

Unlike the Watchers stationed in the ballroom earlier, all twelve soldiers wear grey emblems on their chests, marking them as Protectors. Torches are set in sconces on the walls, casting their light around us.

One of the Protectors, a woman who looks like she exercises for hours daily, glances at my dagger and smirks. Suns, why is my chosen weapon so laughably small?

I open my mouth to warn the others, but it's too late. Time resumes its regular pace as Kadyn and the twins careen down the stairs. One by one, they slam into my back until they all stand beside me. Kadyn is on my left, and the twins are on my right.

More soldiers file in behind us, filling up the stairwell. One of them snatches the torch from my grip. A twin whimpers. I wish I could turn to see which of them made that sound so I could comfort them, but I can't move my eyes away from the swords pointed directly at us.

There's nowhere to run.

"Please," I whisper, letting my useless weapon fall to the ground with a clatter. I open my palms beseechingly. "Please let us go."

Here I am, begging for my life *again*.

How many more times is this going to happen? How many more times will I be teased by a taste of freedom, only to have it be ripped away?

A low chuckle that has my stomach clenching comes from beyond the soldiers.

"Let you go?" The deep voice sounds like it's been dipped in oil, and every part of me wants to recoil. But there are soldiers at my back and my front, and I'm trapped. "Why would I do that when I've been searching all over my kingdom for you?"

As if they're following a silent signal, the guards in front of us split into two groups of six. Striding between them, every bit the dangerous man I've heard him rumored to be is King Andreas Bloodthorn.

"Wren Lilith Nightingale." He says my name as though it's a curse, and for once, I believe it might be true. "I've been looking for you." He fixes his eyes on Kadyn and smirks. "Both of you."

"Why?" I breathe.

I don't even realize the question has slipped from my mouth until it's echoing in the stone corridor. It's a fair question, though. Why search for us? Why not let us go? Why kill the gods-blessed at all?

All these questions feel connected, but there's a missing piece. A hidden connection that has yet to be revealed. Something vitally important standing just outside of my reach.

The king laughs, and the vicious sound is like nails scratching on a chalkboard.

"Isn't it obvious?" His eyes glimmer with malice, and chills run down my spine. "You're *Marked*. Blessed. You carry a gift from the gods in your veins."

This again. I fucking hate this glowing swirl. It feels hotter than before, like flames are licking the inside of my forehead, trying to burn their way out.

The Mark ruined my life, Amelia's life, and now it's about to ruin the twins' lives, too. Gods-blessed? More like cursed and fated to fail.

None of the soldiers have moved, waiting for the king's signal.

I've heard of King Andreas, of course. Everyone knows about the man's bloodthirsty reputation.

No one ever mentioned how *wrong* being in the king's presence feels, though. My skin is crawling, goosebumps have erupted on my flesh, and I'm filled with the urge to flee.

But I can't because swords are pointing at my sisters. Even if they hadn't been in danger before, that's no longer the case.

They could die here, just like all the other Given. Like Amelia. Only this time, it would be because of me.

I meet the king's gaze, swallowing my fear.

"Take me," I plead. "Let them go and take me."

That's what he wants, right?

A long moment passes, during which the thundering of my heart is the only sound I can hear. Even the soldiers are silent, their eyes fixed on the royal.

Then, a booming laugh erupts from the king. His skin glows, and his eyes . . . Oh, suns save me. His eyes are death and darkness and pure, unadulterated evil.

"You foolish little Blessed bitch." He steps towards me, the air thickening. "What makes you think this is a negotiation?"

Marie sobs, and the sound is a dagger shoved into my gut.

I'm going to die here tonight.

The thought slams into me, and I swallow the moan rising in my throat. Midnight must be minutes away, maybe even seconds, but it doesn't matter. I'll never see another birthday, never see another year.

I'll never do anything again.

"Your Majesty, my sisters didn't do anything." Maybe if I take his attention off the girls and focus it on me, I can still save them. "They're innocent. I dragged them into this."

I should have left them in the ballroom. Suns, I never should have even come here. Why did I think I could help anyone?

This is all my fault. I'm the reason the twins are in danger, the reason why the king is staring at them like he's a predator and they're the tiny kittens he's about to devour.

The Hunter was right. I should've run away when I still could. My sisters are better off without me. My family is better off without me.

Maybe everyone is better off without me.

The king doesn't answer me. He opens his palms, gathering magic in his hands. I've never seen magic in real life before, and I never realized it looked so menacing. So dark. So . . . wrong.

Racing footsteps come from down the corridor, and that tugging in my gut returns.

"You will all die tonight," the king says, his words a dark promise.

He pulls back his hand, murmuring something inaudible beneath his breath. Sparks fly, and my heart twists. The knowledge of my impending death is a sinking pit in my stomach.

My sisters are weeping, and I turn to them. Their faces glisten with tears, and they're holding each other.

"I'm so sorry," I tell them. "So fucking sorry."

The words aren't enough. Nothing is fucking enough. How can this be the end?

The king's murmurs cease, and he lifts his hand. Sparks rise off his outstretched palm, and then he speaks a word in a language I don't recognize.

The magic twists in the air, a cyclone of death and destruction.

I wish I could say I feel no fear, staring at the man determined to kill me, but I'd be lying. Every part of me shakes, and my stomach churns.

My Mark is engulfing me in flames from the inside out, but what does that matter when I'm about to die?

Those footsteps get louder, the tugging more insistent.

With a final smirk that speaks to my impending death, the king throws his magic. It sails through the air, a crimson sphere speeding towards me.

I cry another apology, hoping the girls forgive me. "I wanted to help."

I just wanted to save them. Instead, I've doomed them.

The time for words is over. The magic spins, and my death draws near. The soldiers at my back make it impossible to move.

Regret fills my heart for all the things I never had a chance to do. All the places I'll never see. All the life I wanted to live.

Death is coming for me, its cold arms outstretched, when hands slam into my side. The force is sudden and takes me by surprise.

I stumble, crashing into the girls.

A yell claws out of my throat, and I turn just in time to see the king's magic strike Kadyn in the middle of his forehead. It's a perfect shot, and my friend cries out, the guttural sound filling the hallway.

Blood pours from the wound, painting his face in crimson.

Life seeps from his eyes. Fast. It's so damn fast that I can barely process what's happening.

A never-ending second passes, and then he falls over.

Dead.

Oh, suns.

He . . . This . . . That was *my* death. My pain.

And he took it.

Why? Why would Kadyn do that? Why did he push me away?

There's no time to delve into Kadyn's sacrifice because the strangest thing happens. A flash of light erupts from his body, washing the corridor in forest green.

My fingers tingle, and my Mark feels like it combusts into flames.

I'm burning, burning, burning. I am fire, and fire is me.

My heart is racing, my lungs have forgotten how to breathe, and something new settles within me. It's familiar but foreign. New, but it settles within me like an old friend.

Then the light is gone.

My Mark cools, and my brows furrow. Something is different, but I don't know what it is.

King Andreas's eyes flash with crimson rage, and he's vibrating with fury. He growls, "You fucking Blessed, good-for-nothing cunt."

What did I do?

I try to take a step back, to move away from my friend's body, but the tip of a sword meets my back. "I . . . I didn't—"

"That Harvest was mine," the king snarls, gathering more magic in his palms. So much magic. So much death. "And I'm going to make you pay for stealing it. Blessed or not, you cannot take what belongs to me."

"I don't know what you're talking about." I shake my head, my breath coming in short gasps. His words don't make any sense.

This is too much.

Kadyn is dead, and the king is upset, but I don't understand what he thinks I did. He's the one who killed my friend.

Grief looms on the edge of my mind, but I can't focus on it yet. The girls need me.

Those footsteps finally cease, and my heart thunders in my chest.

Gabriel skids to a stop behind the guards in the corridor, his sword gripped in his palm. His face is paler than I've ever seen it. He's lost his mask, and his panicked gaze darts between me, the king, and the bloody body at my feet.

"Well, if it isn't the failed Hunter." King Andreas raises a brow but doesn't look away from me. "I'm glad you're here to see this, Gabriel. She tried to escape me, but she couldn't. No one escapes my wrath. You'd do well to remember that."

The air thickens with the tang of magic. There will be no evading my fate this time. Nowhere to run.

Death is here to claim me.

Only before the king can lob his attack in my direction, a distant toll reaches my ears. One ring. Two . . .

They keep going.

A clock tower somewhere far above us is striking midnight. It seems I made it to my twenty-first birthday after all.

I brace myself for the king's killing blow, but it never comes.

My Mark burns as though imbued with the heat of a thousand suns. Something paints the stones in a brilliant blue sheen, as bright as any star.

A guard curses, and several of them stumble back.

Then I look down at my hands. A strangled cry rises in my throat. Blue sparks, the color of a cloudless sky, dance around my fingers.

"Get them!" King Andreas shouts, his already pale face draining of blood. "Quick, stop them before she—"

I turn my hands towards the king.

All I want is for him and his soldiers to stay away from me and my sisters. I can't let them suffer Kadyn's fate.

I have to keep the twins safe.

A guard steps towards Violet with a growl. That's all it takes.

"Get the fuck away from us!" I scream as the flames erupt within me.

Brilliant blue bursts out of my fingers, filling the corridor. Brighter than any star, it's blinding.

The ground shakes, and I shout. Shutting my eyes, I throw myself between the guards and my sisters, shielding the girls.

Cries fill the air. Grunts of pain. My sisters whimper. Then, a thundering sound, like trees falling, fills the air.

After what feels like several lifetimes, but was probably a few seconds, the blue light dims. I ease up my head, opening my eyes.

Suns, have mercy on me.

I don't . . .

I don't understand.

The guards are charred husks on the ground.

The only ones who seem to have survived are the king, who is hiding behind a crimson shield, and Gabriel, who is staring at me with wide eyes. Blue flames lick the ground near the Hunter but don't touch him.

A blue light is around me . . .

A shield. *My* shield?

A growl rumbles through the corridor, and I drag my eyes back to the king. Oh, suns.

I never knew rage had a color until now. The monarch's eyes are bloodred, and he's trembling with fury.

His lips draw back in a snarl, and he shakes his head, taking a step back. He lifts a hand, and my eyes snag on the golden ring on his left hand.

I didn't notice it before, but now that I've seen it, it's the only thing I can focus on.

"You?" I breathe, staring at the piece of jewelry. I've seen it once before—on my best friend's Giving Day. "You killed Amelia?"

What the fuck is going on? It feels like my entire world has been thrown upside down. My head spins, and a dozen emotions course through me.

The blue flames wreathing my hands grow brighter.

The king stares at my magic, then at the shield I somehow erected around me and my sisters, and sneers. His crimson magic slams up against the shield again and again, but it doesn't make it through.

Fury flashes through the king's eyes, and he draws his crimson magic towards himself.

"This isn't over," he snarls. "I swear to you on all that is holy, you will pay for this."

His last words echo through the corridor as he disappears in a crimson mist. I stare at the spot he just vacated, my heart galloping in my chest.

There's no time to process what's happening, because the Hunter steps towards me.

That's all it takes for me to feel it. A rope in my stomach, drawing me forward.

It's like the sensation I felt earlier, but a hundred times stronger.

It's need and want and a force beyond all reason. I've never felt anything like this, and yet, at this moment, I know my entire life is about to change.

"Little bird," Gabriel breathes.

I lift my eyes to meet his through the shimmering blue shield.

One look. That's all it takes for my entire world to shift.

My Mark erupts into a bonfire, blue sparks burn and pop all around me, and a knowing fills my soul.

In the same way that I know the two suns shine during the day before giving up their seats to the three moons at night, I know that this man—this *Hunter*—is more than just a predator.

He's more than the man who gave me one day's head start, more than the man who chased me halfway across the kingdom, more than the man who I can't erase from my mind.

The fire on my forehead, the twisting in my gut, and the look in his eyes all tell me the same thing.

He's meant to be *mine*.

ACKNOWLEDGMENTS

We've reached the end of another book. How is that possible? It feels like just yesterday I was putting the finishing touches on *Of Earth and Flame*, my first romantasy, and here we are diving into an entirely new world.

I cannot properly express just how much fun I had writing *Given*. The moment Wren and Gabriel came to me and started telling me their story, I knew I would have a blast getting to know them.

And I was right. We had so much fun together, and I can't wait to see where their journey goes next.

Books are so much more than a collection of words—they're full of love and life—and there is so much that goes into them behind the scenes.

Given wouldn't have ever come to fruition without some very special people in my life.

To my alpha and beta readers—Sarah, Ophelia, Demi, Jay, Rachel, and Lizzie—thank you. Thank you for listening to my thoughts, reading rough early drafts, and helping me make the story the best version of itself.

To my editor, Jaime, thank you for helping me clean up this book and get it ready for my readers.

To my husband, Aaron.

I thank you every book, but I don't think it's ever enough. You are the perfect partner for me. Whether it's grabbing a cup of coffee with me in the morning, listening to my midday rants when the characters just aren't doing what they're supposed to do, or helping me work through plot holes in the middle of the night, you're always there.

Thank you for being my person through all of this.

To Britanny and Jack. You guys aren't old enough to read these yet, but one day, you will be, and I want you to know I'm so proud of both of you. I love you more than you'll ever be able to comprehend.

And finally, to you, my readers.

Thank you for reading my words and coming on this journey with me. It means more to me than you'll ever know.

Until next time,
Elayna

ABOUT THE AUTHOR

Elayna R. Gallea is the author of bestselling romantasy series the Binding Chronicles and the Giving Chronicles. A whimsical weaver of words and a lifetime lover of literature, she lives with her husband and two younglings in the enchanting land of New Brunswick, Canada. When she's not writing fantastical stories, she enjoys eating copious amounts of chocolate and cheese, reading, and playing with her dogs and cats. You can find Gallea at @authorelaynagallea.